LIMELIGHT

LIMELIGHT

Graham Hurley

This first world edition published 2020
in Great Britain and the USA by
SEVERN HOUSE PUBLISHERS LTD of
Eardley House, 4 Uxbridge Street, London W8 7SY.
Trade paperback edition first published
in Great Britain and the USA 2021 by
SEVERN HOUSE PUBLISHERS LTD.

British Library Cataloguing in Publication Data
A CIP catalogue record for this title is available from the British Library.

ISBN-13: 978-0-7278-8980-5 (cased)
ISBN-13: 978-1-78029-734-7 (trade paper)
ISBN-13: 978-1-4483-0456-1 (e-book)

All Severn House titles are printed on acid-free paper.

Severn House Publishers support the Forest Stewardship Council™ [FSC™],
the leading international forest certification organisation.
All our titles that are printed on FSC certified paper carry the FSC logo.

MIX
Paper from
responsible sources
FSC® C013056

Typeset by Palimpsest Book Production Ltd.,
Falkirk, Stirlingshire, Scotland.
Printed and bound in Great Britain by
TJ International, Padstow, Cornwall.

To Gerri and Rob
with love

'Remember that, whatever happens, all is well between us forever and ever . . .'

– Edward Thomas, January 1917

ONE

Getting Pavel to Prague was never going to be easy. Pavel Sieger was a screenwriter of genius. Blindness lurked in his family genes and he had recognized the onset symptoms only too well. Determined that his last visual memories would be of somewhere truly special, he took a flight to Prague four years ago when his doctors told him to expect the darkness to descend. He went blind on a winter's night in a pension in the Old Town, and always looked back to that last glimpse of the cobblestones of the Charles Bridge, the city silhouetted against the gathering dusk, and – when he peered over the balustrade of the bridge – the slow green suck of the river below.

We became lovers, a tribute to his playfulness, his imagination, and his raw courage in the face of blindness. Later, he had an accident that broke his neck and left him paralysed from the neck down. What was left – far more than you'd ever imagine – became my glad responsibility. My son's natural father, H, paid for a specially adapted apartment and round-the-clock care overlooking the estuary in Exmouth. I was still living and working in London, but Pavel and I talked daily on the phone, and though a physical relationship was out of the question, I like to think we became even closer. A stroke took Pavel earlier this year, and disposal of his ashes falls to me.

Those ashes have been in my bedroom wardrobe all summer. I keep them in a brown plastic container about the size of one of those glass sweetie jars I remember from my childhood. The container has a screw lid and I've checked the contents. Pavel, when he died, was skin and bone. A thin grey dust, speckled with tiny white fragments of that same bone and something darkly granular, is all that remains. In my head we still talk, and we both agree that there's only one resting place for what's left of him. It has to be a moment on the Charles Bridge, preferably towards the end of one of those smoky autumnal dusks that Prague saves for special occasions. I will unscrew the lid, mutter a line or two from a poem I know he loves, and upend the container. Gravity, and the wind, will do the rest.

And so, this glad September morning, I'm en route to Gatwick Airport with my little black carry-on suitcase and a self-printed boarding card for the 11.55 EasyJet flight to Prague. Malo, my son, has a longstanding date with a couple of mates in Brighton and has volunteered to drop me off on his way. He has no idea why I'm going to Prague, and neither does he bother to ask, and in this respect I'm blessed by youth's unrelenting self-absorption because this is a deeply private expedition and I've no great urge to share it.

We spend the journey discussing the apartment Malo and his girlfriend want to buy. His girlfriend's name is Clemenza, Clem for short, and they've been together now for a couple of years. She's the daughter of a wealthy Colombian businessman, beautiful, gifted, funny and unswervingly loyal. She drives a big Harley Davidson, currently works for a TV production company, and fronts a band in pubs in west London. For a small girl she has a big voice, husky, dark, occasionally wistful, and her weekend gigs attract a substantial following. There's no way that my wayward son deserves a partner like this, and on good days he knows it. See them together, as I often do, and they could be the perfect couple. This, as I've often told Malo, is a tribute to his luck and her patience. Beware, I warn him. Things only last if you take very great care of them.

On the motorway, heading south, Malo wants to know what I've told H about the apartment. This is important because Malo's natural father will be putting up half the money, and Malo knows already that everything will depend on me. H and I go back two decades now. We've only slept together once, and the result was Malo, but recently we've built a friendship that has proved commendably resilient. H owes his wealth to the drugs biz. He was a gifted cocaine dealer back in the day, but his feel for the property market is less certain. Hence his reliance on my verdict.

'So, what do you think, Mum?'

'It's wildly over-priced.'

'A *mil*? You really think so?'

I do. It's a seventh-floor apartment off Ranelagh Gardens. It has two bedrooms, two bathrooms, and views of the Thames. It's a nice enough perch, especially if someone else is footing the bill, but thanks to the wonders of the internet, I know that the current owner bought it for £395,000 just eighteen years ago. Now, he's after a million pounds. Even these days, a profit of £33,000 a year for doing nothing is near obscene.

'It's the market, Mum. You can't argue with it. No one can. It's what people will pay. Plus, it's got really fast broadband.'

'What about Mateo? What does he think?' Mateo, Clem's father, is evidently putting in the rest of the money.

'He hasn't seen it yet. Clem's taking him and her mum round tomorrow morning.'

'And the neighbours?'

'Old. They need new blood. We met the bloke next door a couple of days ago. He was ancient enough to be Clem's grandad, but he couldn't take his eyes off her. It's perfect, Mum. You know it is. That's all you have to say. That's all Dad needs to know.' He shoots me a look. 'Yeah?'

We're on the slipway off the M23, heading for the airport. When he drops me off, Malo gets out and helps me retrieve my suitcase from the Audi's boot. At the kerbside, he looks me up and down. I'm forty-two years old. I'm clad entirely in white, a simple, body-hugging dress in soft mohair that Pavel adored. I toyed with wearing black in view of the occasion but that, I know, would offend him deeply.

'Audition, Mum? Is that it?' Malo grins, giving me a hug. 'You look great. You'll knock 'em dead.'

Knock 'em dead? I give him a wave as he accelerates away, and then step into the terminal building. I have more than an hour in hand, but I always like to get through security before settling down. The queues snake back and forth through a maze of ropes and we shuffle slowly forward until it's my turn to hoist my suitcase on to the belt for the X-ray machine. As I step through the security gate and raise my hands for a pat-down, I'm aware of the woman in charge of the machine looking hard at the image on her screen. She stops the belt and looks up to summon a uniformed guy who I'm guessing is her supervisor. Then her perfectly lacquered fingernail descends lightly on the screen. Look, she's saying. Just there.

Shit, I'm thinking. *Pavel*.

I'm right. As my suitcase emerges from the machine, it's lifted from the belt and put to one side. I identify it as mine and confirm that no one else has had a hand in the packing.

'Open it, please.' This from the supervisor.

At his invitation, I lay everything out for inspection. My washbag. A towel. A light jacket for the evening. A silk scarf in blues and deep reds I especially treasure. A battered copy of a John Updike novel I acquired in a charity shop. Spare undies, plus a pair of comfortable Nikes for a brief walking tour I plan for tomorrow morning. The supervisor is interested in none of this. Instead, his eyes have settled on the container I picked up from the undertaker. I think the superviser's Pakistani, but he could be Indian. Early middle-aged. Nice hands. Single gold ring. London accent.

'What's in there, madam?'

'Ashes.'

'What?' His eyes flick up to my face.

'Ashes. What's left of a good friend of mine.' I start to explain about Pavel, and his passion for Prague, and the mission that will take me to the Charles Bridge, but he cuts me short.

'Can you prove that?' he asks.

'Prove what?'

'That these are his ashes? They could be anything. They could be combustible.'

'They were combustible. That's the whole point. We cremated the poor man.' I nod at the container. 'And that's what's left.'

'But can you *prove* it? Do you have a death certificate? Something from the crematorium?'

'No.' I shake my head. I have no paperwork. I should have thought this thing through, I tell myself. I should have come prepared.

'Open it, please.'

I unscrew the lid of the container and he bends to peer inside, careful to avoid touching this object. His body language gives him away. He's disgusted, and it shows.

He lowers his nose, takes a precautionary sniff, recoils at once.

'No,' he says.

'No, what?'

'No, you can't take it on the flight. We need to get it analysed.'

He gestures at the line of waiting passengers. 'We have a responsibility here. It could be anything.' One of the passengers, a young woman, nods and whispers something to her partner before gathering up her infant son.

'Like what?'

'Like some form of explosive. These things happen. You wouldn't believe what people get up to.'

'You think I want to blow the plane up? With me in it?'

'I've no idea, madam. But it's a risk we can't take. Like I just said, it could be anything.'

'But it's not anything,' I insist. 'It's Pavel.'

'You say.'

'I say.'

The supervisor shrugs and checks his watch. He has a trillion people to get through to airside, and his decision is made.

'You're serious?' I ask him. 'I'm making this special trip to scatter the ashes and I've got to leave them here?'

'Yes. I'm afraid that's pretty much it. Unless you've got some form of proof that they are what you say they are.' He pauses, trying to soften the bad news. 'Why don't you just go anyway? Prague's a lovely place. Especially this time of year.'

'But there'll be no point. I can't scatter ashes I haven't got.'

'I'm afraid that's your problem, madam. We'll give you a proper receipt, of course. The process should take a couple of weeks. We can courier the container back to you but I'm afraid there'll be a charge.'

'And the test? The analysis?'

'We may be able to offer you a discount on that. I'll have to check.'

I'm getting angry now but the passengers behind me are beginning to stir. I'm an actress by profession, and while I'm no stranger to public performance, this particular script is starting to wear thin.

'I've changed my mind.' I reach for the container. 'I'll scatter him somewhere else. Anywhere round here you might recommend?'

My sarcasm is wasted on the supervisor. He makes a dismissive gesture towards the container and turns away. *Poor Pavel*, I think, screwing his top on again, and then repacking my suitcase.

I make my way back against the tidal wave of passengers, escorted by another security guard, and phone Malo from the main concourse. Pavel, I know, would have found the last ten minutes of my life richly entertaining. Ever subversive, he'd have loved the thought of his remains being tested for explosives. All his life, privately and professionally, he'd been unpredictable, dangerous, ignoring conventions, breaking new ground, and even in death, it turns out that his reputation won't leave him alone.

'Mum? You've landed already? That's gotta be a world record.' It's Malo.

'Sadly not.' I tell him about my encounter with airport security.

'You've got his *ashes*? And you want to drop them off some *bridge*?'

'I do.'

'That's gross.'

'That's what the supervisor thought.'

'I don't blame him. Why don't you scatter him on the garden of remembrance or whatever? Plant a rosebush on top? Just like everyone else?'

'Because he wasn't everyone else,' I say firmly. 'And neither am I. We're going to Prague, come what may.'

'We?'

'Me and Pavel.'

'Weird.'

'Listen . . .' I've had time to think this through. I want my darling boy to drive me to Folkestone. We can put his Audi on the Eurotunnel. There are virtually no checks and once we get to Calais, Pavel and I can take a train to Brussels, and then another to Prague.

'And me?'

'You pop back to Folkestone. Job done.' I try smiling at the phone. 'I'm seeing your father next week. We'll be discussing your new apartment.'

Malo mumbles something I don't fully catch about his mates in Brighton. He says he'll have to make a call, then phone me back. I say fine, and then hang up.

Seconds later, I'm looking at a WhatsApp from my lovely friend Evelyn. As a neighbour in Holland Park, she's seen me through countless crises, both marital and medical. She's worked in publishing all her life, becoming the doyenne of London editors with a fine list of authors who all adore her almost as much as I do, but recent retirement has bought her a rather nice bungalow in a seaside town called Budleigh Salterton. She's had a long association with the place, thanks to their annual literary festival, and now – it seems – they want to stage a little welcome to celebrate her settling down for good.

A whole evening of yours truly, she's written. *Sorry about the short notice but it's taken me by surprise, too.*

The event is to take place tomorrow in St Peter's Church, and I can tell by the rest of the message that she very definitely needs moral support. I'm in the middle of replying to her when Malo rings. He has H's bluntness when it comes to bad news.

'Sorry, Mum—' he begins.

'No problem.' I cut him short. 'I've got another date. Best to those mates of yours. I'll take the train back to town.'

I hang up, and then finish my WhatsApp message to Evelyn. Of course I'll come down for the event. Might I beg a bed afterwards?

She's back within seconds, absolutely delighted. Of course I can stay the night – in fact I can stay forever if the mood takes me. The message ends with one of those cheesy emoticons, which is a bit of a departure for Evelyn.

I study it for a moment, and then reach down for my suitcase.

'Later, eh?' I know Pavel is listening. 'Some other weekend?'

TWO

Not going to Prague turns out to be a godsend. Getting back to my apartment in Holland Park, I find a message waiting for me on my landline. My agent, Rosa, has been trying to raise me but without success. I apologize for having my cell phone switched off but she says it doesn't matter. She has some interesting news. One of our favourite BBC development executives has been on. Like me, by some strange twist of fate, he's been thinking hard about ways to mark Pavel's passing and has caught wind of a script, or perhaps a long treatment, he evidently never showed to anyone.

The honchos at BBC drama, bless them, have always held a candle for Pavel, recognizing his distinctive voice and doing ample justice to script after script. Rather than wasting resources on some dutiful retrospective, with warm words and extravagant curtsies from his favourite thesps, they're keen to lay hands on this rumoured masterpiece.

'Any ideas, my precious?'

'None, I'm afraid.' I'm thinking hard. 'Have they got a title? Subject matter? Lead names? Any other clue?'

'Alas, no. They rather thought that you might be able to help.'

'They think he told me everything?'

'They think you were his muse. It might be the same thing.'

'Christ, no. He didn't even tell me he had a son. As you know, the guy had to fly halfway round the world and knock at my door before I twigged that bit of the back story.'

Rosa has a throaty laugh, a tribute to half a lifetime on the roll-ups. Ivan, Pavel's son, teaches world literature at the University of Western Australia in Perth. He turned up in London a couple of months ago to attend a conference. Pavel's obituary, and then a call to Rosa, brought Ivan to my apartment, where I was only too happy to share a story or two about the father he'd never known. That afternoon has stayed with me ever since, partly because Ivan's smile and playful intelligence brought Pavel back to life, and partly because he left with the knowledge that his father's estate was worth at least three and a half million pounds. When I share this news with Rosa, of course she isn't surprised.

'Five,' she says briskly, 'at least. I'm told the French have just come in with a huge rights bid on that Huguenot costume series he did way back, and Pavel's agent is expecting something similar from the Canadians. Have you talked to Claude recently?'

'No.'

'Then maybe you should.' Claude Ransome was Pavel's solicitor, and is now acting as executor for his estate.

'This missing gem . . .' I say, wanting to change the subject. 'I don't even know where to start.'

'His house, maybe? The one in Chiswick?'

'It's gone. Sold.'

'That place you bought him down in the West Country?'

'That went, too.'

'That laptop of his?'

I nod, but say nothing. Before he went blind, Pavel used to write on an Apple MacBook, an object to which he was fond of ascribing almost supernatural powers. A decent bottle of Chablis plus Steve Jobs, he used to say, are the twin keys that will open any fictional door. Latterly, paralysed as well as blind, Pavel acquired a significantly expensive piece of software that would turn speech and dictated stage directions into screen text. This MacBook, I still have.

'I can take a look,' I tell Rosa. 'No promises, though. You knew the man. He buried everything. Layers and layers of deceit, and that was just for the day-to-day stuff. Something like this, something he really wanted to hide, you'd need to be an archeologist, not a muse.'

Rosa grunts something I can't make out. Then she asks whether I've recovered.

'From?'

'Your Dutch *beau*, my precious. The way I heard it, you were lucky to get out of that pub alive. Am I right? Or is this all hearsay?'

'You're right.'

'And might I get the whole story one day?'

'Probably not.'

'Sleeping dogs?'

'I'm afraid so. What's done . . .' I muster a shrug. 'Is done. The bloody man's dead. That's all you need to know.'

'Really?' Rosa doesn't bother to mask her disappointment. 'And that's all I get?'

'That's all you need. I'm off to Devon again.'

'Exmouth?'

'Budleigh Salterton. A different world, believe me. Beware of rumours. They're bad for your health.'

I hang up moments later, after agreeing to meet for a drink once

I'm back in town. When Rosa asks again about Pavel's mystery script, I promise to have a look at his MacBook. Then I'm gone.

West London to East Devon is three and a half hours' drive. I attend to a number of chores I've been putting off and then hit the road. I'm very happy to be seeing Evelyn again and I've packed for the best part of a week. My sat nav delivers me first to Budleigh, and then to a quiet cul-de-sac at the very top of the town. By now it's early evening, and I stand beside the car in the gathering darkness, perfectly still. From far away, I think I can catch the rasp of surf on pebbles. Closer, the sigh of the wind in a stand of elms.

Evelyn has already sent me a couple of photos of her new home, but it seems bigger than I'd somehow expected, a neat but spacious-looking bungalow with double bay windows at the front, and an attic extension upstairs. One side of the property is bordered by a field, while the bungalow next door looks near identical. This is a world away from the muted roar of traffic Evelyn has lived with for the last umpteen years, and I'm still enjoying the absence of aircraft descending into Heathrow when I become aware of a presence behind me.

I glance round. He's tall, gaunt, maybe a generation older than me. He's wearing jeans and a green hoodie and there's something wrong with his face. The bottom half, from the eyes downwards, is latticed with scars which have a bluish tinge in the half-light, but his smile has just a flicker of warmth.

'You're Evelyn's friend?' I detect a flat London accent. 'Come to stay?'

'I am.'

'I'm her neighbour. Lovely lady. We're keeping an eye on her.'

'We?'

'Me and Christianne. She's French, like you. Lots to talk about. You'll love her.' He studies me a moment longer, deep-set eyes under a savage buzz cut, then he digs deep in his jeans pocket, turns on his heel and limps away. No handshake. No opportunity to introduce myself. No chance to ask how he knows I'm French. Just the scrape of his key from the neighbouring bungalow as he opens his front door and disappears inside. Strange, I think, as I lift my suitcase from the boot.

Strange, and a little unsettling. Pavel would have loved this
exchange. Not a good sign.

'His name's Andy. Andy McFaul.'

An hour later, I've settled in. Evelyn is spoiling me with
industrial-strength gin and tonics and a giant plate of canapés.
The canapés are an extravagant riff on her usual theme of olives,
steamed asparagus and anchovies, married to rich twists of
sundried tomato. These are flavours she knows I adore and, apart
from the silence outside, we could easily be back in Holland
Park, with yours truly reporting back after another day on the
showbiz front line. Except that this latest adventure is hers, not
mine, and I'm keen to know more about her neighbour.

'They've been here a while, him and his partner. She's lovely.
Impossible not to like.'

'And him?'

'Difficult.'

'Difficult how?'

'Difficult to like.' Evelyn frowns, reaches for another canapé,
then hesitates. 'No, that's unfair. Difficult to make a judgement
about would be kinder. He's hard to talk to, hard to pin down.
There's lots to admire about him, not least Christianne, and I
know he'll help anyone who really needs it and has the courage
to ask.'

'Courage? Why would you need to be brave?'

'Because he's forbidding. And because he doesn't have much
time for conversation.'

'Is he shy?'

'Not at all. Neither is he lazy. Back in the summer, just after
I'd first arrived, I happened to mention to Christianne a new
flower bed I wanted dug and Andy was on it like a flash the next
day. I explained what I was after and said I was happy to pay,
but he wouldn't hear of it. I thought the work would take the
best part of a week. He did it in a day and a half.' She shook
her head at the memory. 'Remarkable. He never stopped, never
wasted a spade full of earth, sorted every weed, gave me exactly
what I wanted. I offered him lunch on the second day, but he
said no. Fresh lemonade was the closest I got to the man. And
you know something else? Back then, it was hot. He was working

in shorts and that matters in this little story because it was only then that I realized he's only got one leg. Think prosthetic, my love.' She put her hand on my right knee. 'His starts from here downwards.'

'So how come?' I ask, thinking of the scars on his face.

'I've no idea. And to be honest, I haven't had the nerve to ask. I see quite a lot of Christianne, and I'm sure she'll get round to telling me one day, but even so I think it's maybe best to let her make the running. This is a very unusual place, my lovely. I'm sure people here are as nosey as anywhere else, but what everyone's got is *time*. There's a way of doing things, a code if you like. You don't push, you take your place in the queue. It's *de rigueur* in the bakery, and it's the same in conversation. It matters to be patient, to wait your turn, and after a while it becomes rather delightful. I hate to say it, but on reflection London's full of barbarians, even dear old Holland Park. Shove, shove, shove. Yatter, yatter, yatter. Life in your face all the time. How did my neighbour lose his leg? How did he acquire all those scars on his face? I've no idea, but what's certain is that one day someone will tell me.'

'*Comportement,*' I murmur. 'That's what we call it in French.'

'*Exactement.*'

'*Exactement?*' To my knowledge, Evelyn doesn't speak French.

'*Mais oui.*' She's laughing. 'I've joined the Anglo-French Fellowship. We meet once a month in the Masonic Hall, another one of Budleigh's little surprises. Everything in French. Best behaviour. *L'importance du comportement.* Christianne's fault, not mine.'

Much later, a little drunk, I help serve supper. Evelyn has always been a sort of mother to me, a wise neighbour with unlimited patience and an uncanny ability to unravel the endless tangles – both personal and professional – I laid at her feet. She's a small woman, neat, self-contained, unfussy, easy to underestimate at first sight, but a conversation with any of her stable of writers tells a very different story. All of them talk about her editorial judgement, of how acutely she's tuned into the flow and cadence of real conversation, of the nose she has for the faintest bum note in a descriptive paragraph, or a passage of dialogue, and how she can transform a novel's prospects – both commercially and in every other sense – with a bold narrative suggestion, an artful feint that wouldn't have been out of place on a battlefield. One bestselling scribe, impossible to miss at any airport bookstore, once described her as the General Patton among a dying breed of editors. And he meant it as a compliment.

This weight of accolade comes as no surprise because Evelyn's judgement of people and situations is faultless. Over the years, she's been there for me when my marriage collapsed, when my only son deserted me for his scumbag father, and the afternoon when I returned from a hospital appointment with the news that I had a tumour in my brain, and that it would probably kill me. The latter news, on top of everything else, seemed pretty much the end of everything, and yet Evelyn, with the aid of a great deal of malt whisky, gave me just an inkling that there might be an afterlife that had nothing to do with dying. And all this at the hands of a woman who has never married, never had kids of her own, and may – for all I know – still be a virgin.

That latter possibility is something that we've never discussed, but Evelyn is world-class at seeding tiny hints, and just now, as she serves the cheese and breaks out the port, I realize that her gift, like Pavel's, lies in *imagining* life's larger truths. In this regard, I suspect her faith helps enormously. Ever since I've known her, Evelyn has always attended church on Sundays, preferably C of E, but any other sacred space if need be. She once described it to me as a weekly act of surrender in the face of gathering odds ('of growing older, my lovely, and of becoming far too successful'), and this faith of hers goes perfectly with her dislike of display or boastfulness, and with a quiet wit which can – if you're properly tuned in – be a life-saver. The evening when she compared Berndt, my feckless ex, to a dog that even the lamp posts were frightened of was the moment I decided to divorce him.

Now, typically, she wants to listen.

'It was in the paper,' she says, 'what happened in that pub over in Exmouth.'

'To me, you mean?'

'Yes. I imagine you needed a little time to let the dust settle. Which is why I've never mentioned it.'

I nod. Like Rosa, my sainted agent, Evelyn has gathered up the chaff of a difficult summer in my life and now, as a friend, she needs the kernel of that story. The bare facts are bald enough, and that's where I start. Thanks to H, Pavel was living a life of sorts in a spacious penthouse apartment with every piece of equipment that money could buy. Blind and paralysed, he doted on his carer, Carrie, a local woman. Carrie was wonderful in countless ways – kind, loyal, gifted, athletic, luminously beautiful – but, like me, she had a habit of falling in love with the wrong men. In her case, she ended up dead, horribly mutilated, and though I was spared the same fate in that Exmouth pub, it was a very close call.

When I get to the end of the story, we're on our third glass of port and I'm rather hoping that Evelyn can pull all the narrative threads together and tell me where I went so badly wrong. Alas, and all too typically, there's no such easy denouement.

'A mess,' she agrees, re-corking the bottle. 'Thank God you're in Budleigh now.'

THREE

I get up late next morning to find a note from Evelyn lying on the kitchen table. She's popped down to the church to confer with a couple of members of the festival committee ahead of tonight's event. It seems they need to agree how long she'll talk for, and what kind of questions she might like to field afterwards. The latter, of course, will be in the hands of the audience, but the right word in the right ear might prompt a more general discussion. The good news, meanwhile, is that ticket sales have been brisk, and that the festival organizers are anticipating a full-ish church. On her return, Evelyn will pick up *pains aux raisins* from the local bakery. *Le petit dejeuner*, she promises, *sera un régal*.

A treat? No need. I'm pouring myself a second cup of coffee when I hear the chime of the front doorbell. When I get there, I can see a mass of auburn hair behind the pebbled glass.

'Christianne Beaucarne. *Bienvenue à Budleigh. Enchantée.*'

She's a big woman, tall, warm, full of presence. She extends a hand, takes mine, smiles. Older than me? Yes, by at least a decade. In her other hand is a brown paper bag. She nods down the corridor towards the kitchen. She knows the place already. She may even know that I'm here alone.

'Croissants?' She gives the bag a gentle shake.

'*Très bien. Entrez . . .*'

We go through to the kitchen. While I search for plates and maybe even a little marmalade, I nod at the row of mugs above the work surface and suggest she pours herself a coffee. For the first time, she hesitates, eyeing the coffee pot. No. She'd prefer me to do it.

I shrug. *Pas de probleme.* We settle at the table. Already, this could be France, the smell of the coffee, the feel of the plump croissants under my fingertips, the ease with which we relapse into our native tongue. I establish that she comes from Amiens. I happen to know the city but when I ask exactly where she grew up, she doesn't seem to hear me. She's gazing at a box Evelyn keeps on the shelf beside her recipe books.

'We had one exactly like that at home,' she says. 'I loved it.'

The box is old, made of metal. A rural scene – a meadow, sheep, a distant mountain shadowed with clouds – adorns the side that faces us. The colours are beginning to fade, giving it a slightly antique look, and when I fetch it down it's heavier than I expected.

'Can we open it? Would she mind?' Christianne shoots me a look. The question is conspiratorial. We're kids on someone else's territory. Nice.

'Care to hazard a guess?' I'm looking at the box.

'What's inside, do you mean?'

'Yes.'

Christianne frowns, then suggests I know already. I tell her I don't.

'But you're her friend. You had the next-door apartment up in London. She told me.'

'That's true.'

'So, you'd know. Surely.'

'I don't.'

'Then *you* guess.'

The invitation comes with that same hint of mischief. I shrug. I tell her I haven't a clue.

'One attempt, one go.' She won't give up. 'Just one.'

'Bric-a-brac.' I'm staring down at the box. 'Little treasures. Odds and ends she's squirrelled away.' I glance up. 'And you?'

'Buttons.'

'You're sure?'

'Absolutely. Let's see . . .' She extends a hand but has difficulty opening the box. 'You do it.'

The box has a lock. When I point it out, Christianne shakes her head.

'It won't be locked,' she says. 'Just open it.'

I do her bidding. The lid lifts open at the slightest pressure. Inside, to Christianne's delight, we find nothing but buttons: blues, deep purples, plastic, glass, fabric-covered, various metals, all sizes, all shapes. She reaches for the box once again, her fingers drifting among the buttons the way you might sift coins, and when she finally withdraws, I realize her hand is shaking. Excitement, I think vaguely.

'My mother had a box exactly the same.' She's grinning like a child. 'It had to be buttons.'

I pour more coffee while Christianne digs around in the box. A leather-covered button, probably the biggest, earns a special nod of approval.

'Did your mum sew?' She glances up.

'Not really. She read a lot.'

'No button box?'

'I'm afraid not.' I'm about to tell her a bit more about the little Breton house in Perros-Guirec where I grew up when, once again, she performs a conversational swerve and changes the subject. Her croissant finished, she's pushed her coffee to one side and sat back, as if to take a proper look at me.

'I've seen you before, haven't I?'

'Maybe.'

'In the movies?'

'Yes.'

'*The Hour of our . . .*?' She frowns, hunting for the key word. '*Passing?*'

'The one in Nantes? During the war?'

'Yes.'

She nods, beaming, and then extends a hand. She wants to congratulate me, not for being on screen, not for being just a little bit famous, but for the sequence towards the end that Pavel always cherished.

'You were great,' she says. 'We saw the movie last year, when we were still living in Portugal, and I'll never forget you making love to that young guy. It should have been sexy, and it was, but it was more than that. The man knew he was to be arrested and shot. There was no way out. What you did for him made Andy cry and that – believe me – doesn't happen very often.'

'I was younger, then,' I say defensively. 'And with the right lighting, the camera can be kind.'

'That's not the point. I'm a woman. You got it right. You were *parfaite.*'

I'm staring at her. There's something so honest in the simplicity of what she's just said. After a couple of years of multiple disasters, it's good to know that something of mine touched a nerve or two.

'Portugal?' I need a change of subject.

'That's right.'

'You were living there?'

'We were. We had a couple of acres in the Alentejo. You've been there?'

'Never.'

'You should. There are forests of cork oaks. There are wild flowers everywhere. It maybe isn't as pretty as I'm trying to make it sound, but it's real, and it's cheap, and if you'd been where we'd been it feels like heaven on earth.'

I hold her gaze. I want to know more. A tiny gesture of the hand, a lifted eyebrow, is all a conversation like this needs. I want to know where she was living before settling in Portugal. For once, she doesn't change the subject.

'Angola,' she says.

'You mean Africa?'

'Yes. We were there in the nineties, during the civil war. In fact, that's where we met. We were in a little town called Luena, and it was full of limbless kids. I was working for MSF. Andy

was with another outfit. Sometimes I think we fell in love to stay
sane.'

I nod. Médecins Sans Frontières has become a byword for the
best of Western intentions in the chaos of the developing world.
My mum, in an unfortunate phrase, always says she loves it to
death.

'You were a nurse?'

'Yes.'

'And Andy?'

'He was working in the minefields. There were mines everywhere. He'd learned his trade in the army. Afterwards, he joined
one of the mine-lifting charities. Terra Sancta it was called. They
were brave men. A little crazy sometimes, but brave.'

'And after Angola?'

'That was different. Andy did a couple of extra tours with
Terra Sancta in the Balkans, Bosnia mainly, but in the end, he
packed it in. Portugal was a whole new life. Kids with the normal
ration of limbs?' She shakes her head. 'Hard to believe.'

'I'm guessing you liked it out there.'

'In Portugal?'

'Yes.'

'You're guessing right.'

'So why here?' I gesture round. 'Why Budleigh?'

She holds my gaze for a long moment, refusing to answer my
question, and at last reaches for the remains of her coffee. As
she sips it, her hand is shaking again and a little spills on the
table. Then I hear the turn of a key in the front door, and moments
later Evelyn has joined us in the kitchen. She's staring at the
plate of croissants, half-finished. Then she sees the box of buttons,
still open on the table.

'Is this a private party?' she asks. 'Or is anyone welcome?'

That same afternoon, with Christianne back next door, Evelyn
insists on taking me for a walk. I've yet to share the news about
her neighbours' adventures but she's aware that I've never taken
a proper look at Budleigh and she thinks that omission needs
rectifying.

After a grey morning, the weather has cheered up and we walk
arm in arm down the hill towards the heart of the little town.

Exmouth, where I spent a great deal of the summer, is barely five miles away, but this is another world. People are older, richer, better turned out, and their tastes are reflected in the shops along the main street that leads from the top of the town to the seafront: cafes with every table taken, upmarket vintners, a butcher's window brimming with choice cuts of lamb and venison, even a decent art gallery.

We pause in the sunshine outside an estate agent. A particular property catches Evelyn's eye. It has five bedrooms, sea views, a double garage, and half an acre of carefully landscaped garden. The neighbouring house, she says, is even grander and happens to belong to someone she knows.

'Bill Penny,' she says. 'Ex-diplomat. Used to head the embassy in Berlin. Get him off the croquet lawn and you won't meet a nicer man.'

I nod, but say nothing. The pile next door to Bill Penny's is on sale for £1,250,000 and I can't help thinking about Malo's bid to buy a modest perch in Ranelagh Gardens.

'These places are cheap,' I murmur, 'compared to prices at home.'

'Home? Home, my lovely, is here.'

I glance down at her and grin, and tell her she's fallen on her feet, and then I slip my arm through hers, and we set off again. Evelyn, I've remembered, is a West Country girl by birth, brought up in a tiny village on the edge of Dartmoor, and her smile – totally unforced – tells me this seemly little town suits her perfectly.

The beach lies at the end of Budleigh's main street. We pause on the lip of a long curve of pebbles, smooth, grey, dotted with curls of drying seaweed. The pebbles fall sheer to the tideline, and in the distance, beyond the beach, a headland is topped by a stand of trees. I've seen this view in at least three shops in the last half hour, faithfully reproduced on film and canvas, but Evelyn has something else on her mind.

'Did I tell you about Christianne swimming?'

'You didn't.'

'She goes in every day, along with some other chums, mainly women. And you know something else? She does it in winter, too.'

I nod, impressed yet not surprised. Then I tell her about the minefields, and Angola, and the kids with no legs. By now, I have Evelyn's full attention.

'She *told* you all that?'

'She did. I asked a question or two, of course, but she was very happy to talk. Maybe it's a French thing, two women together. Fifteen minutes over coffee and croissants and you can't help comparing notes. Being nosey is our birthright. *Curieux, n'est-ce pas?*'

'And that's where Andy lost his leg? Got those marks on his face? In *Angola*?' Evelyn shakes her head.

'In Kuwait. Up near the border, apparently. First Gulf War.'

'But he still went back to the mines? With one leg?'

'Exactly. And that's where he found Christianne. Life can be odd – disaster one moment, bliss the next. That's her take on it, by the way, not mine. A little further maybe?' I nod towards the distant headland. 'Then a cream tea?'

We're back at Evelyn's bungalow by late afternoon. Twice, she's been stopped on the street, both times by men well past their sixties. There followed a courtly exchange of kisses, one on each cheek, followed by a companionable pat on the arm and good luck for tonight. After these encounters Evelyn supplied a name and other gossipy details, but I know I'll never retain all this. Not that it matters. What's important, I tell myself, is that this little town has settled on Evelyn like the duvet of her dreams. It will keep her snug. It will furnish endless friendships. And who knows, it may even offer more than that.

Back home, she excuses herself to prepare for the evening. She has in mind, she says, a little surprise, a kind of thank you for the festival's generosity in making the event happen. When I press her for more, she plays coy, telling me she has one last phone call to make. This I recognize as my cue to leave her in peace and I make my way upstairs to my bedroom. The window offers a perfect view of Evelyn's back garden, but what catches my eye is the figure next door.

Andy McFaul, in those same jeans and that same green hoodie, is on his hands and knees on a sizeable expanse of lawn. In every respect but one, the grass looks perfect: perfectly laid, perfectly

mowed, perfectly edged. For the man Christianne hinted at –
ultra-rational, obsessed by the smallest detail – the lawn is a
telling metaphor. So why has this same obsessive seen fit to sink
a series of holes, lined with metal, in a random pattern that
stretches from the line of crazy paving at the rear of the bungalow
to the flower bed at the far end?

The answer appears moments later. Christianne is barefoot.
She's wearing a pair of shorts and a long-sleeved T-shirt. The
pullover draped over her shoulders might be cashmere, but in
the fading light it's hard to be sure. She's carrying a golf club,
a putter, and I watch McFaul bring her to a halt maybe a dozen
metres from the first hole. From the pocket of his jeans he
produces a golf ball, then another, and he stands back while she
tries to get her balance over the ball he's laid at her feet. For a
long moment, while she sways with her bodyweight, nothing
happens. Then she takes a tentative, exploratory swing, and misses
the ball completely. The fact that I can hear the soft '*merde*' is
a tribute to the silence of this place, but at McFaul's muttered
suggestion she tries again. Another struggle to get herself properly
balanced. Another stroke that fails to connect.

McFaul is behind her now. Softly, he nuzzles the nape of her
neck before putting his arms around her and taking control
of the club. With two pairs of hands, the ball rolls steadily towards
the hole. It doesn't go in but it's not far short. Christianne gazes
at it, then shakes her head and turns back towards McFaul before
burying her head on his shoulder.

Nearly an hour later, I find Evelyn downstairs. She's had a bath,
and she's treated herself to a dress in soft greys and blues and I
tell her she looks – and smells – fabulous. I fetch her coat from
the hall and make sure she's got the notes she's been working
on. Then, ever punctual, she nods towards the front door and
offers me her arm.

'Is it normal to feel this fluttery?' She gestures down at her
stomach.

'Always.' I give her arm a little squeeze. 'Break a leg, eh?'

FOUR

E velyn need not have worried about performance nerves because the evening in the shadowed spaces of St Peter's Church is a genuine triumph. We attend with Christianne and McFaul, and arrive to find the place already filling up. The festival organizers have installed a lectern on a raised dais in front of the choir stalls. The dais is flanked by an artful collage of Evelyn's favourite authors, faces that need no introduction, and when she settles behind the microphone with her notes, her face is bathed with a soft spotlight.

A member of the festival's organizing committee introduces her as the doyenne of London editors, one of literary publishing's treasures. This accolade brings a tinge of pink to Evelyn's smile, but the moment she clears her throat, briefly checks her notes, and then peers out at the assembled multitude, I know she has this thing nailed.

All writers, she observes lightly, are control freaks, and her opening doff of the cap to one bestselling author's reliance on 50,000-word synopses – the infant book's every breath maniacally detailed – is fond as well as very funny. The audience chuckles in appreciation, the kind of reaction every stage actress prays for, and this sense of immediate companionship sets the tone for what follows. As the minutes speed by, my clever friend shares the highs and lows of three busy decades tucked up with her jar of editing pencils and her stable of *écrivains*.

All writers, she confirms, are needy and demand a bit of TLC, but so is the readership, and it's been her pleasure to build a bridge between the two. By now, we're starting to understand the sheer range of talents a calling like this demands, but the detail is richly delicious. One woman, half-American and still the toast of the Sunday broadsheets, evidently needs an early morning bowl of Thai noodles, fiercely spiked with chilli, to unlock her muse before settling at the PC. Another top-selling scribe, male this time, could never tackle his book's final pages without spending half a day on top of a London bus. You readers, Evelyn confides softly, owe a great deal to the number 38.

The laughter is full-throated and deeply appreciative. The audience adores these gossipy delights, morsels from the feast that is London publishing, but tonight's star is quick to marry them to a shrewd analysis of what makes a good book work. Sheer stamina, she insists, is a given in the world of any novelist. Writing a hundred thousand words isn't a stroll around the block, and trying to get them all in the right order is a huge undertaking, but wrestling the damn thing to the mat isn't all sweat and effort because greatness on the page demands submission to all kinds of strange alchemies. What keeps the reader desperate to find out what happens next doesn't happen by accident and when she tells us that editing – helping the storyteller – can be a mystery as well as a pleasure, heads nod yet again.

This audience, or perhaps congregation, is wise and well-read enough to recognize sincerity as well as a lifetime's uncontested achievement, and Evelyn's final tribute to the men and women she's accompanied to bestsellerdom sparks a standing ovation. Success, she says, can be a lottery but it's her pleasure to confirm that talent – along with patience, fortitude, and sheer determination – will out.

This *aperçu* goes down better than well. Evelyn peers over her lectern at the ocean of beaming faces with relief as well as exultation, and then comes her surprise announcement. Her publisher, Hespera, has offered to sponsor a writing prize open to everyone for at least the next five years. In a nod to Hespera's colophon, the prize will be known as the Golden Nymph, and at Evelyn's suggestion entries will be limited to novellas only. The novella, I know, is a format she's always loved and the news that the lucky winner will get a cheque for £10,000 brings the audience to their feet for a second time. These people, I realize, are canny as well as appreciative. A prize like this will give the festival – as well as Hespera – yet more profile.

The three of us are sitting in a reserved pew at the front of the church, and we're more than happy to sit back and savour Evelyn's moment of glory. Already, she's taking questions from the audience, each one triggering another story, and I'm enjoying

her account of a particularly vicious attack of writer's block,
when I catch McFaul's eye.

What's a novella? he mouths.

Half an hour later, we're back home. Evelyn has been whisked
away for a celebratory meal in a local hotel and when I pause
outside Evelyn's front gate, Christianne invites me next door for
supper. McFaul looks briefly appalled. This is a man who either
won't or can't bother to hide his feelings, but Christianne doesn't
seem to care. It will, she says, be something light and she gives
me a clue or two about what to expect. I tell her I have no
problem with spicy food, news that puts a smile on her face, and
promise to join them as soon as I've dumped my coat. I've bought
a bottle of champagne and stored it in Evelyn's fridge for a little
celebration of our own, but I hoist it out and take it next door.
The evening has been revelatory, even for me, and a glass or two
of Moët seems deeply appropriate.

The bungalow is a muddle inside. Nothing fits. Nothing
matches. The lounge has become a dumping ground for random
bits of furniture and sundry other items. Most of it probably
came from car-boot sales, and some of the furniture is falling
apart. A sagging chest of drawers beneath the window should
really belong in a bedroom, or be consigned to the local tip,
while the one decent armchair, almost intact, is occupied by an
ancient cat I initially mistake for a cushion. It eyes me warily
as I stand by the door, gives one paw a lick or two, and then
goes back to sleep.

Christianne calls me into the kitchen, which seems bigger than
Evelyn's, but here too there's been no effort to make the room
interesting or even presentable. A day's washing-up is lying in
the sink. The waste bin is brimming with potato peelings. The
table where McFaul and Christianne evidently eat their meals is
still cluttered with the remains of lunch. This comes as something
of a surprise. On the evidence of the garden, and McFaul's many
talents, I expected something very different. Does this bit of the
kingdom belong to Christianne? Is my new friend from Amiens
a slut?

While Christianne hunts for glasses for the champagne, I settle
at the table. McFaul has the Moët and his thumbs have found

the lip of the cork. On the way home, we've all agreed that Evelyn has been a star, and I've done my best to explain the concept of the novella to McFaul, but the atmosphere is a little tense – probably my fault for saying yes to Christianne's invitation – and conversation has died.

'So, is this your place?' I say brightly, gesturing round. 'You own it?'

'God forbid,' says McFaul.

'You're renting?'

'Not really. It belongs to my stepbrother. He's in New York just now, investment banker, works for Goldman Sachs. If we nicked the place, put it in our pockets and did a runner, I'm not sure he'd even notice.' He looks at Christianne. 'Four properties? Including the house in Twickenham? Have I got that right?'

'Five. You always forget the apartment down in Malaga.'

'You're right.' He nods. 'Maybe it's time for a swap.'

They exchange glances, say nothing. Christianne has at last found glasses for the champagne. None of them match, and one of them is quite badly chipped, but it doesn't seem to matter. McFaul pops the cork and I propose a toast.

'To your brilliant neighbour.' I raise my glass. 'I just hope Budleigh recognizes what a talent they've got on their hands.'

To my surprise, the latter comment triggers a nod – which I take to be agreement – from McFaul.

'It took guts to do something like that,' he grunts. He tips his glass, the one with the chip, to his mouth and takes a pull at the champagne. He's looking at Christianne. 'Are they all as good as her? At that festival of theirs?'

'I've no idea. We never go.'

'Then maybe we should.'

'*Avec plaisir.*' She shoots McFaul a look. 'You mind if I write that down?'

Without waiting for an answer, she glances at her watch and stoops to open the oven door. I can see a glass casserole inside, loosely covered with foil. She must have put it in earlier because the kitchen suddenly smells wonderful.

'I hope you meant it about spicy food.' She's struggling to bend. 'I've done a big pot of dhal. If you want to know our secret, we live on the stuff.'

'She means it's cheap.' This from McFaul.

'He means it's delicious.' Christianne is looking at me. 'Andy loves it. I meant to get roti, but I forgot. Will plain bread be OK, or shall I toast it?'

I shrug. I don't care. A bowl of whatever's in that casserole dish sounds fine to me. Christianne nods. She's still gazing into the oven. For whatever reason, she seems uncertain what to do next. McFaul empties his glass, wipes his mouth with the back of his hand, and then gets up. He circles the table until he's standing behind Christianne, before helping her to stand upright. In the close confines of the kitchen I can't help remembering the scene in the garden last night, McFaul trying to coach Christianne to sink a putt or two, or just make contact with the ball, and this strange *pas de deux* in front of the oven has the same feel.

'OK?' he mutters. 'You want me to get it out?' Christianne nods, says nothing. 'Serve it? Sort the toast?' Another nod.

McFaul hooks a chair towards him with his foot before trying to settle her at the table. She gazes down at the chair, then shakes her head. She needs to fetch something. She won't be long.

'Like what?'

'It doesn't matter.'

'Of course it matters. We've got a guest.'

'But that's the point. She might be interested.'

'In what?'

'Us.'

She's at the door now, and she's turned to face McFaul. He shakes his head, spares me a brief glance, then joins Christianne as she leaves the room.

'Let me,' he says to her. 'Please.'

Alone now at the table, I'm wondering whether to shut the oven door, or even to get the casserole out myself and do the honours. I've been here before, I tell myself, with my ex-husband, incessant low-level domestic warfare over the silliest things. I'm still wondering where Christianne keeps the bread and the toaster when I hear the scrape of a drawer from the front room. Moments later, McFaul is back with what looks like a photograph album. It's fat with prints and battered around the edges. He puts it squarely on the kitchen table before looking me in the eye.

'Not my idea,' he says.

Christianne returns. While McFaul sorts bread for the toaster, she settles at the table and opens the album. If I'm expecting page after page of carefully mounted photos, I'm in for a disappointment. The album, like the bungalow, is a complete mess. Christianne takes a handful of photos, all different sizes, some in colour, others in black and white, and shuffles slowly through them, like a pack of cards. Then she selects one and slides it towards me across the table.

'Luena,' she says. 'We were younger then.'

I'm looking at the shot. In a dusty street, a bunch of kids are standing around the remains of a car. The vehicle has no wheels and a line of what I assume to be bullet holes stitch their way up the driver's door. The car is empty and the baked earth beside the door is dark with what could be dried blood. The kids don't seem to care. Two of them have lost a leg. Another, the biggest, is holding a football. They're all grinning fit to burst.

'His name was Aurelio.' Christianne's finger has settled on one of the crippled kids. 'We sort of adopted him.'

'Was?'

'He died that same month.' McFaul has barely spared the photo a glance. 'Down by the river. The army swore they'd swept for mines themselves. They said the place was clean.'

'And?'

'It wasn't.'

'And this was when?'

'Ninety-six, going into ninety-seven. Happy fucking Christmas.'

I nod, not knowing quite what to say. More than two decades later, this man is still full of disgust, or perhaps anger.

Christianne has found another photo. This time, it's more intimate. I recognize both Christianne and McFaul. They're sitting at a plain wooden table and Christianne is wearing one of those joke hats you get from crackers. I glance up. In the intervening years, she's put on a great deal of weight.

'Andy mentioned Christmas.' Christianne is smiling. 'We had good times, too. It wasn't all bad.'

I nod. The power of the camera's flash has bleached out the faces at the table but even so I'm looking at a very handsome couple. Christianne is wearing an MSF T-shirt that does nothing to hide her figure, while McFaul is sporting a red bandana. His

hair is longer than now and a sprig of something green is tucked
inside the bandana.

'It was the closest we could get.' McFaul has at last lifted the
casserole from the oven. 'The Angolans don't do holly.'

'It was lovely. Look.' Christianne has found yet another shot.
The lighting, this time, is kinder. It's the same setting but this
time I'm looking at four people, posed beside the remains of a
huge meal. Christianne and McFaul each have an arm around
another couple. The woman is dark, plump, winsome. The man
beside her, a huge grin on his face, has a lighter skin tone and
a mouth full of crooked teeth. A baby nestles in the crook of his
arm and he, too, has laid hands on a hat from a cracker. In the
background, his eyes red from the flash, lurks an enormous dog.

'Celestina and Domingos,' McFaul says. 'We were at their
place that night. Carols round the barbie and goodwill to all men.
That dog was a monster but even he behaved himself. Great
evening. The little man excelled himself.'

'You're telling me he did the cooking?' I'm looking at what's
left of the food in the photo.

'Absolutely not. Men in Africa aren't built that way. No, but
he laid hands on three bottles of Scotch. I couldn't believe it.
Black Label? In the middle of a fucking *war*? How did he ever
make that happen?' He shakes his head at the memory and turns
back to the casserole, making room for three bowls amid the
chaos of the work surface.

'He and Andy worked together in the minefields.' Christianne's
voice is low, like she's sharing a secret with me. 'Andy ran Terra
Sancta in Luena and took him on. He was a lovely, lovely man.
Three kids. Wonderful wife. I've never met anyone so cheerful.'

'Yeah, and sharp as a blade.' McFaul is giving the dhal a stir.
'I trained him up, taught him the basics, then got on to the
important stuff. With that little guy you only had to say something
once. You could hear his brain working. Literally. Tick-tock,
tick-tock. He was brave, too. Never ducked a challenge.'

'Andy used to play football with his kids in the evening before
it got dark. They loved that leg of his. It made him one of them.'

'They were buggers, all of them. Kicked me to death most of
the time. But they were good, they had the knack, natural ball
players, really gifted, little black ghosts, darting around. Most

of the Brazilian teams have Angolan blood. If you know about football, that probably explains everything.'

Little black ghosts. It's a lovely image, totally out of keeping with what little I know of this dour retiree. Maybe I'm missing something, I think. Maybe he's softer than he seems. When I glance up, he's still staring down at the photo.

'And?' I know there's more to come.

'He died,' Christianne says quickly.

'In the minefields?'

'Yes.' She wants to change the subject. 'But Andy's still in touch with Celestina. The kids have grown up, of course. One of them's a teacher in Luanda. Another emigrated to Portugal. We saw him in Lisbon a couple of times when we were living out in the Alentejo. He was working for a bank.'

'And Celestina?'

'Still in Luena.' This from McFaul. 'She's never remarried, and I doubt she ever will. That generation were giants. Listen to people like that, be around them, and you learn so much.'

I'm not quite sure what McFaul is getting at here, and I badly want to find out more, but he's spooning out the dhal and our little interlude with the photos is over. Christianne struggles to her feet, collects the photos and puts the album on top of the fridge. McFaul has found the bread and the smell of burning announces the first slices of toast.

'Co-op white, I'm afraid.' Christianne sits down with a fist full of cutlery. 'I thought there might be a croissant left but I'm wrong.'

It doesn't matter. The dhal is brilliant, warm and earthy with layer after layer of careful spicing. On closer inspection, I find tiny florets of cauliflower, curls of Brussels sprout, shavings of carrot, and tiny dark green fingers of bird's eye chilli, sliced open to free the seeds. I cooked this way after my marriage collapsed, alone in Holland Park after my husband had departed, taking my son with him. My career was also in trouble, and money was suddenly tight, and peasant food like this became a lifeline. Not simply because it was cheap to make but because it was so comforting. Convalescence in a bowl, I remember thinking. And if you fed the saucepan with more veggies, day after day, that kind of solace could last forever.

'Lovely.' I lick my spoon. 'And I mean it.'

When McFaul offers a refill, I shake my head. I've seen what little remains in the casserole and I've realized what should have been obvious all along: this couple are poor. Money is tight. And that must matter in a town where a kilo of decent vine tomatoes will cost you the earth.

'You grow your own veg?' I ask Andy.

'Yeah. I've got half shares on an allotment up by the croquet club. Most of the stuff comes from there. The weed I grow in the greenhouse.'

Weed? This comes as a surprise. The bungalow is full of smells, but not once have I scented cannabis. Christianne, it seems, can read my mind.

'I won't let him smoke indoors.' Her hand suddenly reaches for McFaul's. 'But I've got the feeling that may change.'

There's a moment of silence between them while I watch McFaul's hand tighten around hers, then comes the growl of a car pulling up outside. Evelyn, I think, back from her triumph.

I get to my feet and thank them both for the meal. Christianne looks disappointed. She wants me to stay. I feel guilty at leaving so abruptly but this is Evelyn's evening, not ours, and when Christianne suggests we might take a walk tomorrow, just the two of us, I'm very happy to say yes. McFaul accompanies me to the door. He's looking grim again.

'I'm sorry about all that.' He nods back towards the kitchen. 'All what?'

'The pics. Angola. It's ancient history. Who cares any more?'

He has the door open by now and the car has gone. This is my cue to leave but McFaul has asked a question and I tell myself it's only polite to offer some kind of reply.

'I'm guessing you do,' I say quietly. 'Might I be right?'

Evelyn insists we treat ourselves to a nightcap. Watching her pour two large measures of Armagnac, she reminds me of a schoolgirl returning with the end-of-term report of her dreams. She's passed her exams in the finest style, and her hosts in the restaurant had spoiled her to death. The festival proper is due to start next week, but everyone, she says shyly, seemed to agree that she'd set the bar high.

'You were great,' I tell her. 'We were very proud of you.'

'We?'

'Me and those neighbours of yours.'

The news that I've spent an hour or so next door astonishes her.

'They invited you *in*?'

'Christianne did. I'm not sure McFaul was so keen. Are they married, incidentally?'

'I don't think so. She doesn't wear a ring. What was it like?'

'Inside, you mean?'

'Yes.'

'You've never been? Never paid them a visit?'

'Never.'

This news comes as something of a surprise. Evelyn, after all, has been in residence for a couple of months now and I know for certain that Christianne is used to popping round for a coffee, but then I remember the state of their place.

'It's a slum,' I say. '*En pleine dégringolade.*'

'*En pleine* what?'

'*Dégringolade.*' I do my best to explain the phrase. We French use *en pleine dégringolade* to describe what happens after everything falls apart. Think Paris after a week of strikes, I suggest. Piles of rubbish in the streets, the Metro under siege, the main boulevards choked with traffic, everyone grumpy as hell.

'And that's the way they are? Next door?'

'Yes. It was sweet of her to invite me in, but I have to be honest, that man bewilders me. He's around her all the time, he watches her every move, he won't leave her alone. Is it a control freak thing? Is he jealous to be sharing her with someone else? Just for an hour in the evening?'

Evelyn's looking blank. This is a manuscript that's just arrived in the post, totally unsolicited, and she doesn't know where to start with the characterization.

'But she adores him,' she says. 'I can see it when they walk out together. I watch them sometimes from the front window. She hangs on his every word, she physically clings to him, it's really nice to see.' She's frowning, still trying to make sense of this plot twist. 'Slum's a big word. Is it *that* bad?'

'Worse. And I don't just mean the look of the place. You know

when you can smell trouble . . .?' I leave the thought
unfinished.

For a moment, we just look at each other. I know what Evelyn
wants. She wants me to roll back the timeline. She wants to be
back in that church, enjoying the applause, welcoming the next
question and the question after that. She wants to believe that
Budleigh, this new home of hers, is as cultured and untroubled
as she'd been led to believe. Just now the sun is shining on her
and the presence of a single cloud, especially so close, is deeply
unwelcome.

'I'm sorry.' I reach for her hand. 'You don't need any of this.
You're probably right. They're hopelessly in love but like most
bloody men he plays grumpy.'

'You're making that up, my lovely.'

'You're right. I am.'

'So, what do you really think?'

I frown. I tell her I don't know, and I'm wondering why any
of this can possibly matter when I hear raised voices from next
door: McFaul and Christianne. Then comes the slam of a window
closing, and the volume abruptly fades to nothing.

'Does this worry you?' I nod towards next door. 'Be honest.'

'Yes. She's a lovely woman. She doesn't deserve to be hurt.'

'You think that's what this is about? Him, the alpha male?
Her, the helpless partner?'

She holds my gaze for a moment, then grins. We know each
other far too well to give house room to clichés like this.

'You're right,' she says. 'I'm sure it's much more complex and
much more interesting.' She reaches for her glass. 'Here's to us.'

'To *you*,' I say. 'You were a star.'

We're late to bed. In certain moods, especially when she's relaxed,
Evelyn can be very expansive, and this is just such a moment.
She's looking back at the decision to abandon London for East
Devon, and when she enumerates the countless blessings that
have come her way, I know she means it. Instead of blank faces
in the street and the stink of diesel, warm smiles from passing
strangers and the incessant growl of the surf. Instead of the lash
of editorial deadlines, yet more sunshine behind her parted
bedroom curtains and the glorious promise of an unplanned day.

'This place is full of surprises,' she says. 'I thought the problem might be boredom, nothing much to do, but it's quite the reverse.'

Evelyn has always been a great one for lists and now is no different: the challenge of learning to play croquet, lending a hand at the crafts exhibition, finding decent partners at bridge, attending French conversation classes for beginners, listening to a glorious Haydn string quartet at the mid-summer BMF.

'BMF?'

'Budleigh Music Festival. It was in the Temple Methodist Church. This is supposed to be God's Waiting Room but the players, the quartet, were all so *young*. The local kids are great, too. London pays youth far too much respect, because it's probably easier that way. That's why they're all so bloody moody and arrogant. Down here, they haven't forgotten how to smile. It's a place apart. It's utterly delightful. I'm a lucky girl.'

A place apart? About London, I can only agree. Malo, I'm thinking, and his casual assumption that a million pounds is a fair price for two bedrooms and a view.

Evelyn is still bubbling about the programme for next week's literary festival. In her footsteps, luminaries like Robert Harris and Louis de Bernières will be filling St Peter's Church. Midweek, Hilary Mantel will be in conversation with James Runcie.

'Hilary lives on the seafront.' Evelyn smiles. 'A view like that, no wonder the books are so good. You should stay longer. Wind down a little. A couple of months and we can have Christmas together.'

I tell her it's a nice thought, but I still have the embers of a career to attend to. In the meantime, Christianne and I will be stepping out together.

'Tomorrow morning, you mean?'

'Yes.'

'And he agreed?'

'I don't think she asked him.'

'That'll be nice then.' She drains her glass and then laughs. 'Keep notes. I'm dying for the next chapter.'

We have a goodnight hug and I make my way upstairs. A wash with a wet flannel in the tiny en suite is enough for now, and I linger briefly at the window before getting into bed. This is the first time that I've paid any attention to McFaul's greenhouse.

It's tucked into a corner at the bottom of the garden, and in the darkness I can see the glow of tiny heaters inside. A cannabis factory in deepest Budleigh, I think. Yet another surprise.

In bed, I'm asleep within seconds. I dream, for some reason, about Malo. He's young, barely nine, but already Berndt and I are having trouble getting him to school. He seems reluctant to leave us alone. It's almost, with a rare prescience, that he doesn't trust us to be there when he gets back. I'm in the process of insisting that we love him, that all is well, when a sudden noise returns me to consciousness. I lie quite still, trying to work out what it might have been. Then it happens again, readily recognizable, that same soft clunk, the face of a golf club against a ball.

Curious, I slip out of bed and tiptoe across to the window. McFaul's back garden is bathed in light from his kitchen, and the man himself is crouched over another ball. He's wearing nothing but a pair of ancient-looking shorts and there's no sign of Christianne. For a long moment, he stands immobile, feet slightly apart, head down. A lit cigarette glows between his lips. Then a tiny movement of his wrists sends the ball rolling over the darkened lawn until it slips into the hole.

I watch for a moment longer, and then return to bed. Evelyn, ever-thoughtful, has left a radio beside the bed. The radio has a time display. 03.33.

FIVE

I wake late next morning to the sound of hammering from downstairs. When I finally make it to the kitchen, I find Evelyn preparing two slices of toast for a bacon sarnie. Beyond the open door to the garden, a figure in jeans and a scruffy top is sawing a length of timber on a Workmate.

'This is Presley.' Evelyn does the introductions. 'Enora.'

Presley wipes one hand on his jeans. He says he's glad to meet me. A glorious fall of long, blond, curly hair. A three-day growth of stubble. Light blue eyes, heavily bloodshot. A Viking god, I tell myself, safely ashore after a rough passage.

'You're the actress.' His handshake is firm, lots of callouses from all that sawing.

'What else did she tell you?'

'Not much. But I'm a good listener.'

I step back into the kitchen, glad of Evelyn's offer of coffee. Presley, it appears, is yet another of Budleigh's blessings, a local carpenter recommended by Christianne. Evelyn has used him a couple of times already and has been delighted with the results. Just now, he's making her a couple of bespoke shelves for books she's yet to reclaim from the Exeter warehouse where she's still storing bits and pieces from her London flat.

'Christianne says he's a genius,' she murmurs, 'and I think she might be right.'

Right or otherwise, Presley is certainly a gentleman because he willingly surrenders the first of the bacon sarnies to little me. Under his approving smile, I add a scribble of brown sauce. Too much Armagnac, I tell him, does that to a girl.

'On the hard stuff again?' He's looking at Evelyn. 'That's the problem with you DFL guys. Before it was simple. Beer or beer. Now we're spoiled for bloody choice.'

'DFL?' I'm lost.

'Down From London. Is it the money I'm complaining about? Christ, no. Do either of you lovely ladies bother me? Absolutely not. This was a sleepy old place in my dad's day. Thank God for DFLs.'

Evelyn and I take that as a compliment. Two more rashers of streaky go into the frying pan while I mind the toaster. The second sarnie is coming along nicely when Christianne appears at the front door. It's already half past ten. The sight of me in Evelyn's borrowed dressing gown, way too small, delights her.

'You're going walking in *that*?' she says.

We set out an hour or so later. As we leave, we pass Presley, who's digging around in the back of his van. Christianne catches his eye.

'How's it going?' she asks.

'Fine.' He grins. 'Am I allowed to say you'll love it?'

Love what? She doesn't answer, just blows him a kiss, and as we turn to head down to the town I can't help wondering whether

McFaul might have been watching. Budleigh, I'm beginning to conclude, is no place for the faint-hearted.

We walk first to the seafront. Christianne, it turns out, attracts even more attention than Evelyn. Everyone appears to know her, and most of them insist on stopping for a chat and a catch-up. Christianne seems to get a real kick out of introducing me, and as we progress very slowly down the High Street, arm in arm, she starts telling people I'm in the process of moving down.

'But you know that's not true.' At last, we've made the seafront.

'So what? You're famous, that's what really matters. And you're my friend, too. Can I call you that? Do you mind?'

I shake my head. Of course I don't. We're two French girlies together, a slightly exotic addition to this busy little town, but once again I'm struck by how childlike this woman can be. It's nice. She has a candour, and a simplicity, that I find deeply refreshing. Parisian women, especially, can be far too cool, too detached, too *ironique*, for their own good. Not Christianne.

By now we've arrived at the beach. Five hours earlier, with most of Budleigh still in bed, it turns out that my new friend and her buddies were swimming from the far end of the long crescent of pebbles.

'I'll show you exactly where another time.' She squeezes my arm. 'Today, *ma chérie*? Today, we take the coastal path.'

We set off again. Like many big women, Christianne is slightly flat-footed and we stroll slowly along the promenade in the sunshine while she yabbers on in French. She might be an eager child at school in the queue for lunch, I'm thinking. She blitzes me with questions about movie-making, about celebs I might have met, and most of all she wants a helping or two of my private life. Am I married? Do I have kids? Am I *happy*? There's a pleasing artlessness about this curiosity of hers, and she nods when I briefly describe the wreckage that my one and only husband left behind.

'Men can be *loubards*,' she says gravely.

'You know about *loubards*?' I try to hide my surprise. *Loubard* means 'yob'.

'Yes. Not Andy. Andy is sweet. That man is my rock. He looks after me. He keeps me safe. But other men, especially when I was young, back home . . .' She shakes her head. 'You have someone else now?'

'Had.' I tell her about Pavel's stroke, and try to do justice to the kind of person he was. I tell her about our brief couple of years together, and how his passing – utterly predictable – left me short-changed, as well as bereft.

'You thought he was immortal or something? This writer guy?'

'I never thought he'd die. Not properly. Not forever. Maybe his flesh and blood. Maybe that. But not the essence of him. His ideas. His imagination. What he could do with a single thought.'

It's true. The way Pavel could plait one *aperçu* against another, and come up with something so different, so original, so out there that it would take my breath away, always astonished me. Grown-ups aren't supposed to do that. Only kids and fairies.

'You loved this man? Truly *loved* him?' Christianne has paused for a moment to catch her breath as the path begins to steepen.

'Yes. Not physically, not in the end, because that was impossible, but the answer's still yes. It was unconditional on my part. I just couldn't help myself, and you know why? Because I knew he'd never let me get the measure of him, because there were always bits he'd keep hidden. Mystery's a great aphrodisiac, just like laughter. Don't you find that?'

'Of course. Your friend sounds like Africa. No matter how hard you try, you'll never really get to know it. It's at your fingertips, just there. You can see it, you can sense it, you can smell it, but you can never quite get on top of it. You can't pin it down. Lions and tigers and all that safari stuff is one per cent of the story. Africa makes you bleed. And only then do you begin to even half understand.'

Africa makes you bleed? This is powerful stuff, beautifully put, a perfect gem sieved from the torrent of Christianne's conversation. We're climbing now, the row of houses along the seafront behind us, and the path ahead looks steeper and steeper. Christianne is still hanging on to my arm, but she's stumbled a couple of times and I tug her to a halt.

'You're OK with this?'

'With what?'

'Walking?'

'Of course. If you're tired, we can stop.' She says she feels rain in the air, and she's right. She has an anorak but I'm wearing nothing more weatherproof than a thin cagoule. She gestures up at the clouds and produces an old-style plastic mac.

'Here,' she says. 'Put that on top.'

I do her bidding, and then we forge upwards again, trying to match each other step for step. There's something irresistible about this woman. She's fun, if slightly unhinged. Her habit of zigzagging through a conversation makes me laugh. Between outbursts of her own, she has a talent for listening, which is rare, but there's something else about her that I can't quite pin down. She seems excited, liberated, the way you might be if you'd booked to go away, maybe on a whim. She seems to have somewhere strange and exotic in mind, but at the same time she's given to fleeting moments of near-impenetrable silence when the look in her eyes tells me I've lost her. The more often this happens, the more I'm tempted to ask why, but just now this rapport of ours is too new and too delicate to bear much real weight. All I know for sure is that Andy McFaul is a very lucky man.

The path is beginning to flatten out now, and to the right, beyond the fence, I can see a golf course. Then comes a pressure on my arm as Christianne pulls me to a halt. To our left, there's just the hint of another path – nothing more than a smudged boot print or two – through the tangle of shrubs and bushes.

'There,' she says. 'Follow me.'

She steps into the undergrowth, losing her balance for a moment, and then she recovers, tramping down the vegetation, and I follow, trying to avoid the nettles and the prickly stands of wild rose. Abruptly, this barely trodden path turns to the right to avoid a knot of tree roots, and suddenly we're out on the bareness of the clifftop. This little patch is the size of Evelyn's kitchen, not small, and a dry summer has crazy-paved the ochre soil with deep-looking fissures, but the real headline is the view, which is dizzying. Away to the left, prompted by a jerky wave of Christianne's hand, I can see a mile or so along the coast to the distinctive cluster of trees on Otter Head. In between nestles Budleigh itself, a comfortable muddle of rooftops, while a glance to the right reveals yet another promontory.

'Here. Look.' Christianne pulls me to the very edge of the cliff. The drop, which must be hundreds of feet, is near vertical and I feel a stir of fear in my belly as I peer over. Where the sea washes in against the foot of the cliff, the water has turned the strangest shade of red. We could almost be on Mars – a thought I share with Christianne.

'Exactly.' Another sweep of her arm takes in the entire bay before she grabs my hand. 'Special, eh?'

She and Andy, she explains, discovered this hidden gem within a month or two of moving to Budleigh. On hot summer days, they'd hike up here with blankets and a picnic and a bottle of cheap wine. The people who look after the coastal path had already done their best to seal the place off on health and safety grounds, but Andy, she says, has no time for all that *merde* and they were more than happy to take a risk or two for the sake of privacy and a decent tan.

'It's my favourite place in all the world,' she says wistfully. And looking at her, I know she means it.

By now it's begun to rain but I want to take this image, this view, back to London with me. I get my phone out, holding it at arm's length while I position us both a pace or two from the edge of the cliff. Christianne is hanging on to my arm again, fighting for balance, and I wait for her to settle down before taking the photo.

'*Fromage,*' she murmurs. The command to smile turns us briefly into giggling schoolgirls again, and I take a couple of extra shots before pulling us both to safety. These are images I shall treasure until the day I die, but little did I know on that clifftop just how important they'd become.

SIX

We return to the coastal path. By now the rain is heavier, the path sticky with mud, but Christianne obviously knows these parts intimately. She leads me to a gap in the fence, and we wait for a couple of golfers to finish teeing off before we head across the fairway, and then back towards a copse of trees and a row of houses beyond. The closer we get

to the houses, the grander they look. When Christianne steals a
glance at her watch, I ask her why she doesn't rely on her smartphone for time checks.

'Because I haven't got one.'

'No smartphone?'

'No phone at all. Not to carry around.'

I blink. In my world, this is unheard of.

'Any particular reason?'

'Yes. For one thing, I've always got by perfectly well without
a phone in my pocket. And if you really want the truth, I can't
afford the credit. Even when they give the bloody things away,
you're still paying the earth.'

I nod. I've never given a second thought to my Vodafone
unlimited data plan, but that's irrelevant. I need to find out more.

'Does this extend to computers? Laptops? All that?'

'*Au contraire.* Andy's always been on top of the IT stuff, still
is. He was using a computer way back to log the pattern of the
mines he was lifting, and when we were in Angola he even came
up with a programme of his own. He had a phrase for it I always
forget – predictive something – and it seemed to work. He always
said that particular minefields, the way they're laid, tell you
everything you need to know about the bad guys. Crack the way
they think, and the job takes care of itself.'

This sounds impressive. I've been thinking about my last
conversation with Rosa, my agent. Pavel may well have buried
a script for safekeeping, and although I still have his MacBook
with the clever software he used to dictate stuff, I have no idea
how to disinter this unseen treasure. Whether I can trust this
challenge to McFaul is doubtful, but I nevertheless store the
thought away for later.

We're nearly on top of the houses now, and Christianne has
checked her watch for a second time.

'Where are we going?' I ask her.

'There.' She points at the biggest of the nearby houses.

'Why?'

'I want you to meet someone. His name's Sir William. Sir
William Penny. We're expected for lunch.'

'*Lunch?*' This sounds like an ambush. Christianne ignores my
alarm.

'You'll love him, *chérie*. He's a wonderful man. To be honest, I'm showing off. He adores your movies. I think he must have seen them all.'

I shake my head in disbelief. My trainers are caked in mud. I'm soaking wet. A couple of hard miles have raised more than a sweat. *Lunch?*

'Can't we make it some other time? Like this evening? We could invite him out somewhere. I don't mind paying.'

Christianne shakes her head. We're a little late already. Bill is very forgiving, she says, but she knows his views on punctuality.

'A word about his little dog,' she adds. 'Her name's Hundchen. Bill got her as a stray in Berlin. She's old now, and she's going blind, poor thing, but we all love her.' She smiles. 'Especially me.'

We're in the driveway by now. A green Range Rover, slightly battered, is parked on the semicircle of gravel in front of the house. The name 'Bill' has triggered a memory. One of the estate agents' windows in the High Street, I think. Nothing under a million pounds.

'Evelyn knows him?' I ask.

'Of course. They play bridge together. And she loves Hundchen as much as I do.'

We mount the steps to the front door, and Christianne rings the bell. Inside, I can hear a dog yapping, then the door opens and I'm looking at a tall, thin figure, slightly stooped. He's wearing a pair of salmon-coloured chinos, and a check shirt open at the neck, and after he's submitted to a long hug from Christianne, his gaze settles on me. He has a slight cast in one eye which should be disconcerting but somehow isn't.

'Ahhh . . .' The smile, unforced, is full of warmth. 'Do, please, come in.'

The house smells of furniture polish and fresh flowers. The entrance hall has parquet flooring, and a couple of exquisite rugs. A staircase winds up to a gallery on the first floor, and the walls – a deep green – are hung with antique prints.

Sir William, as I'll call him, takes my borrowed plastic mac and Christianne's anorak, and we both leave our shoes at the door. Christianne touches Sir William lightly on the arm and asks whether she might give me a tour of the house.

'Of course, my dear. You'll know where to find me.' Sir William gives me a cheerful wink and disappears down the hall. Moments later, I hear the chink-chink of cutlery. Already, Christianne is halfway up the staircase. The dog has appeared from nowhere and seems to recognize her scent. It mounts the stairs one by one, wheezing slightly, while Christianne directs my attention to a fall of rich material in blues and browns and whites, hanging on the wall.

'Batik,' she says. 'Bill served in Jakarta for a while. I think it was his first posting as ambassador.'

'How well do you know this man?' Hundchen is sniffing around my ankles.

'Very well. We come here a lot. He's a good friend.'

'We?'

'Andy and I. Bill's a volunteer with the National Trust. He might not look the part but Andy says he's great with mending fences and stiles. That's where they met. That's where it all began.'

'Andy's a volunteer as well?'

'Yes.' We've come to a halt outside a door at the end of the upstairs landing. This is a room, Christianne says, that has to be seen to be believed, and as she opens the door a foot or two and stands aside to let me take a look, I sense an almost proprietary sense of pride. But she's right. The room is huge, washed in grey autumnal light. The windows offer a view out towards the coastal path, and I catch the gleam of the sea beyond. The furniture is French, and one of the armchairs looks original, possibly Louis XVI, but the real jewel is a chaise longue, perfectly angled to take advantage of the view. A glance at the fabric, wonderfully thick stripes of dark blue and grey, tells me the chaise has been recently upholstered, but the rightness of the proportions, the way the back swoops down to join the seat, oozes class. Thanks to my mum's passion for provincial auctions, I happen to know a little about French antique furniture and I know that this chaise must have cost Sir William a fortune.

I gaze at it for a moment longer, wondering whether I might give it a try, if only to enjoy the view, when Christianne touches me lightly on the arm. She's nodding at the double bed wedged against the back wall and I realize someone is curled beneath the embroidered counterpane.

'Who's that?' I whisper.

'Sylvester. Bill's son. He flew over from New York last night. Took a cab from the airport this morning.'

'Exeter?'

'Heathrow.'

'On the meter?'

'Probably.'

'Bloody hell.'

'Exactly.'

We giggle together again, schoolgirls at the feast of someone else's making, then I hear our host calling from below. Lunch is ready. Sir William will be glad to serve us.

We descend to the dining room. The dog is desperate for affection so I stoop to pick her up and give her a brief cuddle as we go back downstairs. The table is laid for four but I'm guessing that Sylvester is still asleep. At Sir William's invitation, we sit down. Lunch is a selection of cold cuts with a crisp green salad, and late-season new potatoes. Our host has readied a bottle of Chablis and circles the head of the table to fill our glasses. The toast, when it comes, is simplicity itself.

'To *Arpeggio*,' he says. 'And all the other treats you've given me.'

Arpeggio is a not-so-recent film of mine, a brooding exploration of guilt and the capricious workings of fate, made with French money and under the direction of a young German director I happen to admire greatly. Sir William, it turns out, had him round to the embassy a number of times in Berlin.

'You'll be glad to know he thought the world of you,' he says. 'Which doesn't surprise me in the least.'

It's a graceful compliment, and I thank him for it. I can sense that Christianne wants me to perform a little, to brighten Sir William's day with tales from various film sets, and I talk at some length about the madness of putting character and story on the big screen.

'Madness?' From Sir William, the word carries an air of slight reproof.

'Madness,' I confirm. 'Insanity. The best directors, the best actors, are often a little crazy. You often shoot out of sequence. The key bits are always in close-up. You have to remember so much, hold the big picture, concentrate on the tiniest details. The camera is unforgiving. If you make the slightest bloop, drop the tiniest stitch, it will always find you out.'

'Golly.' Sir William is carefully removing a thin crescent of fat from his roast beef, 'To be honest, I never quite thought of it that way. My admiration is unbounded. Does that make me naïve? Or simply grateful?'

It's at this point that the door opens and the missing diner appears. For a split second, I'm looking at an older version of Malo: the same tangle of black curls, the same snake hips inside the tightness of his jeans, the same predatory hints in his smile.

'Sorry, Pa . . .' He settles at the table and reaches for the bottle of Chablis. 'New York time tells me I need a drink. Do you mind?' He has a faint American accent which I'm guessing he can turn on and off at will. When his father tells him it's seven o'clock in the morning on the eastern seaboard, he simply shrugs. 'Whatever.' His eyes find mine, and he nods at my glass. 'A little more?'

Christianne and I stay at the table for most of the afternoon, chatting to Sir William. Sylvester, after answering a series of emails on his phone, has pushed his plate to one side and left without a word of apology. This kind of abruptness is so Malo that I can barely believe it, and when I get the chance to stop talking about showbusiness, I ask Sir William about this son of his. Does he live in New York? Work in New York? If so, doing what?

'An excellent question, my dear. He tells me he's in venture finance. I gather that's code for taking very large bets with other people's money. Am I proud of him? Of course I am. Can he be insufferably rude on occasions? I'm afraid so. My only excuse is that he left home at a tender age. Carting him round the world from posting to posting simply wasn't an option. I'm not sure he took to prep school and in various ways he's been paying me back ever since. Guilt, I'm afraid, is harder to bear the older you get, but one day we might be kinder to each other.'

Kinder to each other. I've been here before and I sense that Sir William understands that. By now, after a couple of hours of conversation, I know exactly what has drawn Christianne to this man. He's fluent in a number of languages. He's shrewd, witty, effortlessly charming, and a brilliant listener. Not once has he given us the impression that he might be anyone special. His knighthood, perhaps like his wayward son, was simply an inexplicable accident that happened en route.

We say our goodbyes in the late afternoon. Sir William kisses me on both cheeks, warms my hands in his, and insists I'm welcome any time. When I tell him I have to go back to London, he looks pained.

'Our loss, my dear,' he says. 'God speed.'

Christianne and I dawdle on the way home. She tells me she's tired, and when I suggest a pause at a pub called The Feathers in the High Street, she's very happy to say yes. Two large glasses of Merlot arrive, and when I propose a toast, I notice her hand shaking with the effort of holding the glass. I know she wants me to stay a couple of days more, and in truth I'd like to, but a number of pressing engagements await me in London, and I know I have to get back on the road. When I ask the barman for a pen and a sheet of paper, and write down my contact details, she studies them carefully.

'W11?' she queries.

'Holland Park. Come and stay any time. You'd like it.'

'You mean that?'

'I do.'

'Both of us? Andy, too?'

I say nothing and hold her gaze for a long moment before she finally says she understands.

'It's nothing personal.' I put my hand over hers. 'Nothing to do with Andy. It's just that this, just the pair of us, works so well.'

'You mean that?' she says again.

'Yes.'

Over the wine, we talk a little more about our afternoon with Sir William. When I tell her the man was an utter delight, I mean it, but I'm curious to know about his private life. Was there a Lady Penny?

'Yes.'

'And?'

'She died in a pile-up on the M5. I think it broke his heart, though he'd never admit it. That room I showed you used to be their bedroom. Bill hasn't slept in it since.'

'How do you know?'

'His son told me. Sylvester.' Christianne's gaze has returned to the address I've scribbled. It's still lying on the table between us. 'So what's it like?' The question sounds almost wistful. 'Holland Park?'

'It's London lite. I'm lucky. We had money once, my ex-husband and I, and it bought us all the things we thought mattered.'

'Like?'

'Peace and quiet. Decent neighbours. Good places to eat. It's odd, isn't it? Sort all that, find the right address, a nice place to live, and you think you've got it cracked. We were wrong, of course, but we were young, and far too pleased with ourselves, and that can make you stupid. The real problem comes from here.' My hand closes briefly over my heart. 'I thought I knew the man. How wrong can a girl be?'

'Bad times?'

'The worst. Way beyond bad. Then I got sick, and that didn't help, but the marriage was the real killer. What we did to each other was near terminal. No child on earth needs that.'

Christianne nods. She's nearly finished her wine. 'Evelyn told me,' she says.

'About Malo?'

'About the tumour.' She touches her own head. 'It's gone now?'

'Most of it. I have regular check-ups, every six months. They do a brain scan and my consultant hauls me in and we look at the results together. If you want the truth, it's very odd. The bad bits come out as a kind of shadow. It's in here . . .' My finger briefly settles on my forehead. 'The X-rays and the chemo zapped most of it but there are still little traces and I'm guessing there always will be. I used to press him for some kind of clue, how many years I might expect, but he says it's all guesswork. Maybe something else will carry me away – who knows? He tells me there's no point worrying myself to death and he's probably right. He's a great Churchill fan, my consultant. KBO, he says. Keep buggering on.'

Christianne's smile is wan, an act of politesse. Her lips are moving. She's trying out the phrase for herself. Keep buggering on, she whispers. *Keep . . . buggering . . . on.* Then she shakes her head, reaches for the address and scans it one last time before slipping it into her bag.

'That place of yours sounds nice,' she says.

'You'll come? You promise?'

She studies me for a long moment. She doesn't answer my question but when I ask her again, she summons another smile, warmer this time, reaches for her glass but misses. Embarrassed, she recovers herself and grabs it on the second try. She knows I'm watching her, and I think she can feel my concern, but she says nothing.

We finish our drinks in silence and head for the street. Walking up the hill, Christianne starts to lose her balance again, but I put my arm through hers and we struggle on upwards. Neither of us has the breath for conversation, and when we finally arrive at Evelyn's gate, she gives me a hug.

'Say goodbye before you go,' she says. 'Just promise me that.'

'I will, of course I will. We'll meet again. We'll make it happen. London. Holland Park. There's a Lebanese restaurant down the road. You'll love it.'

'I know.'

'So, you'll come? Make the effort? I'll buy you a train ticket, meet you at Paddington. It won't cost you a penny.'

'That's kind.'

'Do I hear a yes?'

'*Peut-être.*' Maybe.

She disentangles herself from the hug and gently pushes me away before heading for her own gate. Back inside Evelyn's bungalow, I find her arranging lines of books on her new shelves.

'I was starting to wonder,' she says, nodding at the clock on the mantelpiece. 'I thought someone might have carried the pair of you off.'

SEVEN

Next morning, packed and ready to go, it's time to say goodbye to Christianne. I knock a couple of times, and it's McFaul who comes to the door. When I enquire about Christianne, he says she's still in bed. He's very happy to pass on a message but just now wouldn't be the time to disturb her.

'Is she OK?'

'Touch of flu. It happens sometimes.'

'Poor thing.'

'Yeah.'

I hold his gaze. Saying goodbye to Christianne plainly isn't an option.

'Just tell her it'll be fine,' I say. 'Just tell her that.'

'What will be fine? Am I allowed to ask?'

'Of course. She's coming up to town for a couple of days. My treat.' I stare at him. 'Have I said something funny?'

'Not at all.' He gestures vaguely towards what must be the bedroom. 'I'll let her know.'

'That would be kind. Say hi from me, too. And tell her it's been fun.' I pause a moment. For the first time, I catch a waft or two of incense, maybe a joss stick, sweet, pungent. Or maybe, I think later, weed. Already, McFaul is stepping back inside, wanting this conversation to be over.

'Take care.' I hold my ground. 'The pair of you.'

Back next door, I say my goodbyes to Evelyn. She's effusive about me making the effort to come down and give her what she calls 'moral support', but what's pleased her most is the bond I seem to have established with Christianne.

'She's been a bit down lately,' she says. 'You've brought her out of herself. She's become the old Christianne again. I don't know the secret, but it's really made a difference.'

'We're French,' I say. 'That's all you need to know.'

We look at each other for a moment, and then she opens her

arms. 'You've been wonderful, my lovely.' She gives me a long hug. 'What a shame you can't stay forever.'

I'm back in London by early afternoon. I have a mental list of calls to make, bills to pay, and arrangements to confirm, but the moment I step into the apartment I realize how foolish it is to take anything for granted. Three glorious days with Evelyn and Christianne have made me lazy. Real life, as Pavel once told me, never takes a holiday.

Malo, my son, is sprawled on the sofa. At first I think he's asleep but when I dump my coat on the back of the chair, one eye opens. Already I have a feeling of dread. I tell myself something terrible has happened, and it's no consolation to find out that I'm right.

'Clem's left me,' he grunts.

'Again?'

'Yeah. But this time she means it.'

'How do you know?'

'She told me.'

'Has she found someone else?'

'I don't think so.'

'So, what is it?'

'Me.'

My son is seldom this honest. Like his natural father, when the world doesn't do his bidding, he has a reflexive habit of blaming someone else. In the case of H, this has frequently led to violence, always directed against other men, while Malo prefers the long sulk.

Looking down at the line of little bottles beside the sofa, I'm briefly torn between compassion and impatience. Leffe Blonde has its place in any celebration, but beer that strong does nothing for self-pity.

'Are you drunk?' I ask him.

'Yes. A bit.'

'That can't have helped, not with Clemmie.'

A nod signals agreement. Clem doesn't touch the stuff.

'Does it stop with booze?'

'You know it doesn't.'

'What else, then?'

Malo just looks at me, then shakes his head. I try to contain my temper, staring down at him. For some reason I can think only of Sylvester Penny, riding west from Heathrow in a London cab, oblivious of the meter. Reckless. Spoiled. All the usual terms of endearment.

'Consider Clemmie for a moment,' I tell him. 'Poor bloody woman.'

This might be a cue for a much longer conversation but I'm tired after the drive and not having the apartment to myself has come as a bit of a shock. It's been a while since I spent any serious time with my son and while it's nice to catch up, the prospect of him moving back in alarms me deeply. The last time we lived together, his drug of choice was Spice: cheap, addictive, nasty. It turned him into a zombie, an experience I never want to live through again, and it was only the discovery of his real father that gave me my sanity back. H is nerveless on life's tighter bends, and I'm still grateful for the way he took charge of our feckless son.

'Does H know about Clemmie?' I ask him.

'Not yet.'

'Aren't you going to tell him?'

'Yeah. Maybe.'

'What does that mean?'

'Nothing. You know what he thinks of her.'

'He thinks she's wonderful. Like we all do. And like you should.'

'Who says I don't?'

'This does.' I gesture down at the sofa, at the line of empties, at the roll-up still smouldering between Malo's fingers. 'Take a look at yourself. I'm guessing this is what that lovely girl has to come home to every night. Are you surprised she wants out?'

Malo is staring up at me. I can see the surprise in his eyes.

'That's harsh.' He's trying to make me smile. 'You're supposed to be my mum, take my side, make me feel better.'

'Better about what? About making Clemmie's life a misery? In your dreams, Malo. In case you haven't noticed, there are other people on the planet apart from your lovely self and I suggest you spare a thought for them, too. One of them's Clemmie. Another is me. You might start by clearing up after yourself and taking that bloody thing outside. No one smokes in this flat. I think I may have mentioned it before.'

I bend quickly and take the roll-up. Malo is incredulous, as well as angry. He watches me pinch the end of the roll-up between my fingers and step into the kitchen. I drop it in the bin and return to the lounge. He's upright now, sitting on the sofa.

'Well . . .?' I'm nodding at the bottles. 'I'm serious, Malo. If you're really wanting to stay here, if you really think it's over with Clemmie, then we have to get one or two things straight. This is my place. This is where I live. So either you give it a bit of respect, and me too while you're at it, or I suggest you go and live with H.'

Malo gazes at me. It's been a while since I've been this frank with him.

'That might not be possible,' he says at last.

'Why not?'

'Because I *did* phone him. I was going to tell you. When I explained about Clem, he went mad, lost it completely.' He looks pained, bites his lip, then shrugs. 'So, what choice do I have?' He bends to retrieve the empty bottles, then glances up again. 'Spare room, Mum? Like before?'

For the rest of the day, we tiptoe round each other, observing the provisions of what feels like an armed truce. This is deeply wearing for both of us and, mid-evening, after a supper on trays in front of *Call the Midwife*, I break out a bottle of Rioja and offer him a glass or two. This perks him up no end and by the time we say our goodnights, he's behaving like a human being again. He even concedes that I'm probably right about Clem, and that he needs to clean up his act, which – coming from my son – is something of a surprise. Malo, now twenty-one, still has youth, looks, and occasional outbreaks of charm on his side. Confusing this with the hard work it takes to sustain a grown-up relationship has always been his mistake.

Moments before he goes to bed, he admits he's been a dickhead.

'That's something *you'll* have to live with.' I give him a kiss. 'Not me.'

EIGHT

Next morning, I leave Malo to sleep late while I get on with the rest of my life. By lunchtime, I've written a long email to Evelyn, assuring her of a bright future as a public speaker, and have also been in touch with my agent. The good news is that a BBC royalty cheque we've been expecting has at last come through, but it seems they're more eager than ever to nail down Pavel's mystery script.

'You've looked, my precious?' Rosa asks.

'Not yet.'

'Then when?'

'Soon. These things aren't as simple as you might think.'

'Simple? You?' Rosa laughs. 'Why am I not surprised?'

I have lunch with a girlfriend in Notting Hill. A fellow thesp, she feeds me endless gossip from the set of a big feature shooting out at Elstree, and warns me never to open my dressing-room door to the fatter of the movie's two producers.

'The man's a carnivore.' She shakes her head. 'Share a meal with him and all the clues are there. Normally, he never takes his knife and fork to any girl this side of twenty, so maybe I should feel flattered. He didn't even ask nicely. Just dug in.'

This, we agree, is the Zeitgeist. First Trump. Then a small army of grotesques in thrall to their dicks.

'I giggled at the sight of it.' She orders another glass of Prosecco. 'Laugh like you mean it, and the bastard's out the door.'

'Along with your career?'

'Hopefully not. Though these days, that might be a blessing.'

I'm back in Holland Park by late afternoon, fully expecting to find Malo still in bed. Fumbling for my key, I think I can hear voices inside the apartment. I'm right. Malo, fully dressed, is pouring a cup of tea for a suited figure sitting at the kitchen table. This stranger has his back to the door but there's something familiar about the almost seigneurial way he's pushed the chair back and crossed one leg over the other, and the moment he turns to look at me, I know I'm not wrong. Sir William's wayward son.

'Sylvester.' I dump my bag. 'What on earth brings you here?'

'Pa had a book he meant to give you.' He gestures at a Waitrose bag on the table. 'I got your address from Evelyn and volunteered to drop by and let you have it. Your son's been the soul of hospitality. Not just tea but biscuits, too.'

I sense at once that this story of his is wildly improbable, and a glance at the book confirms it. Why on earth would I want to read a novel by Nevil Shute?

Malo has found another cup. He even remembers that I prefer lemon to milk.

'Sylvester's come up for a meeting, Mum,' he says. 'The Twilight Fund? Why on earth didn't you tell me? It's a brilliant idea. Genius.'

Twilight Fund? I haven't a clue what he's talking about.

Sylvester is on his feet now, offering me his chair. Half an hour ago, I was braced for another round of post-adolescent angst. Now this.

'It's Pa's fault.' Sylvester nods at the book. 'He got me reading it a while ago, said it was one of his all-time favourites. I took it to New York, finished it on the flight over. He was right. Shute wrote it yonks ago but it's un-put-down-able, especially now.'

'And this is your father's copy?'

'No, it's mine. But he wants you to read it.'

I'm looking at the cover, then at the synopsis on the back. A nuclear war has ravaged the northern hemisphere and a giant cloud of radioactivity is making its way towards Australia. A US Navy submarine captain is among many of the refugees seeking shelter and awaiting the inevitable, while he falls in love with a local woman. Then comes a faint radio transmission from the US. After all the carnage, there may be survivors. The captain's wife and family are on the eastern seaboard. And so, he must go back.

'They turned it into a movie, of course. 1959. Gregory Peck and Ava Gardner. Pa thinks you could act her off the screen.'

'In a remake, you mean?'

'Of course.'

I nod. This man is a born salesman, I think, a judgement obviously shared by my son.

'The movie's a great idea, Mum,' he says. 'I told Sylvester how many people you know in the business. But the movie's only part of it. Listen to the rest.'

'The rest?'

'The Twilight Fund.'

My gaze goes from one face to the other. Only yesterday, the moment I set eyes on this man, I was looking at an older version of Malo. Now, in the flesh, the similarity is uncanny. It's not just a physical likeness – the same facial bone structure, especially around the eyes, the same disdain for a comb or a hairbrush – but they both have the knack of seizing your attention and not letting go.

I suggest we make ourselves comfortable next door. Sylvester and Malo, peas in a pod, settle on the sofa.

'The Twilight Fund?' I enquire again.

Sylvester nods. When he asks me if I mind him calling me Enora, I say he's welcome.

'Bottom line, we're talking money, venture funding, investment. I've been in this game a while, Enora, and every proposition shakes down pretty much the same way. Life is a market. Think buyers and sellers. What you have to find is something people really want, and in this case Mr Shute's made it very easy.'

'So, what is it? What are you selling?'

'Survival. You've heard of the Doomsday Clock?'

'No.'

'It was dreamed up by a bunch of nuclear scientists after the last war. They wanted to measure how close the world was to catastrophe. The closer we get to midnight, the closer we are to extinction.'

'And now?'

'It's two minutes to. That, believe me, should frighten us all. Before Trump came along, and global warming took off, we had one hundred and twenty seconds in hand. Now, all bets are off.'

'Scary.'

'You're right. And what makes it worse, or maybe better from our point of view, is just how helpless we've become. We're all spectators now. What happens, happens. Unless, that is, you've got a great deal of money.'

His big opportunity, Sylvester explains, came a couple of years ago, when a Stateside road trip with a girlfriend took him across the Midwest. In North Dakota, he came across a roadside advert for apartments with a difference.

'A difference, how?'

'Normally, you build upwards, but the Midwest is full of old silos, big holes in the prairie. They used to house intercontinental missiles. Now most of those missiles have gone to sea in submarines so the silos are empty. Some genius with a black sense of humour decided to start building *down*. These are fully serviced apartments, storey after storey of them. For a lot of money, you get the full survival *shtick*: parking, a supermarket, full sanitation, every movie ever made, medical facilities, the gym of your dreams, the lot. There isn't much of a view, but at least you won't fry.'

'Really?' I'm trying to imagine this proposition. The rest of the world might have gone up in flames, and everything is poisoned for ever, but I ask Sylvester whether it's worth sharing the rest of my life with a bunch of grumpy moles.

'Good question. Excellent question. Terrifying prospect. But that's not the point. Believe me, this thing has taken off. You won't believe how many people are buying in. The silos are everywhere. There's a rash of them, all over the Midwest. Colorado, Nebraska, Montana, you name it. You're buying insurance, you're buying survival; an investment like this lets you sleep at night. Two million pounds to get to old age? If you're rich enough, you think it's a steal.'

'And you're part of this? You're selling these apartments?'

'I have been, yes, but it's like anything. The proposition sells itself and that means that half the bloody world has piled in. Competition's a fine thing but just sometimes life is too short. You know what I'm saying here?'

I shake my head. I'm afraid I don't.

'It's the marketplace, Mum.' This from Malo. 'Too many fingers, not enough pies.'

'Think gold rush, Enora. It's California, 1849 all over again, and you can't move on the riverbank for all those prospectors sieving away. There isn't enough gold to go round. Something has to give.'

'An alternative, Mum. You need to dream up some other way of staying alive. And Sylvester's found it.'

I take the pair of them out for an early supper. Sylvester makes a couple of phone calls to reschedule meetings he says he'd planned for this evening, and the three of us are sitting down to Lebanese mezze before the restaurant has a chance to fill up. This is my favourite local eatery, the one I mentioned to try and tempt Christianne up to town, and the woman who runs it offers us a bottle of Prosecco on the house. A little to my surprise, Sylvester opts for Perrier, as does Malo. To watch my son turn down free alcohol is a pleasure I've never had before, but by now I sense he's keen to impress this man who's just stepped into our lives. So far, we've skirted the small print of exactly what Sylvester might have in mind for the Twilight Fund, but now Malo is keen to press him for details.

'It's simple,' he says. 'You start with the habits of the super-rich. A man makes himself – say – a billionaire. Some of them keep that kind of wealth to themselves, but others need the world to know. Not everyone, of course. You're dealing here with maybe 0.1% of the population. But it's precisely those folk, equally blessed, that you want to impress. This quickly becomes a social thing. You throw huge parties – birthdays especially. You favour the coolest night clubs in the coolest cities. You buy Margaux and Château-Lafite by the case, sometimes for tables of complete strangers. And each of these extravagant little gestures establishes just how amazing you are. Not just talented, not just rich, but *generous*, too. These are boasts, of course, and everyone knows it, but the currency that matters at this level is celebrity, being talked about, and you'd be amazed by how many of these people buy in.'

I'm wondering what exactly any of this has got to do with the Doomsday Clock and the Twilight Fund, when Malo asks exactly the same question. Sylvester breaks off for a moment and puts a hand on his arm.

'Patience, my friend,' he murmurs. 'Just ask yourself one

question. These people adore toys, especially when it's costing them the thick end of seven figures. So what's the must-have, high-end purchase?'

'The private jet?' Malo is frowning.

'Close.'

'The hilltop spread in Tuscany?'

'Nice try.'

'A super yacht,' I say quietly.

'Exactly.' Sylvester offers me a nod of approval. 'Just think about it. Buy something big – wrong, *commission* something *enormous* – and you broadcast just how far your money will stretch. That ticks one box. The others are obvious. You can live aboard, enjoy everything your little heart desires. You can spend the summer sailing from port to port, country to country, continent to continent. When it's party time, you decorate the gangplank, and phone the caterers, and invite your rich friends aboard. And when the shit *really* hits the fan, and the world blows up . . .' He pauses, waiting for one of us to finish the sentence.

'You sail away,' Malo says.

'Exactly. Get it right, and we're not talking survival in some burrow in North Dakota, we're talking the remote Pacific, the far South Atlantic, even the Antarctic if your data feeds tell you that's safest.'

Malo and I exchange nods. I've been on enough Mediterranean film locations to confirm that much of this stuff is true. A week-long shoot in Cannes, or Nice, or Malaga, would often end with all-night parties on some super yacht or other. More often than not, we'd never get to meet the owner, but that wasn't the point. We thesps were part of the offer, along with the buckets of Kristal champagne and the devilled prawn wraps. In fact, Malo himself was conceived aboard a super yacht in Antibes, thanks partly to H's special take on margaritas.

'Survival afloat?' I ask. 'Is that what you're selling?'

'Yes. You've nailed it.'

'So, pretend I'm very rich. What am I buying?'

'Everything you'd normally specify, plus some tweaks.'

'Like?' This from Malo.

'Zero reliance on FFs, for starters.'

'FFs?'

'Fossil fuels. No petrol. No diesel. We have to make assumptions here. Every port, every refuelling facility, will either be rubble or glowing with radiation.'

'Back to sails, then.'

'Sure. That would be safest. Some folk talk about solar, but the jury's still out on the technology and in any case, survivors might be in for wall-to-wall cloud cover. They call it nuclear winter. And if you can't rely on the sun, wind is the only option. That will certainly get you places that will keep you safe. Then there's food and water. Food's no problem. Think NASA. Lots of dried stuff, tinned stuff, high-protein shit. A yacht of the right size, you can stock up for years, and when you need something fresh you can always tow a trolling line and hook a fish or two. Water? A breeze, literally. Wind will charge batteries, and batteries will power a modest desalination rig.'

I nod again. Item by item, Sylvester's prescription for life everlasting is making perfect sense. Then I remember Nevil Shute's cloud of intense radiation, slowly girdling the entire planet.

'What if there's nowhere to hide?' I ask. 'What then?'

'We give you a safe room down below. Lead-lined. Impervious to radiation. You have access to water, food, light, heat, everything you need. Most radioactive elements have a half-life measured in months, sometimes years. We'll keep you alive until it's safe to come out. And that's a promise.'

This, I know, has to be a joke.

'So, who could possibly enforce a guarantee like that? When most of the world is in ruins?'

'No one. But I guess that's the whole point. A tiny, tiny handful of the world's population has the means to cheat the Doomsday Clock. All they need is money. The rest is down to us.'

'You mean you?'

'Me and my company. We like to think of ourselves as enablers, the yeast in the mix that makes the whole thing rise. Having the idea's one thing. Bringing it to market, quite another.'

When I ask him where on earth he'd start, he's looking at Malo.

'Someone told me you organized an expedition a couple of

years back,' he says. 'Took a bunch of paying guests to Normandy aboard an old fishing smack.'

'*Provident.*' Malo's grinning. 'It was a Brixham trawler. We hit a shipping container on the way back and ended up on the beach in Ventnor, but that wasn't my fault.'

'I know. The guy told me that, too. He was impressed.'

'By the boat? The voyage?'

'By you. You had to hook him in the first place and this guy isn't an easy sell. He happens to be rich now, very rich, but he still takes a lot of convincing.'

I can see my son searching his memory for a name from the half dozen faces we took on the voyage.

'Amit someone,' he says at last. 'Indian guy. Has to be him. It was family money and he was big into themed restaurants. He was tight as fuck as well but there was a journalist on board, a woman he fancied, so he came along in the end, although she blew him out. He had a little office off the Tottenham Court Road. Bit of an arsehole, if you want the truth.'

'His name's Iyengar,' Sylvester says. 'And you're right, the man's a monster, but that's why he's rich, just like the rest of them.'

'He's a client of yours?' I enquire.

'A prospect. The way these things work, you put together a bunch of names and then make individual approaches. These people love the personal touch. In fact, they insist on it. Iyengar has a wife he cheats on every day of the week, and a bunch of spoiled kids he's sending to all the right schools. Business is baked into his genes and these last couple of years he's diversified into lifestyle projects, most of which have come good. He's the kind of guy who plans for every eventuality, except the one that's really going to matter, and I'm told that makes him very nervous indeed. He has a super yacht already, but he knows it's not up to the job. Bottom line, he's a family man. They all have to survive.'

'You've talked to him?'

'Only on the phone. That's when he mentioned your son.'

Both Malo and I are beginning to realize exactly why Sylvester Penny has tracked us down. This wasn't a neighbourly errand on behalf of the lovely Sir William, far from it. He's knocked on my door to lay hands on my son. And here we all are.

In these situations, Pavel always counselled what he termed 'full frontal'. Tell it like you think it is, and then see what happens.

'Have you come with some kind of proposition?' I ask Sylvester.

'Of course I have.' He checks his watch, and then looks up at Malo. 'Working with me. Selling top-end survival. How does that sound?'

NINE

F *ar too simple* is the answer. And far too seductive. Under normal circumstances, I'd counsel caution in my son's dealings with Sylvester Penny. Malo definitely needs a sense of direction in his life, especially if Clemmie really has gone, but there are a number of questions I'd like answered about Sylvester's take on venture funding. Is this his own enterprise? Does a market really exist for Doomsday yachts? And what, exactly, is he offering the likes of Amit Iyengar?

I'm half awake, trying to tease some kind of order into this muddle of half-remembered clues from last night, when the phone rings. I roll over in bed and check the time. 04.49.

'Hello? Enora?'

It's Evelyn. She sounds out of breath. She's having trouble getting words in the right order.

'It's Christianne,' she says finally. 'She's gone.'

'Gone?'

'Disappeared.'

She tells me that she woke in the middle of the night to a revolving blue light outside in the street. From the window of her bedroom, she watched McFaul get out of a police car. With an officer beside him, he let himself into the bungalow. They must have been inside for maybe fifteen minutes, then the pair of them reappeared and got back in the car before driving off. Puzzled, Evelyn wondered whether to phone Christianne to make sure she was all right, but when she tried the number – a landline – there was no answer.

'So, what did you do?'

'I went back to bed. Maybe half an hour later, there was a knock at the door. It was still dark, about an hour ago, just gone four.'

'And?'

'It was Andy. He said that he and the police and God knows who else had been looking for Christianne all night. You know how she sometimes likes to swim last thing in the day? She'd gone down to the beach as usual but didn't come back. Andy got worried and went to look for her. Her favourite spot's along towards where the river comes out. That's where he found her clothes.'

'On the beach?'

'Yes. With a towel and trackie bottoms and that cagoule of hers.'

McFaul, she said, had walked back along the beach, thinking she might have got into trouble and been swept along by the current, but found no sign. A couple of people had been out with their dogs. One of them knew Christianne by sight but hadn't seen her.

'Does she always swim alone?'

'In the evening, yes. Earlier, first thing, no.'

'Was there any . . .' I'm trying to avoid the word, but can't. 'Note?'

'Not on the beach, no.'

'In the house?'

'Yes. That's why they were knocking on my door. It was in an envelope, this note. It had your name on, my lovely. It was for you.'

Less than half an hour later, I'm on the road. I've thrown a bunch of clothes into a holdall. I've woken Malo and told him to expect me back whenever. When he peered up at me, rubbing his eyes in the throw of light from the open door, he wanted to know what was going on.

'I've no idea,' I told him. 'I'll phone when I find out more.'

Sunrise finds me on the M25, among the stop-go lines of early-morning traffic. The police, with McFaul's permission, had opened the envelope and read the note. According to Evelyn, it was Christianne saying goodbye. I'd pressed her for the details, but she told me she couldn't do it justice. I had to see it for myself, and in any case I had no choice because the police had decided I was a close friend and now need to talk to me.

'Come down, my lovely. If not for her sake, then for mine.'

Close friend? I've known this woman for a couple of days. We share a language, a background, and in the fullness of time probably much else. But *close friend*? I'm on the A303 now, the road to the south-west, and I pull off at the first service station. I buy myself a big flat white and return to the car to make a call to Evelyn for an update.

'The police are being fantastic,' she says at once. 'Even Andy says so.'

Half a dozen officers, she tells me, are down on the beach searching steadily left and right from where Andy found the pile of clothing. The coastguard has launched the Exmouth lifeboat, and volunteers with binoculars are up on the clifftops that flank the town, scanning the water below for signs of Christianne.

'What's the weather like?'

'It's a lovely day. Sunny, warm, even this early. Andy says the sea's still OK, too. In fact, this time of year's as warm as it gets.'

'You mean she could still be alive?'

'I think so, yes. We haven't given up hope. Not yet.'

'We?'

'Andy and I.'

'How is he?'

'Very hard to tell. He's a man, my lovely. He doesn't give much away. I remember my father when my mother died. Whatever they're feeling stays under lock and key. Maybe it's a generational thing. For a while I thought he didn't much care, but then I found him in tears one day, when he thought no one was looking, so who knows?'

When he thought no one was looking. I can't help thinking of McFaul in his garden in the middle of the night, semi-naked, coaxing ball after ball into hole after hole. Pavel used to talk about everyone's hidden reefs, the defences we all throw up to cope with life's bigger waves, and I'm guessing that McFaul's are higher or perhaps thicker than most.

'Is he back home now?' I ask. 'Andy?'

'I don't know. I don't think so. They've got a police dog on the beach, too. I think Andy rummaged in the laundry and took some extra clothing down. I gather it helps with the scent. I've got a number for you, by the way. Do you have a pen?'

She gives me contact details for the police officer who appears to be in charge of the search. Her name is Inspector Grace Hollick and she'd appreciate a call. I make a note and tell Evelyn I'm still a couple of hours away.

'Of course, my lovely. Drive carefully. I'm sure Christianne will have turned up by the time you get here.'

Inspector Hollick, when I finally get through, seems less certain. She's obviously a woman under pressure because I can hear a chorus of voices in the background, mainly male, and the squawk of seagulls suggests she may be on the beach.

'Any news?' I ask.

'None, I'm afraid. Mispers can be more complicated than you might imagine. We live in hope, though.'

Mispers, I happen to know, is police-speak for Missing Persons. Inspector Hollick asks how well I know Budleigh.

'Hardly at all.'

'We're on the beach. You can't miss it. Drive to the far end. There's a big car park. Look for a white incident van. Ask for me.'

The line goes dead, and I sit behind the wheel for a moment or two, sipping the remains of my coffee. I've had far more contact with the police over the last couple of years than any woman my age deserves, but it's given me a healthy respect for their ability to rise to events. Dial 999, as McFaul may have done, and you'll be amazed at what might happen.

It's mid-morning by the time I make it to Budleigh. I'm tempted to go to Evelyn's place first but decide against it. The incident van is parked in the far corner of the seafront car park, beside a couple of marked cars and an ambulance. A tall woman, uniformed, is in conversation with a suited youth making notes. She's very black, very much in charge, and I'm aware of her eyes settling on me as I approach.

'Ms Andressen?' She breaks off the conversation and extends a hand. Moments later, she's sliding open the side door of the van, and inviting me in. The youth with the notebook is evidently a local reporter.

'That must help,' I suggest. 'Getting the word out.'

My comment falls on deaf ears. The back of the van has the makings of a small office, complete with a comms console. From a file on the fold-down table, Hollick produces an envelope. It has my name on and it's been opened.

'Would you mind?' She hands me the letter. Seconds later, she's talking to somebody on her radio.

I bend to the letter, three typed paragraphs in English on a single sheet of paper, with a light dusting of French phrases when she needs a bit of colour. The tone of voice is unmistakeably Christianne's: direct, unfussy, warm, candid. By the time I'm reading this, she warns me that she'll be gone. How and where to she doesn't say, but the overwhelming implication is that this act of departure, of what she terms 'signing off', is for keeps. Under the circumstances, she writes, all is for the best.

Circumstances? I glance up but Hollick is still on the radio, her back turned.

I return to the letter. The second paragraph is full of regret. If only we'd met earlier in our lives when things were different. If only I'd been in MSF, or she'd been in what she calls '*le showbiz*'. If only we'd had the time to make the most of each other. As it is, she thinks she's been lucky to meet me at all and if she'd ever believed in God, she'd say a little prayer of gratitude for the opportunity to let her guard down and be herself. The last thing she wants is to make assumptions, but she truly believes that I, too, shared this sense of re-discovery. We are what we are, she writes at the end of the paragraph. So thank you for making that possible.

The letter ends on a practical note. She wants me to keep an eye on Andy, and on Bill. They are, she writes, the two men who most matter to her, equally precious, though for very different reasons. *Andy and I*, in an intriguing phrase, have been *co-pélerins*, while Bill has been a surprise *tour nouveau* to a life far richer than she'd ever deserved.

The letter ends with an unsteady scribble that might have been her first name. Underneath, a single cross. I look up again to find Hollick studying me.

'*Co-pélerins?*' She nods at the letter.

'Fellow pilgrims.'

'*Tour nouveau?*'

'I think she means "plot twist".'

Hollick extends a hand and I give her the letter. She scans it for the briefest moment, then her head comes up again. A third question.

'And Bill?'

'I think she means Sir William Penny. He's local. They were friends.'

'That's what Mr McFaul says.'

'Then I'm guessing it's true.'

'You've met this man, Bill?'

'Yes.'

'And how would you describe the relationship between them?'

'I've just told you. They were friends, all three of them, McFaul included.'

'So, what does "plot twist" mean?'

I say nothing. This conversation is becoming an interview, direct questions sharpened by something I can only describe as aggression, and I'm starting to wonder whether we're being recorded when Hollick seems suddenly to relax. I can only guess at her age – early thirties or older – but she clearly works out. She has the skin tone and the physical confidence of a trained athlete, and the last time I saw cheekbones this pronounced was in a fashion magazine.

'Plot twist?' she says again, but more gently this time.

'I've honestly no idea. If you're hinting at some kind of relationship, that would be a guess on your part. In French we use the term to describe a bend in the road. Most of the time it's unexpected. Maybe that's why she uses the word "surprise".'

'But you know this woman. It says so. Second paragraph. She's gone, Ms Andressen, she's disappeared, and as far as we can tell, you're the one person for whom she's left any kind of note.'

'I knew her for a couple of days,' I say quietly. 'It's true we liked each other a lot but it's hardly a lifetime.'

'Two days?' This appears to be news to Hollick.

'A Friday and a Saturday,' I confirm. 'Talk to my friend Evelyn. Check with McFaul.'

'We will.' She nods, scribbling herself a note, and then looks up again. 'First sight? Would that be fair? Accurate?'

'Love, you mean?' I'm laughing now. 'This is bizarre. Two women meet. I'm half-French. She's the real thing. We have a lot in common. We talk. We get on. She shows me around the town. She introduces me to friends. One of them happens to be Sir William, Bill as she calls him. And that's about it.'

'McFaul says you invited her up to London.'

'That's true. I did.'

'Why?'

'Because we liked each other. Because there was a spark there.'

'And?' It's a very good question, much shrewder than I've anticipated, and Hollick gives me all the time I need to frame an answer.

'To be honest, there were things she wasn't telling me.'

'That's an impression you had?'

'Yes.'

'What kind of things?'

I frown. This is harder, more complex. Hollick offers a prompt.

'To do with McFaul? The relationship?'

'Maybe. Maybe not. Hard to tell.'

'Something else, then?'

I shrug. I say I've no idea. Then comes a knock at the door and a face appears. The coastguard coordinating the rescue search at sea has just called in.

'And?'

'Nothing, boss. Nothing from the lifeboat people, nothing from the clifftops.'

She nods. A glance at her watch, and then another scribbled note. The face at the door eyes me for a moment, before disappearing.

'Did you know your friend had medical issues?' Hollick is still writing.

'No.' I shake my head.

'That surprises me.'

'Really? Why?'

'Because she had MND.' She looks up at last. 'Do you know what that means, Ms Andressen? Motor neurone disease?'

I shake my head. I know a great deal about the world of malign tumours, and where that kind of diagnosis can take you, but mercifully I've been spared any brushes with MND.

'It's horrible,' Hollick says. 'A friend of a friend of a friend had it. You're perfectly OK one moment. Then you start getting these strange symptoms, your body out of control. A year or so later, you're in a wheelchair, unable to talk, unable to breathe, just suffocating to death.' She pauses, letting this news sink in. 'She didn't mention it? Not once?'

'Never. But . . .'

'But what?'

I'm thinking of Christianne and McFaul in the garden with the golf club, McFaul trying to guide her every movement. I'm remembering moments in their kitchen, or when Christianne and I went for a walk, and she'd miss her footing, or stumble, or – in the kitchen or the pub – reach for her glass and miss.

'There were clues,' I say. 'Maybe I should have looked harder.'

Hollick nods, says nothing. When I ask how she knows about the diagnosis, she says it came from McFaul.

'It was one of the first things he told us when he phoned in. His call went through to the control room. A misper with serious health issues? That's high-risk, straight off.' She gestures round the van. 'Summon the cavalry. Pull out the stops. Full service. A condition like that, it's the least we can do.' She reaches for her pen again. 'We understand she'd been a nurse. Médecins Sans Frontières?'

'Yes.'

'Then she'd have understood the early symptoms, known what to expect down the road.'

'Hadn't she gone to the doctor?'

'Only very recently.'

'And?'

'You should talk to Mr McFaul. This is a tricky area; I've probably said far too much already. All I need to know for now is whether or not you talked about . . .' She holds her hands wide. 'Any of this stuff.'

'Stuff?'

'MND.' Her gaze is steady. 'Having to cope with something like that.'

'Then the answer's no. We talked about lots of things, but never any kind of illness.'

'But don't you find that strange? Given how close you seemed to have become?'

'Not at all. I'd use a different word. *Courageuse.*'

'Which means?'

'Brave. There were bits of her story she wanted to keep to herself. That was obviously one of them.'

'But isn't that odd? Under the circumstances?' She won't let it go.

'Not at all.' I hold her gaze. 'There's still room in the world for privacy, thank God.'

We part outside the van. Hollick says her stint as Critical Incident Manager is nearly over. Shortly, she'll be handing over the lead in this operation to someone called the LPSM, which evidently stands for Lost Person Search Manager. They will probably be in touch, depending on what happens, but in the meantime she's grateful for me making it down from London.

'Ms Beaucarne obviously meant a great deal to you.' There's no warmth in her smile. 'Friendships are so important, aren't they?'

TEN

Ms *Beaucarne.* Quite why the use of Christianne's family name should come as such a shock is a bit of a mystery but as I drive out of the car park, I'm fighting a gust of deep anger. In truth, I knew nothing of Christianne's diagnosis. Neither, after the last two years, am I a stranger to the innate suspicion which is bred deep into the DNA of any working police officer. As I know only too well, these people patrol the outer fringes of human behaviour, where desperation or misjudgement can sometimes bleed into evil, and no one blames them for taking nothing at face value, yet the logic of what my poor blighted friend must have done is surely obvious.

As I've belatedly realized, Christianne must have been ill.

Soon, she would be very ill. According to Hollick, she was facing the guarantee of a death that would terrify most of us. And so she tinkered with the mechanism of her allotted stay on earth, advanced the hands a little, left her clothes on the beach, and called time on the whole fucking charade. Sylvester's Doomsday Clock. Made real.

Evelyn, when I finally get back to her bungalow, has come to the same conclusion.

'Poor woman.' She shakes her head. 'If we'd only known.'

The fact that she seems to be including me in this act of oversight comes as some comfort.

'And Andy?' I nod outside.

'I haven't seen him, not properly, not to talk to. That's another admission, isn't it? Maybe we should have lived somewhere like this all our lives. Maybe we should keep *closer* to people.'

'McFaul's a grump,' I say at once. 'I'm not sure he needs other people.'

'You really think so? I've seen them together, remember, when they didn't know anyone else was watching. From where I was standing, he doted on her. Go next door, my lovely. Give him a hug. Tell him we're here for him. You're much braver than me.'

This, unusually for Evelyn, has the force of an order and we both know it. When I first knock next door, nothing happens. Only when I try a third time does McFaul finally appear.

'You,' he says. He's rubbing the sleep from his eyes. He looks totally knackered.

I try and explain how sorry I am, how sorry we both are, me and Evelyn, but he simply holds the door open wide and gestures me inside. We go through to the kitchen. To my surprise, it's been tidied up: no mountain of unwashed plates, no smears of grease on the oven knobs, no swing-bin brimming with rubbish, not a single knotted black sack awaiting disposal. The clutter has gone from every working surface and I can even smell the faintest hint of disinfectant.

'It helps,' McFaul says simply. He's noted my interest.

'I'm sure it does. If you want a hand anywhere else . . .' I leave the sentence unfinished.

He shakes his head, puts the kettle on, invites me to sit down. I watch him limping slowly around the kitchen for a moment or two, looking for the jar of coffee he's tidied away. The last couple of days seem to have aged him immeasurably. I'm looking at an old man with barely half a face.

'You never told me,' I say at last. 'About what was wrong with her.'

'You know about that shit? MND?'

'The police mentioned it. I'm just curious why you never did. Either of you.'

'Not my call. Chrissie was a proud woman. In her own good time, maybe, but even then she'd probably keep it to herself. Share news like that, and you were dead already. That's what she thought. That's what she always told me.'

I nod. It fits perfectly with my own impressions of Christianne. A stumble or two? A lunge at the wine glass? Who's watching? And what does it matter?

'When did you know she was ill?' I ask. 'For sure?'

McFaul takes his time answering. He's spooning instant coffee into a couple of mugs. He does it with intense concentration, the way a drunk might, and I'm guessing he must have had this same fierce attention to detail when he was in the minefields. Then, it would have helped save his life, and now is probably no different.

'First signs were in Portugal,' he says at last. 'We'd gone to the coast for a couple of days, camping in the dunes. Chrissie always loved swimming, but she kept falling over. She'd watch the waves coming, and knew how to cope, but it didn't seem to work any more. Her balance had gone. The waves were in charge. At first it made her laugh, me too, then there was other stuff. Back home, she'd miss a light switch with her finger. In the local store, she couldn't get the right change out of her purse. Once, we were standing in a car park and she needed money for the machine. It was always windy down there. The coins were at the bottom and she had to take a couple of notes out first and a big gust took them out of her hand. We both did the chasing, I can see it now, the cripple and his wonky mate. We'd stopped laughing by then. Even Chrissie.'

He'd managed to find a local doctor who referred her to the local hospital in Evora, but the facilities were basic.

'They were good people. The specialist guy suspected MND

from the off, but for a proper diagnosis you need all kinds of shit, nerve conduction tests, MRI scan, an electro-something, and even if you went to Lisbon you'd be waiting for ever. So, when he said we'd be better off going home, we took the hint. He was right, too. The medics here have been brilliant. There's fuck all they can do to cure it, but that's not the point. We wanted an answer, and that's what we got.'

'No cure at all?'

'None. There are cells in the nervous system that stop working, motor neurone cells, and without those you start losing control. There's no magic drug, no magic bullet, so basically, you're stuffed. What's worse is all the guff on the subject. Fifteen minutes on Google scared us to death. Weakening grip, balance all to fuck, rubbish coordination. Then your speech starts to go, and you're slurring like an idiot, and finally even swallowing, even breathing, becomes a problem and so you end up in a wheelchair with a tube down your throat. All that just to stay alive?' He shakes his head.

Scared us to death. Too right, I think.

'Timescale?'

'They told us six months to two years. And that was back in the spring. Chrissie had the patience of a saint but there was no way she was waiting that long. She was a nurse, remember. Once she was sure that they'd got the diagnosis bang on, she knew she wanted out.'

'She told you that?'

'Of course.'

'And?'

'I agreed. Who wouldn't?'

Who wouldn't? McFaul has a talent for cutting to the chase and I'm guessing Christianne loved him for it. In a situation like this, you can wring your hands and share your grief on Facebook for just so long but none of that stops it getting worse. In the end – and 'the end' is *le mot juste* – you have to *do* something. There's an obvious question here, and I know I have to ask it.

'Did you know about last night? Going swimming? Never coming back? Was that planned? Something you talked about?'

McFaul glances up at me, just the hint of a smile on his face. This is a man, I sense, who welcomes bluntness, maybe even admires it.

'No,' he says. 'She'd never have told me, warned me, discussed it. Inside she was very private. Once, quite recently, she said I was never to be afraid. Whatever she did would be for the best. But that was it. Finito. End game. In her own time. When she thought it was right. Strictly no tears. All gone.'

With anyone else, on the page, on screen, or – God help us – in real life, this would have triggered a flood of tears, but McFaul simply holds my gaze. Should I reach out? Should I give him a hug? Should I call him Andy? I do none of those things and when I later ask myself why, I realize that the answer's beyond simple. He doesn't need it.

'So why did you report her missing?' I ask. 'Why not let her drift away?'

'Because it took me a while to realize what was going on. When I found her clothes there was no note. I thought she'd gone swimming, just like always, and I thought she might be in trouble. I went looking for her. I tried to find her. I shouted her name. Nothing. Fuck all. So I made the call and the rest . . .' He shrugs. 'Just happened.'

'Evelyn says they brought you back here, to the bungalow.'

'They did. She's right. Apparently, they always search the home premises. People can be odd, they told me. You think they've gone missing and they turn up in the strangest places, under beds, in wardrobes, up in tree houses, weird shit like that. I told the guy he was wasting his time, but he found that note for you, so maybe I'm wrong.'

'Where did she leave it, as a matter of interest?'

'On the bathroom floor, beneath the basin. She probably propped it against the mirror. Pull the door shut, and the draught would do the rest.'

I nod, swallow hard. McFaul might be immune to grief but I'm not sure I am. He watches me for a moment, then asks me if I'd like something to drink. When I nod, he struggles to his feet and limps next door before reappearing with a bottle of brandy.

'Neat?' he says.

'Neat,' I agree.

He pours two glasses, slides one across to me, and proposes a toast.

'She was an incredible woman,' he says softly. 'And nothing any of us can do will ever bring her back.'

McFaul and I spend the rest of the day together. A second brandy follows the first but after that he caps the bottle and suggests we go out. We head down towards the seafront, pausing en route to buy a big bag of chips. Both of us, it turns out, are famished.

Walking through the town centre, to my surprise, McFaul appears to know as many people as Christianne. Most of them are tradesmen, middle-aged or younger, buried in the back of a white van or working high on a scaffold. Word has gone round about Christianne, and McFaul accepts condolence after gruff condolence with a grunt and a nod of the head.

'They'll find her,' murmurs a pensioner emerging from the bakery. 'Bet your life on it.'

At the car park, we head for the incident van. Instead of the icy Inspector Hollick, another officer has taken charge. He's older, voluble, slightly overweight, and introduces himself as Paul Bevan. He has a light Welsh accent and seems nerveless in the face of near-impossible odds. Had Madame Beaucarne really gone swimming, he agrees, then the outlook would be grim. The water might still be warm, and it's a glorious day, but even so there are limits to survival time in the English Channel.

'You think she never went in? Never left the beach?' McFaul asks.

'I'm saying I don't know, can't be sure. We're into elimination here, Mr McFaul. We've had the lifeboat out all night, and the police chopper was up at first light. With infra-red, even deceased, we'd still find her. The guys who understand these things have plotted the tidal flows. We have eyes on the clifftops, blokes on the beach clear round to Straight Point. Agreed, she might have taken weights into the water, stones from the beach say, but if that was the case she'd have gone under close in. As I understand it, high tide last night was around the time you found her clothes. In which case her body would have washed up later. So . . .' He nods towards the beach. 'Maybe she wasn't swimming at all.'

Headquarters, he's glad to report, have allotted a couple of extra officers to the search, and with their help his team are moving from beach hut to beach hut, and combing gardens along the seafront, in case – for whatever reason – Ms Beaucarne has chosen to hide herself away.

'But why would she do that?' McFaul again.

'You want the truth? I have no idea. This job teaches you many things and one of them, I'm afraid to say, is never to discount the impossible. Eliminate everything else, like I said, and you're probably left with the truth. Does that sound unduly philosophical? If so, you have my apologies. If and when we find something, you'll be the first to know.' He pauses. 'No mobile? Am I right?'

'Yes.'

'My congratulations, Mr McFaul. One day, when the penny drops, the rest of us may kick the habit, but somehow I doubt it. Armageddon is more likely than surrendering our smartphones. You're a lucky man, sir. Stay sane and we'll do our best to find your partner.' He turns away to confer with an unseen voice on a proffered radio. When it becomes clear that this is another conversation he finds hard to finish, we turn away.

'You want me to leave him my mobile number?' I ask McFaul. 'Just in case?'

'Sure,' he says. 'Why not?'

We settle on the beach. The tide is out now, and I can feel the warmth radiating up from the huge, egg-shaped pebbles. A huddle of swimmers in the shallows, all of them women, are preparing to take the plunge and further down the beach an elderly couple are scolding a child for feeding the seagulls.

At length, McFaul stirs. He's obviously been thinking about Christianne. 'The last time we went to the GP was back in the early summer,' he says. 'She's a lovely woman but every medic has the same problem with MND.'

'Meaning?'

'Meaning it's incurable, meaning there's nothing they can really do. That's not what they're there for and so they fob you off with forms. That was the real killer. The bloody form. It's called a DS1500. I'll remember that forever. She gave one to Chrissie. Signed. Stamped. Witnessed. Everything.'

'And?'

'It tells anyone who needs to know that you won't survive

beyond six months. I'm sure it's really useful, and I'm sure it opens all kinds of doors, but Chrissie was gutted. She called it an advanced death certificate and I guess she was right, but that wasn't the point. It wasn't being dead that mattered. It was what lay behind all those doors.'

'Like?'

'Like all the benefits you can get, all the care packages, all the blokes who are going to turn up and fit grab rails in the bathroom, and wheelchair ramps, and all the rest of it. The GP talked about the hospice, too, how Chrissie could make drop-in visits to begin with, just to get used to the place, make friends, see what's on offer. People talk about The Journey. I'm sure they mean well, but what fucking choice do you have?'

I nod, and agree it must be horrible, but McFaul hasn't finished.

'Voice banking?' he says. 'Is that a phrase you've ever come across?'

'Never.'

'Again, it's useful, obvious, really helpful. A bloke comes along and records a whole load of phrases while you've still got the power to speak. Your own voice. Your own way of putting things. Then, later, when you can't talk at all, you use this special machine, pretending you're someone that you're not, someone who's long gone. Chrissie couldn't get her head around it. The thought of someone having to cut her food up and feed her was bad enough, but this was way off the scale. She never cried, never. That morning, outside the surgery, she was all over the place. No way, she told me. No fucking way. You understand now?' He nods at the water, and then gestures back towards the car park and the incident van. 'So you see why everyone's wasting their time?'

ELEVEN

At my insistence, the three of us go out to dinner. On Evelyn's recommendation, I book a table at the local Indian restaurant and we spend a quiet-ish evening trying to cheer McFaul up. It doesn't help that a couple at a nearby table are discussing the day's developments on the beach and when they agree that the whole thing – the husband uses the word 'pantomime' – is a huge waste of public money, I'm half-expecting McFaul to thump him. Far from it.

'He's right,' he grunts.

Back home, McFaul mumbles a thank you and disappears into his bungalow. Evelyn and I share a nightcap or two and agree that only time will resolve what might have happened to Christianne. When I tell Evelyn about the form from the GP, and how distressed she'd been at the thought of what lay in wait, she nods.

'We went shopping a couple of weeks ago,' she says. 'I drove her over to Exmouth and we dropped in at the big Tesco. There was a woman there with a zimmer frame on wheels. She wasn't old, not at all. Christianne couldn't take her eyes off her, barely said a word on the way back.' She runs her finger around the glass of port. 'Should I have been nosier? More intrusive? And what on earth are we to do with Andy?'

This, of course, is the million-dollar question. Try as I might, I can't get that final paragraph of Christianne's letter out of my mind. Whatever else I owe her memory, I need to keep an eye on the men in her life.

Next morning, I find a number for Sir William Penny and make the call. To my surprise, he recognizes my voice.

'My dear,' he says. 'How's life up there in the real world?'

When I tell him I'm back in Budleigh, he appears to be delighted. Then he wants to know why.

'It's Christianne,' I tell him. 'You must have heard, surely?'

'I have. Of course I have. Is it a tragedy? Alas, yes. Am I surprised? Sadly not. I was talking to Andy early this morning. The poor man's in a bad place. On his behalf, one can only hope, of course. It's grand to see the police making such an effort, and here's hoping it all pays off, but I fear she's probably gone forever. A lovely, lovely woman. I'll miss her like hell.'

If anyone else knows why Christianne chose to end it all, I think, then it has to be Budleigh's distinguished ex-ambassador, not that Sir William wants to dwell on the matter.

'Where are you just now?' he asks brightly.

'I'm staying with Evelyn.'

'Pay me a visit, then. I'm just round the corner.'

This is confusing. Like most women, I have an uneasy grasp of geography, but Sir William's pile has to be at least a mile or two away. When I check to be on the safe side, he roars with laughter.

'I'm doing a spot of gardening on Andy's behalf,' he says. 'Ask Evelyn how to get to the croquet club. They're forecasting rain so bring a brolly.'

Evelyn supplies the directions. Andy, she says, has one of the allotments adjacent to the croquet pitch, though this is the first time she's had Bill Penny down as a gardener. When I finally make it to the croquet club, I find him on his hands and knees beside a row of lettuces, hunting for slugs. Gardening, he readily admits, isn't altogether his thing, but given Andy's current situation it's the least he can do.

We take coffee and a toasted bun in the clubhouse. By now, Sir William has emphatically become Bill. He wants to know whether I've seen McFaul since what he delicately calls 'the incident'.

'Yesterday,' I say. 'We spent the afternoon together.'

'Really? Brave girl. That man can be difficult.'

That man? This doesn't marry with Christianne's take on their relationship.

'I thought you two were close,' I say lightly. 'I thought you spent lots of time mending stiles on the coastal path.'

'We do, we do. And what a pleasure that is. I meant difficult with the fairer sex, my dear. Andy's a one-girl man, and I suspect he always has been. Courtly? No. Awash with *politesse*? Sadly not.'

'Who cares?' I shrug. 'Just tell me Andy made Christianne happy.'

'Very. He made her exceptionally happy. You know about their time in Angola?'

'Yes.'

'Then you'll understand what they'd been through together. All wars are bad but civil wars are worse. After an experience like that, very little upsets you. I'm not sure this is an appropriate metaphor, but as a couple they had extremely low blood pressure. They got by on very little – no money, no real security, no place to call their own – but it never seemed to matter, and that kind of *timbre*, that kind of fortitude, that degree of *bottom*, earns you serious brownie points in a little town like this. People here, dare I say it, have the means and the education and perhaps even the breeding, the self-confidence, to turn their backs on the world, but Chris and Andy pulled exactly the same trick with barely a penny to their names. Serious respect, my dear. And not only from yours truly.'

I duck my head and reach for my cup. I've bumped into men like Bill Penny once or twice before in my life. He happens to have made his name as a diplomat. A couple of others I know have earned a fortune in the city, or – like Pavel – become a byword among thesps who recognize genius in the opening scene of a film script. On first acquaintance, they can appear undistinguished, ordinary, even a bit of a disappointment, but what they all have in common is a steely concentration of talent and effort that gives them what I can only describe as X-ray vision. They have no time for imposters. They see through *faux* bonhomie. And they celebrate life's genuine articles when they swim into focus. Which takes us back to McFaul.

'Do you like him?'

'Yes. Very much. I'd do anything for the man, and he knows it. I even offered him money once, a sizeable sum, no strings attached, and I'm sure you can guess his response.'

'He turned you down.'

'Worse than that, or perhaps better. He just laughed, and you know what, my dear? I cherish that moment. This was recently. I happened to know they were barely making ends meet and on top of that Chris had just had the diagnosis. You'll be aware of the details, because I'm guessing Andy has told you, and so you can imagine the kind of state they must have been in. But there it was. A significant sum of money. Enough, perhaps, to buy them a treat or two before the curtain came down. Yet he just laughed. Not unkindly. Not to insult me. Quite the contrary. It just struck him as funny. Or perhaps absurd. Either way, I take my hat off to both of them. This world of ours hasn't got much space left for people like Andy, and like that wonderful girl of his, and that's our loss. God speed, eh? And *bon voyage*.'

I can only agree. *That wonderful girl of his* is a perfect summing-up of the woman I so briefly knew. I'm about to press him further about Christianne when he changes the subject.

'Sylvester,' he murmurs, 'was impressed.'

'With Malo? My son?'

'With you, my dear. Malo, I gather, is a work in progress. What did you make of the Twilight Fund? Dare I ask?'

'I thought it was interesting.'

'That's a politician's answer.'

'Intriguing, then.'

'That's no answer at all, though intriguing has undertones of mischief, which might be closer to the mark than you think.'

'You're serious?'

'Yes.'

'So, what are you telling me here?'

'Nothing. Yet,' He smiles. 'You, first. The Doomsday Clock? An Armageddon yacht at your beck and call? A nuclear bunker afloat? What do you make of it all?'

I do my best to gather my thoughts and sort them into some kind of order. It doesn't help to know that this man has spent most of his life engaged with brains far bigger than mine.

'I don't understand his input, where he starts, who he talks to, what – exactly – he's selling. He strikes me as an ideas man. Showbiz is full of them and he's right to be excited because the best ideas can earn you a fortune. But what happens next?'

'A very good question, and one I've asked him myself.'

'And?'

'He gives me all the buzz words. Vertical integration. Synergies of effort. The visionaries marching in lockstep with the boffins and the builders.'

'Visionaries?'

'I gather that's the term he's reserved for himself. My son was never one for understatement.'

'And is that where his real talent lies? Selling himself?'

'In one, my darling. You should take up croquet.' He nods at a group of players on the lawn outside. 'Straight through the hoop, no messing. My son could easily have been a waster, or even something worse. Thank God for the word visionary.'

'But you think it will work? The Twilight Fund?'

'I think it may keep the wolf from his door. It may not be the same thing. Sylvester has always had a predatory streak. He can sense weakness at a thousand miles. What he's after, what he needs, are people with a great deal of money who are sufficiently alarmed and sufficiently gullible to take fright at where the world is taking us. It might be war, a proper war, the real thing, or it might be global warming, which is the same catastrophe slowed down a little, but either way – says my son – there are fortunes to be made. That's where it begins and ends for Sylvester, though it pains me to say so.'

He sits back, picking the crumbs from his gardening shirt, while I wonder what qualifies as weakness in Sylvester Penny's eye.

'Are you telling me my son's at some kind of risk?' I ask. 'Does Sylvester think he's gullible?'

'God forbid, quite the contrary.' He's beaming at me now. 'I gather they're brothers-in-arms. It's a love affair, my dear. They both want to get very rich indeed. Which may not be the best news you've heard all day.'

TWELVE

E n route home, hurrying to get out of the rain, I get a text from Rosa, my agent. Bill has given me a bag of allotment veggies for Andy, mainly salad stuff, and I pause beneath Evelyn's umbrella to read the text.

Rosa, I can tell at once, is losing patience with yours truly. *Halligan's pressing for sight of the Pavel masterpiece. It would be good to know if it even bloody exists. Any chance of a clue or two, my precious?* No sign off. No line of kisses. Just a peremptory shove to stir me into action.

Back at the bungalow, I share this news with Evelyn. Charlie Halligan, I explain, is the commissioning editor who can green-light the project.

'And you have access to this machine of Pavel's?'

'It's upstairs. I brought it down with me.'

'And have you looked?'

'I tried. Did my best. But lots of stuff is locked down and I haven't a clue what to do.'

We discuss options. Evelyn herself is as clueless about IT as I am. The latter years of her editing career, she says, put her on handshake terms with the Word programme but anything beyond that gives her panic attacks. She even fights shy of internet banking, fearful that half the world might be watching. Better, she says, to nip down to the Nationwide in the High Street. Nice girl called Debbie.

This takes me nowhere, and when I ask about friends of hers who might help me out, she looks dubious.

'What else is on the computer?'

'Everything, I imagine. Half his life. Maybe more.'

'Then shouldn't you be talking to some kind of relative? Otherwise it sounds a bit intrusive to me.'

She's right, of course, but Pavel had only one relative that I was aware of and he lives in Australia.

'Then phone him. Ask for his permission. Everyone obsesses about data protection these days.'

It's a great idea, deeply sensible. I shared an afternoon with Pavel's son a couple of months ago, and we exchanged phone numbers before we parted. My call finds Ivan at home in Perth, nursing a glass of Shiraz after a rugged day with the new intake of first-year students at the university where he teaches. He seems genuinely glad to hear me and after a brief catch-up, I tell him about the Beeb's interest in whatever his dad might have been hiding. As far as I know, probate on Pavel's estate has yet to be finalized and Ivan is the chief beneficiary. This – if I find the mystery file – could be very good news.

'Do I smell money?' Ivan is laughing.

'Lots, if I look under the right stone.'

'Then do your worst. Fifty per cent? Half and half? Does that sound fair?'

I tell him he's crazy, and suggest he opens another bottle. With his blessing, I'll put Pavel's MacBook in hands I can trust, someone who knows what they're doing, and report back. This, he says, sounds like a plan. Go ahead. Do your worst. Then he's gone.

It's at this point that I remember Christianne telling me about McFaul's cyber talents. Next door lives a man who wrote his own computer programme to make life just a little sweeter in the minefields. Surely, he could take a look at Pavel's machine?

Minutes later, I'm standing at McFaul's front door. I've wrapped Pavel's MacBook in a Waitrose bag against the rain and I'm beginning to think that McFaul might be out when the door opens. McFaul, for some reason, has worked up a light sweat.

'Come in.' He's looking at the Waitrose bag. 'What's that?'

I tell him it doesn't matter, not yet. First, I want to know the latest about Christianne. Has he been in touch with that nice Inspector Bevan?

'Yeah. He phoned me on the landline earlier. They've got more hands to the pump. Has anyone mentioned the Force Support Group? Bevan's like a pig in shit. He says he's reorganizing the search the way he always wanted. I told him there was no point, but these people never listen. He thinks she's out there. And he's sure he's gonna find her. Does that sound like optimism? Or early dementia?'

He shakes his head. We're still standing in the hall and through the open door I can see the big lounge at the front of the property. Last time I took a look, it reminded me of an auction house before they get everything sorted, a jumble of mismatched items dumped in the hope of a sale. Now, the battered furniture has been tidied into a single corner of the room, chairs piled on chairs, cardboard boxes brimming with stuff that nobody will ever buy.

'Time for a sort-out,' he says.

'Someone's coming round?'

'Yeah. Tonight, fingers crossed. Coffee?'

I follow him into the kitchen. I also have his veggies from the allotment, which I leave on the table. Instead of the jar of instant coffee, McFaul spoons ground coffee into a new-looking expresso machine. The smell alone tells me this man is into serious spring cleaning. Good, I think. Good, and maybe long overdue. A disease as vicious as MND takes many victims, and not all of them die.

At his invitation, I unpack Pavel's MacBook and do my best to explain. Pavel ended up imprisoned in a body that didn't work, but his brain was as huge as ever and he could still talk,

just. H spent a great deal of time poring over the specialist
literature and finally laid hands on the software that could turn
speech into text on screen. This was no use to Pavel, who was
blind, but I tell McFaul it helped the rest of us no end. No
longer need Pavel keep his best ideas to himself. We could all
share them.

This little quip raises barely a flicker of amusement. McFaul
picks up the MacBook, examines the various ports in the back
and then takes me next door. The master bedroom lies at the
back of the house. It's a biggish space with a scatter of Afghan-
looking rugs on the polished floorboards. The walls, sea green,
are patterned with carefully framed black and white photos
and a plain wooden cross hangs above the double bed. I'm
looking at the photos. I've seen these faces before, all of them
young, all of them black.

'Angola? Am I right?'

McFaul nods, says nothing. Already, he's taken a seat at a
smallish desk in the corner of the room, away from the light
flooding in through the window. His own laptop lies open and
the screensaver, beyond a torrent of icons, shows a dusty yellow
landscape rolling away towards the far horizon. A stand of trees
casts long shadows, and a lean-looking mongrel dog lies sprawled
on the parched grass.

'Africa, again?' I nod at the screen.

'Portugal. That was the view from our kitchen window.'

'And the dog?'

'Vasco. He was always wandering off, little bugger.'

He's found the cable he's after. Moments later, he fires up
Pavel's MacBook and bends to the keyboard. A flurry of
commands opens Pavel's screensaver. Unsurprisingly, I'm looking
at a lovely shot along a bridge at dusk, the blackness of the
cobblestones shiny under a thin rain.

'Prague,' I murmur. 'I should have been there last week.'

'And?'

'They turned me back at the airport. I had Pavel with me.'

'I thought he was dead.'

'He was. That was the point. Never try and smuggle ashes
through an X-ray machine. Body remains turn out to be on the
restricted list. Pavel would have died laughing.'

McFaul shoots me a look, says nothing. He's into a long list of files now, some of which I recognize. These are scripts from way back, stepping stones that finally took Pavel to fame and fortune.

'*Scapa Flow*?' McFaul's peering at one of them. 'What's that about?'

'He wrote a movie for the Germans. They scuttled their fleet at the end of the First World War. It's about a grandson revisiting his grandfather's death aboard a battleship called the *Hindenburg*. It was the last one to sink and it took our hero's grandad with it. They flew Pavel up to the Orkney Islands and had him dive on the wreck. They kitted him up and took him down there. He told me he mapped that battleship by touch alone, and I believed him. He was blind, couldn't see a thing. Trying to imagine a whole battleship through your fingertips? Can you get your head around that?'

The question earns another look from McFaul. He's scrolling down through the endless list of files.

'You've got a title?' he says at last.

'No.'

'A date?'

'I'm guessing it'll be the last one.'

'And he died when? Exactly?'

'This year,' I say. 'Sunday, twenty-eighth of April. He had a huge stroke. By the time I made it to the hospital, he'd gone.'

McFaul makes a note of the date and returns to the screen. He reconfigures the files in chronological order, then frowns.

'Something's not right,' he says. 'Look . . .'

I join him in front of the laptop. He's pointing to a file that carries an asterisk but no name. A series of commands fail to open it.

'February the fourteenth?' He's peering at the screen. 'Does that ring any bells?'

'Valentine's Day,' I say automatically. 'I remember phoning him.'

'And?'

'We talked. Like we always talked. Blew kisses on the phone. Laughed a lot.'

'Did he mention a file? Something he'd written? Finished? Saved?'

'No. But that means nothing. Pavel always told me he was born in darkness and that's where he ended up. He was an underground creature. He squirrelled everything away. Maybe that file was meant to get him through the next winter. Nourishment for the soul. Sadly, it failed.'

This moment of reverie is wasted on McFaul. He eases his chair back from the desk and tells me he'll have to start from scratch.

'What does that mean?'

'It means I'll need to go into the code, untangle one or two things, understand how it all hangs together. Nothing's impossible. I'll crack it in the end, but it might take a while.'

'You don't mind?'

'Not at all.' He nods at the screen. 'What else is on here?'

'Most of his life, I imagine.' I do my best to summon a smile. 'And bits of mine, too.'

Late that same afternoon, I phone Malo. This morning's conversation with Bill Penny has persuaded me to trust McFaul, but I'm not at all sure about my son. The news that he's found a soulmate in the shape of the wolfish Sylvester isn't altogether a surprise, but when Malo gets himself revved up – in H's phrase – pretty much anything can happen. In the right company, like Clemmie's, Malo can be a dream. In the hands of someone older, and less caring, he starts to lose his bearings. I'd like to blame it on the lure of untold wealth, but it's way more complex than that. Malo can be reckless, especially on the tighter bends, and what he adores more than anything is the prospect of an adventure or two. As he's told me himself, he gets bored all too easily. Attention deficit? Being ignored as a kid by his busy, busy parents? Too many treats instead of a family life? All of the above.

My call finds him at the wheel of his car, a rather stylish Audi convertible that came as a present from H. He's driving down to Southampton to take a meeting with a guy about the Twilight Fund. 'Take' is new. I've never heard Malo use it in this context before. It must come from Sylvester.

'So, who is this man?'

'His name's Karl. He's a bit older than me, but not much. He used to work for one of the big super-yacht outfits, based down in Poole, but he's started a consultancy of his own. He's awesome, Mum. Sylvester met him at the Monaco Yacht Show. This is a guy with a line to everyone who matters.'

I smile. In these moods, at full flow, my son is impossible to interrupt. The sheer momentum that carries him from sentence to sentence, from proposition to proposition, from dream to dream, is irresistible. Nothing can stop him, and it's nice to hear.

'You're having dinner?' I manage at last.

'Big time. Karl's booked us a table at some incredible place in Hamble. A couple of other guys are coming. Pool our expertise, and we cover the entire reservation. We'll have it nailed by midnight.'

'What? What will you have nailed?'

'The project.'

'Who says?'

'Karl. He thinks Twilight's great. He's already told me. Huge potential. History on our side.'

'He *said* that?'

'He did. He's half German, Mum. Speaks five languages. He's got a contacts book you wouldn't believe, a CV to die for. *History on our side?* Don't you love it?'

In a way, I do. As a phrase, it weighs nothing, means nothing. It's lighter than air, the perfect lure to tempt rich punters on to the hook. Pavel, I know, would adore it.

'So, what are *you* bringing to the table?'

'Our database, Mum. Sylvester's spent the best part of a year getting it together, doing the research, pressing the flesh. More than a thousand names. Tally all that wealth and you end up in the trillions.'

Tally. Another rogue verb.

'Don't Karl and his friends have these names already?' I enquire.

'Shit, no. That's the whole point. That's our USP. These are people who haven't been near the ocean all their lives, and you know why? Because they've been so busy. Busy, busy, busy, Mum. Sylvester calls them virgins. They're ours for the taking. None of them would dream of setting foot on one of these monster yachts. Not unless we can give them a very good reason.'

'And that's your role?'

'Absolutely. We're selling Doomsday. The end of the world. It's either the bomb or global warming or maybe some pandemic or other. You take your choice. All three are on the schedule. If the Americans don't blow the world up first, then you can rely on climate change or the demon virus, bet your life on it, or your kids' lives, or their kids'. There's a neat little pictogram Sylvester's designed. It's a graph line, basically, and by the time you get to the bottom of the page, we're all dead. Scary stuff, Mum.'

'Unless you have a super yacht.'

'Exactly. And not just any old super yacht. We're talking survival, as well as plunge pools and walk-round peninsula beds. Did I ever mention the cache plan? We pre-position supplies at remote locations around the globe. Access by membership only. Layer after layer of security. State-of-the-art cyber-coding. "A" list stuff. Believe me, Mum, only the rich will make it through.'

Only the rich will make it through. This, it occurs to me, is a rather bleak view of our collective future, but Malo's sell thunders on, numbing my brain as well as my ear. I have no idea what a walk-round peninsula bed might be, but I realize it doesn't make the slightest difference. Bill Penny is right. His clever son, like most of the world's richer folk, is peddling a dream, or in this case a nightmare, and it's taken no time at all for Malo to tune in.

At last, thanks to some decisions he's got to make about the best junction to take him off the motorway, what passes for our conversation comes to an end. Malo promises to give me a ring tomorrow, once he's got a deal to take back to his new friend, and we leave it at that.

I've made the call from my bedroom upstairs in Evelyn's bungalow. She appears at the door with a cup of tea and when I ask, she says I'm welcome to borrow her PC. I know it's downstairs in her lounge. I settle at the keyboard and Google 'super yachts UK'. As any actress knows, the key to a new role is research. Pay attention to the script. Get inside this person's head. Explore every nook, every cranny. Figure out what makes them tick.

The first surprise is just how many players this game has attracted. Shipyards in Southampton, Poole, Plymouth. The days of building proper vessels in the UK – cargo boats, ocean liners – have clearly gone. Instead, the go-to market demands something smaller and infinitely more luxurious.

I choose a firm at random and settle back to watch the presentation. It's slick, polished, and wildly aspirational, a collage of gym-honed bodies aboard yachts that belong in a Bond movie. The sell is pitch-perfect: paths less trodden, horizons unexplored, pristine beaches, coral reefs in the rudest health. A lone super yacht arrows towards yet another perfect sunset, while a line of guests linger at the bar. These lucky few, we're given to understand, are risking it all, making it all, enjoying it all. Beyond the material things in life, murmurs the voiceover, lies the sublime.

This, I know, is wealth porn, a glitzy tribute to the power of cool, married to unimaginable wealth. This is what you're worth, and this – by implication – is what you deserve. By scrolling left or right, up or down, I happen on jewel after jewel from this Aladdin's cave: fantasy cabins, the work of interior design superstars poached from leading five-star hotels; bespoke vanity areas, hi-tech private saunas, state-of-the art Jacuzzis; a hand-made spiral staircase in bubinga hardwood, linking all three decks; a sky lounge with a retractable roof for late-night stargazing and – should you be up for an extra million or two on the construction bill – a tastefully integrated landing pad for the private chopper.

The sell is relentless, and my eyes begin to blur. This is a world away from the modest little shag pad in the Antibes marina where H and I conceived our son, and I've never realized just how much money there is in the world, yet the crushing weight of all this opulence suggests that Malo and Sylvester might be on to something. If you're willing and able to pay ten million pounds for one of these toys, wouldn't you write a bigger cheque to make sure you got the better of Doomsday?

I put the question to Evelyn over an early supper. So far, I've resisted the temptation of sharing Malo's latest fantasy career, but the realization that it might conceivably work prompts a rethink. I tell her about Bill's son, about the Twilight Fund, and about Malo sitting down to dinner with three strangers he thinks will change his life. Evelyn knows Malo well. She's been kind to him in all kinds of ways over the years and has a kinship with him that, to be frank, I've always envied. After the meal, at her insistence, I load up the site I've just watched, and leave her to it while I deal with the washing-up. When I return to the lounge, she's turned the PC off.

'Obscene,' she says briskly. 'And you can tell him I said so.'

That evening, we watch old episodes of *Location, Location, Location*. This is a world away from peninsula beds and on-board tables laid for twelve, but Evelyn is a huge fan and admires the way that clever camerawork can turn a humble terrace into the home of someone's dreams. Earlier than usual, we share a hug and retire. As I climb the stairs to bed, I wonder again where Malo might be headed. H, it has to be said, is a rich man. Half a lifetime in the cocaine trade has brought him a 300-acre spread in West Dorset, and Malo is no stranger to the goodies that money can buy. Yet this new world into which he's stepped represents a totally different dimension of wealth, a far bigger swamp, and I just hope he's clever enough not to get sucked under.

I'm showered and ready for bed when I become aware of voices from next door. I turn off the light and stand by the window. A white van is parked outside McFaul's bungalow, the back doors open. I recognize Presley, the young carpenter who made and fitted Evelyn's new bookshelves. He's looking at a small mountain of furniture piled on the pavement and, as I watch, two other figures join him. One of them is McFaul. The other, a woman, I don't know. The stuff on the pavement must have come from McFaul's front room. He rummages around for a moment or two and then gives up. Presley, meanwhile, has clambered into the back of the van.

'OK, Andy?' This, very faintly, from Presley.

McFaul grunts something I don't catch. Then he's at the back of the van, taking the weight of a sizeable piece of furniture Presley is pushing towards him. The woman joins McFaul and together all three of them manhandle the object out of the van. A streetlight beside the van gives me a perfect view as the lifting party struggles across the pavement and through McFaul's front gate. As they edge carefully towards the front door, I recognize the distinctive curve of the backrest, the glorious blue and grey stripes, the plumpness of the upholstery, the beautifully turned little legs. Then they pause a moment, while the woman readjusts her grip, and I have a second or two to make absolutely sure. The chaise longue, I think, from Bill Penny's once-cherished bedroom.

THIRTEEN

It's mid-morning the next day when McFaul knocks at Evelyn's front door. His face rarely gives anything away and today is no exception.

'You've done it? Cracked it? Opened the file?'

'No.' He shakes his head. 'I tried but he'd managed to embed a self-destruct.'

'A what?'

'It's a coding thing. I've no idea what was in that file but he never wanted anyone to see it. It's like wiring your bell push to a stick of dynamite. The minute I wanted to get in – boom, the file disappeared.'

'Gone?'

'Yeah.'

'Forever?'

'Probably. I'm going to have one last go, but don't hold your breath. In Angola, in the minefields, we'd call it a tripwire. Same principle.'

'You looked elsewhere? Back-up, maybe?'

'I looked everywhere – I've been up half the night.' He stifles a yawn. 'I'm guessing the guy mattered to you.'

'You're right. He did.' I hold his gaze. 'One other favour?'

'No problem.'

'This has nothing to do with computers, I promise. I happened to see that chaise delivered last night. Am I right that it belonged to Bill Penny?'

'Yeah. How did you know?'

'I saw it in that huge bedroom of his. It's an amazing piece. I'm a bit of a nerd around French antique furniture. Would you mind if I popped in for a closer look?'

He gazes at me until I begin to feel uncomfortable. He clearly wants to say no but can't quite work out how.

'Sure.' He shrugs. 'Why not?'

I'm knocking at his door maybe an hour later. He shows me into the lounge where I find the chaise artfully placed a metre or two back from the bay window. Apart from this single piece of furniture, and a small occasional table, the room is bare. I can smell disinfectant again, bleach this time.

'May I?' I'm nodding at the chaise.

'Help yourself.'

I kick off my sandals and pause to run my fingers over the upholstery where the swell of the seat folds into the backrest. Clever, I think. Half a lifetime ago, when I was still living at home in Perros-Guirec, my mother encouraged me to try my hand at upholstery and it wasn't until I had a go at re-covering an ancient armchair she'd stored in the garage that I realized how difficult it was.

'Beautiful.' I glance up at McFaul. 'Don't you think?'

He nods, says nothing. Then he mutters something about Pavel's MacBook. I can take it, if I want. He's had another look but he honestly doesn't think that the file I'm after still exists.

'Not worth another go? Just one? If you've got the time?'

He's frowning now, and I sense he'd prefer if I took it and went, but I still haven't tried the chaise. I settle in the corner, leaning slightly back, feeling the support of the back and the arm exactly where it should be. Then I pivot on my bum and extend my legs, half-closing my eyes, trying to conjure the view from Bill Penny's bedroom, and I'm still wondering why he's parted with a piece like this when there comes a rap on the door. McFaul, I realize, has been staring at something out of the window. Already, he's in the hall.

I hear voices, McFaul's and someone else. A conversation develops. Then, after a brief silence, I'm looking at two faces peering round the door. One of them is middle-aged, maybe older. His greying hair is carefully parted on the right-hand side and he's wearing glasses. With his rumpled suit and hints of exhaustion around the eyes, he looks like an accountant troubled by far too many clients. The other face, much younger, I know. His name's Brett Atkinson, and he's a detective.

'Ms Andressen.' He has Malo's easy smile. 'We meet again.'

I nod. I've yet to move from the chaise. Earlier this year, this young man was responsible for keeping me safe from a fate that still – just sometimes – keeps me awake at night, and I like to think we bonded as a result. That little episode ended with Brett getting badly glassed in a pub fight in Exmouth, and I can still make out the scar across his throat.

The other man's name is Frank Bullivant. According to the ID dangling from his lanyard, he's a DI, short for detective inspector. He's gazing at the bareness of the room, aware of the little indentations still visible on the carpet from last night's furniture.

'You've cleared this place out, Mr McFaul?' Flat accent, difficult to place.

'Yes.'

'Why?'

'Too much stuff, gets on top of you, time for a change.'

'And where's it gone? This stuff?'

'The tip, I expect.'

'You don't know?'

'Not for sure, no.'

'So, who took it?'

'A mate of mine.'

'When?'

McFaul shakes his head. He wants to know what all this is about. Bullivant studies him for a moment, then produces a small pad.

'His name? This mate of yours?'

I'm looking at a stand-off. I can see it in McFaul's face. No way is he going to oblige these two strangers who have walked into his life.

Bullivant is looking round again. Then he sniffs.

'Is that bleach I can smell?'

'Yeah.'

'You've been cleaning up? Giving the place a seeing-to?'

'Yeah.'

'All of it? Everywhere?'

'Yeah.'

'You mind if I take a look?'

'Help yourself.'

Bullivant leaves the room. It clearly falls to Brett to clear up behind this implacable boss of his, and he's still doing his best to update McFaul on the status of the current search for Christianne when Bullivant reappears.

'A MacBook and a laptop in the bedroom.' He's looking at Brett. 'Bank statements in the top drawer of the same desk.' He turns to McFaul. 'Your phone?'

'It's in the kitchen.'

'I meant your mobile.'

'I haven't got one.'

'You haven't got a mobile?'

'Never. Can't stand the things. But you guys know that. I told you last time you were here.'

'It's true, boss.' This from Brett. 'It's in the log. Neither party had phones.'

Bullivant nods. First I sense incredulity, then disbelief, now disappointment. And all this with barely a flicker of visible emotion. Dead eyes. An upper lip thin enough to be virtually invisible. A mask instead of a face. This man is beginning to frighten me.

'That MacBook you mentioned?' I say lightly. 'I think it's probably mine.'

'So, what's it doing here?'

'I'm taking a look at it,' McFaul grunts. 'Helping her out. It's a neighbourly thing.'

'You live next door?' Bullivant's eyes haven't left my face.

'I'm staying there. With a friend of mine.'

'The letter, boss,' Brett again. 'The one we seized last time. Enora's was the name on the envelope.'

'And that's you? You're Enora Andressen?'

'That's right.'

'Excellent.' The hint of a smile at last. 'In that case we'll need to talk to both of you.'

At this point, McFaul kicks off. He demands to know what's going on, and when Bullivant invites him back to the police station in Exmouth, he shakes his head. Over the last couple of days, he's had a thousand conversations. He's very happy to help but there's nothing more to be said. His partner has gone. Her decision. End of.

None of this has any effect on Bullivant. Should McFaul refuse to attend for interview, then only one option remains. The word 'arrest' makes me blink. How come the conversation has so suddenly taken a turn like this? A moment ago, I was wondering about putting the kettle on. Now, I'm thinking handcuffs.

'You have to have grounds. There has to be a reason.' McFaul has taken a step closer.

'You're right, Mr McFaul.'

'So why threaten me with arrest?'

'Because we think you may have murdered Miss Beaucarne.'

'You have grounds for that? Evidence?'

'That remains to be seen, Mr McFaul.' He gestures round. 'It might be wise to leave us with the key. The forensic boys hate putting doors in.'

FOURTEEN

McFaul is unbending. Bullivant asks him twice more to submit to a voluntary interview and when McFaul shakes his head, he's arrested and formally cautioned. Budleigh police station has been abandoned and so we drive to nearby Exmouth. McFaul is now handcuffed to Brett, and they sit wedged together in the back of the unmarked Ford. It has squeaky brakes and smells of cheap air freshener, and by the time we get to Exmouth I'm getting slightly nauseous. I know the police station well, thanks to events earlier in the year, but being back in the green-washed corridors, beneath the soulless glare of the neon lights, makes me feel like a recidivist.

Exmouth's top cop is a uniformed inspector called Geraghty, a big, untidy woman, much shrewder than you might think, whom I got to know and like.

She greets me at her office door. 'Welcome to Operation *Bulldog*,' she says. 'Still a splash of milk, is it? No sugar?'

Her coffee is beyond awful and she laughs when I say no. We share a moment of chit-chat and she asks how I'm coping without Pavel around. When I confess that his last stroke was a blessing, she puts a big hand on my arm and says she understands. Brett, she promises, will sort me out. 'Have a good day.'

Have a good day? By now, McFaul has disappeared, hand-cuffed to a uniformed officer. I follow Brett along the corridor and into an office at the end. There's no name on the door, and not much inside: a desk, a metal filing cabinet, and a faintly gothic poster on the wall portraying the tell-tale signs of domestic violence. Brett waves me into the chair in front of the desk, but for the time being I stay standing.

'Operation *Bulldog*?' I want to know more.

'That's right. Every major enquiry gets a codename. This one happens to be *Bulldog*. We have a suss death on our hands. We need to bottom one or two things out.'

'But there's no way he killed her,' I say hotly. 'Absolutely none. This whole thing is a charade. Your time? Our money? Need I go on? The poor bloody woman was dying. In case no one's told that boss of yours, let me be the first to break the news. She had motor neurone disease. It strangles you to death. Can you imagine that? Can you imagine going to bed every night, listening to your body pulling the rug from under your feet? Can you imagine what it's like waking up every morning, wondering whether you can still talk properly, still swallow, still put one foot in front of the other? Does any of that figure in this investigation of yours? Just nod. Just give me a clue. *Does* it?'

Brett is sitting back. He looks slightly pained, embarrassed even. My guess is that we're still friends, at least I hope so, and once I've calmed down I hear myself apologizing.

'No problem.' He's watching me taking a seat. 'This whole thing is tricky. Like I said, we need to bottom it out. Your mate McFaul did himself no favours. He could have said yes to another interview. If he's got nothing to hide, that would have been rational. People we arrest step into a whole new ball game.'

'So, where is he? Where's he gone?'

'We've taken him to the custody centre in Heavitree. He'll be booked in, photographed, fingerprinted, you know the way it goes. We'll hold him for twenty-four hours at least, maybe thirty-six, maybe longer.'

'And you really think he did it? Killed her? Be honest. Just tell me.'

Brett holds my gaze, says nothing, and for the first time it occurs to me that this search of theirs might have stumbled on a body.

'You've found her? Is that it?'

He shakes his head, like he's not going to tell me, and I turn away, trying not to imagine Christianne's body rolling around in the surf.

'I read that note she left you,' he says at last. 'You seem to have got really close to her. Would that be fair?'

'Yes. Within limits.'

'Limits?'

'A couple of days, to be exact. Nobody was counting, least of all me, but that's pretty much the time we spent together.'

'Good mates, though?'

'Yes. Being half-French helped. You tune into somebody, and hers happened to be a frequency I know very well. She'd made her own way in the world, done stuff, been brave, often very brave. She never boasted about it, barely mentioned it at all, but I knew what it had cost her.'

'How?'

'McFaul told me.' I explain about their years together in Angola, children they'd loved and lost to the minefields, a particular run-in with a local warlord who'd taken a fancy to this comely young nurse. 'She was very lucky not to have been raped.'

'McFaul told you that?'

'Yes. He was there, too.'

'And you believed him?'

'Every word. Every syllable. Do yourself a favour, Brett. Let your guard down. Trust people a little. Give us all a break.' I shake my head, study my hands. This is terrible dialogue, a scene I never want to play again as long as I live, but I owe it to McFaul to open these people's eyes. 'Goodness still exists in the world. And you've just banged a decent man up.'

'All that stuff he got rid of,' Brett says. 'Why would he do something like that?'

I do my best to explain. MND had turned Christianne into a slut, I tell him, and he couldn't bear to live with the evidence a moment longer.

'Shaz, wasn't it?' I've remembered the name of Brett's partner.

'Still is.'

'Then try and imagine that this horrible thing has happened to her. She's changing in front of your eyes, in front of her own eyes. The life you've always taken for granted has become a nightmare. You find yourself living in conditions the pair of you would never have put up with for a moment. Never. But there turns out to be nothing you can do about it. She's sensitive. She's proud. So every time you try and clean the place up, she loses it, yells at you, tells you to fuck off back to the garden. That's what happened, Brett, and that's why he's just had a bit of a spring clean. Do you blame the man? Wouldn't you get the bleach out? Under circumstances like that?'

'But she might come back,' he says softly.

'She might. You're right. But she won't.'

'How does he know?'

'Because they've lived together for more than twenty years. Because they've worked in places that would scare the likes of you and me shitless. And because he knows exactly what she'd decided to do.'

'Disappear?'

'Yes.'

'Do away with herself?'

'Yes.'

'Can you prove that?'

'Of course not. That's your job. All I'm doing here is putting in the bits none of you appear to have noticed. In my business, we'd call it back story, stage directions, whatever. You need the whole picture, Brett, and I'm happy to help.'

Brett has produced a pad. He scribbles himself a note, then stares at it for a moment or two, and looking at him I begin to doubt that they've found a body.

'They were poor, this couple . . .' He taps the pad with the end of his pen. 'Would that be right?'

'In the smallness of their wants? No. That made them rich. In cash terms? You're right, they were flat broke, totally skint, barely a penny to their names.'

'You *know* that?'

'I inferred it, built a picture, if you like. You don't need too many clues. No one drinks own-brand coffee, buys white sliced bread, gets by without a mobile, not if they can help it. As it happened, I doubt whether any of this much bothered them, especially when she was healthy, but that's a different story.' I pause. 'Why do you ask?'

'Ms Beaucarne had a bank account. We've accessed the details. Someone paid a sizeable sum of money into that account only a couple of weeks ago.'

'How much?'

'I can't tell you.'

'Thousands?'

'Go on.'

'Tens of thousands?'

Brett nods. Bill Penny, I think. He loved them both. He wanted to help them out. His first offer went to McFaul. When he said no, he must have turned to Christianne. But the story, it seems, doesn't end there.

'The money stayed in her account for three working days. Then she wrote a cheque.'

'To whom?'

'McFaul. He cashes it, and a week or so later he tells us she's disappeared. I know you think we always assume the worst of people, but . . .' He shrugs and tosses his pen on to the desk. 'Have we got this wrong? Isn't there just a tiny possibility there might be more to this story than meets the eye?'

It's my turn to shrug. I have nothing to say, and it's certainly not my part to bring Sir William into this squalid little fantasy.

'Well?' Brett insists. 'Don't you agree?'

I shake my head. I tell him none of us have the right, or even the imagination, to understand what it must be like to live with something as grotesque as MND.

'I assume you've talked to her GP?' I say.

'Of course.'

'And they confirmed the diagnosis?'

'She did, yes.'

'And what else did she say? About Christianne's state of mind?'

Brett gazes at me, and when he shakes his head the implication is all too clear. Do I really expect him to share a conversation like that?

'OK,' I say. 'If you want me to go through the whole thing

again, I will, though an hour or so with McFaul should make your boss a wiser man. He knows a great deal about MND and I'm sure he'll love to share it.'

Brett reaches for the pen again. He wants to change the subject.

'This friend of yours.' He glances down at his pad. 'Ms Warlock.'

'Evelyn,' I say. 'I call her Evelyn.'

'Our control centre took a 101 from her nearly a month ago, August twenty-third to be exact, three minutes past midnight. I gather she'd only moved in a matter of weeks before.'

'And?' 101 is the non-emergency number.

'It was a neighbour call. She was worried about some kind of domestic going on next door. Raised voices. Breaking glass. A woman in tears.' He gestures up at the poster on the wall. 'Naturally, we sent a car round.'

'This was McFaul? And Christianne?' My heart is sinking.

'Yes. By the time we got there, it had quietened down.'

'Was Christianne hurt?'

'No.' A sudden smile, the old Brett. 'But *he* was. They'd had a set-to and she'd thrown a couple of glasses at him. The car was single-crewed. I talked to the bloke who attended only yesterday. He remembers the incident very well, perfect recall. He says McFaul had a nasty cut over one eye, quite a lot of blood. By the time he got there, they'd both calmed down and she was doing her best to stop the bleeding. He says the place was a tip, shit everywhere, terrible smell. He thought they might have been pikeys to begin with, but that wasn't the case. Neither party wanted to make a statement and when he checked with your friend next door, she said she was mortified. She'd heard all the rumpus and assumed the worst but now she had nothing but regret. Big time. She wanted the incident buried. She asked us to wipe the record clean. Lovely neighbours, she told us. The best.'

I nod. Evelyn has never breathed a word about any of this, and listening to Brett I can understand why.

'So, you get it now?' I ask him. 'The state of the place? How keen you'd be to clean up afterwards?'

'Afterwards?'

'After she'd gone.'

Brett tries to hide another smile, but I don't let him.

'What's so funny?' I enquire.

'You really believe it, don't you? This story of his?'

'I do, yes. Have you got a better one?'

'No, not yet, but my boss is someone you'd be wrong to underestimate.'

'I'm not sure I'd dare.'

Brett laughs. He's genuinely amused and for the first time I start to wonder about the ethics of attaching him to this enquiry. We are, in a way, good friends. After the night he nearly bled out in the pub, I visited him a couple of times in hospital, and met his partner, Shaz. I also told every senior policeman what a star he'd been, endorsements that had probably got back to him. The fact is that we owe each other. Doesn't his presence behind this desk represent a conflict of interest? Or has he deliberately been assigned in the hope that I might mark his card, betray a confidence or two, stitch McFaul up?

'This boss of yours,' I say. 'Tell me more.'

'Bullivant? The man's a one-off. He's a very effective copper. "Driven" doesn't do the man justice. He's been in and out of the Major Crimes set-up for most of his career but just now he's attached down here.'

'Age?'

'Early fifties, and that's the point really. He'll be retiring early next year and I know he wants to go out with a bang. This job fell into his lap. He'll never keep it out of Major Crimes, not the way it's going, but I'll bet he'll bloody try.'

'Major Crimes? You're serious?'

'I'm afraid so.'

'So, you *have* found her?'

'No, and that's significant, believe me. We've put a lot of resources into the sea search. You can never be absolutely sure, but the odds are huge.'

'Against what?'

'That she ever went swimming.'

'You think he's lying?'

'Yes.'

'So, you think she's still alive?'

'No. Given the background, what we know from the GP, from

McFaul himself, we accept she's probably dead. What we need just now is a body. And some kind of steer to what might have happened.' He bends to the pad again and reaches for his pen. 'We always start with a timeline. Helps no end. We have multiple sightings of her last Saturday, some of them walking with you. McFaul reported her missing on Monday night. That leaves Sunday and most of Monday. Exactly where were you over those two days?'

'I went back to London,' I say at once.

'You can prove that?'

'Of course. Talk to my son. His name's Malo. He was there in the flat when I got home. On Monday, there's someone else you might talk to. Sylvester Penny. I took him and Malo to supper. Mezze. Holland Park Avenue. You want the number?'

I fetch out my phone, and give him the name of the owner, too. Brett writes all this down, then glances up.

'So, when did you last see Ms Beaucarne?'

'Christianne?' I'm thinking hard. 'It would have been Sunday, before I left for London, we would have said goodbye. Wrong. I'm wrong. McFaul said she was in bed, asleep. Rough night, I think, or maybe flu. I left it at that.'

'So, the last time you saw her . . .?'

'Saturday. We spent most of the day together, ended up in a pub called The Feathers. After that I walked her home. That's when I really began to notice.'

'Notice?'

'The little things. The way her balance was starting to go. The way she didn't trust herself with a glass or a cup. Just a hint of slurring when she talked. At the time you put it down to a million things, especially when you've been in the pub, but now . . .' I frown, angry at not drawing the right conclusions earlier.

Brett wants to know more about their relationship, McFaul and Christianne, and for the next hour or so I encourage him to picture the life they must have led together before the onset of MND. The years in Angola, and later Bosnia. Moving to the remoteness of rural Portugal. Getting by on very little except each other. I can tell he doesn't entirely buy this idyll because policemen aren't made that way.

'So, what happens next?' I ask. Brett is checking his watch.

'We put forensics into the bungalow,' he says. 'Box it off, room by room. That can take days, literally.'

'And you're looking for?'

'Anything that can build the story. The physical search is already winding down. The inspector in charge released the Force Support Group this morning. Now we're left with McFaul himself, and anyone else we can lay hands on.' That smile again. 'Any names you might like to share?'

'None,' I tell him. 'I'm a stranger down here, remember.'

Brett holds my gaze for a moment, then gets to his feet. I do the same. He reaches down to tidy the pages of his notepad, and as he does so, I notice a date circled in red ink. Saturday, 14 September. The day Christianne and I went walking on the coastal path. The day she showed me the view from the clifftop. The day we had lunch with Bill Penny. Is this where Operation *Bulldog* has settled? Is this where Bullivant and Brett believe the truth might lie? In the hours after Christianne returned from the pub? Or maybe later that weekend?

I turn away from the desk. On the back of the door hangs a leather suit, and a helmet, the kind that bikers wear, and tucked neatly beside the skirting board are a pair of leather boots.

'You've got a motorbike?'

'Christ, no. Never. That kit belongs to Bullivant. He rides a big Kawasaki, has done for years. He's a lay preacher, too. Doesn't drink, doesn't smoke, so maybe that's where the bike comes in. How does all that fit together?' One last grin. 'You tell me.'

FIFTEEN

The news that I've just spent a couple of hours with the police appears to startle Evelyn.

'They've found dear Christianne?'

'Alas, no.'

'Then what on earth's going on?'

I've been tempted to gloss over the small print of my interview with Brett Atkinson, but the sight of two vans outside McFaul's bungalow, one of them marked *Police Forensic Unit*, has rather blown my cover.

'They seem to think there's more to all this than meets the eye,' I mutter.

'More to all what?'

'Christianne going missing. You never told me about the little fracas you reported.'

Evelyn stares at me. She looks deeply ashamed.

'That was a mistake,' she says, 'on my part. I thought they'd forgotten about it, buried it. Andy didn't talk to me for days, weeks, not that I blame him. Ratted him out? Isn't that the phrase?'

'But he was the one on the receiving end. At least, that's the story I got.'

'It's true. It wasn't bad enough for stitches, but you'd never wish a bruise like that on anyone. Poor man.' She nods towards the vans at the kerbside. 'And now all this nonsense.'

It's gone six when I get the call from Bill Penny. He has a talent for giving you his full attention, and now is the perfect example. On the spur of the moment, he says, he's decided to host a modest little soiree, nothing alarming, just a handful of chums, and he would be flattered if I could find the time to pop over.

Soiree? Chums? Flattered? Pop over?

'You mean this evening?' I ask. 'Like now?'

'I'm afraid so.'

'Lovely,' I say. 'What time?'

'Seven would be perfect, but don't break a leg, eh?'

I arrive fifteen minutes late to be met at the front door by Bill. There's no sign of his precious little dog and when I ask, he says she's gone missing.

'She was out sniffing around for rabbits all morning, poor thing. At her age, I'm afraid she's doomed to disappointment, not that it seems to matter. Either way, she hasn't come back.'

'But you think she will?'

'We live in hope.'

Already, as I step into the house, I can hear the murmur of conversation through the open door that leads into the lounge, and a murmured comment about the country being safe in the hands of Comrade Corbyn raises a collective chuckle. According to people in the know, we're barely months away from a general election, though I doubt that Budleigh will be troubled by a rash of Labour posters.

To my surprise, there are only half a dozen armchairs around the log fire. Presley, I already know, and I vaguely recognize the figure sipping a glass of wine in the adjacent chair. She must have at least a decade on Presley but she's very striking: loose pantaloons the colour of blood, a pair of sandals in worn black leather, and a gorgeous Indian-looking *kurta* I once glimpsed at a Bollywood launch in Leicester Square. Last time I saw this woman, she was wearing a pair of trackie pants and helping manhandle the chaise longue into McFaul's bungalow.

'Beth.' Presley gets up to do the introductions. 'My other half.'

We shake hands. Lovely wrists. Lots of silver bangles. She holds my hand for a moment longer than strictly necessary.

'You're Evelyn's friend,' she murmurs. 'I thought she was fabulous the other night. So fucking *wise.* She really fired me up.'

'I'll tell her.'

'Do. I'd love to meet her. Seriously . . .' She gives my hand a little squeeze. 'Can you fix that?'

'Of course. My pleasure.'

The other stranger in front of the fire gets up to introduce himself.

'Nathan Kline.' He looks me up and down.

'Golfer extraordinaire.' Bill is circulating with a bottle of Château d'Auzanet, as solicitous as ever. 'We'd be lost without him. A treasure beyond compare.'

I think I sense irony in this comment but, if I'm right, it's lost on Nathan. He's taken his seat again. He wants to know whether I play at all.

'You mean golf?'

'Of course. Is there any other game? Any mention of bloody croquet, and I'll have Sir William throw you out.'

I tell him I've never played golf in my life, and probably never will. Beth and Presley nod in agreement and exchange glances. At first sight, this tiny gathering seems a strange assortment of people – different generations, different dress codes, different tribal markings – and as we get deeper into the evening, I start to wonder what on earth possessed our host to bring us all together.

Around Bill's magnificent antique dining table, which looks to me like rosewood, Nathan holds forth about the current state of the legal system. He spent most of his working life in and out of court, mainly in London, and as an ex-QC he considers himself more than qualified to pass judgement on a succession of recent justice ministers. These people, he tells us, are dwarfs compared to previous holders of the office, and he's shocked at the way a Tory government has allowed the system to fall apart. These days, he says gravely, you can get away with murder. The police, both of them, are otherwise engaged. The law courts are overwhelmed. The prisons are run by the inmates. And the probation service has been sold off to some bloody corporation. The result? Anarchy.

Beth mimes applause. She quite likes the idea of anarchy, though she's not entirely sure it'll catch on. Too foreign-sounding, she murmurs, too hard to spell. Beth's wit comes as a relief after Nathan's bombast, and I get up to help Bill clear the table for the cheese course. Our host has readied an impressive selection in the big kitchen and tells me where to find the bottle of port he's been saving.

'For what? Am I allowed to ask?'

'For tonight, my dear. I knew it had to happen. I just didn't expect it so soon.'

So soon? I follow Bill back to the dining room. The port is a Quinta do Noval vintage, and wins qualified approval from Nathan. He studies the label, sniffs the cork, then looks up at Bill.

'I had some of this last year in LA. Picked up a bottle at the airport on the way home. North of a hundred dollars? Am I getting warm?'

Bill, bless him, doesn't stoop to discuss the price he paid. Instead, he watches the bottle pass from hand to hand, and then raises his glass.

'To Christianne,' he says softly. 'Good luck and God speed.'

A murmur of voices repeat the toast, after which comes a

slightly uncomfortable silence. Is this my cue to share the news about McFaul's arrest? In truth, I've no idea, though it turns out at least one of them knows already.

'I had a call this afternoon.' Nathan is looking at me. 'Constabulary headquarters. A chum of mine. Plays off a three handicap. Only took the bloody game up a couple of years ago. Operation *Bulldog*? Would I be right?'

'You would.'

'And is it true they arrested him? Young Andy?'

'Yes.'

'And you were there?'

'Yes.'

'But you need grounds for arrest. What were theirs?'

This blizzard of questions is beginning to irritate me. I might be wrong, but I thought I'd been invited to a social event.

'Suspicion of murder.' I hold his gaze. 'They seem to think he killed Christianne. It's nonsense, of course, and I told them so.'

'You volunteered for interview?'

'Yes. Christianne left me a note. I was rather flattered, if you want the truth. I think she needed to say goodbye and for whatever reason, she chose me. The police wanted to know more about that, not that I had much to offer. We'd only just met. In one sense, I barely knew her.'

'And in the other?'

'We'd bonded. Definitely.'

'You had, my dear.' This from Bill. 'I could sense it when she brought you round.'

I nod, chiefly because it's true, but Nathan hasn't finished with me.

'Was it a long interview?'

'Mine, you mean?'

'Yes.'

'Not really. Maybe an hour. Maybe less.'

'And did you form any impression of the case they might be trying to make against Andy?'

This question belongs in a court of law. Part of me wants to ignore it, to change the subject, maybe even tell Nathan to mind his own business, but I'm aware of the interest on other faces around the table.

'They're puzzled by the absence of a body,' I say at last. 'They've looked and looked but they can't find her.'

'And that's it?'

'Yes. As far as I know.' This, of course, is a lie but I've no intention of embarrassing Bill Penny. The money that went to Christianne may well have come from our host but it's not going to be me who breaks the news.

Nathan, at last, appears to have finished with his cross-examination. In the silence that follows, I reach for my glass.

'This must be bloody hard on Andy,' I murmur. 'Losing your partner's one thing. Getting accused of killing her, quite another. I'm sure there's no case to answer. They've probably released him already.'

Heads nod around the table. Beth wants to talk about Christianne. She says they'd first met within days of her arrival from Portugal. She'd signed up for the Wednesday evening Zumba class at the Masonic Hall and she and Beth had shared a bottle of wine in The Feathers afterwards.

'I think she knew even then,' she says, 'even before the GP sent her for all those tests. She told me it was payback, though I never understood what for. She carried a lot of guilt. You could sometimes feel it.'

'You became friends?' I want to know more.

'Mates. I think she trusted me, and she certainly needed someone to talk to. Andy's a lovely guy but he can be a bit remote. If I had MND, I'm not sure he'd be the person I'd want to be tucking me in at night.'

'That's unfair.' Presley is sitting opposite. 'It crucified him. It broke the bloke in half. He'd coped with all kinds of shit for most of his life, and then this comes along. He was in denial at first, as I guess we'd all be. Only when she got the diagnosis did any of that change.'

'Change how?'

My question sparks an exchange of glances around the table and I sense that these people are trying to explore how far to take this conversation. Finally, it's Beth who breaks the silence.

'I knew,' she says. 'Chris told me last week.'

'Told you what?'

'Told me she was going to do it. They had a plan, in fact they always had plans, they were that kind of couple, but this plan was different because there'd be no coming back. She loved the water, the ocean, swimming every day, and when even that started to get tricky, she knew the time had come. I remember her telling me. I remember the phrase she used. "I want the ocean to take me away," she said. "I want it all to stop."'

'And that's when she went swimming? Off the beach?'

'No.' Beth shakes her head. 'Not there.'

'Somewhere else?'

'Yes.' She looks across at Presley, and I catch the faintest smile on his part. *Go ahead*, he's saying. *Tell them.*

Bill is sitting at the head of the table, with Beth beside him. His hand settles lightly on hers. 'You don't have to do this, my darling. Not if you don't want to.'

'I know, but we're friends, right? And this is about a woman we all loved, yes?' Beth's looking at the faces round the table.

'Bill's right,' I say. 'If it's easier, I'm sure we can change the subject.'

'But I don't want to change the subject. Politics? Would that make us feel better? Brexit? Boris fucking Johnson?' There's colour in Beth's face now. She has an intensity I hadn't quite grasped at first, and now she's very angry. 'We all know why we're here,' she says. 'We all held a candle for that lovely, lovely woman. So maybe the least we can do is honour the way she chose to go. Do I hear a yes? Or am I stepping out of line?'

'Tell them, Beth.' Presley is playing with his glass. 'Just tell them what happened.'

'OK.' She picks at a fingernail for a moment, then looks up. 'It was Sunday last. Chris had been in bed most of the day. I knew it had been getting bad because she'd told me last week, but apparently it took a turn for the worse. She'd tried to peel a banana, spent hours at it, had to give it to Andy in the end. A banana? Something as simple as that? Dear God . . .' Beth shakes her head.

'She phoned us,' Presley goes on. 'She wanted to talk to Beth.'

'That's right. It was the evening, gone eleven. We were nearly off to bed, but Chris was in tears. That was a first. She'd been a strong woman for so long, always on top of it, always looking on the bright side, but it was like I was suddenly talking to someone else. She wanted me to come round with the car. She said they needed a lift, the pair of them. I said fine, I'll come down and pick you up. They wanted to go over to Exmouth. Fifteen minutes, tops. A doddle. No problem.' She breaks off, biting her lip, and for a moment I think she's decided she can't go on but I'm wrong. 'The moment I saw them, I knew they were pissed. They must have been drinking most of the day. Do I blame them? Absolutely not. In any case, it didn't matter. They still wanted to go to Exmouth, so I got them both in the car. That was strange, or maybe sweet's a better word, because they insisted on sitting in the back, side by side. Andy had a bag. I could see them in the mirror. They were holding hands. They were all over each other. Nice. That was nice to watch.'

She breaks off again. Nathan wants to know about Exmouth.

'So, where did you drop them? Where were they going?'

'They wanted to go to the dock. You know where the Stuart Line puts in? The tourist boat? Down beyond the Rock Fish restaurant? That's where I took them.'

'Why?' Nathan again, our guest QC. 'Why the dock?'

'That's what I asked them. Andy wouldn't say a word. Chris was crying. They had a bottle in the bag, wine I think, and she kept taking mouthfuls, big swigs. Then they both got out, and I did, too. It was cold that night, and quite windy, no one around, the whole place completely dead.'

I nod. I know the dock. Pavel's apartment block was a couple of minutes away, at the end of the marina, and I often walked the path that skirts the little beach beside the dock entrance.

'The tide,' I ask. 'What was happening to the tide?'

'It was rushing out.' Beth has turned to look at me. 'You know the strength of that tide? It was like a river. I remember looking down at it. It was dark, of course, but there are lights around the corner on the prom and you could see this torrent of water pouring out to sea.' She shivered at the memory. 'Horrible.'

'You guessed what they were up to?' Nathan can't let this go.

'I guessed what she was up to, yes.'

'And Andy?'

'He was just holding her. Keeping her away from the edge.'

'He didn't want her to do it?'

'He didn't want me to watch. In fact, he didn't want me there at all. He asked me to go.'

'And?'

'I went. Just drove away. Left them to it. Came home.' She pauses, shaking her head. 'Andy phoned me in the middle of the night, said she was at peace. He told me he'd walked back from Exmouth. Starry night, he said. Not a cloud in the sky . . .' Her voice begins to catch, and she fumbles for a tissue as Presley gets to his feet to comfort her.

For a moment, no one says a word. Then Nathan seizes the bottle.

'Christ,' he says. 'What a story.'

SIXTEEN

I lie awake for most of the night, haunted by the image of Christianne's body being carried away by the ebbing tide. I've ridden that tide myself. I was aboard a sizeable sailing boat, outward bound for Brittany, standing on deck, yet I could still feel the fierce tug of millions of tons of water, emptying into the open sea. Drunk, helpless, Christianne would have been carried deep into the darkness, way beyond the curl of the beach and the red and green buoyage lights that flag the deep-water channel. She may have jumped with some kind of weight belt. She may have died hours later, miles out to sea. Either way, I'm praying she found just a moment or two of peace.

Next morning, exhausted, I'm debating what to do with this story of Beth's. Before we left Bill's house last night, he'd slipped a CD into his audio system and asked us to spend a minute or two just remembering what a remarkable woman we'd lost. The music was Brahms. *Schicksalslied*, the Song of Destiny. Christianne, Bill said, had fallen in love with it.

Afterwards, the music over, we collected our coats and all met in the hall for something I can only describe as a group hug. It happened spontaneously, an unvoiced pledge that we'd respect Christianne's departure and keep the knowledge of what had really happened to ourselves. In the darkness outside, I briefly fell into step beside Nathan.

'Nightmare.' He shot me a glance. 'Can you imagine doing something like that?'

'Yes,' I said. 'I can. But I'd have to be very drunk.'

'Just like her, then.' He shook his head. 'Poor soul.'

Now, soaping myself in the shower, I'm thinking about McFaul. DI Bullivant, I know, will do his best to take him to court. With whatever evidence he can muster, he'll try and prove that Christianne was killed by her partner, either out of desperation, or for gain. Isn't it therefore down to me to prove that she went of her own volition? At a moment of her choosing? By jumping to certain death off that bloody dock? Wouldn't that get McFaul out of the clutches of Operation *Bulldog*?

I phone Brett Atkinson after Evelyn has fed me toast and a pot of tea. When I press him for a meet, somewhere private, he suggests the car park beside Exmouth's leisure centre. He'll be in a white Ford Focus. He'll be watching out for me.

I leave the bungalow with plenty of time in hand. The presence of the forensic team has been reduced to a single van. The curtains on the bungalow's front windows have remained closed since the team's arrival, but I've watched enough prime-time TV to imagine these men trying to conjure a story from microscopic particles of God knows what. Poor bloody McFaul, I think. Fate, indeed.

Brett turns up late, blaming a meeting that overran. When I ask him how things are going with Operation *Bulldog*, he pulls a face. McFaul, he says, has struck lucky with the duty solicitor. She's an old hand, aware of the lack of truly hard evidence, and has advised her client to say nothing. So far, he says, the interview team has failed to get beyond 'No comment', and the case against McFaul has barely progressed at all. The on-call superintendent has approved another twelve hours of custody, but after that *Bulldog*'s prime suspect will probably walk free.

'What about the forensics?' I enquire. 'The search team at the bungalow?'

'They're still on the case.'

'And?'

'You have to be kidding.' Brett is looking pained. 'I'm here because you've got something to tell me. If I thought this was a fishing expedition, I'd never have come.'

This is a reprimand, and we both know it. Back in the summer, circumstances may have made us friends, but just now we're in a very different place. There's a protocol here, a quiet little game of give and take, but I have to remember the rules.

'You rely on cameras a lot,' I mutter. 'CCTV. Am I right?'

'Yeah. Right place, right time . . . yeah.'

'So, what would happen if I could prove that Christianne killed herself?'

'How?'

'By drowning. By throwing herself in.'

'Budleigh beach, you mean?'

'No, somewhere else.'

'Somewhere *else*?' The thought appears to appal him. All those wasted hours for the search teams. All that overtime. 'What are you telling me here?'

'I'm telling you she did what she said she'd do. Except not quite where we thought.'

'And McFaul knew that?'

'Maybe. Maybe not. But let's pretend he did.'

'Then we'd have him. Stone bonker. Perverting the course of justice. Wasting police time. You're aware of the bills we've been running up here? A chopper? The lifeboat? The rest of the circus? A search like that doesn't come cheap, believe me.'

'But at least he didn't kill her. Doesn't that matter?'

'Of course it does, but it means the bloke's been dicking us around and, believe me, that's nearly as bad. Laying false trails? Hiding what he knew to be true? I'll check if you like, but last time I looked the phrase was criminal intent.'

I nod, realizing already that I've just walked into a trap of my own making. En route to the car park, I made a detour to the dock to check for CCTV. One camera, mounted on a pole on the dock, seemed to offer the view that mattered. But the moment I head Brett in that direction is the moment I land McFaul in serious trouble. Perverting the course of justice is a phrase I've come across before, and given circumstances like these, I suspect he could be looking at a lengthy prison sentence.

'Fine.' I'm reaching for the door handle. 'Just wanted to check.'

'And that's it? You're going?'

'Yes.'

'But you were serious? About McFaul?'

'No.' I give him a brief peck on the cheek. 'I get in a bit of a muddle sometimes. Let's pretend this never happened.' I'm halfway out of the car when I have another thought. Rosa has been on to me again. She's getting impatient. She badly needs word about Pavel's missing masterpiece. 'That MacBook of mine you seized,' I say. 'When can I have it back?'

Brett studies me a moment. Then he smiles, and reaches for the ignition key.

'It's on the download list,' he says. 'But the queues for full analysis these days are beyond belief. Could be a month or two.' He shrugs. 'Maybe longer.'

Shaken, I drive back to Budleigh. Over the last couple of years, I've had far too many dealings with the police, and I should have learned by now to be more circumspect. The business of law and order is very black and white, but in the shape of young Brett Atkinson I thought I might have found a little room for manoeuvre. Not only was I wrong, but from now on he'll probably think I'm as bent as McFaul. Or, much worse, an airhead.

I take my frustrations out on Evelyn.

'If we lived in Holland,' I tell her, 'none of this would bloody have happened. They're civilized people. Get something like MND, and you have the right to call it quits. Killer injection. Final curtain. Huge applause. Gone. So why can't we have some of that? Why couldn't Christianne?'

Evelyn is a woman of faith. Choosing to end your life, she thinks, raises issues that might be a little more complex.

'Like?'

'Like it might not be your life to end.'

'Then whose is it?'

'God's. Life is a loan, my lovely. It comes with strings attached, duties, obligations, responsibilities. One of them is not to waste it. Another is never to throw it away. Life is a sacrament. A precious gift. We should understand that. We should treasure it.'

'But if it hurts? If it turns you into someone you don't want to be any more?'

'Then that is simply another of God's plans. He loves us, Enora. He truly does.'

Evelyn very rarely calls me by my Christian name and it's a mark of the nerve I've touched that she should be doing so now. I've always respected her deeply, and I always will, but all I can think of just now is DI Bullivant. He, too, has evidently put his trust in the Lord and look what's happening.

He turns up in person a couple of hours later. I hear the Kawasaki first. I'm lying on my bed upstairs, trying to have a nap, but the high insect whine as the bike powers up the hill towards the cul-de-sac draws me to the window. It's definitely Bullivant. I recognize the leathers. He parks behind the forensics van and removes his helmet before going to the front door. I hear a brief conversation, and then the door closes behind him. I linger at the window for a moment before returning to bed.

Half an hour later, maybe longer, I jerk awake to hear McFaul's front door opening again. Back at the window, I watch Bullivant and one of the forensic team manhandling the chaise longue into the back of the van. The chaise is covered in heavy duty polythene, and both men are wearing blue gloves. The rear doors closed, there's a brief kerbside conference before Bullivant taps his watch. Moments later, with his helmet back on, he's astride the big bike and away.

Hours later, over supper, it turns out that Evelyn had also witnessed this little scene. The chaise has taken her eye, too, and she wants to know more. I tell her what little I can, that it was probably some kind of present from Bill Penny, and leave it at that.

'And what about the chap with the motorbike?' she asks.

'He's a man of God,' I say bitchily. 'But he's unforgiving.'

SEVENTEEN

Next morning, the work of the forensic team is apparently over. The van has gone, the curtains at the front of the bungalow are pulled back, and the only evidence that McFaul's life has been picked apart is a neat stash of folded cardboard beside his wheelie bin.

I go for a long walk along the seafront, climbing the coastal path that I'd discovered with Christianne only a week ago. At the very top, before the path zigzags down towards the holiday park at Sandy Bay, I pause beside the fence that separates the path from the golf course. A party of four have circled a nearby hole and I'm watching one of them lining up a difficult putt when I realize that another of these men is Nathan Kline. He's recognized my yellow anorak, and he saunters across.

'Difficult evening the other night.' He's inspecting me over the fence. 'Your take on that story of Beth's?'

'I thought it was very sad.'

'Indeed, but all too plausible I imagine. A state like that, I'm sure you'd reach at every straw.'

Quite what he means isn't clear, but I get the feeling I'm somehow being put to the test. This man has an almost lordly presence, *de haut en bas* as the French like to put it, and years of cross-examination have definitely left their mark. We wring our hands a moment or two longer over Christianne's final hours, agreeing that a bottle or two of decent red would ease the pain, before a whistle from one of the golfers summons him back to the business in hand.

'Staying down here a while longer?' he says.

'I might. It depends.'

'Well, let's hope so.' He pauses, ignoring another summons back to the game. 'Ever fly at all? Ever tried it? Little planes? Up and away?'

'Yes,' I say. 'And I loved it.'

'Excellent. I've got shares in a Cessna out at Dunkeswell. East Devon from the air is a real treat. We could have a bite to eat afterwards. The pleasure would be mine.'

He produces a calling card and scribbles a mobile number on the back before striding back to the hole. I watch him seize a putter and miss the simplest of shots before I slip the card into the pocket of my jeans. My acceptance of this little come-on appears to be a formality.

After lunch, Evelyn takes me down to the public hall where a writer called David Barrie is appearing as the literary festival comes to an end. As a thank-you for last week's *tour de force*,

Evelyn has the pick of events that aren't fully booked but, in the light of last night's exchange, she's spared me a talk on British cathedrals which I happen to know she'd been keen to attend.

This is typical Evelyn, generous to a fault, but David Barrie more than makes up. His forte is animal navigation and he treats us to a grand tour of the mysteries of the natural world. Dung beetles that steer by the light of the Milky Way. Ants following patterns of light invisible to the human eye. Sea turtles tuned in to the earth's magnetic field. Birds of passage that can find their nests on a tiny island after crossing an entire ocean.

Emerging back into the daylight, sharing a brolly against a thin rain, I can't help thinking of Malo and the Twilight Fund. Christopher Columbus was undoubtedly a genius and GPS, I'm sure, is a miracle of technology, but the image of the super-rich fleeing certain death, thanks to Sylvester Penny, fills me with despair. Humans have no sense of direction, I think. Unlike a thousand other species, we're lost.

As a thank-you for the talk, I treat us both to afternoon tea. L'Image is a café in the High Street that I know Evelyn loves, and the minute we step in I understand why. It's a stylish essay in creamy-grey décor and elegant wicker chairs, and the scatter of tables are surrounded with displays of women's couture. This combination shouldn't work but somehow it does, and it reminds us both of similar places we used to haunt together off the Bayswater Road. Evelyn has already commandeered a table beside the window but I linger for a moment, running my fingers through a rather nice chenille sweater dress. I have my back to the door, and feel the draught on my bare legs as it opens.

'My dears, I knew I'd find you here.' It's Bill Penny. Like us, he's been to listen to David Barrie. 'I saw you as you were leaving,' he says. 'I waved but you weren't looking.'

He joins us at the table and while we wait for service, we agree that the natural world holds secrets we can scarcely comprehend.

'It's so easy to confuse knowledge with wisdom,' Evelyn says. 'If we're really so clever, then why are we so stupid?'

'Wisdom?' Bill isn't sure. 'Is the sea turtle wise? Or the dung beetle? Might a better word be instinct?'

Evelyn nods, and so do I, and within seconds we're talking about Christianne again.

'What she did was instinctive,' I say. 'She was listening to her body. Listen hard enough, and in her situation, I doubt you have much choice. You follow the path that seems most right, most natural, and who is anyone else to stand in her way?'

This little *aperçu* has put me, once again, on a collision course with Evelyn's religious beliefs and I'm desperately trying to come up with a change of subject when Bill asks me whether I've heard any more about Andy.

'I gather they're still talking to him,' I say. 'You know the man much better than I do, but I sense he doesn't scare easily, especially when he's upset.'

'And they really arrested him?'

'They did. And that might have been a mistake on their part. Andy strikes me as very territorial. I know he resented the way they barged into that bungalow of his, and the same will be true of his life as a whole. My guess is he'll say nothing. Which is his way of telling them to bugger off.'

'Shrewd.' Bill is smiling.

'Of him?'

'Of you, my dear. A shrewd judgement. Work with the man *en plein air* and you can't help admiring his qualities. Show him a stretch of that coastal path that needs a bit of TLC, new risers, replacement timberwork, whatever, and he's utterly undaunted. I just hope the police recognize the genuine article when they see it. In my book, the man can't lie to save his life. Just wouldn't see the point.'

The waitress arrives and takes our order. Bill declines to stay for the full cream tea but beckons us closer before he leaves.

'We've been mulling over ways to mark Christianne's passing,' he murmurs. 'Something simple, the kind of farewell we think might put a smile on her face. She's been gone for nearly a week, so now might be the time for a little get-together. *En plein air*, again. In a setting of which she'd undoubtedly approve.'

'Today, you mean?' Evelyn gestures out at the rain.

'Tomorrow. The forecast is much better. I took the precaution of checking.'

'Where?'

'On the beach. Down at the far end where Andy found her clothes. We'll have a little gathering on the beach first. Beth has a couple of ideas on that score. After that, one of the local fishermen will be only too happy to take us offshore. We're having a wreath made up. Beth's idea, again. She's been talking to the girls whom Christianne used to swim with. There's a line of buoys a hundred metres out, a kind of fence they had to touch before they went back to the beach. A prayer *in situ*? Maybe in French?' He's looking at me. 'And then a moment or two of silence after we cast the wreath on the waters. How might that sound?'

Both Evelyn and I are thrilled by the idea. Back at the bungalow, we agree that this gesture is pitch-perfect, neither a showy act of collective grief, nor a passing nod to register an event that has clearly touched so many lives. Best of all, it puts Andy's arrest in exactly the right context. No one is questioning the rights of the police to investigate a death like Christianne's, least of all in this little town, but the wider context remains far more important. She took her own life in the fullest knowledge of how it would otherwise end. And while everyone will miss her, everyone will – or should – understand.

Evelyn and I eat a late supper and raise a glass of Chablis to tomorrow's get-together. We're settling into *Match of the Day*, which Evelyn adores, when I hear a car pulling up outside. Her beloved Man City are playing Watford. After the first fifteen minutes, the home team are already four goals up and, given Evelyn's passion for Kevin de Bruyne, she's totally absorbed.

At the window, curious, I check through a tiny gap in the curtains. McFaul is getting out of a taxi. As I watch, he bends to the driver's window and hands over some money. Then, without another word, he's limping slowly towards his front door. The cab driver pulls a three-point turn and moments later the street is empty again. One of Evelyn's windows is open and I can hear the scrape of McFaul's key in his front door. The man has just spent two and a half days in police custody, I think. The last couple of nights, he'd have slept in some cell, and now he must confront the emptiness of a bungalow he probably never liked in the first place. And all this without the company, the solace, of a woman I'm certain he loved.

I steal a glance at Evelyn.

'Goal number five.' She's kicked her shoes off, and her legs are tucked beneath her, like a child. 'Otamendi, can you believe that?' She spares me a brief glance, pats the sofa beside her. 'It could be six,' she says, 'and we're only fifteen minutes in. You can't miss this.'

I try and explain about Andy coming home but I doubt whether she's heard me.

'I won't be long.' I tap my watch. 'I'll leave the door on the latch.'

I let myself out and go next door. The lights are on in the front room, but the curtains have been pulled tight. I ring the bell twice and, when nothing happens, I venture into the flower bed and tap on the window.

'Enora,' I call, 'from next door.'

Andy lets me in. He looks terrible: pale, drawn, a man close to defeat. I want to put my arms around him, give him a hug, make some of this terrible, terrible loss just a little easier to bear, but there's still something forbidding about him, a tacit expectation that the rest of the world will keep its distance and leave him alone.

'So, what happened?' I ask. It's the best I can do.

He's staring at me. I know he wants me gone but when I make no move to leave, he shrugs and holds the door a little wider.

'Come in,' he mutters. 'Why not?'

We go through to the front room. I can smell the sharp tang of chemicals hanging in the stale air, and when I look hard, I notice a crust of whitish powder where the carpet laps against the skirting board.

'So, where's my fucking chaise?' he asks.

'They took it.'

'They?'

'Bullivant, the DI. And one of the forensic people.'

'When?'

'Last night.'

'You talked to those bastards?'

'I watched them from next door. My guess is they want a closer look.'

'At that chaise.' He nods. 'Too fucking right. You know what these people do? They take hostages. It can be a bit of furniture or your whole bloody life. They never know when to stop. And even when you give them the time of day, or even an answer or two, they never believe you. He comes from a dark place, that man. God's truth, I'd never want to be in his head.'

'You mean Bullivant?'

'Yeah. Or that mate of yours, the younger guy.'

'Brett?'

'Yeah, him. Arseholes. The pair of them.'

I nod. I've no idea what to say. I've come here to offer comfort, or at least a listening ear, but this man is beyond reach.

'Is there anything left to drink in this house?' I ask.

'*Left?*' he says hotly. 'You think I've necked it all? Is that what you think?'

'I'm just asking. I'm sorry.' I pause for a moment while he looks away. 'Well?'

'Well what?'

'Maybe just a glass before I go?'

'Why? What would be the point? You want to know what happened? I'll tell you what happened. They banged me up for session after session. They wanted to know everything about the pair of us, the way we'd been together, what had taken us to Africa, to Portugal, what had brought us back here. They're convinced we'd crashed and burned. They were like a pair of pervs, sniffing around, sniffing at our lives. They're convinced I'd been beating her up, threatening her, robbing her blind, making her life a misery. They think all the business on the beach was some kind of set-up. They think it was me who put the clothes there when all the time she was back here, brown bread, while little me dreamed up ways of getting rid of her.'

'Brown bread?'

'Dead. The phrase they're using is crime scene. Here. Where we stand. *Crime scene.* Can you believe that?'

There's a long silence. Dimly, from next door, I think I catch the roar of a crowd from Evelyn's TV but I'm not sure.

'So, what did you tell them?' I manage at last.

'Nothing. I told them fuck all. In the end they had to let me go. And you know why? Because fuck all means fuck all. And that's all they've got.'

I nod. I have something to say, something important, but I'm
not at all sure how to put it.

'There might have been an easier way,' I suggest.

'Like what?'

'Like you could have told them what really happened.'

'*What?*'

McFaul is staring at me. I'm about to re-phrase what I've just
said when he puts a finger to his lips and gestures wildly round.
Moments later, he has me by the arm and we're heading for the
front door. Outside, the rain has stopped and it's much colder.

'That's your car?' He's nodding at my ancient Peugeot.

'Yes.'

'You've got a key?'

'Yes.'

The key is in my jeans pocket. Within seconds, we're sitting
together in the front.

'What's this about?' I'm feeling the first prickles of what might
be apprehension. 'You want me to drive you somewhere?'

'Not at all. They'll have bugged the house. It's what they do.
Microphones. Transmitting gear. Tune in and help yourself. It
never fucking fails. Park up down the road there, go round the
corner. They may be watching the place, too.'

I hold his gaze for a moment, and then shrug. Paranoia, I think.
We've gone about a quarter of a mile, down towards the town
centre, when he points to an area of semi-darkness between two
streetlamps.

'There,' he says. 'But keep the engine on.'

'Why?'

'I'm freezing. This heater works?' He fiddles with the controls
and I feel a gust of hot air rising between us. McFaul is checking
the road behind us.

'Anyone there?'

'No one. But that means sod all. Say what you've got to say.
Just tell me.'

'OK.' I nod. 'I had dinner with some people you know the
other night. God knows why they invited me, but they did.'

'So, who are they? These people?'

I list them in order, faces around the table, starting with Bill
Penny. McFaul is gazing out through the windscreen.

'And?' he asks. His voice is stony.

'We were talking about Christianne. They asked about you, obviously, and about not finding a body, and about the arrest, but then Beth explained what really happened. I'd no idea. Truly none.'

'So what did she say?'

'She said they'd taken a call late. It would have been Sunday night. You both wanted to go to Exmouth.' I hesitate. Something's wrong here, I can feel it. 'You remember that call? To Beth and Presley? Asking for a lift?'

'Go on.'

'She came round, picked you both up, took you over to Exmouth. You were sitting in the back of the car. Christianne was quite emotional. Apparently, she'd had a bad day.' I pause again. 'The banana? You remember that? Not being able to peel the bloody thing?'

Nothing. No nod. No confirmation. Just another grunt.

'So, what happened? When we got to Exmouth?'

'You wanted to go to the dock. There was a big tide. It was late, no one around . . .' I shrug. 'So she did it. Threw herself in. Disappeared out to sea. Beth had gone by then, but you phoned her after you walked back home, told her what had happened.' Still he doesn't react. I'm frowning now, trying to choose my words carefully, trying to sieve the facts from something rather darker. 'You remember all this?' I catch just the faintest hint of a nod. 'Is that a yes?'

'Could be.'

'Right. So Christianne threw herself in. A tide like that, there's no getting out.' I pause for a moment, ashamed to be setting this little trap. 'Stone-cold sober, that's a brave thing to do. We agree?'

'Yeah.'

'She hadn't been drinking?'

'No way.'

'And you?'

'No.'

'OK. So why did you leave the clothes on the beach? That Monday night?'

He looks away, gives the question some thought.

'To protect Beth,' he mutters at last. 'Isn't it fucking obvious?'

*   *   *

I'm back home within minutes. I've parked the car outside Evelyn's and Andy has disappeared into his own bungalow without a word of farewell or even a backward glance. I linger behind the wheel, trying to make sense of Beth's story.

This woman, I can sense already, can't resist the grand gesture. The way she dresses, the way she carries herself, the trophy *beau* she lives with, all speak to a passion for drama. She needs to be noticed, to be listened to, and if she feels that Christianne's last hour on planet earth might call for a bottle or two of decent red, then so be it. This was her account, her moment in the spotlight around Bill Penny's table, but the question that begins to shape itself deep in my brain is deeply troubling. Was it *all* a lie? And does McFaul know that?

I find Evelyn still on the sofa. She appears to have adopted the recovery position and when I enquire further, it turns out that Man City have put no less than eight goals past the luckless Watford. Not only that, but the clincher, in the eighty-fifth minute, came from – yes – Kevin de Bruyne.

This, she says, calls for a modest celebration. I do her bidding, glad to forget about Andy for a moment or two, and return from the kitchen with two glasses and the remains of the bottle of Armagnac. We toast the sainted Kevin, and then someone called Pep, and we're on our second glass of brandy before she asks me where I've been.

'Next door,' I say.

'You're telling me Andy's back?'

'Yes.'

'Safe and sound? A free man?'

'Police bail. He has to report twice weekly while they make further enquiries.'

'They still think he killed her?'

'I suspect they do, yes.'

'And can they prove it?'

'Obviously not.'

'And you, my lovely?'

'I was there to listen. And maybe try and help.'

'I meant London. Earlier you thought you might go home tomorrow. After we all meet on the beach.'

'I know.'

'And?'

'Second thoughts, I'm afraid.' I reach for the bottle, thinking once again about Beth's story. 'Maybe later in the week.'

EIGHTEEN

Next morning, as Bill had promised, the weather behaves itself. The rain and the murk have gone and the sun is heavenly as Evelyn and I make our way down through the town. The road dips suddenly towards the big car park at the end of the beach and already I can see a knot of people gathered on the pebbles. They're standing beside a splash of scarlet, deep in conversation.

Walking on the beach is awkward, thanks to the size and smoothness of the pebbles, and I take Evelyn by the hand, steadying her when she loses her footing. The splash of scarlet turns out to be a couple of towels, carefully rucked. Beth is talking to Bill Penny, but she breaks off when we approach. She's wearing an ankle-length cotton dress that stirs in the wind off the sea. Her feet are bare and a patterned bandana gives her a faintly warrior look.

'This is where Christianne left the clothes?' I nod at the towels.

'Yeah. It's as close as I can get. Andy gave me the rough directions.'

'Isn't he coming?' I'm looking round.

'He said he might.'

'*Might?*' I can't help frowning.

'Yeah . . . you know . . . it must be tough for him . . .' She steps a little closer and takes me to one side. 'Maybe we need to remember what really happened. That man is hurting. Can't you feel his pain?'

Really happened? I say nothing for a moment. Sooner or later, this woman owes me a proper conversation, but not here, not now.

Nathan Kline has arrived. Knife-edged flannel trousers, crisp white shirt, black tie, Golf Club blazer. He, too, wants to know about the towels.

'They represent fire,' Beth says. 'It's a Native American thing. It's one of the projects I'm working on. Fire as a cleanser. Fire as the essence of nature. Fire as the presence of Wakan Tanka.'

'Who?'

'The Great Spirit. Christianne is with him now. As we all will be.' Beth presses a hand to her chest and briefly closes her eyes, tilting her face upwards to the sun. A group of women, none of them young, are standing nearby. They're watching this little performance, unsure quite what to make of it. All of them are carrying towels of their own, and I ask Evelyn why. More disciples of Wakan Tanka? More spiritual kindling for Christianne's fire?

Evelyn laughs. 'I expect they'll be going in for a dip later.' She nods down towards the curl of waves on the wet shingle. 'These are the women Christianne used to swim with. It's nice to see them here.'

Beth has abandoned Nathan Kline and is back with her partner, Presley. Presley is dressed entirely in black – jeans, T-shirt, leather jacket – and watching them together it's easy once again to see who bosses the relationship. I suspect Beth is at least ten years older than this partner of hers, and it shows. She's forever touching him, a hand on his arm, her lips to his ear, a commanding physical intimacy she wants us all to see, but she's definitely kept her looks, and the longer I watch her, the more I begin to sense something slightly Aztec in the planes of her face, and the sallowness of her complexion, and that thick, lustrous fall of jet-black hair beneath the bandana. A beautiful woman, I think. Lucky Presley.

Moments later, she checks her watch and does a head count, and calls us to order. The time has come, she says, to start proceedings, but then she spots McFaul making his way along the beach.

'No pressure,' she says. 'Let's wait for who really matters.'

There's a mumble of agreement as people follow her pointing finger. There must be a couple of dozen of us by now, young as well as old, and I realize that the make-up of this little impromptu gathering, the sheer range of ages, is a tribute to Christianne's cheerful sense of fellowship. Evelyn recently told me her neighbour could strike up a conversation with anyone in this little town and, feeling the warmth around me, I can only believe her.

All eyes are on McFaul, poor man. He's wearing an old pair of khaki shorts and a grey T-shirt, and with his prosthetic leg he's finding it hard going on the pebbles. Part of me wants to break ranks and give him a hand, but I know he'd hate it and so he limps slowly closer, his head down, checking the lie of the big smooth stones, trying to spare himself a fall. Was this the way you'd survive in the minefields? Have those years in Angola seeped deep into his muscle memory?

Finally, he's with us. He accepts Bill Penny's outstretched hand, but it's Nathan Kline who leads the round of applause. This is a gesture I find rather touching, but McFaul's curt shake of the head tells me he's embarrassed. For him, I'm guessing this must be the most private of moments. In fact, looking at him now, I'm amazed he's here at all.

Beth has broken off again. She's spotted another newcomer, a much younger figure in a rumpled grey suit. I've seen his face before but it's a second or two before I realize where. This was the young man who was talking to the fearsome Inspector Hollick beside the incident van, that first day of the police search. Beth is bringing him across.

'Enora Andressen.' Her hand is on my arm but she's talking to the newcomer. 'I expect you'll know the name. A very good friend of Christianne's. I'm sure she'd be happy to spare you a moment afterwards? Is that OK, Enora? You don't mind sharing a memory or two?'

I say nothing. I'm looking at the camera looped over the young man's shoulder. Then my gaze wanders to the ID card dangling on the lanyard around his neck.

'*Exmouth Journal*?' I query.

'That's right.' Local accent, ready smile. 'Beth invited me down. Very happy to be here. Wonderful way of saying goodbye.'

Beth squeezes my arm and then takes her young reporter to meet Bill. Bill, like me, is plainly surprised that a private event like this should have suddenly become public property but – gentleman that he is – he does his best not to let it show. The reporter shakes his hand, then retreats to a nearby fold of pebbles and begins to take shots on his camera while Beth asks us to form a loose circle around the scarlet towels.

This morning, she says, we can all feel the warmth and the

presence of the spirits. She gestures up towards the sun, out towards the sea, and then reassures us that Christianne is in good hands, the best of hands, and that the purpose of us being here together is to celebrate not just her life but the way she chose to bid us farewell.

'Darling?'

Presley answers her summons. From the depths of a rather nice calico bag he produces a smallish china pot. He removes the lid and gives the pot to Beth. She studies it a moment, raises it to her nose, inhales deeply, and then extends it like an offering.

'This is a paste,' she says. 'I made it this morning. It's based on an ancient Hopi recipe. It begins with dried yam and tumbleweed and crushed sage, and includes all kinds of unctuous yumminess, but I wouldn't recommend it on toast.'

The joke, in a setting like this, falls flat. People are nervous now. They've come for remembrance, not a masterclass in Native American rituals, and they begin to exchange glances as Beth circles with her pot of magical potion, moving from person to person, anointing forehead after forehead with a small greasy dot of – I assume – spiritual awakening. No one says a word. No one refuses or withdraws. But the spell that brought them here – that debt of gratitude they owe Christianne – is somehow broken. Only the reporter, framing shot after shot, has bought into this nonsense. And given the impact it will make in next week's local paper, who can blame him?

It's my turn.

Beth hesitates a second. 'I expect you've done this before,' she says.

'Never.'

'Not even on stage?'

'Never.'

'A first then. My privilege.'

She dips a finger. The gunk, dark green, is granular and oily and I catch the harshness of the crushed sage. The dot feels cool on my forehead but before she moves on, I beckon her closer.

'Andy might say no,' I murmur. 'If that happens, you should respect it.'

'He won't.' The smile is knowing. 'I promise.'

And she's right. Andy inclines his head and submits to a dot of his own. Is he tuned into the Great Spirit? Or, for once in his life, is he being polite? I try and catch his eye but he's avoiding every gaze.

Beth has returned the china pot to Presley. She closes her eyes and raises her face to the sun again, her arms held wide, and then begins to chant. No one, least of all me, has a clue what any of this means but it must go on for at least a minute. Beyond the chanting, I can hear the mew of the seagulls and the click-click of the reporter's shutter. More shots for the *Journal*. Then, suddenly, complete silence before Beth's arms come down and she opens her eyes. The spirits, she says, are in attendance. And now we must propitiate them.

Propitiate them? At another nod from Beth, Presley produces a small speaker connected to his mobile phone. He swipes the screen a couple of times, dabs at an icon, and we hear music, mainly drums and some kind of wind instrument.

Beth widens the circle, asking people to step backwards. When she has enough room, she begins to dance slowly around the towels, the faux flames, moving slowly from foot to foot, her body swaying above the hips, her lips moving in some silent prayer. Then comes a change of chord in the music, a tiny pause, and she reverses the dance, circling the other way. From time to time, she beats her thighs with the palms of her hands, one after the other, before the tempo of the music quickens, some form of promise, or maybe release, shaping itself in the harshness of this muddle of notes. Then comes a sudden climax, and she stands rigid for a moment, totally immobile, before jumping over the towels with a wild yelp I can only describe as animal.

Watching the faces around me, it's impossible not to sense how appalled these people are. Must we do this? Will it be our turn next? And I, too, a seasoned performer, am dreading the moment she claps her hands again and tugs us into this crazy piece of theatre. But I needn't have worried. This isn't Beth's plan at all. She's standing on the far side of the circle, her body limp, a strange smile on her face.

'Done.' She gestures down at the towels. 'Finished.'

People stir. You can almost taste their relief that this strange rite of passage is over. Even Evelyn, always fair-minded, can't resist a shake of the head and a muttered confidence.

'What total crap,' she says.

Bill, mercifully, has taken over, appointing himself MC for the rest of the proceedings. Ever the diplomat, he thanks Beth for the time and effort she must have put into what we've all had the privilege of witnessing, and then indicates a smallish boat that has beached below us.

'Room for six,' he says. 'To avoid disappointment, I'm afraid the places are pre-allocated.'

Bill tallies off the names of those who will be dropping the wreath. To my surprise, five of us shared Thursday evening around his dinner table.

'And the sixth?' This from Nathan.

'Sylvester. My son. If he deigns to show up.'

The news that Sylvester may be joining us is totally unexpected. I'd somehow assumed that he was far too busy to bother himself with a provincial occasion like this but, minutes later, he proves me wrong. Bill spots him first, a tallish figure in a track top and shorts, moving at some speed along the promenade. On the beach, he bounds across the pebbles to join us. He, too, is carrying a rolled towel and – to my surprise – is barely out of breath.

'Sorry, Pa. Misjudged the time.' He's looking at Bill.

'Again.'

'Again. *Mea culpa*. Lovely day. Perfect.' He looks around. He has his father's beam, his father's seeming openness. 'Enora!' He gives me a hug. 'We must talk about that lovely boy of yours.'

We must indeed, I murmur to myself, but not quite yet. Bill is already marshalling what he calls his 'Adieu Team' and leading them down to the waiting boat. Christianne's swimming chums, meanwhile, are getting changed. They, it turns out, will be escorting us out towards the deeper water where Bill intends to drop the wreath. We all clamber aboard the boat while everyone else clusters around the stern to push us off. One by one, the swimmers don their tight white caps and wade into the sea. Then, on a command from the skipper, a mighty collective heave launches us off the beach. Christianne's fellow swimmers are breast-stroking gracefully seawards as the skipper throttles back to slow us down. Sylvester happens to be standing beside me.

'You brought a towel.' I nod at the water. 'Not tempted?'

'Later.' He smiles. 'Once everyone's gone.'

'You swim a lot?'

'Most days, as long as I can find a pool.'

'You find it helps?'

'Worse than that, I *have* to do it. Some days it's a penance. Other times, it makes me feel great. Today will be one of those days, I know it already.'

'*Have* to do it?'

'Yeah. I'm in training.' Another grin. 'An iron-man triathlon. Only career masochists need apply.'

Iron-man triathlon? My knowledge of extreme sports is very limited but even I know that triathlon is code for a great deal of pain.

'Pa says you're giving us a reading.' Sylvester, like his father, knows exactly when to change the subject.

'That's right. It's an excerpt from a letter. Your dad wanted something in French and I'm very happy to oblige.'

I have the text in my pocket. It was Pavel who first drew the letter to my attention, and since then it's travelled everywhere with me.

Sylvester is looking at the dog-eared fold of paper. He wants to know more.

'It comes from the war, Paris – Fresnes prison to be precise. That's where the Nazis banged up the Resistance people. This was written by a young guy they'd arrested in Bordeaux. They suspected him of blowing up a troop train and they were right. They shipped him up to Paris to make an example of him. The death sentence was a formality. They knew that and so did Marcel. He's in his cell. Tomorrow, at dawn, they'll take him down to the prison yard and put him in front of a firing squad.'

'So, what does it say?' I've touched a nerve here. I can tell.

'You speak French?'

'Yes.'

'Then you'll have to wait. In fact, we can go one better than that. After I've finished, you can explain what it was all about.'

He nods, and smiles, and I sense he's pleased to be given a role. By now we're approaching the line of offshore buoys. The skipper slips the engine out of gear and brings our little boat to a halt. The swimmers, perfectly choreographed, form a wide semicircle off the landward side. On the beach, I can see the young reporter raising his camera for yet another shot.

'Enora?' Bill wants me to perform.

I peer down at the letter. I've read it so many times, I'm word perfect, but this is a very special occasion and I'm determined to do it full justice.

'This comes from a young man who knows he faces certain death,' I glance up. 'Under the circumstances, I imagine he might have something important to tell us.'

I bend to the text and begin to read. I've no idea how many of this tiny gathering can follow my French but in a sense it doesn't matter because Sylvester's translation will come later. What's more important is getting the delivery right, that subtle, complex balance between raw emotion and something close to solace. By the time I've finished, both Beth and Presley are in tears. Neither of them, as I later discover, can understand a word of French.

'And now for what it all means . . .' I turn to Sylvester. He, too, has been visibly moved.

'Extraordinary,' he begins. 'What a perfect choice.'

'So what's he saying? What's this young man telling us?' This from Nathan.

'He's alone in his cell,' Sylvester says. 'His name is Marcel. He's a *Resistant* and tomorrow he will be shot. He has no quarrel with the verdict. He hates the occupation, he's no friend of the Germans, but he understands the brutal logic of the Occupation. *C'est vrai?*' He's turned briefly to me.

'*Exactement.*'

'And so he's resigned to his own death. More importantly, he accepts it, even welcomes it. Why? Because he knows he's done his duty, done his best, for himself, for his family, *pour la France*. And that, in his own words, is enough for any man, any woman. Indeed, it makes him lucky. Because his life has had a direction, a purpose, and he'll now die in the knowledge that he can do no more.' Sylvester looks up. 'The letter, as a matter of interest, is written to his mother. Women, dare I say it, are probably wiser in this respect than we men. Christianne, whom I like to think I knew, was wise. And she, too, understood the importance of making that final peace.'

Sylvester's timing is immaculate. He stands in silence for a long moment, then folds the letter and returns it to me before nodding at his father. Bill is holding the wreath. The balance in the boat shifts a little as he steps towards the side, and people instinctively cling to each other.

Bill is looking down at the splinters of sunshine on the water.

'*Bon voyage, notre cherie*,' he murmurs. '*Et bonne chance.*'

He hesitates a moment, and then launches the wreath into the semicircle of waiting swimmers. A couple make the sign of the cross. Another blows the bobbing wreath a kiss. For a timed minute, we drift slowly inshore, all of us, the boat, Bill's Adieu Team, and the swimmers. That long moment, with the boat alive beneath my feet, will stay with me forever, regardless of what was later to come.

Bill is looking at his watch. A nod to the skipper stirs the engine into life and we putter back towards the beach to make a landing. Only when I'm back on shore, climbing the pebbles towards the knot of mourners we'd left around Beth's towels, do I notice the figure sitting at the top of the beach, his back against the wall. He's peeled off the top half of his leathers but in this weather he must still be baking. His legs are clad in motorcycle boots, and he's steadying a pair of binoculars as he tracks our approach.

DI Frank Bullivant, I think. Watching us.

NINETEEN

Bullivant departs within minutes of our return to the beach, zipping up his leathers and straddling his Kawasaki. The bravest part of me wants to confront him, to ask what's happening to Operation *Bulldog*, to demand exactly what he thinks lies behind Christianne's disappearance, but another voice in my head tells me we've said our goodbyes, that she's gone, and that – in all probability – we'll have nothing left to mark her departure.

This is certainly McFaul's take on the morning's events. He, too, has seen Bullivant.

'Didn't I tell you?' he says. 'They're dogs with a bone. Nothing puts these guys off. Bother them with the truth, and they still don't believe you.'

McFaul leaves shortly afterwards, limping away across the pebbles. The letter I read in the boat appears to have drained some of the anger he's had since his release on bail, and he even half-nods at my suggestion that I might buy him a drink or two before I go back to London. Now, I'm sitting on the pebbles, minding Sylvester's clothes while he swims along the line of buoys. Earlier, I'd found it difficult to believe that I was looking at an extreme athlete, but watching him churning up and down, eating up kilometre after kilometre, there's no doubting his fitness.

He joins me more than an hour later. He's wearing those little Speedo trunks that certain kinds of Frenchmen adore and his physique, to say the least, is impressive. He dries his hair and then spreads the towel on the warm stones.

'I used to come here as a kid,' he says. 'Even then I was sitting on the bones of my arse. When God invented sand, he forgot about Budleigh.'

He's right about the stones. They're unforgiving. When I ask him about coming here as a kid, he says his dad used to rent a place for a month in the summer. Only in the past ten years has Bill lived in the town permanently.

'You like it down here?'

'I love it.'

'So why do you do all this triathlon stuff?'

'Because it keeps me sane. I get bored easily. Just ask my pa. I need a challenge. Dreaming up ways of earning a living's good for starters, but once you're on a roll, like recently, you realize there has to be something else. Success is great but it's easy to repeat yourself. Ask the hardest questions. Always.'

'Of whom?'

'Yourself.' He's been lying full length, trying to get comfortable, letting the sun dry his chest and legs. Now his eyes open. 'You know who I last said that to?'

'Tell me.'

'Your son.'

'And?'

'I think he understood. At least he said he did. It was Friday, just a couple of days ago. He'd come back from a meet on the south coast and we got together at that apartment of yours. I'm living at a hotel at the moment, and Holland Park's perfect for a quick ten miler so I brought my kit along. He's a quick study, your boy. Tell him once . . .' He taps his head. 'And it's there.'

I nod. I agree. Under the right circumstances, in the right company, Malo can be deeply impressive. It was one of the first things that H noticed about him, which is no surprise because he's got the same knack of mastering a complex brief and then turning it to his own advantage. In the cocaine business, this talent made him rich. Malo appears to be selling something very different, but the principle's exactly the same.

'You went running in Holland Park?'

'Yes.'

'From my apartment?'

'Yes. And you're right, I used the shower when I got back.'

'You're very welcome,' I say lightly. 'And Malo?'

'He asked me about runners. Not just footwear but lightweight kit, on-board nutrition, warming-up routines, the whole shtick. I thought he was kidding to begin with, but he was on the internet Friday night, getting himself sorted. You'll see the stuff when you get home. I'm not sure I'd have chosen pink runners but that boy's definitely his own man, and in my line of business there's no better place to start. No one without self-belief ever sold anything.'

'Even when it comes to pink runners?'

'Especially when it comes to pink runners.'

This, need I say it, is very good news indeed. When I ask rather delicately whether he's thinking of recruiting Malo to the cause, he rolls over and laughs.

'You mean agreeing a deal? Paying him?'

'I guess so.'

'Then the answer has to be yes. I'll be offering him a month's trial on a daily rate. If it all works out, we'll agree a basic wage and a commission scale. In the meantime, I'll be holding him to his word.'

'About what?'

'Getting fit.' He pauses a moment, and his gaze strays towards the sea again. 'That letter you found was pretty amazing,' he says quietly. 'You mind if I photocopy it?'

'Why would you want to do that?'

'Because it would make a great selling tool.'

'*Selling* tool?'

'Yes, and you know why? Because it makes death so vivid, so real. The way the guy wrote it, anyone can imagine themselves into that prison cell. And that's where we are now, all of us, thanks to Trump, and Putin, and far too many nukes, and global warming, and Australia on fire, and all the rest of the pantomime. Your boy got that at once. Doomsday? He's totally up to speed. All he needs to do now . . .' That same slow smile again. 'Is get rich.'

Sylvester is on his feet now. He's knotted the towel around his waist and he's reaching for his shorts.

'That Beth woman,' he says. 'How well do you know her?'

'Barely at all.'

'She's a fruitcake.' He's wriggling into his shorts. 'Take it from me.'

TWENTY

Next morning, I tell myself I have one last port of call before I pack my bag, say my goodbyes, and return to London. For long periods of the night, I've thought of nothing but face after anointed face staring at the figure in the patterned bandana as she circled and re-circled her little heap of scarlet towels. Fruitcake? Sylvester may have nailed it.

Beth's shop is in the High Street between an estate agent and a funeral parlour. It's mid-morning and a lingering glance through the front window confirms what Evelyn's already told me. Until recently, this business apparently ticked along on a modest selection of eternity rings, retro watches, and that something special for the diamond wedding anniversary. Now the offerings in the window include a viper brooch in eye-catching yellow enamel, a rather lovely bracelet made of what looks like plaited wire with jewelled insets, and a pair of huge look-at-me earrings in shiny red plastic. Budleigh's demographic is changing fast, Evelyn tells me, and here's the living proof.

Inside the shop, I ask for Beth. The girl behind the counter is young, barely out of school.

'She's in rehearsal just now.' She yawns, then checks her watch. 'You know the public hall?'

I do. Evelyn and I were there on Saturday, listening to David Barrie. The entrance at the side of the building is open, likewise the door to the hall itself. Two days ago, as the Literary Festival came to an end, it was a full house, row after row of chairs. Now the floor space is empty except for a couple of chairs and a table. I don't recognize the figure at the table, hunched over what I assume to be a script, but there's no mistaking the woman on stage.

Beth is wearing dark green dungarees over a matelot T-shirt. Also, a pair of yellow-framed dark glasses, just a little too big for her face. As I tiptoe into the shadows at the far corner, she's in the middle of some kind of monologue, and as far as I can judge this is an emphatically solo performance. A single spotlight pins her to the very centre of the stage, and from time to time she steals a glance at the script in her hands. I have, of course, absolutely no idea what this play might be, but it's immediately obvious that Beth can't act. No colour in her voice, no sense of rhythm, none of those little tricks that can grab an audience, and make it your own.

'Was it my fate to be given in marriage? To bear this husband of mine four children? Did I ever foresee the pneumonia that bore him away? Or your letters, my beloved? Or this . . .?'

As she pauses, I watch the figure at the table reach for his mobile and cue a piece of piano music. The music comes from a speaker beside the script. It's soft, quietly playful, full of tenderness, and unlike what I've seen of the performance on stage it's immediately compelling. Pavel, I think, as the pianist recapitulates the major theme, and then lets his right hand dance away into a series of light-fingered variations.

Beth, meanwhile, has abandoned both the script and the spot-light and is circling the stage in a trance-like series of flourishes that remind me of yesterday's performance on the beach. Returning to the front of the stage, still borne by the music, she suddenly catches sight of me at the back.

'Stop!' She freezes as the music dies, then removes her glasses for a better look. I'm already halfway to the table, penitent, full of excuses. Sorry for barging in. Sorry for stopping the rehearsal in mid flow.

'Enora?' She's shading her eyes with her hand. 'Is that you?'

'It is. *Mea culpa.* I shouldn't be here.'

'Nonsense.' She leaves the stage and gives me a hug. 'This is Stephen. It's his script. His idea.'

Stephen must be in his eighties. Age has been kind to him and he has a nice smile. He struggles to his feet and offers a courtly handshake.

'A pleasure.' He nods down at the script on his desk. 'It's a sketch for something more substantial. We're just trying out ideas at the moment. Words and music.'

'Beethoven.' Beth seizes the script, and insists I take a look. 'Next year's his two hundred and fiftieth anniversary. Everything plays into a woman called Josephine, letters, memories, music, everything we can lay our hands on. This woman is the love of his life. He worships her. He composes for her. But she's forever having other men's babies. It's the saddest thing. Drama-wise, the possibilities are endless. Everything will be there in Stephen's script, but most of all we will hear it in the music. We're calling it *Immortal Beloved.* Is it a celebration? Of course it is. But will we weep as well? Alas, yes . . .'

Without a further glance at Stephen, she threads her arm through mine. Moments later, we're sitting in a room outside the main body of the hall while she pours two mugs of coffee from a Thermos.

'Black OK?'

'Black's fine. You play Josephine, am I right?'

'That's the plan, yes. Stephen's idea, not mine. This is lovely, having you here.' She nods towards the open door that leads to the hall. '*Immortal Beloved.* What did you think?'

'Very interesting idea.'

'But seriously?' I can almost taste her need for approval and I think she senses this because she suddenly changes the subject.

'That lovely friend of yours,' she says. 'Evelyn. I meant it when we first met at Bill's place. I thought she was fabulous in St Peter's the other night. So wise, so funny, so *authentic*. Can I ask you a huge favour?'

'Of course.'

'I'm doing a series of short stories at the moment, all linked to a developing theme. I've called it *The Water's Edge*. Do you think she might spare the time to take a look? Tell me how crap they are?'

'I'm sure she'd be delighted.'

'You'll ask her?'

'Of course.'

'You're a star.' She's beaming at me. 'How's the coffee?'

I tell her the coffee's fine. I also get up and close the door. This appears to alarm her.

'There's no one here,' she says, 'apart from us.'

I say that doesn't matter. I want to talk about Christianne.

'You mean yesterday?'

'I mean Christianne.'

'Same thing, isn't it? I thought it all went really well. That letter you read . . .' She shakes her head. 'Pure class.'

I choose to ignore the compliment, partly because the phrase 'pure class' is so poorly chosen, but mainly because I've realized that I've been right about her, that everything in this woman's life is a performance. Yesterday on the beach wasn't about Christianne at all. It was about her, and now about me. Wrong.

'That story you told us at Bill's the other night. Getting the phone call. Driving over to Christianne's place. Picking them both up.'

'Yes?' She's doing her best to look blank but failing completely.

'Remind me again,' I say.

'About what?'

'About how drunk they were.'

'I told you. They were totally wasted, the pair of them. It's obvious isn't it? Would you ever do something like that *sober*?'

'I agree, but that's not the point.'

'It isn't?'

'No.'

'Then what are you telling me?'

'I'm telling you that none of it happened.'

'You think I'm lying?' She's staring at me, outraged.

'I think you made it up. I talked to Andy last night. They released him. He's out on bail.'

'And?'

'He said they hadn't touched a drop. Either of them.'

'Then he was kidding you.'

'I doubt it.'

'But did he deny being there? On the dock? Watching her go?'

'Not exactly.'

'What the fuck does that mean?'

'It means he went along with the story. Sort of. But gave himself away at the end. This gives me no pleasure, but I set him a little trap.'

'About the booze?'

'Yes.'

'A *trap*?' She's open-mouthed. 'His partner's committing suicide, ending it all, and you set him a *trap*? Who are you? Some kind of cop?'

I hold her gaze, trying to decide whether the anger is genuine, and I realize the answer has to be yes because she lacks the talent to fake it.

'There's something else,' I say softly. 'There's CCTV on that dock. Perfect field of view. Everything covered.'

'Shit.' She briefly turns away. 'And you've seen it? Seen the footage?'

'I have.' I'm lying, but it feels right.

'How?'

I shake my head.

'Then you *are* a fucking cop.'

'*Au contraire.*' I fake a smile. 'Ways and means. Better me than them.'

She nods. Her next question is obvious. To both of us.

'So what did you see? What did it tell you?'

'Nothing. You were never there. Not the car. Not you. Not Andy. And certainly not Christianne.'

She nods. She's biting her lip.

'You're denying it?'

'No.'

'So, you made it up? The whole thing? Driving over? The pair of them pissed? The darkness? The tide?'

'Yes.'

'Why?'

She holds my gaze for a long moment. The anger appears to have gone.

'We thought you didn't believe him.'

'Andy?'

'Yes. You *said* you believed him but we assumed you were thinking what the cops are thinking. Big fucking search. No trace of a body. Therefore, he must have done something terrible.'

'And did he?'

'No way. God's truth.'

'So you did it for him? Lied for his sake? Is that it?'

'Of course. That's what he needs, what he deserves. Protection.'

I nod. I can see the logic. Just.

'And this "we" you keep using? Who's *we*?'

The question hangs in the air. I can tell she doesn't want to answer it, not here, probably not ever, but I ask her a second time, and then a third.

'All of us,' she says at last. 'Around that table.'

I leave the public hall minutes later. Beth does her best to pretend that nothing's changed between us but we both know that's not true. I've no idea what really happened to Christianne, and that degree of ignorance – or perhaps bewilderment – is hard to accept, but my thoughts are with McFaul. I've absolutely no doubts about his courage in the minefields, and the fierceness of his commitment to Christianne, but just now he's slipped his moorings. Beth, to her credit, has found *le mot juste*. He needs protecting.

The nearest shop selling mobile phones is in Exmouth. I drive over and part with a modest sum in return for a pay-as-you-go Doro. I register it in my own name and load it with £150 worth of credit. Back in Budleigh, I park outside Evelyn's bungalow and knock on McFaul's door. When he finally appears, he looks wrecked. There's a darkness beneath his eyes and he doesn't smell good. He blinks, stares at me, rubs his face, and then stands aside and says I'm welcome to come in, but I shake my head. I have to go back to London, I tell him, but before I hit the road, I have a little present I want to give him.

He stares at the box that contains the phone, then glances over his shoulder as if someone's watching and shepherds me on to the pavement.

'Why do I want one of those?' he asks. 'I hate the bloody things.'

'Just take it, Andy.' I give him the pre-loaded Vodafone card. 'There's quite a lot of money on there, and no one can trace it to you. I don't know why, and I don't know when, but one day you're going to need it. Here's my number. Phone if you need me.'

That's it. I don't want to say any more. Seconds later, I'm gone.

I say my goodbyes to Evelyn, promise to phone her the moment I get back home, and then set off. Try as I might, I can't get the image of McFaul out of my mind. After maybe half an hour, still deep in East Devon, I spot a place to stop and pull over.

My call to Bill Penny is answered within seconds.

'Enora,' he murmurs. 'What a lovely surprise.'

'It's Andy.' For once I have no time for small talk. 'You need to keep an eye on him.'

'Might I ask why?'

'Maybe you should go round and take a look at him. See what you think. Promise me you'll do that? Please . . .?'

TWENTY-ONE

Lunch with Rosa next day comes as a relief. Back in London, I feel suddenly rooted again. Normal is taking a cab to our favourite eatery in Covent Garden. Normal is ordering a bottle of decent Chianti to go with the scallops to come. Normal is listening to my lovely agent listing the treats that lie in store if only I can lay hands on Pavel's elusive final opus.

'Charlie wants to mount a retrospective. He says he's got the backing for it, but he needs just one last bullet for that gun of his.'

'The missing file.'

'In one, my lovely. Are you absolutely sure it's gone?'

Charlie Halligan, as I've already explained to Evelyn, is the commissioning editor whose magic wand hovers over Pavel's considerable body of work. He has a great deal of clout in the BBC Drama department and I need no convincing that he can deliver on this homage to one of his favourite writers. Just as long as I can somehow retrieve the bloody file.

'So where is it? Exactly?'

This is a trickier question than you might think. Rosa can smell a lie at a thousand metres.

'The police have seized it,' I confess.

'It's that bloody good?'

'Not the file. Pavel's MacBook.'

'Remarkable. Do dead men break the law? Is your Pavel even naughtier than we thought?'

My Pavel – I like that, a lot. Rosa always knew the way to my heart. I explain about meeting Christianne, about our brief friendship, about her sudden disappearance after onset MND, and about the police turning up to seize anything they could get their hands on.

'And this included the MacBook?'

'I'm afraid so.'

'Should I enquire what it was doing with this man of hers?'

'He's a computer nerd. I asked him to try and find the file.'

'And?'

'He says it self-destructed. Blew itself up.'

'Golly.' Rosa looks impressed. 'Can files do that?'

'Apparently so. The guy used to lift mines for a living. He's good around explosives.'

'Christ.' Rosa is picking at her asparagus starter. 'So do we believe him?'

I tell her I don't know, can't be certain, and Rosa spends the rest of the meal reviewing the hole that Pavel appears to have left in the BBC Drama department's forward offerings. We both know that this is a wild overstatement, but Rosa never got rich by sticking to the truth and we part outside on the pavement

with me promising to have one final go at laying hands on Pavel's
MacBook.

'That might be very wise, my precious.' She's looking for a
cab. 'And who knows? The bloody file might turn out to be
crap.'

Back home, I put a call through to Brett Atkinson, but he's not
picking up, so I leave a message. The lunch has been a delight,
as have several glasses of Chianti. 'It's me,' I announce playfully.
'Your favourite suspect. Any chance of returning my stolen
property?'

A second call finds Malo in his Audi. He's returning to London
after a weekend with H, his natural father, and he can't wait to
share the good news.

'About what?'

'I'll tell you this evening.' He names a restaurant in Bayswater
that he knows I love. 'Half six? On me?'

This is beyond astonishing. I can't remember Malo ever inviting
me for supper *à deux*.

'You're serious?'

'Get real, Mum. Of course I'm serious.'

'And you'll be coming back afterwards?'

'No need, and no time either. I'm selling the end of the world,
Mum. That's why we have to eat early. You won't believe how
busy I am.'

He's laughing now, a sound I always cherish, and after he
rings off I pocket my phone and drift across to the window.
Young mothers are still pushing buggies round the nearby park.
A delinquent spaniel is chasing a gaggle of seagulls. Big, fat
passenger jets are lining up to land at Heathrow. If the end of
the world is that close, there are few clues in Holland Park.

Avventura is an Italian place I've been going to for years. It's
family-run, unpretentious, utterly reliable, and serves the best
acqua pazza I've ever tasted. Two Italian meals in one day is
slightly over the top, but Malo even remembers the wine I like
to go with my favourite dish, and orders a bottle while we're
still en route to the table.

My son's lost weight, and he's taken to proper shaving. Best of all, his eyes are bright and there's a blush of colour in his face.

'You're still doing it? Running? Swimming? Whatever?'

'Running, mainly. Dad couldn't believe it. I was down there for three days, found a really neat circuit, back down the drive, then left through the woods, out round the pond, back via that track he used for the motocross, then twice more. I did eight K the first morning. An extra lap the second. H thought I'd gone for a smoke at first. Can you believe that?'

'And booze?' I nod at the bottle of San Pellegrino the waiter has just delivered.

'Never touched a drop all weekend. H thought I must be ill.'

The waiter has returned with a bottle of chilled Greco di Tufo.

'You'll be helping me out, I hope?' I nod at the two glasses already on the table.

'Afraid not, Mum. Training's training. You do it or you don't.'

'Is that Sylvester I'm hearing?'

'Could be. The man's a machine.' He lifts his glass of fizzy water. 'Here's to the end of the world.'

We clink glasses and I press him for news from Flixcombe Manor. H's spread in the depths of West Dorset was the bait he used to lure his newly found son into the beginnings of a proper relationship. Like everyone else who's ever been there, me included, Malo fell in love with the views, and the peace, and the glories of the wondrous Georgian house that dominates the estate.

'You told H about what you're up to? This Doomsday thingy?'

'Of course I did. He thought it was a crazy idea to begin with, then this morning he gave me a list of prospects. Said he'd been working the phone for most of last night.'

'You mean you sold it to him? The idea? The concept?'

'I did. Big time. And now he's after a thirty per cent commission for every introduction that comes good. In your dreams, Dad.'

Malo laughs and steals a look at his watch. Already we've agreed to skip starters in the interests of his hectic schedule, but Avventura has an open kitchen and the smells tell me we're only minutes away from eating.

'So tonight?' I query.

'Lebanese guy. Used to be a pro footballer in France. PSG and then Monaco. Made a bit of money and invested big time in top-of-the-range rental property. Really nice bloke, and clever, too. Fabulous wife. Two kids. Big duplex in Shoreditch. Rich people hate surprises, and DD is definitely the biggest. Insurance again. Get yourself a way out. Buy a bunker that floats. Join the SC. Never fails.'

'DD?' I query.

'Doomsday.'

'SC?'

'Survivors' Club.' He rolls his eyes, then changes the subject. 'Sylvester mentioned he saw you at the weekend. Bunch of people and some wreath or other? What was that about?'

I tell him briefly about saying goodbye to Christianne, but I sense he knows most of this already. What really interests him is McFaul.

'Sylvester says he used to clear minefields for a living.'

'Sylvester's right. He worked in Africa, the Balkans, the Middle East.'

'Lifting mines?'

'Yes.'

'That sounds like DD every day of your working life. Brave or what?'

'Good question.' I'm thinking of my last sight of McFaul. 'Brave is where you start. Brave takes you to a job like that. But what's happening now is probably worse. Losing a leg he seemed to deal with. Losing Christianne is a different story.'

'How well do you know him?'

'Barely at all. He's a difficult man. Conversation isn't easy.'

'But I'm guessing you managed OK.'

'Just. Enough to know the guy's slipped his moorings. Strange, isn't it? You spend most of your life coping with stuff that you and I can barely imagine, then you end up in that sleepy little seaside town, and it all falls apart.'

'He's got mates? People he can trust?'

'He's got people he knows. Christianne was his mate. I'm not sure he's ever been keen on the plural.'

Malo nods. The food arrives and we tuck in. Poached sea bream in white wine, capers and parsley never fails to lift my spirits. Not that Malo isn't, by some truly magical transformation, the best company.

He wants to know more about McFaul. Has he anyone to turn to? Now that his partner's gone?

'There are one or two people, friends of Christianne, but he's a loner, really.'

'Bit of a one-off?'

'Definitely.'

'And right now?'

'Unhinged. Displaced. All at sea. Slipped his moorings. Like I just said.' I look up, genuinely curious. 'How come you're suddenly so interested in other people?'

'Goes with the territory, Mum.' My lovely son has the grace to smile. 'The trick with selling anything is to make friends. Listen hard enough and it's easier than I ever thought.'

'Good.' I'm back with the remains of the fish. 'I'm pleased.'

We part on the pavement. The meal, if brief, has been a delight. Luca, the waiter, has corked the half bottle of Greco I've yet to drink and my flat is only a ten-minute stroll away. Malo is about to get into his Audi when he suddenly straightens at the kerbside.

'One thing I forgot, Mum.' The grin is back, wider than ever. 'Clem's all over me. Must be those runners I bought. Pink? When she's so into those dark reds? Who'd have thought . . .?'

'You're back together?'

'Big time. I'm on a yellow card as far as the booze is concerned, and I think she's going to start running with me, just to check I'm not making it up. Aside from that, I can't put a foot wrong. If she's still awake tonight, I might ask her to marry me. Depends.'

'On what?'

'On how this evening goes. Fingers crossed, eh?' He gives me a hug, which is better than nice, and I'm still trying to work out whether he's joking about Clem when he slips into the car, pulls a savage U-turn against the onrushing traffic and roars away.

Back at the flat, I settle in with the rest of the bottle of Greco. I'm half-expecting some kind of reply from Brett Atkinson, but I've no missed calls and there's nothing in my texts. Still buzzing after Malo's news about Clem, I resist the temptation to wallow in brainless TV and put a call through to H. To my slight disappointment, he knows about Clem already.

'He's a lucky boy,' H grunts. 'She should have given him the push months ago.'

'That was the old Malo,' I tell him. 'This one's close to irresistible. If I was Clem's age, I think I'd forgive him, too. You know about his new friend? Sylvester? I'd like to say we owe him a big drink but I gather he's teetotal, too.'

'You've met him?' H wants to know more.

'I have. He's older than Malo but they could be brothers. His dad's a treasure, an ex-ambassador, though you'd never know it, truly a gentleman. Sylvester even looks like Malo. It's uncanny.'

'And you think he's kosher?'

'Meaning?'

'All this Twilight Fund crap? The Doomsday thing is right on the money. In fact I'm amazed it hasn't happened already. We just need to know he's genuinely selling what he's selling.'

'Malo seems to think so.'

'Malo's still a kid. He rolls over easy.'

'But he told me you gave him a list. Prospects? Isn't that right?'

'Yeah. But that's because I'm checking the guy out. The people on that list can spot dodgy from way out. Let's hope Malo's right.' He pauses. 'You OK?'

'I'm fine.' I drain my glass. 'I've been down in Devon with my friend Evelyn. Not her fault but it's been a difficult few days.'

TWENTY-TWO

Next morning, I wake early. A thin grey light is washing through the venetian blinds and a glance at my bedside clock tells me it's 06.23. I lie still for a moment, trying to imagine what might have woken me up, when there comes a flurry of knocks at my front door, and a raised voice.

'Police. Let us in. Police. Last call before we do the door.'

I struggle into my dressing gown and head down the hall. I

can hear voices outside, at least two men, and when I put my eye to the peephole I count no less than four bodies. Two of them are in body-armour: helmets, visors, shoulder pads, the full ninja-gear. The others, partly hidden, are wearing suits.

I open the door and step back. One of the ninjas thrusts a document at me. This, it seems, is a search warrant. He steps past and gestures for his mate to follow. They move quickly from room to room with shouted warnings and raised weapons. Once each room is declared empty, they end up in the lounge. At first, this had felt like a film set, a piece of well-rehearsed hokum, but now it's beyond intimidating. As the ninjas check out the space behind the sofa and peer out of the window, I'm looking at the men in suits. One of them is DI Bullivant. The other is Brett Atkinson.

'What's going on?'

Bullivant ignores the question. He wants a contact for the firm that manages the apartment block.

'You've got CCTV in the car park. There's also a video phone at the entrance. We need the pictures.'

'Why?'

'Just do it.' A thin smile. 'Please?'

I hold his gaze for a moment or two, and then find the number. One of the ninjas has abandoned his weapon and is going through the bin in the kitchen. He spots the empty bottle of Greco and lifts it out.

'You had company last night?'

'No.'

'Drank it all by yourself?'

'Yes.'

The other ninja emerges from the spare bedroom and shakes his head.

'Nobody slept there, Skip.'

'What is this?' I'm looking at Brett. Bullivant's on the phone to the twenty-four-hour security desk at the management company.

'Bit of a development, I'm afraid.'

'In Budleigh?'

'Yeah.'

'You've found her?' I'm staring at him. 'You've found a body?'

'No. It's your friend McFaul. He failed to show at the nick

yesterday morning. He's in breach of his bail conditions and we think he's done a runner.'

'Up to London, you mean? You thought you'd find him here?'

'It's a possibility.'

'And now?'

'We have to check everything out. Any digital devices, I'm afraid we'll need to seize them. PC?' He's looking round. 'Laptop? Tablet? Mobile phone?'

'Help yourself.' I'm staring at him. 'This is unreal, you know that? You haven't got a shred of evidence, not one, yet here you are, four of you, armed to the teeth, barging in. You mind if I make a phone call? Is that allowed?'

'You can do it from the station.'

'*What?* You're arresting me?'

'Only if we have to. Best if you volunteer for interview.' He's meeting my gaze at last. Then he relents. 'Who do you want to phone?'

'A friend,' I say. 'And he happens to be a lawyer.'

Brett is spared having to make a decision by the arrival of another figure. He's tallish, pale, balding, and wears a nicely cut suit. He doesn't offer a name, or a rank, but his body language suggests he probably outranks everyone else in the room.

Bullivant has finished with his phone call. The newcomer wants to know about my bank statements, cards, and – most important of all – passports.

'We understand you're half French, Ms Andressen.' He's turned to me. Impeccably neutral accent. Impossible to locate.

'Yes. I was born there. Brittany. Perros-Guirec.'

'You have a French passport?'

'Yes. And a British passport, too.'

'I'm afraid we'll need sight of them both. Plus any old passports you've kept.'

'Now?'

'Yes.'

'You mean you're seizing them?'

'Yes. You'll get them back, of course. Once we're finished.'

'Do I have any choice here? Can I say no?' I'm looking from face to face, already guessing the answer.

*   *   *

They drive me to a police station half an hour away. The place feels like a fortress, but I'm allowed to make a phone call from the desk where they book you in. Tony Morse is an old ally of H from his Pompey days, a successful and rather stylish solicitor with a huge profile in Portsmouth. We first met a couple of years ago and bonded at first sight. Keeping H one step ahead of the men in blue made Tony a legend in Pompey, as well as rich, and I've always marvelled at what I can only call his *sang froid*. Tony Morse panics at nothing, least of all a call from his favourite screen actress.

I tell him where I'm being held. So far, Tony has only been half-listening but the name of the police station appears to change everything.

'You're kidding me,' he says. 'Why?'

'Good question. Do you mind coming up?'

'No problem.' I hear a door close in the background. Then he's back on the phone. 'You know the drill?'

'I do.'

'Good. Whatever you say, say nothing.'

He arrives in time for a late-morning coffee in the tiny, windowless room assigned to interviewees. In the meantime, photographed and fingerprinted, I've been watching the custody sergeant going through my records. Arrested by Dorset Police, the year before last. Detained and questioned by one of the Devon and Cornwall Major Crime Investigation Teams only a handful of months ago.

'You're giving showbiz a bad name.' Tony waits for the door to shut behind him, and then settles at the desk. 'Murder, is it? Or some other Class-A rap?'

'I've no idea. They haven't arrested me, so that might be a clue, but I don't trust these people.'

'Very wise.' Tony produces a yellow legal pad, and I give him a full account of events to date. Finally he looks up. 'They'll think you're close, you and . . .' He gestures at the pad, '. . . this McFaul. That's the first thing that pops into their little heads.'

'Close as in good friends?'

'Close as in shagging. Have you, as a matter of interest?'

'Christ, no. The man was in love. That's the whole point.'

'And he's done a runner?'

'That's what they're saying.'

'So do you know where he's gone?'

'No idea.'

'Good. So why are you their first point of call?'

'You tell me. They may have kicked in every door in Budleigh. They may have arrested poor Evelyn. These people are out of control. The DI is the one we have to watch. He's a lay preacher. Brett thinks that's significant.'

'Brett?'

'The young one. His sidekick.'

'You know him? This Brett?'

'I do.' I explain about the pub fight in Exmouth, and Brett ending up in hospital. On that occasion I didn't call on Tony's services, largely because I'd become a key witness. Now, though, is different. Now, as I'm trying to explain, I get the feeling that I've become the target of some malevolent force. First McFaul, then little me.

'The woman was under sentence of death,' I tell Tony. 'She had MND. She did away with herself. That's all anyone needs to know.'

'A body would be helpful.'

'That's what they say, the police, Bullivant, Brett. People are allowed to disappear . . .' I'm frowning now. 'Aren't they?'

'Tricky question. Our CID friends like to tidy up. People going missing offends their sense of neatness. It probably sounds anal but sometimes it turns out they have a point. Our first job is getting you out of here in one piece. They're pushing for two interviews. The first will relate to McFaul. You won't be under caution. My advice is to answer their questions unless I advise otherwise. Can you live with that?'

'Of course,' I say. 'And the second interview?'

'That could be trickier.'

'No clues?'

'Not yet, alas. There are still disclosure issues to resolve.'

'You mean they think I've done something else?'

'That's the impression I'm getting.'

I shake my head in disbelief. The last few hours have turned my life inside out and I very badly want this man's support.

'Am I wasting your time?' I ask. 'Be honest.'

'Christ, no, my darling. I'd have preferred a meet in a decent pub, but just now we don't have the choice.' He gets to his feet and checks the time. '*Allons-y?*' he queries.

I gaze up at him. Gorgeous suit. Such a subtle stripe. And that familiar tang of the cheroots I know he smokes.

'My pleasure.' I try to summon a smile, joining him at the door.

The first interview is led by Bullivant. Brett Atkinson, for the most part, takes notes. What they want is a full account of my movements since the weekend, with supporting names and contact numbers where appropriate. I walk them through my lunch with Rosa, my return to Holland Park, and then my date with Malo at Avventura. Brett's biro is racing from line to line.

'Malo?' Bullivant asks. His dead eyes have been locked on mine.

'He's my son,' I say. 'We talk from time to time. It's a kind of family thing.'

The sarcasm, way too heavy, is wasted on Bullivant. When he asks when I last saw McFaul, I describe our brief encounter at the front door of his bungalow.

'What was that about?'

'I came to say goodbye. And good luck.'

'Good luck how?'

'Good luck coping.'

'With what?'

I hold the stoniness of his gaze and resist the temptation to say 'you'. Instead I give him a prim little sermonette on the trauma of losing someone you love very much.

'You find yourself suddenly alone,' I point out. 'The person you love has gone forever and the bungalow is empty, barely a stick of furniture. Can't you imagine that? Can't you understand how that must *feel*?'

'I'm afraid that's not for me to answer. The absence of furniture, to be frank, is troubling. And all the deep-cleaning he's been doing also gives us pause for thought.'

'And is that why you took the chaise longue?' I'm aware of the pressure of Tony's foot on mine under the table but I can't help myself.

'McFaul told you about that?' Bullivant is beginning to look animated.

'Absolutely not. I watched you carrying it out the other night. Is that working for you? Have you found the missing clue?'

'To what, Ms Andressen?'

'To whatever brought you to my door at half six in the morning. Nothing better to do?'

I fancy I can see the ghost of a smile on his face, but I might well be wrong. Brett takes up the running with a series of questions designed to test my earlier answers, then Bullivant's mobile begins to emit a Bach cantata and he leaves the room without a word.

Tony asks Brett to formally confirm that he and I have had, in Tony's phrase, 'previous'. The word makes Brett smile. His fingers stray to the scar on his neck and he confirms my account of what happened in the Exmouth pub.

'Do we scent a conflict of interest at all?' Tony has the lightest touch.

'Between myself and Ms Andressen?'

'Yes. I understood you became friends afterwards. Didn't she visit you in hospital a couple of times? Helped you get better?'

'She did, and I was grateful. You're thinking that might colour our relationship now? Me giving her an easy ride?'

'Not at all. I'm thinking you might take advantage of that relationship.'

'How?'

'By getting her to lower her guard. Easily done, DC Atkinson, but a little harder now we've established the rules of engagement. Just a word in your ear, my friend. The world is full of temptations, but I'm sure you'll be fighting this one.'

I'm looking at my hands, fighting the urge to applaud. Tony has wised me up to this tactic before. The police put family liaison officers into major enquiries, attaching them to traumatized wives or girlfriends of suspects under arrest. They sympathize, they listen, they befriend, and they keep notes which go straight back to the incident room. Neat. Obvious. And, in Tony's phrase, often bloody effective.

Brett, I know, is about to be scandalized by the very

suggestion that he might have used our friendship for leverage, but Bullivant has returned. He's had a chance to review the highlights from all the CCTV footage in my block of flats, and evidently he's found no trace of McFaul.

'I could have told you that,' I say. 'In fact, I did. Twice.'

'And no phone calls? Texts? Emails?'

'You've seized everything. Look for yourself.'

'We will, Ms Andressen. But you haven't answered the question. Has he been in touch at all?'

'No. Not a peep.'

'Does he have your number?'

'He could get it from Evelyn. She's a friend of mine. She lives next door to Andy.'

'Again, please answer the question. Did you ever give him your number?'

I hold his gaze, and then – in the absence of any pressure from Tony – I nod.

'Yes,' I say. 'I gave him my number on Sunday, that last time I saw him.'

'But this is a man without a mobile, isn't that what he told us? When you were there?'

'That's true.'

'So why give him a number?'

'Because he's still got a landline.'

'And did you give him anything else before you left?'

'Like what?'

'Money? Material support? Anything to help get him on his way?'

This time, Tony tells me not to answer, but I choose to ignore him.

'On his way?' I enquire coldly. 'Do you really think that man wasn't lost enough already?'

This first interview ends within minutes. A uniformed officer appears at the door and escorts me to a holding cell while Tony disappears for another meeting. A thick steel door opens to a bigger space than I'd expected. I'm guessing the cell has recently been refurbed because I can smell just a hint of fresh paint. A Perspex domed window in the ceiling admits floods of sunshine, and the walls have been painted a cheerful shade of yellow. I count two cameras recessed into the ceiling, and there's another in the toilet. This room, from personal experience, wouldn't disgrace any number of budget hotels, and I settle on the easy-clean blue mattress to await developments. There's even a couple of Harry Potter novels, much thumbed, on the shelf over the sleeping plinth.

I'm still wondering about the people who might have spent time in this cell before me when the officer returns. He takes me back to the tiny, airless room where Tony and I first met. Now, he's sitting behind the desk.

'Well?' I ask.

He nods at the other chair. I sit down.

'This is what they call a TACT suite. Has anyone mentioned that?'

'TACT?'

'It's plod-speak for the Terrorism Act. Anyone nicked on suss terror charges in the Met area comes here. You're in esteemed company, believe me.'

'They think I'm a terrorist?' I'm astonished.

'They think you might be tainted.'

'Tainted?'

'By association. It means you've been keeping bad company. To be honest, I sense they don't really have very much. This is going to be a fishing expedition. All they know is what they don't know. My guess is they've found something on one of your devices. That's where they'll start.'

'But there's nothing to find.'

'You're sure?'

'I am. Listen to me, Tony. Watch my lips. I'm not a terrorist. I've never even auditioned for the fucking part. Blowing stuff up? Hacking people apart? Running amok? I wouldn't know where to start.'

'Don't pull a face, my darling. This is more serious than you might think. Just the mention of terrorism, just a whiff, opens doors you wouldn't believe. No government can keep their fingers off this scab, least of all the bloody Tories.'

I shake my head. This is absurd. Then I think of Rosa. Put the word 'terrorist' on my CV, and she'd be hitting the phones within seconds. My little Enora, she'd say. Certified freedom fighter. I'd have the pick of any number of star roles.

'So, what do I do? When they start asking questions?'

'Tell them the truth. If they start taking liberties, leave it to me.' Tony reaches across the desk and gives my hand a squeeze. 'Happy with that?'

The second interview is very different from the first. In charge is the nameless suit who came late to my flat this morning and asked for my passports and all the other stuff. With him is a younger woman with a face that would grace any cover of a certain kind of magazine. *Tatler*, perhaps. Or *Country Life*. She carries an air of perfectly honed entitlement that's impossible to miss, but I quickly sense that this masks a vivid intelligence. She doesn't smile much.

The suit at last introduces himself. He says his name is Deneuve and way back I suspect he might have been French. Tony has already told me these people are MI5, tasked to man the nation's ramparts, not police at all. The woman also offers a name. Lucy Cavendish.

From the start, the tone is conversational, not a hint of aggression or disbelief, and after the earlier session with Bullivant, this comes as a relief. Deneuve wants to know about what he calls my 'relationship' with McFaul. How long have I known him? How long have we been friends?

I trouble them with the facts. My knowledge of Evelyn's neighbour extends to barely a week and a half. Christianne, I like to think, quickly became a friend. McFaul, her partner, I hardly knew.

'But you'd have talked, surely . . .?'

'When?'

'After she disappeared. A situation like that, you'd need support, perhaps a listening ear. Am I wrong?'

'Of course. And you're right, we did talk.'

'About?'

'All kinds of things – Christianne mainly, and Africa, too. The pair of them were working out there. That's how they met.'

'And the minefields? He talked about the work he was doing out there?'

'Yes.'

'And your impression?'

'I don't understand what you're getting at. *Impression?*'

Deneuve doesn't answer. Cavendish clears her throat and stops playing with her fountain pen.

'We believe McFaul . . . how can I put this . . . was an angry man. Would that be accurate?'

I give the question some thought. Then I nod.

'Yes,' I say. 'Angry would be right. You'd see it from time to time. He'd flare up. He's not an easy man at all. Not on others and not on himself.'

'Easy, meaning . . .?'

'Companionable, relaxed, laid-back.'

'Tense, then? Is that the picture we're getting?'

'Yes.'

'And why would that be? Might you hazard a guess?'

I'm tempted to laugh. Where do I start?

'He spent years in the minefields,' I say carefully. 'He saw what these things can do to an arm, a leg, a child, a mother. He lost half a leg himself, and that would have hurt his professional pride, but he never stopped trying to clean the place up, even though he knew it was impossible.'

'And that would have angered him?' Deneuve this time.

'Of course.'

'Why?'

'Because all this stuff is man-made. People design these things, put them together, sell them, make a great deal of money. There are millions of them. Some will be there forever. He thought that was incomprehensible. Another word is obscene.'

'Is that him talking?'

'Me, as it happens. Though I know he'd agree.'

'A meeting of minds, then?' Cavendish is making herself a note. 'Would that be fair?'

'On this issue, definitely.'

'And others? Was the system to blame? The profit motive? Corporate interests? The whole shebang?'

At last, probably far too late, I twig where all this idle chatter is leading. McFaul and little me have obviously been tucked up in some grand conspiracy to blow Western capitalism apart. Tony, too, is getting disturbed. He says he has an issue with this line of questioning. Please stick to the known facts. This is deeply supportive on Tony's part, but I'm determined to clarify what I'm trying to say.

'You're right about McFaul.' I'm looking at Deneuve. 'He has lots of anger. He's also difficult, solitary, and bloody hard to be with. He wants to keep you at arm's length. I doubt he trusts anyone. He thinks life's ganged up on him, he thinks he's been fighting impossible odds, and then his partner, the woman he loves, falls ill with MND. She's been disintegrating before his eyes for months. This is one of his mines exploding, but in slow motion. Anger's probably too small a word. Bewilderment? Incomprehension? Would that cover it? In real life I happen to be an actress. My job is getting inside other people's heads, most of them fictional. McFaul's, if it's of any relevance, I can barely imagine.'

There's a long silence. I think I detect just a hint of approval, or maybe even admiration, in the blankness of Deneuve's face. Then Cavendish flicks back several pages on her notepad and leans forward over the table.

'You bought a mobile phone on the twenty-third of September at the Vodafone store in Exmouth. The purchase was logged at one-eighteen p.m. You paid for a hundred and fifty pounds of credit. We looked for that phone this morning, but we couldn't find it.' She looks up. 'Might you tell us why?'

'Because I gave it to McFaul.'

'For what reason?'

'Because he doesn't have one. And because a man in his situation should be able to talk to others if and when he needs to.'

'And you gave him your number?'

'Of course.'

'And has McFaul phoned?'

'No.'

'So you've no idea where he might be?'

'None.'

'Do you think he has support? Some kind of network?'

'He had Christianne. That's all he needed. Now she's gone he could be anywhere.'

'That wasn't my question.' She's frowning now. 'Did he ever mention Calais? The refugee camp they called The Jungle?'

'Never.'

'Not even second-hand? *En passant?* As a talking point?'

'Absolutely not.'

'Did he ever mention Syrian friends he might have made? Here or abroad? Refugees, perhaps? Asylum seekers?'

'No.'

Cavendish scribbles herself another note and glances at Deneuve.

'You spent some time in Syria yourself,' he says. 'According to one of your passports.'

'Palmyra,' I say at once. 'Before they blew it up.'

I explain about the film I made there, six magical winter weeks in the desert surrounded by thousands of years of history.

'The movie bombed, I'm afraid, but those February sunsets were unforgettable.'

'You made friends in Syria?'

'I make friends everywhere.'

'But you support their cause?'

'I don't pretend to understand it. Do I feel sorry for those people? For what happened to them? Of course I do. Have I ever discussed any of that with McFaul? Alas, no.'

'Alas . . .?'

'He's gone . . .' I spread my hands wide. 'And for his sake, I just hope someone finds him.'

The interview continues for the best part of an hour. We criss-cross the same terrain time after time, Deneuve and Cavendish putting exactly the same questions a million different ways, much like McFaul in his minefield probing for hidden little parcels of high explosive. They seem to want to believe that this maverick do-gooder has set up some kind of terrorist safe house deep in leafy East Devon, and my refusal to take them seriously comes as something of a disappointment. Only when the interview has come to a formal end, and I'm free to leave, do I return to the one issue that has surprised me.

'Calais?' I ask. 'The Jungle? You want to tell me more?'

Deneuve wants me gone. He has the lightest handshake, the merest touch of flesh on flesh.

'Sadly not,' he says. 'But thank you for your time.'

*   *   *

Tony and I retire briefly to a pub in the Edgware Road. By now it's late afternoon. I settle at a table in the corner and wait for Tony to return from the bar with the drinks. Crossing swords with MI5 doesn't happen every day in his busy, busy life and I get the impression he's rather enjoyed the experience.

'Well?' I enquire, as he hands me a packet of crisps.

He shoots me a look. He hasn't got much time and he wants to start with Bullivant and Brett Atkinson.

'This is a game,' he says. 'From where I'm sitting, they've got bugger all, and that's not in the job description at all. Your guy McFaul does a deep clean? Gets rid of all that crap furniture you described? Accepts a cheque from his partner? That barely even qualifies as circumstantial. You're right about our Mr Bullivant. The man is unforgiving. He has iron in his soul. He needs to believe that McFaul killed his partner and – even worse – he's become the prisoner of his own hunch. In other words, our Mr Bullivant's banged up with the darkest side of his own nature. Look at the man. And on top of everything else, you tell me he's a lay preacher. Can you imagine anything worse?'

Banged up with the darkest side of his own nature. I store the phrase away for later, thinking especially of Berndt, my ex-husband, and when things got very bad indeed, of Malo. But Tony Morse hasn't finished.

'The other lot might be more problematic. MI5 don't do proper disclosure. Secrecy comes with the job, in fact secrecy *is* the bloody job. These people have powers you won't believe, and digging anything out of them is a no-no. If they thought you were a terrorist, you'd still be talking to them but McFaul's a different matter. They've obviously got something on him. He's obviously in the frame.'

'You're serious?'

'I am. And so are they. These people don't fuck about, believe me.' He pauses, then reaches for his gin and tonic. 'Just an aside, but can you think of *any* reason why your friend might attract this kind of attention?'

In truth, I can't.

'Do terrorists work in minefields?' I ask him. 'Do they try and keep Angolan kids in one piece? Do they retire to deepest

Portugal and keep their heads down? Has that poor bloody man come back to Budleigh Salterton to blow the country up? This is bizarre. Turn it into a drama and even Channel Four wouldn't screen garbage like this.'

Tony nods, seeming to agree. Then he empties the remains of his glass. He has to be back in Pompey to sort out mitigation pleas for tomorrow's Crown Court. It has, as ever, been a pleasure. He gets up, checks his hair in a nearby mirror, and then gestures me to my feet. I submit very readily to a hug, and then thank him for making the effort.

'Any time.' He gives me the trademark squeeze. 'You've got my number.'

'You think they'll be back for more?'

'I very much doubt it.'

TWENTY-THREE

C oping with MI5 as well as the police has exhausted me, but I have two precious days of doing virtually nothing before I must attend a read-through for a Beeb radio play. A phone call from Rosa assures me that we have more time on the Pavel submission than she'd anticipated. Better still, a production company on the Champs-Élyséés has acquired screen rights to a crime novel that has taken France by storm and is excited about the prospect of casting yours truly as the older of the two female leads.

'Excited', in this context, is normally showbiz-speak for a low opening offer on the fee, but I've had dealings with these people before and I trust, as well as respect, them. They have a track record of excellent adaptations and most of the production money they spend ends up on the screen. Rosa is keen to courier the scripts to me and just now I can think of no better way to fill my time.

The scripts arrive less than an hour later, and I spend all of Wednesday and most of Thursday morning exploring them scene by scene. *Dimanche* is the story of a series of murders that take place week by week, always on a Sunday. Corpse by corpse, this terrifyingly metronomic outbreak of lethal violence builds a pattern which the two cops leading the enquiry must first recognize, and then squeeze for vital clues. I'm deep in the final script, which is truly excellent, when the video entry phone begins to buzz.

I abandon the sofa and go down the hall to see who it might be. At first glance I don't recognize the face on the screen. He's oldish, suit and tie, neatly parted hair, dark blue blazer, slightly military bearing. He rings again, shifting his weight from foot to foot, and as he does so, he looks directly at the camera. It's Nathan Kline. Retired QC. And stalwart of the East Devon Golf Club.

'What a surprise,' I say. 'Do come in.'

He's out in the corridor, knocking at my door, before I have a chance to tidy up. I let him in, apologizing for the mess in the lounge before he's even got there. He doesn't seem to be listening.

'Young Evelyn gave me your address,' he says. 'I hope you don't mind.'

'Not at all. Coffee? Tea? Something stronger?'

'Tea would be fine.' He follows me into the kitchen. 'Nice place.' He's looking round. 'All yours?'

'All mine.'

'Lucky girl. I had you down as married, somehow, but it seems I may be wrong.'

This is not a good start. In less than a minute, this man – whom I hardly know – has barged into my nest with a sense of entitlement I can only describe as seigneurial. Just now, he's running his fingers along the work surface. Next, he'll be inspecting the contents of the dishwasher. Either he's nervous, I decide, or simply thick-skinned.

The latter proves to be the case. I shepherd him through to the lounge, tidy the script, and settle him on the sofa. By the time I return with the tea and a plate of chocolate chip cookies, he has the script open on his lap.

'You mind terribly?' He looks up.

'I do, as it happens. My mum always told me to ask first. Especially with strangers.'

'Is that what I am? Good Lord, I hope not.'

He struggles to his feet to help me with the tea. I tell him it's OK, that everything's fine. Please sit down.

Back on the sofa, he reaches for a biscuit, uninvited, and then brushes the crumbs from his lap.

'Ever get lonely?' He's looking round again.

'Never.'

'Excellent. You know the secret to a happy life? Independence. It can be financial. It can be up here . . .' He taps his head. 'Or it can be this.'

'This?'

'A good-looking woman making her own way. I admire that, I truly do. Rare as hen's teeth, in my day. Ten a penny now. Still . . .' He reaches for another biscuit. 'I expect that counts as progress. You mind me asking you a question?'

'Not at all.'

'McFaul.'

'What about him?'

'The chap's disappeared. I imagine young Evelyn told you.'

'She did. She mentioned it last night.'

'Gone. Fled.'

'She didn't say that. She just said she hadn't seen him for a while.'

'So, you don't know?'

'Know what?'

'That he broke his bail conditions? That he's on the bloody run? Every copper in the land keeping an eye out?'

'My goodness.'

'Exactly.' He watches me pour the tea. 'And you're telling me you really didn't know?'

I take my time answering. I'd kept my conversation with Evelyn on the brief side, just a call to make sure she was OK. I'd no intention then, or now, of sharing my little adventure in the TACT custody suite with anyone in Budleigh Salterton. Enough, I've decided, is enough.

'Well?' Nathan wants an answer.

'Maybe he's gone away for a few days,' I say lightly. 'Or maybe it's more serious than that.'

'Serious how?'

'The last time I saw him, he looked awful. Maybe he's had some kind of breakdown.'

'That's what Bill thinks. He went round to check at the start of the week, Monday I think, said exactly the same thing. The man's heading for the buffers, he said. Poor bastard.'

'Did he offer any help? Bill?'

'Money, I suspect. He's generous that way. Poor bugger's on his uppers. Christianne was the one who kept the show on the bloody road and now she's gone. Terrible business. Frightful shame.'

'You think . . .' I'm frowning now. 'Think he might have done something silly?'

'Like Chris, you mean? More than possible. In fact, likely, I'd say. Chap like that, he'd take himself off, find somewhere nice and quiet. Shotgun, probably. Time will tell.' He plucks at the crease in his trousers. 'And you, my dear? What's your take on this sorry little saga?'

'I have no take.' I nod at the script. 'We thesps live in a world of our own.'

'Really?' He looks affronted. 'And that's the best you can do?'

'Yes, I'm afraid it is.'

I manage to get him out of the house shortly afterwards. He lingers in the hall for a moment or two and wonders whether I'd like to join him for dinner. He says he's staying at his club, The Reform, wonderful grub, much-envied cellar. I'd be more than welcome. When I turn the invitation down, he looks disappointed.

'Better offer?'

'Not at all.' I nod back towards the lounge. 'I'm planning a quiet evening in.'

He's gone moments later, and I linger at the window, watching him clamber into a sleek-looking Mercedes in the visitors' section at the far end of the car park. Acting teaches you a great deal about the way people behave, those little giveaway signs when they're faking it, pretending to be someone or something they're not, and the performance I've just witnessed is a perfect example. If Nathan Kline wants to play the bluff country misogynist, awkward, clumsy, then he should have spent a little longer prac-tising the role. He's a bright man, and probably a bully, and I suspect he has friends in high places. So why did he take the trouble to track me down? And play the provincial buffoon he so patently isn't?

To this, I have no answer. I circle the flat for a minute or two, touching this, adjusting that, a routine I developed in the darkest days after the collapse of my marriage. This is my fortress, I tell myself, this is the little tiny patch of west London real estate that I've truly earned. Kline's visit has been an intrusion, no question, but my job now is to put it out of my mind and pretend it never happened.

And yet. And yet . . .

I'm looking at the cheap mobile I've bought as a stand-by for the Samsung seized by the police. It's lying on the low occasional table beside the sofa. I have an overwhelming desire to phone McFaul, to touch base, to make sure he's OK. He's a man, I tell myself, of untold inner resources. No way would he walk into the woods with a shotgun and a handful of shells. Just a clue is all I need. Just one tiny moment to confirm that I've got this thing right, that he's still alive.

I pick up the mobile. Without the number stored on the Samsung, of course, I'm helpless, but then I remember the paperwork from the Vodafone store in Exmouth. McFaul's number will be there. I'm sure it will.

I spend a fruitless half hour going through the flat, cursing the police. They – or the MI5 people – have taken everything: my laptop, Malo's iPad, an old tablet I still use from time to time, together with reams of bank statements, credit card records and sundry other documents. Then I remember my Peugeot in the car park downstairs. I have the dimmest memory of stuffing the Vodafone paperwork into a door pocket. I find the keys and clatter downstairs. My ninja friends, thank God, have ignored my car. And exactly where I thought, I find the Vodafone number.

I take the lift back to the top floor, hopelessly conflicted about making the call. In truth, my visit to the TACT suite has disturbed me more than I like to admit. The police I've learned to cope with, just, but the intelligence services are way scarier, and for that reason alone the last couple of days, absorbed in a French cop drama, have been a real blessing. It's distanced me from the world of Budleigh Salterton, of MND, of the acrid tang of chemicals in the bareness of McFaul's front room. Yet that same world has just paid me a visit, sparked fresh questions, stirred new fears, and I know myself sufficiently well to recognize what I must do.

Back in the flat, I key McFaul's number into my new mobile. For a long moment, nothing happens. Then the number begins to ring. It goes on and on, and I'm about to hang up when the ringing stops and I hear a voice.

'Who is this?' Faint, but definitely McFaul.

'It's me. Enora.' I hesitate a moment. 'You're OK? That's all I want to know.'

'I'm fine. Baking, but fine. Take care. And thanks for phoning.' The line goes dead.

Baking? He's alive. He's somewhere hot. How did he ever get there without a passport? I've no idea. But, at least for now, he's ahead of the game. That night, unusually, I sleep like a baby.

TWENTY-FOUR

The next two months, almost to the day, are equally blissful. As west London surrenders to late autumn, I put McFaul and all of Budleigh behind me and get on with my life. Rosa conveys my congratulations to the Paris-based screen writer on doing such a fine job on her adaptation of *Dimanche*, and within days word arrives from Paris that the role of the lead cop, Danielle Colbert, will very probably be mine. As soon as the Exec Producer has returned from a shoot in the Adriatic, he'll be in touch.

In the meantime, back home in Holland Park, I have a couple of days intense prep on the Beeb radio script before we gather for the read-through in the bowels of Broadcasting House. This is a period piece, a political drama exploring some of the murkier outcomes of the Bristol slave trade. I play the wife of a wealthy merchant and a complex set of events leaves me on the verge of taking my own life. This moment of crisis finds me in the Avon gorge. The tide has peaked and I can't swim. To die or not to die?

I have a longish passage of angst-ridden monologue to resolve this dilemma and as I try voicing it a couple of ways, I can't help thinking of Christianne. She, of course, found herself in a far uglier trap, but the essence of acting is a wholesale surrender to the character and the situation, and once I've managed to fine-tune the performance I think I've glimpsed the relief that comes with taking a decision like that. The producer certainly thinks so.

'Christ,' she says. 'It's like you've actually done it.'

Should I be flattered? I think not. Life, as Pavel once told me, deserves a great deal of contemplation. Look hard enough, and there are no secrets left.

The play is broadcast at the end of October on the evening the clocks go back, and excites mild interest on Twitter. Evelyn has put the word around in Budleigh and comes up to town a week or so later for a couple of days *chez moi*. *Rites of Passage*, she tells me, has done my reputation no harm. Bill Penny loved it, and even Nathan Kline spared the time to listen.

'What did Beth make of it?'

'She wouldn't say. She wants to talk to you personally.'

'Like when?' Beth appears to have forgiven me.

'That's what I said, but you know what she's like. She has to put her own smell on everything.'

Her own smell on everything. Perfect.

'And that dog of Bill's? The one she was crazy about?'

'Hundchen? Still missing, I'm afraid. Missing, presumed lost. Beth, of course, won't have it. She had these posters printed, got a photo from Bill, plastered them everywhere. She talked to the local paper, too, insisted the wretched animal was still alive. That woman would die without publicity, I swear it. She needs to be centre stage. All the bloody time.'

'And does that matter?'

'Not in the least. She's a character. And we like that, don't we, my lovely?'

Indeed, we do. A couple of weeks later, Rosa calls with news from Paris. After a precautionary look at my show reel, the Exec Producer of *Dimanche* has confirmed I'm to be his pick for Danielle Colbert. So far, so good, but Rosa has also been talking to the BBC Drama department. Our favourite commissioning editor has been badgering her again and it appears that it's his last call for Pavel's missing masterpiece. Most of next year's development budget has now been spent and there's precious little left to invest in whatever I might be able to find.

'What do you think, my precious? Worth giving that nice policeman a call?'

I do her bidding, not simply on Pavel's account but because I'm genuinely curious about the fate of Operation *Bulldog*. Last time I checked, Bullivant's enquiry was still at full throttle. In the absence of a body, can we now lay our memories of Christianne to rest?

To my surprise, Brett Atkinson seems pleased to hear me.

'Shaz caught that play of yours,' he says at once. 'She's mad for proper radio.'

'And?'

'She loved it. Especially the bit at the end.'

'When I try and do myself in?'

'Yeah. Drowning, wasn't it? Some place in Bristol?'

This is an easy cue to take us to Operation *Bulldog*, and Brett is more forthcoming than I'd expected. It helps that he's at home, on a rare day off.

'NFA,' he says at once.

'Meaning?'

'No Further Action. Relax. You're off the hook.'

'And McFaul?'

'That's different.'

'How?'

'He's broken his bail conditions, for one thing. That means he's on a nicking. The man has questions to answer. Do a runner, and there has to be a reason.'

'You'll find him?'

'Of course we will.'

I nod. Now is definitely not the time to enquire about abroad, though I've been thinking hard about what might happen after Brexit. Will European arrest warrants still work, when and if we leave? Or can someone like McFaul simply drop off the radar?

'And Bullivant?' I query instead. 'Has all this made him a happy man?'

'Christ, no. He's having to tidy up a couple of other jobs at the moment, but he can't leave this one alone. He's nearly done his time. *Bulldog* was his little retirement present, but unless we lay hands on your bloke before March, he's gonna be disappointed.'

'My bloke?'

'McFaul. That's Bullivant speaking, not me.'

'He thinks we . . .?'

'Yeah. I told him there was no way, but he never listens.'

'Tell him again.' I'm far from amused. 'And tell him he's got McFaul wrong, too. That man never laid a finger on Christianne. Not in the way he thinks.'

'You say.'

'I do. Absolutely. That lovely woman had luck on her side. Just drifted away. Can you imagine a sweeter end? For someone with her prognosis? Brilliant, says me. Gone. Disappeared off the face of the planet. Perfect. Say hi to Shaz for me, promise?'

'No problem.'

'And that Apple MacBook of mine?'

'Still in the queue for analysis, I'm afraid.' He sighs. 'Sorry.'

Malo turns up in Holland Park at the beginning of December, but turns down the offer of tea. An ankle problem has clipped his wings as far as training is concerned, but he's in the hands of a physio he trusts and with luck he'll be back in Richmond Park before Christmas.

'We're looking at a house in Twickenham, Mum. Clem loves it. Ten minutes, tops, and I'm in the park.'

I blink. Houses in Twickenham cost a fortune. As do physios.

'What happened to that apartment off Ranelagh Gardens?'

'Dreadful. You were right. Way overpriced, and in any case it's gone.'

'And Twickenham?'

'Two-bedroom terrace. Six hundred thou. Clem's taking her mum round tonight. H saw it last weekend.'

'And?'

'Perfect.'

'Do I get a look?'

'Of course you do, that's why I came over.'

We take the lift to the ground floor to spare his ankle and he drives me to a quiet street on the Hounslow side of Twickenham. The current owners, who are young, are in the process of putting their infant daughter to bed, but the woman obviously has a soft spot for Malo and is happy to show me around. Malo's right. Two reception rooms downstairs. Galley kitchen. A couple of decent-sized bedrooms. Plus private parking at the back. Perfect.

Once again, Malo insists on taking me to supper. Pizza Express will never hold a candle to Avventura, but I'm not complaining.

'And Sylvester?' I enquire. 'Still smitten?'

'Him or me?'

'The pair of you. Last time we had a proper conversation, you were on a month's trial. I take it you passed muster?'

'Sort of.'

'What does that mean?'

'It means he pays me a wage, keeps me going, points me in certain directions.'

'Like?'

'Prospects, mainly. We're developing Doomsday packages. Quite a lot of money gives you access to a boat that meets the right spec, plus onboard crew. You don't have to own anything. Just turn up when the time is right.'

'I don't understand.'

'Putin makes a move on Estonia? The Israelis take out key bits of Iran? Trump drops a bomb on North Korea? This stuff writes itself. I could go on all night.'

'OK.' I nod. 'So, I'm one of your prospects. What am I paying?'

'Depends on the level of cover. Top end, ten thousand a month premium will buy you and your family a private jet to your POE.'

'POE?' My son is showing off.

'Port of embarkation. From then on, it's all taken care of. Passage costs. Full crew. Access to fuel and food caches. Lead-lined safe room if the shit really hits the fan.'

'And I can access all this any time?'

'Christ, no. Every potential situation is calibrated. On a scale of one to ten, you have to be at nine.'

'Situation?'

'Crisis, Mum. Flashpoint. Very bad stuff happening, like I just said. Sylvester's setting up an international panel of experts to make the judgement call. It's a bit like the Doomsday Clock. They adjust it every January. Next year, it's the twenty-third. Currently the clock's at two minutes to midnight. Sylvester's running a book on that, too. Ask nicely, and he'll give you odds on their decision. Easy money, if you know what you're doing.'

'Really?' I assume he's kidding. 'You're betting on the future of the planet? Is that altogether appropriate?'

'It's business, Mum. Money. Don't take it so seriously.' He's seized a menu. 'The spiced beef pizza looks OK.' He glances up. 'Sloppy Giuseppe? For two?'

I say yes to the pizza without even looking, largely because my son has rather shaken me. I don't doubt for a second that any cloud, in the right hands, can have a silver lining, but it takes a great deal of nerve, as well as the blackest sense of humour, to dream up a business like this. The speed with which Malo has mastered the small print, coupled with his sudden addiction to running, is doubtless a tribute to Sylvester, and for both I'm truly grateful, but deep in my feeble brain I'm beginning to wonder just where all this is headed. There's something else, too. Malo seems to have developed an ongoing interest in McFaul. I've explained the way we met. I've shared a little about his previous life in the minefields. Sylvester has already told him about Christianne going missing. But now he wants to meet the man.

'You can make that happen, Mum?'

'Alas, no.'

'Why not?'

'He isn't around at the moment.'

'You've got a phone number?'

'No.'

'So, where is he?'

'I've no idea.'

This, I'm rather hoping, will be the end of it. Sadly, it simply piques Malo's interest further. He wants more details, more clues, and when I tell him enough's enough, he takes absolutely no notice.

'Is this something private, Mum? You're shagging him?'

'Certainly not.'

'What, then? What is it?'

'I can't tell you. Private's a good word, but not in the way you think. Let's get that waiter back. I'm not sure I'm hungry any more.'

On the way back to Holland Park, Malo is more than solicitous. Am I feeling OK? Is it something I've eaten earlier? Would I like to stop for a drink? To every question, I offer nothing more than a shake of my head. It'll pass, I mutter. It's nothing.

Outside the flat, Malo gets out of the car and helps me on to the pavement. This is very sweet of him and makes me feel very old. He gives me a hug and then holds me at arm's length.

'I'm right, aren't I?' He's beaming. 'You *are* shagging him.'

TWENTY-FIVE

Thursday, 12 December. Election day. I've overslept for once and it's nearly ten o'clock when the phone rings. I roll over, groping for my mobile. I recognize Evelyn's voice at once. When she's upset, she has a tendency to gulp.

'What's the matter?'

'Are you there? Enora?'

'I am. What's going on?'

'Something's happened. I don't know what. Bill just phoned me.'

'And?'

'He said to watch the news. The TV news. And to tell you to do the same.'

'But why? Why would he say a thing like that?'

'I don't know. You'll phone me back? Promise?'

I say yes. Already I'm out of bed and heading for the lounge, trying to remember the channel number for BBC rolling news. Seconds later, it's there in full HD, queues of voters at polling station after polling station, live injects from reporters in Leeds and Plymouth, on-screen reminders of the shape of the evening to come. Prime Minister Boris Johnson, we're told, has already voted. And here's a clip of Jeremy Corbyn doing exactly the same thing. The nation holds its breath. Anything could happen.

And it has. We've left the electoral battlegrounds and a news summary takes us to the coast of East Devon where, it seems, something rather bizarre has happened. The studio presenter throws to a reporter airborne in a helicopter. He bellows something I can't quite understand and then the camera pans to reveal a vast scar in the cliff face. This stretch of coast, the reporter tells us, is notorious for cliff falls and this one has happened overnight, thousands of tons of rock and soil deposited on the beach. I'm staring at the screen, at the shape of the cliffs. The colour is the giveaway, a rich ochre, pinking the waves that curl on to the beach. Budleigh Salterton, I think. Just where the coastal path runs beside the golf course.

But the cameraman hasn't finished. He's tightening the shot, until all I can see is a close-up of the rubble at the foot of the cliff. At first, I can't make sense of the object in the very middle of the picture. It's oblong, probably man-made. It looks like a long box, and as the cameraman tweaks the focus, I'm guessing it once had a lid. Then, as the shot tightens even further, I feel the blood in my veins begin to ice. It's not a box at all, it's a coffin. And the shrouded object inside, a grubby white, is a body.

'You've seen it?' I'm talking to Evelyn again.

'Yes. I'm watching now. Horrible. Ghastly.'

'Is it what I think it is?'

'Yes.'

'Do we have a name?'

'Not yet. Bill says there's a recovery team en route.' She pauses. Another gulp. 'Can you come down, my lovely? Can you do that for me?'

I don't leave at once because I can't tear myself away from the TV. After another interminable trek around the nation's polling stations, we're back with the news roundup. By now, events in East Devon are leading the running order. News crews have established a presence on the foreshore and from a respectful distance, we're watching a pair of paramedics bent over what is definitely a coffin. Barely metres offshore, a lifeboat is wallowing in the swell, but there's no attempt to transfer the shrouded body.

The camera pans slowly upwards, tracing the line of the cliff fall, and then we cut to another shot, this time on top of the cliff.

I stare at it, transfixed. The rawness of the scar in the turf is new, but I recognize the shape of the surrounding bushes, the half-hidden remains of a path, and – most important of all – the view across the bay. This is where Christianne took me the morning we walked up beside the golf course. This is her very favourite place in all the world.

'Well, my lovely?' It's Evelyn on the phone again. 'You're on your way?'

'Not yet. I'm still watching. You've got it on? The TV?'

'Yes.'

'They're on the clifftop?'

'Yes.'

'And you've seen what's on the beach?'

'Yes.'

'It's Christianne, it has to be.'

'What?'

'Christianne. In that coffin. She didn't go swimming at all. Someone buried her there.'

It's early afternoon by the time I make it down to Budleigh Salterton. There are old posters for the Military Wives Choir on the approach to the town and Christmas lights hang across the High Street. In the big car park at the foot of the hill beside the beach, I count half a dozen media vans, including three with satellite dishes. A far corner of the car park has been coned off, and I watch a figure in a high-vis tabard guiding in a small helicopter. The chopper raises a dust cloud as it rears up and then touches down. With the rotors still turning, a cameraman jumps on to the tarmac and heads for one of the satellite vans. Christianne, I can't help thinking. Yet more pictures.

I park. Before I head up to Evelyn's, I want to find out as much as I can. The promenade, predictably, is thick with people. Many will be local. Many won't. The weather is foul, grey, windy, rain in the air, but nothing, it seems, can keep people away from an incident like this.

I head west, towards the curl of beach where the cliff fall happened. The police have sealed off the seafront where the coastal path begins the long climb up towards the golf club, but I jump down on to the smoothness of the big pebbles and keep going. Beyond a line of fishing boats, there's more tape, more spectators, more pointing fingers. A uniformed cop is turning away the braver souls who try to duck beneath the tape and I scan the nearby faces, looking for someone I might know. Then comes the lightest pressure on my shoulder.

'Enora. What a bloody awful thing.'

It's Bill Penny. He's wearing an overcoat that's seen better days and he's looking pale and drawn. His head is bare and what little hair he possesses has gone rogue in the wind.

I look at him for a long moment. A nod is all the confirmation I need. He puts his arms round me while I press my face into his coat. Despite my tears, and Hundchen's long absence, I can still smell dog.

'Shit.' I surface for air. 'I'm sorry.'

'Don't be.' He offers me a handkerchief.

I cry a little more, telling myself this is useless, that it will make fuck-all difference, but that reduces me to tears yet again. Get a grip, I tell myself. You're better than this, stronger than this. Think of Christianne, of McFaul. Dignity. Grace. Man bloody up.

'So, what happened?' I manage at last.

'To be honest, I don't know.' Bill is gazing along the beach. 'Beth called me half an hour ago. God knows how, but she managed to get along to the site of the fall. The police are there now. They wanted a firm ID.'

'And?'

'It's Christianne.'

I nod, say nothing. There are a million questions we all need to ask but here and now doesn't feel right. The jumble of sandstone rock and gravel at the foot of the cliff is maybe half a mile away, and I count at least a dozen high-vis jackets in attendance. The lifeboat is still holding station offshore and I'm guessing that Christianne's shrouded remains will end up on board. Better a dignified recovery, I think, than four men struggling with a stretcher through hundreds of oglers.

As we watch, I catch the bright flare of a camera flash, then another.

'They're treating it as a crime scene,' Bill murmurs. 'As I imagine they might.'

'So . . .?' I'm trying to work out what might have happened, but I leave the question unvoiced. Bill, as ever, can read my mind.

'I don't know,' he says. 'I truly have no idea. Someone obviously buried her.'

'McFaul?'

'That would be a reasonable guess.'

'By himself?'

'I doubt it. He's a remarkable man, but even he has his limits.'

'But you think that's why he disappeared? Fled?'

Bill takes a little step to his left, trying to shield me from the wind. A brief smile ghosts across his face.

'That would imply he saw the fall coming.' He puts his arms around me again. 'Which would be truly astonishing, even by his standards.'

TWENTY-SIX

Evelyn is glued to the TV when I finally make it up to her bungalow. The white shroud has disappeared into a grey body bag and four paramedics in bulky suits are manhandling it through the shallows towards the waiting lifeboat. The process looks beyond awkward, despite the calm sea, and the bearers are up to their chests in the wavelets before the job is done. I watch the lifeboat back slowly seawards and pivot on its axis before the water, still pink, churns at its stern and the boat heads for the open sea. Christianne afloat at last, I think. But not quite in the way we all thought.

'Bill says they'll be doing a post-mortem.' I'm still watching the TV.

'I'm sure he's right.'

The conversation dies. We're watching the lifeboat from the clifftop now, barely a speck in the ocean with its little white tail of wake. In our separate trades, albeit second-hand, Evelyn and

I are all too familiar with the grim consequences of sudden death, that miasma of suspicion and conjecture that thickens and confounds and keeps bums on seats, and pages turning, but this abrupt development is suddenly all too real. The TV coverage has returned to election day by the time someone knocks on Evelyn's door.

It's Beth. I hear Evelyn inviting her in. I'm still in the lounge, one eye on the screen, when Beth appears at the door. She seems surprised to see me.

'She looked so peaceful,' she says at once. 'You wouldn't believe how peaceful she looked.'

There are shots of Plymouth on the TV. Thinner voter turnout so far in the south-west than expected. I mute the sound and turn back to Beth.

'How did you get through the police barrier?' I ask.

'I told them I had an idea who it was. The guy stopping me made a call on the radio. I even got an escort.'

'But what made you think it was Christianne?'

She stares at me, confused, and I realize she doesn't have an answer.

'I just did,' she says at last. 'It had to be.'

'But why?'

'Why? Why bloody not? A woman goes missing? No one can find her? Then a body turns up on a beach? Am I inventing any of this?'

I realize we're back in the side room at the public hall, a couple of months ago, the last time I was trying to pin her down. The same quick flare of anger. The same outrage that someone might doubt her word.

'I'm sorry,' I say. 'I'm just asking, that's all. Let's call it a hunch on your part. Let's leave it at that.'

This should do the trick, but it doesn't.

'Why are you always so difficult?' she says. 'Why are you here at all?'

I do my best to defend myself. I've known Evelyn for years. She's precious to me. And when she wants a little TLC, a little support, I'm very happy to drop everything and drive down.

'You don't think she's made friends of her own? Local people? Me and Presley, for example? Bill?'

'I'm sure she has lots of friends. That's the way she's made. She's a lovely person, always has been.'

'Then why not leave it to us?'

This, to be frank, leaves me speechless. Don't I have a right to get in my car and come to the aid of one of my closest friends? Has someone thrown a fictive border around this town? Does my name belong on a list of undesirables?

'This is crazy,' I say. 'We don't need this, we really don't, not today of all days.'

'You started it.'

'Nonsense. I was simply asking why you thought that coffin, that shroud, had Christianne inside it.'

'But wasn't I right?'

'You were. My question was why?'

She doesn't answer, but the way she's looking at me is deeply revealing. Christianne, and everything her disappearance has spawned, has become Beth's property. She, more than anyone else, has rights of ownership. *Her* friend. *Her* fathomless grief at what's happened. *Her* smell all over this suddenly huge development. One of Budleigh's leading figures identifies the body on the beach. Hold the front page.

Evelyn has arrived with a tray of tea. I suspect she's overheard most of this conversation from the kitchen because she's determined to change the subject.

'So, what happens next?' she's asking. 'What do the police do now?'

We get an answer within hours. Another knock at Evelyn's front door reveals a uniformed officer. He hands me a search warrant. By now it's dark but I recognize the face in the suit behind him. Brett Atkinson.

'This is about Christianne?' I'm gazing at the fold of paper in his hand.

'Yes. We're serving a number of warrants this evening, as you'd probably expect. It shouldn't take long. Is Ms Warlock at home? She'll need to sign for anything we seize.'

This is wearisome. I ask what connection Evelyn could possibly have with today's incident on the beach, but he won't tell me. All that matters is getting the search done. An hour. Tops.

'But what are you looking for?'

'The usual.' He risks a smile. 'With your experience, I'm sure you can guess.'

'We're talking documents? Devices?'

'Both.'

'Nothing forensic?'

'Not yet.'

'Not *yet*?' My heart sinks. Evelyn is a fascist when it comes to keeping her new home, indeed *any* home, spick and span. She has a horror of funny smells, and always has an air freshener or three readied for emergencies. The aftermath of a full forensic search, with its crusty residue of chemical leavings, would horrify her.

'You really think that might be necessary?'

'I've no idea. There might be ways round it.'

'Really?' I've caught the tiny come-on in his voice. 'You want to tell me more?'

He beckons me out into the darkness while the officer steps inside to explain the warrant to poor Evelyn. We stand beside his car, the unmarked Ford I last saw in the leisure centre car park over in Exmouth.

'Well?' I'm looking at Brett. Thankfully he cuts to the chase.

'This is as big as it gets for Bullivant,' he says. 'He's got a body at last. He's all over the bloody media. He's back from the dead. He's been proved right.'

'Back from the *dead*? Is that a helpful phrase?'

'You know what I mean. There's no holding the man down. You know how many search warrants we're serving this evening? I counted them up just an hour ago. Seven. And I expect he's putting a couple more before the magistrate as we speak.'

'And what's he expecting to find?'

'Evidence of a conspiracy.'

'To bury Christianne?'

'Yeah. And he's probably right. McFaul couldn't have done that by himself. The site's remote. There are no approach roads and even when you're on the coastal path you have to battle through the Mato fucking Grosso to get to the clifftop. You want to see what those brambles can do?' For a moment, I think he's going to roll up one trouser leg, but he has second thoughts.

'But might you be able to spare Evelyn the full treatment?' I'm looking at the bungalow.

'Yeah.'

'How?'

'We're thinking you might know more than you've let on.'

'We? You and Bullivant?'

'Of course. Pictures speak louder than words. Isn't that what they say?'

Louder than words? It takes me a moment or two to untangle this little clue. Then I remember the young reporter on the beach that Sunday when we said our goodbyes to Christianne. He must have taken dozens of shots and I know at least one of them made the local paper because Evelyn later sent me a copy.

'You're thinking Christianne had some kind of funeral party? Bearers? All that?'

'We think McFaul had help. Either way it's a conspiracy.'

'To what?'

'To murder. If that's what the PM tells us.'

PM is police-speak for post-mortem. The temperature out here on the grass verge has suddenly dropped several degrees.

'You still think McFaul killed her?'

'Yes. Either that, or he helped. Both would put him in front of a jury.'

'Along with all his mates?'

'Yes.'

'Including me?'

'Only you know that.'

I nod. The unspoken deal here couldn't be clearer. Brett thinks I was one of those sturdy yeomen who carried Christianne to her grave. And a name or two would save us all a great deal of trouble. Including, of course, Evelyn.

I study Brett for a long moment, and then I beckon him closer until I can whisper in his ear.

'I haven't a clue what you're talking about,' I murmur. 'And even if I did, you lot would be the last to know.'

This is brave, and possibly foolish, but I have no other choice, partly because I know far less than Brett and Bullivant assume, and partly because I have no intention of ratting anyone out. Back in the bungalow, Evelyn is in a tizzy. The uniformed policeman is both patient and courteous, but she hates strangers riffling through the drawers in her bedroom. After half an hour, sooner than expected, the search party departs with a laptop, a mobile, and a handful of documents.

'Christ.' Evelyn sinks into her favourite armchair. She's normally a strong woman, resilient, but I can see she's close to tears. She looks up at me and blows her nose before gesturing towards the bungalow next door. 'What has that bloody man started?'

What, indeed? That night, from my bedroom upstairs, I put a precautionary phone call through to Tony Morse. I catch him on the motorway, driving back to Portsmouth, and when I mention the body on Budleigh beach it turns out he's been following the news coverage for most of the day.

'I was down there myself,' I tell him. 'This place has become a circus. Every man and his dog.'

'I'm not surprised. The pictures were amazing. Tell me it wasn't her in the box, that friend of yours.'

'It was.'

'You're sure?'

'Absolutely.' I'm nodding. 'I'm afraid I need a bit of a steer, Tony.'

'About?'

'Euthanasia. This is getting yourself killed, right?'

'A mercy job, yes.'

'So, either you do it yourself, or someone else helps, or someone does it for you, yes?'

'Correct.'

'And is that legal?'

'God, no. We lawyers call it murder, or sometimes manslaughter.'

'And the penalty?'

'Up to fourteen years. That's life to you and me.' He laughs. 'The polls close in twenty minutes. Phone when you need me.'

'When or if?'

'When.'

TWENTY-SEVEN

Next morning, I awake to the confirmation that Boris Johnson has romped home to a victory that even he didn't expect. The Labour Party is routed, the Brexit Party have folded their tents and stolen away, and our newly elected prime minister is standing on the door step of Number Ten looking, if anything, a bit sheepish.

Mitch Culligan phones me shortly afterwards. He's an investigative journalist I was close to several years ago and I think I still count him as a friend, but all that matters this morning is that he hates the fucking Tories. We haven't talked for months.

'Did I get you up?' he grunts.

'No.'

'I pulled an all-nighter.' He's groaning now. 'I thought that exit poll had to be a piss-take. Eighty-four seats? Someone was having a joke.'

'Wrong. It's a nastier country than even you ever thought.'

'Impossible. And nasty doesn't begin to do it justice, if you want the full conversation.' He smothers a yawn. 'Still slumming it in Holland Park?'

'Budleigh Salterton, since you ask.'

'Budleigh where?' He pauses. 'Hang on, haven't they just found a body there?'

'Right. That's why I'm here.'

'You're a journalist now? A paramedic? An undertaker?'

I start to laugh. Culligan is a journalist of real talent. He has a doggedness and a fierce sense of right and wrong I've always admired. He writes like an angel, gets most of the facts right, and has a sour wit I've always found irresistible. I suspect it's kept him afloat through some seriously dark times, but now he wants to know more about the body on the beach.

I give him a brief account of what I've been up to. He's met Evelyn a couple of times, when she was still my neighbour in west London, and he's intrigued by her choice of retirement destination.

'Why on earth Budleigh? From what I remember, she had a lovely flat. London on her doorstep? A neighbour like you? What's not to like?'

I tell him about the literary festival, and about how quickly she's come to love her new home.

'She adores the place,' I tell him. 'She thinks it's one of God's best-kept secrets.'

'Not any more, it isn't. Not with a story like that on your doorstep. You're telling me you knew this woman?'

'Yes.'

'And it's some kind of mercy killing?'

'Probably.'

'Shit.' He stifles another yawn. 'Does your friend have a spare bedroom?'

Later that morning, over a late breakfast, I broach this question to Evelyn. She remembers Mitch Culligan very well and says she'd be happy to have him stay. Her third bedroom is on the small side, but I assure her that Mitch is oblivious to home comforts.

'He lives in his head,' I tell her. 'Like all the other interesting people we know.'

This little *aperçu* sparks a brief conversation about Beth. Evelyn, it turns out, has spent half the night worrying about our little spat when she turned up yesterday afternoon. Like me, she has reservations about Beth, but she thinks her heart's in the right place, even if she wildly overestimates her other talents.

'Her writing is abject,' she says. 'You remember that short-story collection you mentioned? *The Water's Edge*? She brought them round. I was very happy to read them. She's not short of imagination, and she has bags of confidence, but she's never made a friend of language. It doesn't work for her on the page. She has no feel for rhythm, for character, for description. I hate to say it, but what I read of the work was wooden beyond belief. Maybe she should have been a carpenter. Like that nice Presley.'

Evelyn is doubtless right, especially when it comes to self-belief. Bill has told me a little about Beth's determination to lay her hands on the missing *Hundchen*, and when I ask about the lengths she's gone to, Evelyn is happy to oblige.

'Anyone half sane would call it an obsession. I've seen her with the dog. She used to take it for walks sometimes, to help Bill out. It even used to spend the odd afternoon in that shop of hers. It was a yapper, that little animal, and it never knew when to stop. Anyone new, you had to watch your ankles.'

'A bit like Beth?'

'*Touché*, my lovely. Like attracts like. Maybe they were both obsessives. In any event, when the bloody thing went missing she told everyone it had to be found. For her sake as well as the dog's. Listen to her, and you'd think she'd lost a child. Posters? Door–to-door enquiries? Stuff in the papers? Even a piece on the local radio station? Totally manic and – dare I say it – wholly of a piece with the person she undoubtedly is. The dog couldn't bear to be ignored. And neither can she. There. Am I as horrible as I must sound? Probably worse. Be honest.' She beams at me. 'More toast?'

In the afternoon, I insist we go for a walk along the beach. I can sense Evelyn suspects that part of this new life of hers in Budleigh has been stolen by the media – all those pictures, all those head-lines, all that fuss and bother – and it's my job to convince her that this little flurry of attention, this grossest of intrusions, will pass. Media storms blow themselves out, I tell her, because we punters – like the seagulls pecking at the tideline – simply move on. Nothing lasts forever, especially now, and within a week or two Budleigh will sink into its normal state of torpor.

'Torpor? Is that how you view us? Fat? Lazy? Overindulged? Too wealthy for our own good?'

We're sitting peaceably in the thin sunshine, gazing out across the pebbles. None of the above, I assure her. Poor choice of noun.

'Think of another, then. The devil's in the detail, my lovely. Always was. Always will be.'

I accept this little slap on the wrist in the spirit Evelyn intends. Language, as ever, is sacred.

'Contentment? Would that be better?'

'Worse. It makes us far too pleased with ourselves.'

'Secure, then?'

'Better. In fact, perfect. Communities like this, dare I say it, are the exception now. We're lucky to be at the end of the road, end of the bus route. Once you get to Budleigh, there's nowhere else to go. That makes us think just a little harder about who we are, what we've got, how important it is to keep an eye out for each other. That's rare these days, and in a little town like this it helps no end to admit it. Perhaps even to be proud of it. There's far too much noise these days, too much *clamour*. People end up shouting because they're terrified of not being heard, of not being noticed. We don't do much shouting here, and I doubt these people ever have.'

'And Beth?'

'Beth?' A gloved hand descends on my lap. 'Beth, my lovely, is different.'

We walk towards the start of the cliff path. The line of police tape across the beach has gone, though in the distance I can see two bulky police officers standing watch over the pile of fallen debris from the cliff face. The fact that the beach is nearly empty after yesterday's chaos is welcome news for both of us, and when Evelyn suggests popping into L'Image for a spot of afternoon tea, there's a hint of celebration, as well as relief, in her voice.

The café, like the beach, is virtually empty, only a couple of the tables occupied. The two figures bent over slices of carrot cake are all too familiar. Beth glances up as we open the door, and at once grabs for her bag and gets to her feet. She offers Evelyn a nod as she sweeps past but blanks me completely. Nathan Kline, on the other hand, gives us both a courtly kiss.

'Lovely.' He rubs his hands together. 'I apologize for my young friend. I'm afraid that events have rather overwhelmed her. Carrot cake, anyone?' He nods down at Beth's untouched plate. 'Such a shame to waste it.'

We settle at his table and talk, inevitably, about yesterday's events. He says he's been talking to Bill and both of them agreed that digging the grave and burying Christianne was a huge tribute to McFaul.

'How ever did he do it? God knows. It must have been days in the preparation, maybe weeks, maybe longer. If the poor bugger's still alive, I wonder if he's seen those pictures.'

'You think he's dead?' Evelyn sounds shocked.

'I think he may be. I was saying to Enora a while back, before
he bailed out and left us, he had a certain look about him. You
can see it in the tightness of the mouth, in the eyes. Someone's
been in there and turned the lights off. Depression? Despair?
Grief can do funny things to people. I truly think he'd had
enough.'

I nod, say nothing. Since I first made contact on the phone
with McFaul, I've tried twice more. On the first occasion, he
didn't pick up. Five days ago, we had the beginnings of a conversation. He's still somewhere hot, and he sounded relaxed. I think
I caught the clatter of a tram in the background, but I could have
been hearing things. Either way, my guess is that yesterday's
news coverage will catch up with him. A story like that, a bust-
open coffin on a beach, will reach every corner of the planet.

Evelyn wants to know about Beth. She hates it when people
start falling out. Nathan is all sympathy.

'She's a sensitive soul, Beth. Personally speaking, I've never
had a problem with her. In fact, I think she's brought a bit of *je
ne sais quoi* to this little town. Most of the stuff in that shop of
hers isn't to my taste, but my wife loved it. Been a long time
coming, she used to say. God bless her. Red plastic earrings were
never *de rigueur chez moi*, but I suppose there's no accounting
for taste.'

I know these little crumbs of French are tossed in my direction, but I choose to ignore them. Like most lawyers, I suspect
Nathan Kline QC has many faces and I certainly prefer this one
to the boorish clown who turned up at my door in Holland Park.
At least he's not trying to drag me out for supper, and whatever
else he might have in mind for afterwards. Or so I'm foolish
enough to assume.

'That little Cessna of mine.' He's caught my eye. 'The offer's
still there if you ever fancy it.'

I drop a verbal curtsey, tell him I'm grateful. One day, maybe,
but not quite yet. Then I have another thought.

'How many seats does it have?'

'Four. Two up front. Gawkers in steerage. You have a pal in
mind?'

'I might. Would that be OK?'

'Depends whether they're as lovely as you, my dear . . .' He's trying to mask his disappointment. 'Though two Enoras might ask too much of me.'

Evelyn mentions our visit from the constabulary last night. Given Nathan's vast courtroom experience in these matters, what does he think the police might do now?

Nathan gives the question some thought, as if it's the first time he's had a chance to ponder it.

'They'll obviously want to know what happened,' he says at last.

'To Christianne?'

'Of course. People, thank God, rarely die without due cause. The virgin birth? Wildly improbable. A virgin death? I think not.'

He probably means this as a sophisticated little joke, but I know it upsets Evelyn. I watch the colour rise in her face, and she bites her lip and looks away. Strange how even the brightest people, people who should know better, have so little regard for faith.

'What will a post-mortem reveal? What do they look for?' I ask.

'Evidence of physical violence, blunt object trauma, strangulation, puncture wounds, big or small.'

'As small as a hypodermic needle?'

'Certainly. If the evidence still exists.'

'And?'

'Body fluid analysis, bloods, tissues, stomach contents, all sorts. They call it tox. If she died from injection, like you're suggesting, they'll be looking for whatever killed her.'

'And this stuff will still be there in her body?'

'Certainly. I've prosecuted cases where the victim has been exhumed years after death. In one case, the pathologist was able to reconstruct his last meal. Poor Christianne has been dead barely a couple of months. The evidence should still be there.' He gives us one of those creepy smiles, and then reaches for his coat. 'Wondrous carrot cake, *n'est-ce pas*?'

TWENTY-EIGHT

Mitch Culligan turns up in time for a late breakfast next day. The last time I saw him behind the wheel, he was driving an ancient Renault 4 van, the model favoured by French postmen in rural areas thirty years ago, and beneath the wreckage of the bodywork – dents, scrapes, missing trim – I suspect it's the same vehicle. Nothing's changed in personal terms, either. He's still a shambling bear of a man, flat feet, full beard, knitted red scarf tucked into a tatty grey anorak. His one concession to style is a rather wonderful messenger bag, looped over one shoulder, in a shade of sea green I adore at once. It turns out to hold a pair of striped pyjamas, as well as his laptop, a serious-looking camera, and a store of notepads.

Evelyn busies around the kitchen, while Mitch and I compare notes on the last forty-eight hours. The post-shock dust has begun to settle on the wreckage of Mitch's beloved Labour Party, and – says Mitch – the outlines of a new political settlement are beginning to appear.

'Johnson's fucked,' he says at once. 'He never expected a win this big and he knows it'll come back to haunt him. All those pissed-off Leavers in the north have believed his promises and now he'll have to deliver. No excuses. Nowhere to hide. Total nightmare.' He stabs a fork at his second egg and mops up the spill of golden yolk with a finger of toast.

Evelyn, who I know votes Tory, is looking bewildered. She wants to know about the NHS. Especially sorting out proper care for the elderly.

'It's madness down here.' She's buttering more toast. 'I've got a friend whose mother broke her hip. She's eighty-seven and they're trying to send her home. Her daughter works in London. Her son's in Dubai. She's got no immediate family, so she'll have to rely on her neighbours and people like me. She can barely move, poor thing. She should be in hospital for as long as it takes. Treating people that way is beyond belief.'

Mitch is looking sombre. His plate, with its puddles of tomato sauce, looks like a crime scene.

'Tell our new masters,' he says. 'They've promised to deliver and now the bills are due. Will they sort the NHS? Social care? Of course not. Why? Because the math doesn't work. There are too many of us, and we're too old, and in any case there's no money. Labour? Tory? Green? Yellow? Makes no difference. Even with his precious eighty seats, Johnson's fucked, and he knows it.' The sight of the toast puts a smile on his face. 'Do I hear the word marmalade?'

After breakfast, Mitch and I retreat to the lounge. For reasons I understand only too well, he wants a proper briefing. Budleigh Salterton, once you get to know it, is a simple proposition, but every newcomer has every right to ask a question or two.

'Blacks? Browns? Fat mums? Kids?' Mitch, it turns out, took a drive up and down the High Street before finding the bungalow.

'Very few of the above,' I admit, 'though the primary school seems to be thriving, and there's a decent Indian if you fancy a curry.'

'But it's a time warp, isn't it? God obviously had a passion for the Fifties and preserved it here. Did a nice job, too. Good choice of location. Great beach. No litter. All the dogs on leads, and most of the husbands, too. Aspic's the word that comes to mind.' He catches Evelyn's eye. 'Am I on the money here? Is this God's waiting room? Or has London rotted my brain?'

I sense that Evelyn likes this man even more than last time they met. He's brought a gust of irreverence to the tidiness of her little home in the west, and she admires a well-turned phrase. At first, the stream-of-consciousness that is Mitch rather alarmed her, but now she's more than happy to give it house room.

'You need a little time, dear,' she says. 'Then you'll settle in.'

Mitch has never mastered settling-in, never begun to understand what it means. He's been a moving target as long as I've known him, relying on quick feet and a ready intelligence to keep out of trouble. By nature, he can't help himself. He's selectively honest in his dealings with others and is extremely hard on himself. He sets the journalistic bar very high, questions everything, all the time, and was probably born subversive.

We sit together on the sofa, two outsiders in this little community. I tell him about meeting Christianne, and McFaul, and their joint efforts to get on top of MND.

'But you can't,' he says at once. 'That's the whole point, isn't it?'

'It is,' I agree, 'and that's probably what put her on the beach.'

'You mean a mercy killing? Early doors?'

'More than possible.'

'So how would that work?'

I tell him I don't know, not the details, which happens to be true. I also resist the temptation to share my mercifully brief encounter with MI5.

Mitch has found Budleigh on Google Earth. I'm looking at a jigsaw of streets and cul-de-sacs surrounded by the rich greens and reds of rural East Devon. Mitch follows my finger as I point out the highlights. Evelyn's cul-de-sac of bungalows. The High Street. The big car park on the seafront. And the long shallow crescent of cliff away to the west.

'About there.' My finger comes to rest on a tiny splinter of beach at the foot of the cliff. 'That's where she ended up.'

'And here?' Mitch has tracked inland.

'That's a golf course. The poshest part of Budleigh is right beside it, but none of the roads come down as far as the coastal path and the cliff. A good friend lives around here . . .' I think I've found Bill's house. 'He was our man in Berlin for a while. I think that was his last job before he retired. He knew Christianne well. I ought to introduce you.'

'He was an ambassador?'

'Yes. I expect Budleigh's full of them. But he's still a nice man.'

The distinction puts a brief smile on Mitch's big face. He's taking another long look at Google Earth, tightening the focus, teasing out the detail. What seems to interest him most is the golf course.

'Popular?'

'Very, as far as I know. While the daylight lasts, this is a very active little town. Tennis, croquet, bowls. And golf, of course.'

'And after dark?'

'A grave.'

*   *   *

At Mitch's insistence, we go for a walk so he can scout the ground. En route to the seafront, a couple of passers-by pause for a brief chat, much to Mitch's amusement. The talk, inevitably, is of Thursday's events, and what might happen next, but what takes his fancy is the fact that I've made friends already.

'They can't all be fans of arthouse movies,' he says.

'No need. A place like this, you don't even have to try. Conversations come easy. People look you in the eye, even strangers. At first, it felt almost menacing. Then I wondered if people were taking advantage somehow, being slightly forward. Now, it's just the norm. Come with me, *mon brave*, no one's going to hurt you, I promise.'

I reach for him on purpose, knowing he hates physical contact, but for once he relents and we march down towards the seafront arm in arm. The earlier sunshine has gone. A thick duvet of grey cloud has appeared in the west, and the wind appears to be freshening by the minute.

We pause for a moment on the promenade. The waves are beginning to break out at sea, sporting brief little collars of white spume, and offshore I can see a lone windsurfer, stitching up and down, riding the magic carpet beneath his feet. From time to time, he takes off on the bigger waves, making tiny adjustments to his weight on the board before skimming off on another tack.

'Amazing.' Mitch is shaking his head. 'Someone under fifty, has to be.'

I ignore the dig. The willowy figure beneath the scarlet sail belongs in a circus, and the harder I look, the more I'm convinced I know him.

'His name's Presley,' I tell Mitch. 'I think.'

We elect to settle on the nearby wooden bench. From his messenger bag, Mitch has produced a pair of binoculars. He tracks the lone windsurfer for a minute or two, smiling at his wilder tricks, then hands the binos to me. I'm right. I recognize the hair streaming out in the wind, the breadth of his shoulders, the sheer reach he seems to have. Definitely Presley.

For a long time, like the spectators we are, we enjoy the performance. Then comes a wave that is too big, and too mean, even for Presley. His board rears up and he briefly fights to control it before the next wave dumps him in the sea. He must be two hundred metres out, maybe even more. Through the powerful binos, I can almost touch him as he struggles to flip the sail across the board, but this is a battle even Budleigh's superman doesn't seem to be winning.

'What do we do?' Mitch is looking worried.

'We wait. He's good. Let's see what happens.'

I've still got the binos. Presley has finally flipped the rig and a brief lull between waves gives him the chance to get both feet into the straps and let the filling sail pull him upright. For a full minute, he's arrowing out to sea, cresting wave after wave, getting smaller by the minute, then comes an opportunity to haul the board around, and suddenly the black shape is getting bigger and bigger. He's riding the wave train now, the wind at his back, fighting to maintain his balance as the board plunges into trough after trough. I'm no expert but this, I suspect, is a real test, even for someone as accomplished as Presley.

'You mind?'

I give the binos back to Mitch, but I don't need them anymore. Presley is approaching the beach at an alarming speed, his body braced for impact. Twenty metres out, the waves are rearing and breaking but he bursts through an explosion of spume to wrestle the board off the wind and let the sail collapse in the pounding surf. For a moment, I assume the next wave will claim him and drag him back, but he's even stronger than I think, limping over the pebbles, dragging the board up the steepness of the beach.

'I think he's hurt himself.' I'm on my feet, jumping off the promenade and on to the pebbles. There are fishing boats hauled up on the beach and I do my best to keep running as I dodge the litter of crab pots and coiled rope. I can see Presley's head and shoulders now, as he struggles up towards the fold of pebbles that overlooks the tideline, and then comes a corner of red sail, and finally the whole rig.

He's sitting on the pebbles rubbing his right leg before I make it down to him. When I ask him whether he's OK, he squeezes the saltwater out of his eyes and nods.

'Blew up quicker than I thought,' he says wryly.

By now, Mitch has joined us. I introduce him to Presley, and the two men exchange nods. Then Mitch stares at the wall of breakers thundering on to the beach.

'Madness.' He shakes his head. 'What you did was insane.'

'Coming back?'

'Being out there at all.'

'Yeah?' Presley is rubbing his leg again. 'Has to be done, sometimes. You know what I mean?'

Mitch doesn't, but I think I get the drift.

'Did you get a visit last night?' I ask him. 'Our friends in blue?'

'Big time.'

'And?'

'They went through that workshop of mine. Walked away with a load of timber, plywood, screws, even sawdust off the floor. Same with Beth. Paintbrushes, mainly, plus some sampler pots she'd been using.'

'Any explanation?'

'None. I got a receipt, though, if I could only read the bloke's writing.'

Mitch has torn himself away from watching the waves.

'You're a carpenter?' he asks Presley.

'I am.'

'And you knew Christianne?'

'Yes. Lovely woman. She had a go at this once in sensible weather.' He nods down at his board. 'She did better than I thought. Dodgy balance but swam like a fish.'

Like a fish.

Mitch and I carry that thought back to the promenade and along to the beginnings of the coastal path as it rises towards the golf course. I explain in detail about the search mounted to try and find Christianne after McFaul had reported her missing.

'But she hadn't gone at all? Is that what you're saying?'

'Yes. I didn't think so at the time, but I was wrong. I took the man at his word, just like the police did. He was playing games. I'm guessing he wanted some kind of alibi.'

'For what?'

'For her death. No body. No clues.'

'You think he killed her?'

'I think he played a part. Is that the same thing? I gather the law says it is, more or less. McFaul's disappeared now, I never mentioned that.'

'Very wise. Do you know where he is?'

'No. He was on police bail. One of the things he had to surrender was his passport.'

'Are you in touch?'

'No. McFaul has nerves of steel. I doubt any of us will ever see him again, least of all the police.' I'm lying about McFaul, and I suspect Mitch knows it. Hours ago, back in the bungalow, I knew I'd sparked his interest, but now he's definitely hooked. When he truly engages with a story, he has a habit of clamming up. No more small talk. No stream of consciousness.

By now we're approaching the semicircle of police Do Not Cross tape that seals the path to the site of the cliff fall. A young PC stands in front of it, the collar of his high-vis jacket turned up against the first flurries of rain.

'Any chance?' Mitch shows him his Press Card.

'None, sir, I'm afraid. Visits by appointment only.'

'Who do I talk to?'

'There's a DC on the enquiry. Part of the Major Crimes team. Call the main force number and ask for DC Atkinson.'

'I know Brett,' I say at once. 'I'm sure he wouldn't mind.'

'Brett?' The young PC looks amused. 'And you are?'

'My name's Andressen. Enora will do.'

'Fine.' The smile widens. 'I'll pass your compliments on.'

TWENTY-NINE

Disgruntled, Mitch steps back on to the coastal path and we trudge on. Soon, we're walking beside the golf course, which is largely deserted.

'It's Christmas,' I tell him. 'I expect they're all buying presents for their wives.'

'Yeah?' Mitch wants to know about my friend Bill. Might this be the moment for a surprise visit?

'Of course,' I say lightly. 'There's a hole in the fence up here. We can get to his place across the golf course.'

The rain is much heavier now, and by the time we finally make it to *chez* Bill we're both soaked. The rain has brought with it an early dusk and the lights are on inside Bill's house as we step in from the road. Parked on the sweep of gravel drive is a police forensics van, and when I look up to the first-floor window, I catch a glimpse of a hooded figure clad in a grey one-piece, peering at something in his gloved hand.

Bill comes to meet us at the door.

'What's going on?' I gesture towards the van.

'Routine enquiries, my dear. Our friends in blue earning their crusts. Come in. You're soaking wet. Just like last time.'

I introduce Mitch and step inside, grateful for the sudden warmth. Bill departs in search of towels and we stand in the hall. Upstairs, through an open door, I can hear a low murmur of conversation and then the hiss of an aerosol, while Mitch seems more interested in the pictures on the wall.

One of them is a watercolour. Rocks in the foreground frame the view beyond. Pine clad hills descend to a valley. It must be autumn because little patches of deciduous trees have turned golden in the thin sunlight, and the soft swell of a mountain on the far horizon is shrouded with an eiderdown of greyish cloud.

'The Harz Mountains – you know them?' Bill has returned, silent as a ghost.

'*Ja. Das ist die Blocksberg am Horizont?*'

'*Die Brocken, ja. Sprechen sie Deutsch?*'

'*Ich spreche ein wenig.*' Mitch is still gazing at the watercolour. 'You painted this?'

'You're too kind, but I'm afraid not. We used to walk in the Harz at weekends, my wife and I. October was always our favourite, just a nibble of winter in the air. I saw that painting in a gallery in Bad Harzburg. Far more than I could really afford, but I had to have it. To do justice to a view like that in watercolours is remarkable.' He smiles. 'My compliments, Mitch. You're only the second person who's ever put a name to that view.'

'And the first?' It's a question I can't resist.

'Christianne, of course. Come with me. You'll catch your death here.'

We have tea in Bill's cavernous kitchen. He's careful to shut the door. From upstairs comes the faint whine of something that sounds like a Hoover.

'Maybe they're tidying up,' I say brightly. 'Maybe it's a housecleaning visit. Getting you ready for Christmas.'

'Sweet thought.' Bill is rummaging for a tin of biscuits. 'They only appear to be interested in that one bedroom, the one you liked so much. That, I suppose, is a blessing.'

'Have they told you what they're after?' This from Mitch.

'God, no. A word of explanation would have been more than welcome, but you never get beyond the old excuse.'

'Which is?'

'"I'm only obeying orders, sir. Better ask my boss."'

'And have you?' I ask.

'I'm afraid not. There are special treats I save up for the weekend, but talking to DI Bullivant isn't one of them.'

'You've met him?'

'No, but Nathan has. Water off a duck's back, he says. Man's as tight as a clam. Barely gives you the time of day.'

'They're searching Nathan's place, too?'

'No. I gather he had to meet them this morning at the golf club. I don't think they parted friends. Ahh . . .' He's found the biscuit tin. 'Only shortbread, I'm afraid, but help yourselves.'

While Bill pours the tea and opens the doors on the Aga for more warmth, Mitch asks him about Christianne. What was she like? He makes the question sound innocent, but I know this is simply bait on the line. He's in full investigative mode now, and Bill seems to sense it.

'Interesting question.' He sits down at the big, bare table. 'You'll know she wasn't well, but part of the magic of that dear, dear woman lay in the fact that she had guts as well as guile. She needed guts to cope with the thought of what was to come. And she needed guile to pretend that none of it much mattered.'

I chime in here and tell Mitch what a surprise it was to learn from McFaul just what an impact the disease had already made on their lives. She'd reach for a wine glass and miss. She had problems with her balance. Her legs obviously hurt her some-times. But always there was a reason, an excuse, symptoms lightly dismissed, her body telling her she was simply getting older.

'I had a friend with motor neurone disease,' Mitch says.

'Had?'

'He's dead now. He died last year at a hospice in Bristol. Horrible death. You somehow think that palliative care means what it says on the tin, that there's nothing that can resist all the drugs we've dreamt up, but that's just not true. He died in agony, physical, mental, spiritual, the lot. I was there at the end, supporting his partner. The guy thought it was unspeakable. I think it opened his eyes.'

'To what?'

'To just how unprepared we really are. Death's become a commodity, almost a lifestyle choice. You can have a good one, or a brilliant one, or it can sometimes happen without you really noticing. No one ever tells you it really bloody hurts.'

Bill nods. The Hoover noise upstairs has gone, and we can hear nothing except the stir of the wind in the trees outside. We exchange glances around the table. Mitch helps himself to another biscuit. Then comes the lightest tap on the door and a face appears. It's one of the forensic team. I've seen him before outside McFaul's bungalow.

'All done, sir.' He might have been laying a carpet or attending to the central heating.

'And?'

'Not for me to say, sir. I expect someone from the MIR will be in touch.' The MIR, as I know from my previous dealings with Brett Atkinson, is the Major Incident Room.

Bill gets to his feet. As courteous as ever, he accompanies the investigator across the hall and sees him off the premises.

'Happy Christmas to you and yours,' he calls, before shutting the front door.

Back in the kitchen he resumes his seat with a sigh.

'This becomes a little tiresome after a while.' He's looking at me. 'Don't you find that?'

'I do. Of course I do.' I hesitate a moment, wondering if this is the time and place. 'That lovely chaise longue of yours. You know they've seized that, too?'

'They have?' This news appears to come as a surprise. 'So where is it?'

'Wherever they keep these things. Some laboratory or other? I've no idea.'

'I gave it to Andy.' He's frowning now. 'It was meant as a souvenir really. Christianne always adored it, and he knew that. Better in his little place than mine. Still . . .' He shrugs. 'Maybe they'll return it one day. Who knows?'

Mitch wants to get back to Christianne. He's familiar with MND. He knows it's unsparing, remorseless, beyond the reach of any known cure, and on those grounds alone he's astonished at Christianne's evident resilience.

'Was she religious?' he asks.

'Not at all. She was raised a Catholic, went to Mass every week as a child, got confirmed at fourteen like most of her classmates, but I gathered from Andy that Africa put an end to all that, and not – in his book – before time.'

'This is McFaul?' Mitch is looking at me.

'Andy? Yes.'

'And they were close? The pair of them?'

'Very.' Bill again. 'Andy was never the most demonstrative of men, but I know he thought the world of her. He and I worked on the coastal path together, Enora may have mentioned it. He told me in the summer that she could hold her own against any man he'd ever met, and praise from Andy, believe me, comes no higher.'

'Hold her own how?'

'Physically. Mentally. Spiritually. In every way you can ever imagine, that woman was an inspiration. She had the light inside her. You'd follow her to the ends of the earth. Andy never used those words, but that's what he meant.'

Mitch nods. I can almost see him making mental notes. He's in the middle of another question, about Budleigh this time, and what on earth the pair of them were doing here, when the kitchen door opens again. Another face I recognize.

'Sylvester.' I get to my feet, give him a hug.

He's rubbing his face – says he's taken a nap. I introduce him to Mitch.

'Bill's son,' I tell him. 'And Malo's saviour.' I turn back to Sylvester and then nod at the rain streaming down the window. 'Not out running? Is that guilt you can feel?'

I go into far too much detail about Sylvester's athletic prowess until even Bill is suggesting I shut up.

'Malo is Enora's son.' Sylvester is looking at Mitch. 'And now part of a little business of mine.'

Mitch nods, and then raises an eyebrow. When he first met Malo, three years ago, my son was zombied out on Spice and God knows what else, but H took him in hand and helped sort him out. This is the first time Mitch has heard about a full-time job.

'So what do you do?' he asks Sylvester.

'We market survival packages. Think Doomsday. That's where everything begins and ends.'

This is a wonderful come-on and I know Mitch wants to press him for more, but it's Sylvester who changes the subject.

'You know they're getting married? Clemmie and your boy?' He's looking at me. 'Congratulations, Mum. He popped the question last night. Put February the fourteenth in your diary. Doomsday permitting.'

Mitch and I say our goodbyes to Bill in the hall. He's found an umbrella he says we're welcome to keep, and he gives me the warmest hug before extending a bony hand to Mitch.

'What's your family name, by the way? Do you mind me asking?'

'Not at all. It's Culligan. We were Irish, back in the day.'

'Ahhh . . .' Bill nods. 'And you're a journalist?'

'Yes.'

'The *Guardian*, am I right?'

'Yes. From time to time.'

'I see. And you're here for some kind of colour piece?' He nods towards the watercolour of the Harz mountains. 'Travel section? The glories of East Devon?'

Mitch holds his gaze. He says nothing but smiles and then shakes his head.

'Excellent.' Bill steps towards the front door. 'I rather thought not.'

Mitch and I spend the evening with Evelyn. Mitch orders a takeout from the Indian restaurant and drives down to the High Street to pick it up. En route, he stops for a pint at The Feathers to sample Budleigh on a Saturday night. Back with Rogan Josh, chicken jalfrezi, and a delicious prawn biryani, he's evidently bewildered by the rules that govern the skittles alley. Evelyn does her best to help him out, but it's quickly evident that Mitch isn't as pubby as I once thought. But there's also good news. On the way back, though he can't be absolutely sure, he thinks he may have seen a black man. This, he says, makes him feel much more at home.

Over dinner, we carefully avoid any mention of Christianne. I share the news about Malo's coming betrothal, fed up that he hasn't bothered to tell me, but Evelyn tells me not to worry. At worst, it's simply an oversight. At best, he's saving it for a surprise. Either way, we all agree that it's the best possible news. Clemmie has been through a great deal with my son, and a lot of it would have killed the relationship stone dead with any other woman, so the fact that she's going to be part of our little family fills me with something I can only describe as joy. Mitch excuses himself when we've finished the curry and goes upstairs to make a few notes. I share a pot of coffee with Evelyn, and then tell her I can wait no longer.

'What for, my lovely?'

'I have to phone him. Just to make sure Sylvester's not making it up.'

She smiles and wishes me good luck. Upstairs, I have the bigger of the two spare bedrooms. For whatever reason, I've always had a talent to move around very quietly, even as a kid. My mother, not altogether in jest, used to call me *le fantôme*, the ghost. Now, at the top of the stairs, I can't help pausing outside Mitch's door. He's on the phone, I'm guessing to a contact on some paper or other.

'This is about what's gonna happen down the road,' he's saying. 'And in most respects, it's fucking perfect. This place is a waiting room. Most people have come here to die. Don't get me wrong, it's lovely, and I'm sure they've made the perfect choice, but imagine the way we're all gonna be in ten years' time, in twenty years' time. It's Johnson's England writ small. There'll be blow-back from that body on the beach, I guarantee it, and how this place copes will tell us all a great deal.' He pauses. I can hear a voice at the other end, but I can't make out what he's saying. Then Mitch is back on the line. 'You heard it here first, my friend.' He's not laughing. 'Stay tuned, eh?'

THIRTY

By the time I get down in the morning for breakfast, Mitch has found what he's after on YouTube. Quarter past eight in the morning is a little early for hardcore footage like this, but it seems I don't have a choice. The video comes from a hospice appeal in California. The featured patient is a forty-six-year-old former university lecturer, married, with three children. He was, we're told, a marathon runner before MND ambushed him and took him down. He's now been in the hospice, which is in Palo Alto, for just over a month, and looking at the footage, Mitch suspects he's nearing the end of the road.

The sequence we watch is heartbreaking. The patient's name is Adam. He's sitting in a wheelchair, trackie bottoms and a white T-shirt, his thin body twisted, his knees clamped together, his head at a strange angle. The challenge is to transfer him into a seat at the table and, according to the voiceover, Adam is determined to achieve this simple manoeuvre by himself. It's obvious, though, that this will be impossible. Two attendants, one of them male, hover on either side of the wheelchair, ready to catch him as he falls, while a third figure – evidently a nurse – kneels in front of him. She's concerned about Adam's throat.

'It's beginning to constrict,' Mitch mutters. 'That's what happens.'

'Constrict?'

'Barely function. You can't swallow. You can't even breathe properly.'

This appears to be the case, and what makes it worse is that Adam can't talk, either. Whatever he's trying to say comes out as a long slither of grunts and other half-formed noises. Finally, the doctor realizes he needs water. His throat is burning. Please put the fire out.

One of the attendants steps away. Very slowly, Adam's huge head comes round, trying to track what he's doing, while his long, thin arms first flail and then twitch in a grotesque parody of some tribal dance. This, I think, has all the makings of an epileptic fit in slow motion, every limb moving inch by inch through the glue that is motor neurone disease, Adam's mouth gaping open, his head thrust back, then forward, then very slowly sideways as the attendant reappears with the kind of plastic non-spill cup you might offer a small child.

Adam is still in the wheelchair, his hands plucking at thin air, and then the nurse comes closer, trying to calm him, trying to tease the lip of the cup into his open mouth, but the sheer weight of this poor man's head is beyond his control, and it rolls back and forth until the male attendant physically steadies it, both hands, and then gently tips it back, allowing the water to trickle down Adam's throat.

Evelyn has joined us. She stands behind the sofa, staring down at the laptop. The frozen image of Adam's tortured face hangs on the screen, and then come contact details for the Palo Alto hospice foundation while a warm American voice urges us to be generous with our contributions. The voice repeats the contact details, then we hear Adam again, a faint gargle of agreement, or perhaps a thank you for the water, or maybe something else – some strangled plea for help that none of us will ever fully understand.

'Ghastly.' Evelyn is appalled. 'Everyone should see this. Send the link to Beth. She'll know what to do with it.'

At midday, at Mitch's suggestion, all three of us go up to the golf club. I take the precaution of phoning Nathan in advance, and he says we're very welcome to join him for drinks at the bar, and perhaps lunch afterwards. I find a space in the car park and help Evelyn out of the car. Mitch, as ever, sees no point in sartorial compromise, even here. A steady drift of players in Glenmuir shirts and Ryder Cup trousers are making their way into the clubhouse from a morning on the links, while Mitch has no intention of abandoning his jeans, Doc Martens and scruffy grey anorak.

The bar is already busy. Nathan, I suspect, has been watching out for us and spots me at once. When he insists on buying a round of drinks, Mitch asks for a pint of Guinness. He seems to know already that Mitch is a journalist and I'm still wondering whether Bill has marked his card when he appears at my elbow.

'Blind guess, I'm afraid.' Nathan hands me a large gin and tonic. 'But might I be right?'

Evelyn gets the same treatment. The pair of us settle at a table in the corner of the bar, while I try yet again to get hold of my errant son. Is he really getting married, as Sylvester seems to believe? And if so, when? His number rings and rings, and in the end I have to leave a message that's more curt than I'd like. *Married already? Ring me.*

I reach for my glass, returning to the business in hand. Mitch is already working the room, towed from introduction to introduction by the tireless Nathan. This is fascinating. Mitch is clearly an outsider, a virus in Budleigh's body politic. Nathan, on the other hand, has an almost imperial presence, touching arm after arm, ignoring the archest of glances and side looks at Mitch, encouraging conversations, validating his guest's abrupt appearance in this most familiar of settings. A friend of mine, he seems to be saying. Talk to him. Lower your guard. Make him feel at home. In a bygone age, yonks ago, Nathan might have been walking in front of one of those early steam engines, carrying a red flag. Take care, but give thanks. This new creature in all our lives won't hurt you. *Au contraire.*

I've never seen Nathan like this, performing with such guile, and as I watch I begin to understand what must have made him such a successful QC. He has, after all, got the common touch. He's also a superb salesman. Mitch's boots? Mitch's beard? The way he bends into a new conversation, immediately engaged, listening, nodding, filing everything away in that giant brain of his? No problem. For a day or two, after the cliff fall, this is the way life's going to be. This is one of our brighter scribblers. Enjoy the man. Talk to him.

And they do. Evelyn's aware of it, as well. In a whispered aside she confesses that this is the first time she's been to the golf club, but scanning the bar, she identifies face after face. A leading neurologist, recently retired, with a handsome spread in the same avenue as Bill. The new owner of the loveliest address in East Terrace, a rumoured financial wizard who recently sold his Mayfair-based hedge fund for untold trillions and acquired a trophy American wife after the briefest dalliance on the Aspen ski slopes. A rag trade entrepreneur, absurdly young-looking, who apparently made a fortune in high-end sportswear.

All of these people are incomers, DFLs, and between them – according to Evelyn – they can scarcely summon a decade in residence, yet I get the feeling that Budleigh has settled on them in some unfathomable way. They've formed little circles of like-minded buddies, refer to the town's butcher by his Christian name, agree how lucky they are to have the best fish and chip shop, and the best literary festival, on the south coast, and argue about the toughest hole on the course beyond the picture windows. They might have been here forever, I marvel, and I'm guessing very few of them will ever leave.

'Budleigh?' Mitch has re-joined us, and on the evidence of his little tour of the bar I've asked him what he makes of Evelyn's new home. 'It's a state of mind,' he mutters. 'It's monied, it's nice to look at, and I'm betting the house prices have dug a moat around the place. If you want to settle down and turn your back on all the other shit that's going on, you could do a lot worse. These people know what they're about. They're used to making their own decisions. I bet some of them are risk-takers, too, and that gets in the blood.'

'So, what did you talk about?'

'Your French friend, mainly. It's hard not to.'

'And?'

'There's a big thumbs-up for that guy of hers. The one who did a runner. No one seems too bothered about how she ended up buried on the top of the cliff, but I get the feeling they think he made the right decision.'

'By doing a runner?'

'By helping her die. That's an assumption, of course, but these people have been around a bit. One or two of them knew him personally. Said he was bloody difficult but always his own man. Coming from these people, that's a compliment, of course. Fair, do you think?'

'Very. Especially the difficult bit.'

Nathan joins us with a bottle of wine and four glasses. The last half hour has put him in a new light. I shared this thought with Evelyn when he was busy hosting Mitch and she thinks his previous gaucheness was down to not knowing quite how to cope with me. This might be a compliment. If it is, I'm not sure I altogether agree with her, but either way it doesn't matter. There's roast beef on the menu, medium rare, and Evelyn can't wait.

Nathan, in keeping with his new role, is the perfect host. Charm, it turns out, comes easy to him, and he coaxes Mitch to open up about the life of a London-based investigative reporter. Mitch, as I know only too well, is world-class when it comes to professional camouflage, preferring to watch and listen rather than talk, but he allows Nathan a peek or two at just how tough the media business has become. Try to sell anything these days, he says, and you join the race to the bottom. Everything's going tabloid. No one has any time, nor – when it comes to making a living – do they have any money.

'Which I imagine puts the onus on you?'

'Of course. Big time. You have to find the sweet spot. You have to touch the right nerve. I used to spend weeks, sometimes months, getting on top of some really complex stories.'

'Like?'

'Financial scandals, mainly. Sometimes corporate stuff, sometimes international tax issues, sometimes huge political fuck-ups, often around procurement, and the figures involved would blow your mind. It was worthy and fascinating but a complete waste of time. You end up talking to yourself because no one's listening.'

'And why might that be?'

'Because you have to concentrate to understand this stuff, and because – in the end – no one gives a shit. It either boils down to fraud or incompetence, and both turn out to be like the weather, just a fact of life. Always was, always will be. Get over it. Have another drink. That's great if you happen to be minted but sadly most people aren't, and it's them that sad old bastards like me start worrying about.'

'Which makes you a socialist?'

'Of course. And that's another car crash. Especially after Thursday.'

'Bit of a shame, I imagine.'

'Fucking disaster. Do I blame Brexit? Yes. Do I blame Corbyn? Yes. Do I still have a living to make? Yes.'

Nathan nods. I can tell he's enjoying this. I also sense he has just a grain or two of admiration for Mitch's candour.

'Race to the bottom?' he muses. 'Where does that take you?'

'Don't ask. Benjamin Franklin once said that nothing matters in life but death and taxes, and in my book he got the first bit spot-on. Death sells. And so does sex. And so do cooking programmes. We've hit peak obvious, peak in-your-face. Everyone dies. Everyone wants to get laid. Everyone's after something different on their plate. Address any of those, and you'll probably earn a quid or two. Tax havens in Monaco or the Caymans? Forget it. Consultants trousering billions on government contracts? *So* retro. Vagina-scented candles? Bring 'em on.'

This, in my book, is a *tour de force*. I want to clap, and judging by the grin on her face, so does Evelyn. Not only has Mitch turned a career crisis into the blackest humour, but he's also right. We are, by any civilized measure, doomed.

'And Christianne?' Nathan isn't smiling.

'Very dead,' Mitch agrees.

'And might that make your point?' I ask.

'Point?'

'That we all face death? That death can bloody hurt? That some of us might choose not to wait? Regardless of the law?'

Mitch is eyeing the lengthening queue at the buffet. Like Evelyn, he can't wait to get his hands on the glistening side of beef.

'Indeed, it might.' Mitch's gaze settles on Nathan. 'Do your guys make their own horseradish sauce here?'

After lunch, Mitch peels off. Over plum duff and custard, he's secured the offer of a flight in Nathan's Cessna and agreed a take-off time early tomorrow afternoon from Dunkeswell Airfield. He needs to take shots of the cliff face scarred by the fall, and of the pile of debris on the foreshore where Christianne's coffin came to rest. I'm very welcome to come, too, but Evelyn has declined. Commercial flights, she told us, frighten her witless. The very thought of entrusting herself to anything smaller is out of the question.

And so now, with Nathan's blessing, Mitch shambles away across the golf course, oblivious to a party of four teeing-off nearby. I watch him from the car park for a moment or two, wondering about the call I overheard last night. Despite his bluntness at the table, I know he'll never join the race to the bottom. Like McFaul in some ways, he's too difficult, too prin-cipled, too stubborn. He understands what sells only too well, but he's a great deal brighter and more honest than most journalists I've met. In the shape of the coffin on the beach, an image that has gone around the world, he has the best possible start to whatever he ends up writing, but I know he'll take the story way, way further.

Back home, Evelyn announces that she'd appreciate a little time alone in St Peter's. On Sunday afternoons, she says the church is empty and when she says she needs a bit of peace and quiet to have a think about things, I tell her I understand completely. Peace and quiet, of course, is Evelyn's private code for a prayer or two, but I know the aftershocks of Thursday's cliff fall have hit her badly, and if God can help, then so much the better. She gives me a hug before she leaves.

'I don't know how I'd have coped without you, these last few days,' she says. 'Why don't you move down full time?'

Why not, indeed? Alone in the bungalow, I do the thesp thing, abandon real life and plunge myself into the world of make-believe. I've taken Evelyn's advice, turned my back on London and what's left of my career, and traded Holland Park for Budleigh Salterton. What would I gain? And what, perhaps more importantly, would I lose? Could I really flourish in the company of the kind of people I've been watching at the golf club? Would I do a Christianne, and take the plunge with the other year-round swimmers? Could I really build a life on bridge parties and a twirl or two around the croquet lawn? Might, in short, there be a little niche for a still-working divorcee with a dormant tumour in her brain and a French cop series to nail? The answer, I conclude, is an emphatic no, and I'm about to browse Evelyn's new bookshelves in search of something to read when I hear a knock at the door.

I take a precautionary peek through the bay window. To my surprise, it's Beth. She sees me at once and smiles. Knowing I have no alternative, I open the door and invite her in. She gives me a hug. This is surprise number two. The last time I saw her, she blanked me. Now this.

'Coffee?' I hear myself saying.

'Water will be fine. Tap, please. Nothing from a bottle.'

I fetch a glass of water and we sit together in the lounge. Beth apologizes at once for, as she puts it, being such a cow to me. On reflection, she's decided my need to question her story about the way Christianne really died was meant in good faith, and in some respects she doesn't blame me. As an outsider, she says, I must find this whole thing really puzzling, and she doesn't blame me for that, either.

I nod, say nothing. The really interesting thing, then and now, is that she lied to me, and to the others, but I somehow assume she's made her peace with them as well. Maybe she claimed artistic licence. Maybe that night at Bill's table she was simply drunk. Either way, she's right. It's over. Done. Gone.

'That hospice footage Evelyn sent me,' she says. 'Who's Mitch?'

'A friend of mine.' The news that Mitch is a journalist, London-based, grabs her attention at once.

'And his second name?'

'Culligan.'

'Should I know him?'

'Only if you read the *Guardian*, or the *New Statesman*, or happen to pull up his website. He's a dying breed, a threatened species. His kind of journalism will be extinct before long.'

'Really? And he has connections? Contacts? Still gets into print?'

'Yes. I think it's getting much harder for him, but there are still ways and means.'

'So what's he doing down here?'

'He's a friend of mine,' I tell her again. 'But he'll be back in a minute, so you can ask him yourself.'

Mitch takes longer to make it back from the golf course than I'd anticipated. It's raining again, and he's soaking when he finally turns up. Beth has been pressing me for location gossip from my last movie, but the moment she hears the knock at the door, she breaks off and gets to her feet. This afternoon's outfit, a mash-up of Budleigh *bien pensant* and middle-aged vamp, perfectly showcases her figure. Normally she wears loose outfits that leave a great deal to the imagination, but not on this occasion. For a woman who must be in her forties, she's in extraordinary shape.

'This is he?' she mouths.

'It is.'

I sort out Mitch on the doorstep. He removes his Doc Martens, which are thick with mud, while I field his anorak and shake off the excess rain. I'm about to take him into the lounge but Beth has beaten me to it. She's standing in the hall, looking winsome.

I do the introductions. Mitch is studying her with some interest.

'Your name again?'

'Beth. I came to say thank you.'

'For what?'

'That link Evelyn sent. It's exactly what I've been after. You must have read my mind.'

I retreat to the kitchen with Mitch's anorak and leave them to it. By the time I get back to the lounge, they're both sitting on the sofa. Beth has her legs tucked beneath her, a faintly yogic pose, while Mitch has stockinged feet propped on Evelyn's beanbag. Mitch has a real talent for putting people at their ease, for sensing how best to get them talking, but with Beth he's spared that effort. All he has to do is listen.

As I settle into Evelyn's armchair, she's telling him about the impact the hospice footage made on her. Powerful, she says, doesn't begin to cut it. Ever since Christianne disappeared, she's been trying to find a bunch of images that might explain why someone with her problems, someone confronted with the guarantee of an ugly, ugly death, might take things into their own hands. She's tried the Dignity in Dying people. She's poked around the internet. She's even been in touch with survivors – wives, husbands, best friends – who might have taken a photo or two as the end approached. But in every case, she's hit a brick wall.

'People don't want to talk about it, don't want to tell you how horrible it is, won't let you close enough. It's like the end is some kind of secret. So tell me, be honest, how crazy is that?'

'Very crazy.' Mitch is examining a hole in his sock. 'So, what happens next?'

'I develop that hospice footage, put it to good use.'

'How?'

'I don't know yet, but I'm well placed, believe me. We're a

tight little community. When the call comes, we rally round. Would a literary festival be good? It happens. Might we do something similar on the music side? No problem. Last year we got that amazing young cellist, Sheku Kanneh-Mason. Can you believe that? Sleepy little Budleigh Salterton? So, stuff happens, not by accident but because we *make* it happen. It's going to be the same with Christianne, with MND. The will of the people, isn't that the phrase?'

Mitch is nodding. He's abandoned his sock.

'You're thinking some kind of public showing? For that footage?'

'Of course.'

'And copyright?'

'No problem.'

'How come?'

'Listen, Mitch.' Beth's on fire now, I've seen her this way before. Her eyes are alive, there's a blush of colour in her face, and she's bent forward on the sofa, offering Mitch a perfect view of what my mum would call her *embonpoint*. 'I emailed the Palo Alto people as soon as I saw the footage. One of their stakeholders came back to me about an hour ago. I didn't even have to explain about last Thursday and the cliff fall and Christianne and everything because she'd seen the pictures already. I told her we'd like to spread the word, seed a campaign, and that those pictures of Adam might be key. Adam is dead now but she's going to contact the family and get back to me. I said we'd be taking a collection locally if we're allowed to use the footage and send her the proceeds. She thought that was neat.'

'Campaign for what?'

'Mercy killings. Euthanasia. That's where it begins and ends, Mitch. That's the opportunity we're staring in the face.'

'Thanks to Christianne?'

'Of course. And you.'

'Me?'

'Yeah. For two reasons. Number one, the link you found. Number two, that wonderful piece you're going to write.'

'About?'

'Us. Chris. MND. And Budleigh bloody Salterton. This is going to be a turning point, Mitch, in that whole fucking debate.

And you guys in the media are still the ones who write the first draft of history. Isn't that the truth?'

She sits back at last, feigning exhaustion, but I can see that Mitch is impressed. I suspect what he needs is a lock on this story, a way of making it his very own, and in the shape of Beth he appears to have exactly that.

'And I get exclusive rights?' he murmurs. 'Is that what I'm hearing?'

Beth nods. In these situations, as I'm beginning to recognize, she's never less than impulsive.

'Yours,' she says.

'Why? Why not look further? Why not sell those rights? You've got the mainstream rat pack all over you. Why not have a conversation or two? Earn yourselves a big fat cheque?'

'Because we're not like that, Mitch. Not down here. And because Enora says you're the best. An endorsement like that, what choice does a girl have?'

It's a bravura performance on Beth's part, and she gives him a lingering hug before she steps out into the hall. I go with her, opening the front door and standing aside. I tell her that giving Mitch the inside lane will best safeguard Christianne's interests, as well as protecting the heart of the story from the grubby fingers of the tabloid press.

Beth nods. She couldn't agree more.

'Exciting times.' She nods towards the lounge. 'And a lovely guy, too.'

I smile, agree, and then plant a kiss on her cheek. An image of vagina-scented candles has drifted into my mind, but I do my best to resist it.

'He's gay, my love. Nice try, though.'

THIRTY-ONE

Bitch, bitch. Me, not Beth.

I sleep, once again, like a baby, not because I'm especially proud of my little doorstep adieu, but because I

know full well that Beth will dismiss it. One of her true strengths,
I've realized, is the sheer thickness of her skin. She has a gift
for total focus: on the next big thing, and then the one that might
– fingers crossed – follow after that. Once engaged with whatever
it might be, nothing can distract her, least of all anything that
little me might have to say. That kind of certainty, that total
commitment, is a huge asset when it comes to any kind of cause
and just now I realize we're very, very lucky to have her. Today,
with luck, Mitch and I will be largely alone. Thanks to Nathan,
we'll float over East Devon and descend on the scene of the
crime to give him the photos he wants. After that, Beth will
doubtless take over, but for now I have Mitch to myself.

Wrong. By the time we finally make it to the airfield at
Dunkeswell, Nathan has already arrived. I recognize his Mercedes
parked beside a pert little aeroplane with a red stripe down the
side. He has one of the covers up on the aircraft's nose, and he's
pouring oil into a plastic spout that disappears into the engine.
The sky-blue overalls rather suit him. With a leather helmet, and
perhaps a silk scarf, he could audition for any number of movies.

I join him beside the nose of the aircraft and give him a kiss
once he's put the oil can down. I tell him we're really grateful
for the flight and insist on helping out with the costs. The offer
seems to amuse him.

'This is the least I can do,' he says. 'I gather there's a crusade
in the making.'

'Crusade?' I'm momentarily lost, but then he closes the engine
cover and nods up at the windscreen. Beth already occupies
one of the two rear seats. She's busy on her phone but she gives
me a little wave.

'She was insistent on sitting up front.' Nathan laughs. 'I had
to defend Mitch's turf.'

Beth, it turns out, has caught wind of our outing from Bill,
and invited herself along. We take off shortly afterwards,
bumping over the frost-hardened turf and then lifting over the
onrushing line of trees as Nathan eases the control yoke back.
The weather, after yesterday's rain, is near-perfect: the bluest
of skies with just a scribble or two of cloud, plus a chilly wind
from the north-west. The visibility, in Beth's phrase, is awesome.
Nathan announces that we're levelling off at six thousand feet,

and from here we can see the rich green spread of the whole of East Devon.

We head due south, the sunshine already splintered on the enfolding embrace of Lyme Bay. To the right I can see the coast stretching away towards a distant headland while beyond the Exe Valley – according to Nathan – are the smudgy brown shoulders of Dartmoor. Beth, too, has brought a camera, and as we begin to lose height, I recognize the shape of Budleigh filling the windscreen. She takes shot after shot, shifting her weight in the cramped space, a gesture of excitement and – dare I say it – ownership. Nathan has given each of us a pair of headphones so we can talk above the steady cackle of the engine, and now he dips a wing to bring us in from the landward side of the golf course.

Mitch is gazing down. He's yet to raise his camera and he seems intent on grasping the geography of the course. To me, it looks like a moving version of the image I've seen on Google Earth, but Mitch asks for another circuit, a bit wider this time.

'You want more of the golf course?' Nathan checks.

'Yeah. Bit off to the left.'

By now we've cleared the jigsaw of fairways and greens, and for the first time I realize just how close the course is to the clifftop. We're much lower now, and as we race over the coastal path I briefly spot the tangle of undergrowth and bushes that surround the patch of flattened earth where Christianne must have been buried.

'Bloody hell,' Nathan says. 'There's been another land slip, maybe last night. See that?'

I follow his pointing finger as he drops a wing again for a closer look. Nathan is right. There's a fresh spill of debris on the beach at the foot of the cliff, and the dark reds of the Devon sandstone have turned the lapping waves a frothy pink.

'England bleeds.' Beth is taking more shots. 'This is fantastic, Nathan. Can you go any lower?'

England bleeds? It's an extravagant metaphor, Beth at full throttle, but she's right. The latest slip has left another wound in the face of this ancient cliff. Nathan is tightening the turn, giving both cameras a perfect view of Christianne's last resting place, and Mitch mutters his appreciation. I'm watching the aircraft's shadow dancing across the ochre planes of the cliff as Nathan climbs again to offer Mitch another angle on the golf course.

This time, it's perfect. Mitch fires off a series of shots and checks the results. Satisfied, he asks for one last pass over the sea at a thousand feet, Budleigh bathed in pale winter sunshine, the tide full, the promenade dotted with locals making the most of the weather.

'Done?' Nathan needs to know we're finished.

Both Mitch and Beth give him the thumbs up, and my stomach lurches as he drops a wing again and hauls the aircraft round in a 180-degree turn. We're heading west now, still over the sea, the long curve of the cliffs away to our right. Dunkeswell, I'm pretty certain, lies in the other direction.

'This is for Enora.' Nathan must have read my mind. 'A little trip down memory lane.'

I haven't a clue what this might mean, but already we're approaching the rich yellow spaces of Sandy Bay, with Exmouth visible beyond. Exmouth proper begins at a headland called Orcombe Point. We're slightly lower now, and I can see a string of horses splashing through the shallows, towing a gaggle of yapping dogs, and then Nathan is easing right again, following the curve of the beach, and through the windscreen I can see the oncoming dock entrance and the marina ringed with houses and apartments in various shades of New England pastel. Beyond the marina, on the very nose of the shingle spit that juts into the estuary, are two apartment blocks, slightly older than the rest of the development, and as Nathan begins to circle I find myself looking down on one of them.

The penthouse apartment at the top of the building used to belong to H and myself. This is the place we acquired for Pavel when we brought him down from London. The views, which are sensational, were wasted on my lovely friend because he was blind, as well as paralysed, but he'd spend night after night with his balcony doors open, listening to the soundtrack of this extra-ordinary stretch of water. The curlew was his favourite soloist, but he loved the yap-yap of the sandwich terns, and the honk of the Canada geese, and when we talked on the phone he was able to conjure an entire landscape from these clues.

Nathan is tightening the turn now, the penthouse slowly rotating beneath us. This is kind of him, and I appreciate the gesture, but what's slightly creepy is the fact that he knew where to come. I've never mentioned Pavel to him. Neither have I talked about his wonderful penthouse apartment.

He throws me a glance back across his shoulder. He wants to know if he got the right property.

'You did,' I say. 'So how come you knew?'

He shakes his head and chuckles. He won't say. And when I put the question again, this time with an edge of irritation, he murmurs something about the right friends in the right places. This could mean anything, which is probably why he said it, but I'm left with an uneasiness which refuses to go away. We're flying up the estuary now, with a perfect view of this vast sheet of water, but it's minutes later, back on course for Dunkeswell, before I hear Mitch on the intercom.

'You had a visit on Saturday.' He's talking to Nathan. 'Operation *Bulldog*? A couple of DCs?'

'You mean the golf club?'

'Yeah. I understand they wanted to know about your CCTV. Is that true?'

If Nathan is troubled by any of this, it doesn't show. On the contrary, unlike yours truly, he doesn't even ask for the source of this information. Instead, he compliments the police on their thoroughness.

'Smart move,' he says. 'They need to cover every base.'

'But why? What were they after?'

'I have no idea. I imagine it must go back to that weekend when Christianne disappeared. Unfortunate, really.'

'How come?'

Nathan breaks off to make a radio call to announce his descent into Dunkeswell. He throttles back and I feel the aircraft begin to sink beneath me. Only then does he return to Mitch.

'What they wanted were pictures from CCTV in the car park. Shame, really.'

'Why?'

'We have no cameras.'

THIRTY-TWO

Back on the ground at Dunkeswell, we all agree it's been an amazing flight. We say our thank-yous and our good-byes, and Nathan tells Mitch he's welcome up at the golf club any time. When he enquires how long Mitch might be staying in Budleigh, Mitch asks why.

'We may need to lay in more supplies of Guinness.' He pats Mitch's shoulder and nods at the camera. 'Glad you got the shots you need.'

Nathan chocks the aircraft wheels, locks the cabin door, and we linger to watch him joining Beth in the Mercedes. There's a complicity between them, something slightly arch and unspoken, and I know Mitch senses it too.

'Pub,' he grunts. 'We need to talk.'

It's lunchtime now, and I've anticipated this. On Evelyn's recommendation, we drive to a pub called the Drewe Arms in Broadhembury. Christmas is getting closer by the day and the bar is a riot of decorations, tinsel, and a big cardboard reindeer where locals are encouraged to leave presents for the staff. While Mitch finds a discreet table for two, I join the crowd at the bar and order a Guinness and a small glass of Merlot. By the time I join Mitch, he's got hold of a menu, and settled on hake and chips.

'So are they at it? Nathan and that crazy woman?' Conversationally, Mitch has no time for foreplay.

'It's possible, I suppose, but I doubt it.'

'He's married? Nathan?'

'Separated. He told me his wife's gone back to London. Never quite kicked the habit.'

'Budleigh didn't do it for her?'

'Not at all. Though I get the impression Nathan doesn't much care. Evelyn thinks he plays the field. He's got the money and he can be charming when it suits him so she's probably right.'

'And Beth?'

'Beth's in a seller's market. Presley does her very nicely indeed. Fit young man? Budleigh's trophy windsurfer? Just what she needs.'

Mitch is smiling. To my surprise, he seems to be warming to the soapier end of Budleigh Salterton.

'Life's a fucking game, isn't it? Even down here.'

'Especially down here. These people have time and money. Bill Penny told me that was the most dangerous combination in the world, and he's probably right.'

Mitch mentions a man called Harry Lupitt.

'Know him at all?' he asks.

'No.'

'I met him at the golf club. Interesting bloke. Can't stand our Nathan.'

'Interesting how?'

'He used to be a commander in the Met Police. Only retired a couple of years ago. His favourite detective superintendent joined the Devon and Cornwall lot, and now runs one of their Major Crime outfits. Thanks to him, Harry's up to speed on this *Bulldog* thing. He says they're concentrating on access.'

'To?'

'The clifftop. They think the coffin probably came over the golf course. In some kind of van, obviously.'

I nod, remembering the broad green spread of the golf course we'd seen from the aircraft. I've walked up the coastal path enough times to imagine how tough it would be to carry a coffin up there. Using a van to cross the golf course would be the obvious solution.

'I get the impression they think the grave was pre-dug.' Mitch hasn't finished. 'Once you get to the edge of the golf course it's obviously a carry, but with enough help that wouldn't have been a problem. Apparently there's a DI who's been driving *Bulldog* from the off, complete nutter, total obsessive, won't leave it alone.'

'His name's Bullivant,' I say at once. 'Frank Bullivant. He's a DI and he's about to retire.'

'One last job? Mention in despatches? Name in lights?' Mitch laughs and scribbles the name on the back of the menu before glancing up again. 'When I walked back yesterday, I was looking for tyre marks on the course itself, but we're probably talking months ago. In any case, Harry thinks the vehicle would have taken a special route, keeping off-piste.'

'Meaning Nathan was on board?'

'Yeah. Or someone else from the golf club. What I did yesterday was concentrate on the fence, the one between the golf course and that coastal path. From where I was standing it was easy to see the taped-off bit, and you know what? Exactly opposite, nearly touching distance, the barbed wire had been replaced, brand-new strands where someone must have cut the original. Bullivant would have seen that. You couldn't miss it. I'm assuming that's what took him to the golf club in the first place.'

I nod. Mitch has developed a sudden interest in the menu but the last thing I feel is hungry. He suggests we put an order in, and he's about to get to his feet, but I extend a restraining hand.

'You remember Presley? The windsurfer?'

'Yeah.'

'He's got a van.'

'Yeah?' Mitch sits down again. 'And he's with Beth, have I got that right?'

'You have.'

'She's arty? She paints?'

'Paints. Performs. Writes. Sends emails to Palo Alto. Anything to keep her in the limelight. This is a woman who can't help herself. Show her an audience, and she's on her feet.'

'Interesting.'

'Why?'

'Because Harry had a couple of other things for me. He told me there was something strange about the coffin. In the first place it was really basic, just marine ply, strong enough to carry the weight of a body but light to carry.'

'And the other thing?'

'The inside of the side panels were painted. Not just a wash of colour, but figure work, patterns, weird hieroglyphics. *Bulldog* thinks they were modelled on the Pharaohs. Think pyramids. Think Cheops.' He pauses, then checks the bar again. 'What do you think? Hake or the veggie option?'

I elect for neither. Presley has been raided, too, I remind him. *Bulldog* seized tools of his, and paints belonging to Beth. Then

I remember the brief conversation Presley had with Christianne, the morning she and I set off for the walk that took us to her favourite clifftop site. Presley was rummaging round in his van, parked outside Evelyn's bungalow. Catching sight of Christianne, he'd asked her whether she'd love it. At the time, I hadn't a clue what he meant. Now I'm beginning to suspect he was talking about the coffin he might have put together. In terms of decorative motifs to accompany Christianne to the afterlife, an Egyptian theme, to Beth, would have been beyond irresistible.

'Yeah?' Mitch doesn't seem to have understood me. He's on his feet now, looking towards the bar.

'I'd go for the hake,' he says. 'While there's still some left.'

After the pub, we drive slowly home, keeping to the country roads. Detective work has always fascinated me, and some of the best roles early on in my career came from cop thrillers. Cri-fi did the same for my ex-husband and Berndt ended up putting stellar Scandi scripts on the big screen, but in real life Mitch is exceptionally good at it. He knows which relationships to nurture, which investigative paths to follow, how to marry character strengths and weaknesses to an emerging pattern of clues. Christianne's death, and everything that's followed in her wake, has really caught his interest, not least because he senses wider ripples beyond the backwater that is Budleigh Salterton.

'Beth's on to it, too,' he grunts. 'Did you hear what she said in the plane? When we were looking at all that red muck in the sea? The soil from the cliff? *England bleeds*, she said. Credit to her, it's a great phrase. Every nation has a jugular and this one's no different.'

'You mean the UK?'

'No, *England*. That's what this story is about, and Beth knows it. I doubt she does loads of reading. I doubt she's up to speed on the demographics, and the wealth gap, and in-depth Brexit voter profiles, and all the rest of the *Economist* shit, but she doesn't have to be. All she has to do is take a deep breath and look around her. We're getting older. One per cent of us are getting way richer. Another ten per cent are doing just fine, and this Budleigh of hers is where a lot of them end up. Their dream is a ripe old age but they're starting to have a serious think about

what happens afterwards and what none of them want is a diagnosis like your Christianne's. That, dare I say it, would be a
major piss-off. Lots of these people will be offended, and you
know why? Because they've made their own decisions for most
of their lives, and now comes the biggest one of all, but – guess
what – the law is telling them what they can or can't do. Beth
gets that. These people are fighters. They have the money, and
the time, and the breeding, and the sheer balls to stand up for
themselves. They want the government out of their face. Nathan
gets it, too. The word he used was crusade.'

Crusade? I raise an eyebrow. This sounds just a little over-
the-top, Mitch at full throttle, but mention of our pilot has
prompted another thought.

'That little excursion to Exmouth this morning,' he says. 'You
were wondering how Nathan knew where to go.'

'And?'

'It turns out he also has a mate at police headquarters. Harry
hasn't got a name, but he seems to think it's someone at the top
of the organization.' He throws me a look. 'Would that make any
sense?'

It would, indeed. What happened back in the summer would
have gone to every corner of the organization, along with Pavel's
address. Millions of pounds' worth of cocaine? A body bleeding
out on the carpet of a local pub? A young DC glassed to within
an inch of his life? No wonder Nathan Kline knew where to
point his little plane.

'Thanks, Mitch.' I mean it. 'So, what happens next?'

THIRTY-THREE

Arrests, I later learn, are deliberately timed for six o'clock
in the morning. At that hour, few of us are in a good
place. Dazed, and a little hungover after sharing half a
bottle of brandy with Mitch last night, I open the front door in
Evelyn's borrowed dressing gown. There are two of them, both
middle-aged, both plain clothes, and the woman appears to be

in charge. She's looking me up and down. The dressing gown is way too small, and I'm freezing.

She asks me to confirm my name. I hold the door open and invite them in. The light in the hall is dim, but the woman knows the caution by heart. I'm to be arrested for conspiracy to murder. Anything I say may be taken down and used in evidence against me. Evelyn has left the radio on in the kitchen, a habit she's adopted to keep the bad guys away. These *are* the bad guys, I suspect, and we stand there for a moment, listening to some carol or other, before the woman volunteers to accompany me to my bedroom where I might like to get dressed.

We mount the stairs, and she turns her back while I pull on whatever comes to hand. Police stations are normally warm, so I resist the temptation to bring an extra woolly.

'Toothbrush? Flannel? Soap? Towel?'

I collect all four from the bathroom downstairs, wondering quite how long a stay these people are anticipating, and then hesitate outside Evelyn's bedroom door.

'Enora? Is that you?' It turns out she's heard the voices in the hall.

I put my head around her bedroom door. She's already found the switch for the little lamp beside her bed.

'What's happening?' she asks. 'What's going on?'

I explain I've just been arrested. Back soon, fingers crossed.

'Arrested for what?'

'Conspiracy . . .' I manage to muster a smile. 'To murder. Do you mind telling Mitch?'

Outside, it's still pretty dark. The woman handcuffs herself to me in the light from the door before we walk to the waiting car. Together, we sit in the back while the other detective takes the wheel. His driving, given the lack of traffic, verges on the sedate. Neither of my two companions has any interest in conversation and the journey passes in silence. Conspiracy to murder. Giving Christianne a helping hand. Bizarre.

By the time we get to Exeter, the rising sun is throwing long shadows over the car park behind Heavitree police station. This is where they took McFaul, back in September, I tell myself.

This is where he batted every question away with a tight-lipped 'No comment'.

I'm arraigned before the custody sergeant, who gets a complicated booking form on screen and types in my answers to a long list of questions. Down the nearby corridor I catch just a glimpse of Bill Penny in the company of a stout turnkey and I start to wonder how many other bodies have ended up in Operation *Bulldog's* trawl net. Conspiracy is an elastic term. Three? Half a dozen? *Le tout* Budleigh? I can hardly wait.

The custody sergeant wants to know about legal representation. I shake my head when he suggests the duty solicitor and give him Tony Morse's phone number which, thank God, I've memorized. The news that Tony will have to drive from Portsmouth puts a scowl on the sergeant's face.

'The duty's very good,' he says. 'I can recommend her.'

'Mr Morse, please. And give him my regards.'

'You're sure?'

'I am. That's his office number. I'm afraid no one's there before nine.'

He shrugs, checks his watch, makes a note. Next, I'm photographed and fingerprinted, a process that must be the briefest audition ever. Twice, deliberately, I keep my mouth open, incurring more wrath from the custody sergeant's assistant, but in truth I don't care. My faith in British justice, given the circumstances, is remarkably intact. Unless I've imagined the last three months, I have nothing to fear. Dragging me from my bed and arresting me on any grounds is a declaration of war.

The custody cell, by comparison with my brief stay in the TACT centre, is rudimentary – a bed plinth, a thin blue plastic mattress, a loo smelling of bleach, a smallish window high in one wall, and a glassy stare from the camera in the corner. The turnkey tells me the whole operation will shortly be moving to brand-new premises at force headquarters. Bigger cells. Hi-tech everything. Plus coffee to be proud of. I nod, barely bothering to feign interest. I plan to be here no more than a single night, if I'm unlucky, perhaps two. Then these people will never have to bother with me again.

The turnkey is about to leave when I ask him if there's anything to read.

'Sure,' he says, 'I'll see what I can find.'

He's back within minutes, holding the second in the *Shades of Grey* series. With as much grace as I can muster, I tell him I've read it. It's a lie, of course, but I'm not sure it matters.

I manage to snatch a little sleep. I dream of being airborne again, no aircraft, no wings, no company, just little me. I dive and swoop and twirl, giving the seagulls a run for their money, and wherever I look – up, down, left, right – the sky, or the ocean, or the cliff face are exactly the same shade of pinky-red. *England bleeding*, I think, as I finally jolt awake. Beth, bless her, is right. As, in his own furious way, is Mitch.

My watch has been taken away, doubtless a ruse to disorientate me, and so I have no idea of the time when the door opens and I'm led to a nearby office to conference with Tony Morse.

'Nearly half past one,' he says, after giving me a long hug. 'Afternoon already. The longer we can string this out, the better. You're doing well.'

We settle down, a desk between us in the bareness of this little room. He's already talked through disclosure with one of the *Bulldog* team, and he tells me at once that I've got nothing to worry about. The dates they're interested in are 15 and 16 September, and as long as I can alibi myself for that weekend, then my stay will be on the short side.

'So why arrest me at all?' I ask him.

'They're still concerned about the note Christianne left you. They think she told you what she planned to do, what it might involve, and that's information they don't have. But tell me what you got up to that weekend. That's where they'll start, and hopefully it'll go no further.'

By now I've had a chance to try and remember exactly what happened that September weekend. Christianne and I went for a long walk through the town. We ended up on the coastal path, and then she showed me her secret spot.

'Secret spot?'

'Where she and Andy used to spend long afternoons. It was beautiful. No one else ever went there. Think blanket, think picnic, wine, cheese, think whatever else goes with a place like that.'

'And this is where the cliff collapsed?'

'Yeah. And that's where she ended up. At least for a couple of months. There was another landslip the night before last. The whole cliff is falling apart.'

England again? I'm smiling now.

'Amazing TV pictures.' Tony is shaking his head. 'Pompey doesn't do cliffs.'

Back on the coastal path, I explain, Christianne took me to meet a friend of hers, Bill Penny. We stayed for most of the afternoon, then we went to the pub before going back to the bungalow. Christianne and Andy McFaul lived next door. I was staying with my friend Evelyn.

'And you were there all night?'

'Yes.'

'And the next day?'

'I went next door to say goodbye to Christianne, but Andy said she was still in bed.'

'So, you didn't see her?'

'No.'

'And then?'

'I drove back to London.'

'Anyone there when you arrived?'

'Malo. My son.'

More names. More notes. Finally, Tony looks up.

'This Andy McFaul?' He glances down. 'They haven't found him?'

'Not to my knowledge.'

'Excellent. No wonder they're taking as many hostages as they can.' He opens his briefcase and extracts a file, before reeling off a list of names. 'Sir William Penny? Sylvester Penny? Nathan Kline? Presley Philpott? Beth Beddoes?' He looks up, 'Are these names any surprise to you?'

'You're telling me they've all been arrested?'

'Yes.'

'And they're all here?'

'Yes. Separate cells, of course, but they've all done what you've done. Insisted on their own legal representation. Very wise.'

'And you've talked to their solicitors?'

'Yes.'

'And?'

'I'd anticipate the usual.'

'No comment?'

'Exactly.'

'And me? You want me to do that?'

'I want you to tell them exactly what happened that weekend but only as far as you're concerned. Tell them what you told me. They'll use that as a springboard, but resist the temptation to give them anything else.'

'Pleasure.' I offer a wan smile. 'I'm not in the mood for conversation.'

My first interview takes place nearly an hour later. I haven't seen Bullivant for a while, but he hasn't aged a second. The same dead eyes. The same parchment skin drawn tight over the bones of his face. The same meticulous attention when he presses the start button on the recording machine, and announces the time, date and persons present around the bareness of the table.

Brett Atkinson sits beside him, the assigned taker of notes, intervening from time to time to seek clarification on a name or a contact detail. After fifteen brief minutes, I've walked them both through that first and last weekend I ever spent with Christianne, and when they begin to press me on other issues – my rapport with Bill Penny, my dealings with Nathan Kline, what I make of Beth and Presley, how close I might have been to Andy McFaul – I do my solicitor's bidding and offer no comment.

As a working thesp, I'm trained to recognize the tiny facial clues that work so well in close-up on the big screen, and despite his attempts to mask it, I can sense Bullivant's growing frustration. He's developed a giveaway flicker just beneath his left eye, partly hidden by the thick black rim of his glasses. This, I know, is a key tell and I'm delighted when he pushes his pad to one side and leans forward over the table.

'I assume you'll remember that note Christianne left you?'

'No comment.'

'It was fond, wasn't it? Even intimate?'

'No comment.'

'So, are we really to believe she didn't confide in you? About how sick she was? About what she and her partner might have in mind to do about it?'

'No comment.'

'By your own admission, she showed you that patch of ground on the clifftop, the one that meant so much to her. No whisper of what she might have in mind? Not even a hint?'

'No comment.'

This game, which is more tiring than you might think, occupies the rest of the hour. Finally, Bullivant gets to his feet, mutters something to Brett, and then leaves the office without a backward glance. The three of us sit in silence while Brett studies his notes. When Tony enquires whether Operation *Bulldog* might be seeking a twelve-hour extension beyond the current twenty-four, Brett thinks it's more than possible.

'Everyone arrested has asked for their own lawyers,' he murmurs, 'and most of them have to come down from London. If you're looking to stall the interview process, good luck, but that has consequences, as you might imagine.'

Tony nods and shoots me a look. Then he reaches for a pen and scribbles me a note on his pad. *I have to be at Winchester Crown Court first thing tomorrow*, he's written. *So let's hope they wind this thing up.*

Bullivant returns moments later. He has my phone and he lays it carefully on the desk in front of him. He eyeballs me for a second or two, and then accesses my photo gallery.

'Do you recognize this photograph?' He shows me the phone.

I'm looking at a selfie I took of Christianne and me that Saturday she showed me the coastal path.

'Well, Ms Andressen?'

I glance at Tony. 'No comment' sounds a bit silly when I'm looking at myself. Tony shrugs. Go ahead.

'That's Christianne,' I tell Bullivant. 'At that favourite place of hers.'

'And the plastic mac you're wearing?'

'Christianne lent it to me when we were on our walk. It was starting to rain.'

'We seized that mac when we searched your friend's bungalow,' Bullivant says.

I nod. I remember. I say nothing. There's a longish silence, then Brett takes up the running.

'Sir William Penny,' he says. 'Can we assume you know him?'

'Of course.'

'You're friends?'

'I'd like to think so.'

'He has a dog, doesn't he?'

'Had,' I say. 'He had a dog. Little thing. Hundchen. Old. Sweet. Going blind. It wandered off somewhere.'

'How do you know that?'

'Bill – Sir William – told me.'

'When? When did this happen?'

'I can't remember. It must have been back in September, when I first came down.'

'When your friend Christianne disappeared?'

'Yes.'

Tony Morse is beginning to stir. I can sense he's getting uncomfortable with this line of questioning. I, too, haven't a clue where it might lead, but Brett is only too happy to help us out.

'We recovered the dog,' he says.

'Really? Where was she?'

'In the coffin. Beside your friend. Dead, I'm afraid.'

Process, in its modern usage, is a verb I've learned to despise. Way too American. Far too managerial. But just here and just now it's the perfect description of me trying to get on top of this latest little aftershock. Christianne plunging into the afterlife surrounded by Egyptian hieroglyphics? Sharing her coffin with a *dog*?

'You're telling me you found him on the beach?' I check with Brett that I've got this right.

'Yes. In the coffin, like I said. The dog and your friend were buried together.'

I nod. I can't think of anything to say.

'No comment?' Brett is playing games now.

'None.'

'You knew the dog, Ms Andressen?' Bullivant has permitted himself the ghost of a smile.

'I saw her once. Just once. That same Saturday afternoon.'

'Did you have physical contact with the dog?'

'I can't remember. She was a pathetic little thing. Did I cuddle her? I might have done.'

'We think the answer is yes. We recovered hairs from that dog on the plastic mac but the real question is this. Was she alive when you gave her that cuddle? Or was she dead?' Bullivant checks his watch again, then gets to his feet. 'We have a great deal to get through, I'm afraid.' He's looking at Tony. 'I'd like to take a break for a while, reconvene a little later.'

There's no negotiation, not a whisper of apology. Seconds later, both he and Brett have gone.

THIRTY-FOUR

This is a game-changer. A gentle confirmation of my watertight alibi has suddenly become something very different.

'They're looking to put you alongside the body,' Tony says.

'You mean the dog?'

'Christianne. They seem to think you were there when it happened.'

'Happened?' I'm still dazed.

'When she died. That's where they're taking all this. If they can make a case that you witnessed her death, then they can put you in front of a jury. What happens thereafter will be out of Bullivant's hands, but that doesn't matter to him. He's looking for a scalp. Our job just now is to make sure it isn't yours. The media would have a field day. And so would Bullivant.'

We're back in the windowless little office, looking glumly at yet another polystyrene cup of thin coffee.

'So, what do I do?'

'No comment. Definitely. Give them absolutely nothing. Bullivant's on a roll. He thinks he's got the measure of you. But a couple of dog hairs won't take him very far, believe me. He'll have to come up with a great deal more than that.'

I nod. I've been thinking very hard about that plastic mac. For one thing, I'm certain I took it off at Bill Penny's place before Christianne and I went upstairs with the dog. And for another, Christianne herself probably wore it. Lots.

When I share both thoughts with Tony, he scribbles himself a
note. Then his head comes up.

'He's trying to shake you, upset you. It's a tactic.' He taps his
pad. 'Well remembered.'

'Thanks. But tonight? Once they've finished with me? You're
really going back to Portsmouth?'

'I'm afraid so, but don't worry, I've got a couple of numbers
I can ring. Someone else will be with you tomorrow if they go
for an extension.'

I gaze at him for a moment. I'd love to say that this last
exchange in the interview room hasn't frightened me, but I'd be
lying. It takes very little to fabricate a plausible story, as I'm
only too aware. In the theatre, or on screen, fictions of one sort
or another have served me very well, but just now the lure of a
made-up story feels very different. Conspiracy to murder is
a very ugly phrase, and I'm suddenly aware that the next
twenty-four hours could put me inside for a very long time.

'Don't worry, my darling.' Tony's hand has closed over mine.
'These are early days.'

The next episode of this developing nightmare takes place
mid-afternoon. Bullivant and a different detective join us in the
interview suite. This is a face I haven't seen before. She's young,
and overweight, with a fall of reddish hair and rather fetching
dimples. Lose a few pounds, I think, and you could transform
your prospects. Bullivant introduces her as DC Annie Leadbetter.

'Do you recognize this item of furniture, Ms Andressen?' he
says.

I'm looking at a photo of Bill Penny's exquisite chaise longue.
My instinct is to say yes but Tony Morse has his shoe on my
foot.

'No comment.'

'Have you seen it before?'

'No comment.'

'Are you aware that it used to belong to Sir William Penny
but ended up in Andy McFaul's bungalow?'

'No comment.'

'I'm asking these questions, Ms Andressen, because we believe
this chaise may have been a crime scene. We recovered more

dog hairs, and there were also traces of Ms Beaucarne's DNA. Might you be able to account for those? Given that the chaise ended up in McFaul's bungalow?'

Bullivant's use of Christianne's surname chills my blood – so formal, so cold. But far more important is the chronology here.

'He's got it wrong,' I whisper to Tony. 'I need to tell him.'

'No way.' Tony shakes his head.

'But—'

'I said no.'

I stare at him, and then blink. Just whose liberty is on the line here? In the interests of the next fourteen years of my life, shouldn't I correct this gross mistake?

'My client declines to answer that question,' Tony murmurs.

'Ms Andressen?' Bullivant's eyes haven't left my face.

'No comment.'

'So be it.' Bullivant writes himself a note. Tiny handwriting. Each letter perfectly formed. Anal bastard. 'Our point is this, Ms Andressen. We think your friend may have died on that chaise, and our working assumption is that the dog would also have been put to sleep. There was obviously a coffin readied for the two bodies. I think we can say that with some assurance. Can you confirm that, Ms Andressen? Was the coffin delivered to the bungalow on that Saturday night? Under cover of darkness? And were you in attendance when Ms Beaucarne, the victim, died? That letter she left you suggests a very close, a very *warm* relationship. You tell us you only knew the victim for a couple of days. I'm afraid we only have your word on that. Might you care to explain how long you'd really known her? And why you lied to us in this regard?'

The word 'victim' does it for me. I scarcely heard the rest of the question.

'Victim is right,' I say. 'Much more right than you know. Was she suffering? Yes. Was she picked on? Again yes. But by MND, motor neurone disease, not me, nor anyone else. Do you understand that distinction? Or should I try again?'

'By all means, Ms Andressen. And why not tell us a little more about you and Ms Beaucarne, while you're at it.'

I'm angry now, and he knows it. So does Tony Morse. The pressure of his foot on mine is nearly unbearable. *Button your lip. Wind your neck in. Like I told you before, this man is playing games with you.*

'Well, Ms Andressen?' Bullivant is still waiting for an answer.

'No comment,' I mutter, ducking my head.

The next flurry of questions pass in a blur. Tony's right. By losing what little cool I have left, I've fallen into this man's trap. He's touched a nerve that matters to me, and from my point of view, this second session has turned into a car crash.

Over the next few minutes, while I stonewall every question, Bullivant tries to wind me up again. How difficult it must have been for me to watch a close friend dying. How I may have rationalized what remains a crime, told myself I was doing what I was doing with the very best of intentions. How, indeed, I'd taken up the cudgels against the law of the land on my friend's behalf.

'Might any of that be the case, Ms Andressen? Couldn't you feel her pain? Feel it your duty to send her on her way? Wasn't that, dare I say it, a *Christian* thing to do?'

This, I know, is deliberately provocative. Evelyn would be over the table by now, scratching his eyes out.

'No comment,' I mutter.

'That's a shame.' It's Leadbetter this time, her first contribution to the interview, her first stab with her little *banderilla*. 'Was it guilt you felt? Or sympathy?'

'That's an absurd question.' It's Tony's turn to be angry. 'Your assumptions are grotesque. My client deserves an apology.'

Leadbetter says nothing. Another hint of a smile from Bullivant.

'Let's recap, shall we?' Leadbetter is studying the notes she's made. 'Our contention is that you knew Ms Beaucarne a great deal better than you're prepared to admit. Quite how you first met her isn't clear, but no one I know would write a note like that on the basis of a single weekend. So, we think the friendship goes back a while. And we think you also knew about her illness, about the MND. And even if you didn't, our understanding is that you should have been looking harder because – by all accounts – the evidence was there in plain sight.'

I duck my head, partly in shame. *By all accounts* is a killer. Leadbetter might be young, she might take better care of herself, but she's right. They're obviously talking to other people they've

arrested – Bill, Beth, Nathan – and all of them probably knew
the truth about Christianne. That she had this terrible, terrible
disease. And that she was doomed.

'You're right,' I whisper. 'I should have realized from
the start.'

'I beg your pardon?'

'No comment.'

This is getting ugly. For once my assigned role couldn't be
simpler – just two words – but I keep losing my place in the
script. Tony's foot is back on mine. He's fast losing patience.

'Let's talk about Ms Beaucarne's partner, Ms Andressen.'
Leadbetter again. 'I imagine you must have known him pretty
well, too.'

'No comment.'

'Would you describe yourself as friends?'

'No comment.'

'Did you think it was your duty, your responsibility, to give
him support? Lend him a hand when the time came?'

'The time?' I can't help myself.

'Yes, Ms Andressen.' This from Bullivant. 'When the time
came to end it all. And that, of course, is where we get to the
real nub of what happened. No one's pretending for a moment
that this wasn't a deeply tragic situation. No one would deny
that for a second. But the law's the law and it's our job to gather
evidence when we think the law's been flouted. Is this one of
those occasions? We suspect it is. Might there be mitigating
circumstances? Of course, but that's not for us to judge. You
might think that all of this serves no purpose, all our questions,
the precise circumstances we're trying to establish, but you'd be
wrong. The reason we're here, the purpose served by your arrest,
is to try and tease out the truth. And once we've done that, it
will be for you to have your say in front of a jury.'

This is like being back at school, I think, listening to one of
those kindly lectures from the teacher who's about to make your
life a misery. I so want to have my say here and now. I so want
to explain to these people just how wrong they are, but the fact
that I can't just makes me feel even more helpless.

I reach for Tony's hand, shake my head, fight the tears. Not
of pain but of frustration. Tony, bless him, asks for a brief recess,

a private moment or two, and after an exchange of glances my tormentors agree to leave us in peace.

'Ten minutes.' Bullivant is at the door. 'I'll arrange for coffee to be sent in.'

Coffee is the last thing I need. Tony Morse is being stern, telling me to get a grip, telling me simply to obey orders for once in my life, but I barely hear him. Nothing computes any more. Not the setting, the airlessness of this hideous room; not the memory of the faces at Evelyn's front door pre-dawn this morning; not even the knowledge that two grown-ups who should know better seem to believe I'm capable of murder. Just how do I draw this nightmare to a close? And what does this surreal script have in store when the curtain rises for the next act?

It gets worse. Bullivant and Leadbetter return. Leadbetter has the coffees, which she seems to regard as a peace offering, but I ignore them. Bullivant starts the recording machine again and announces the resumption of the interview. With a voice as flat and colourless as his, he'll never make it as a DJ, but I expect he knows that already. In any event, he has a new word to table.

'Fentanyl?' he asks. This appears to be a question.

'No comment.'

'We've been able to access your medical records, Ms Andressen. Fentanyl is an opiate. It's a very powerful painkiller. But you'd know that, of course, because it was prescribed when your condition was at its worst. Am I right?'

'No comment.'

'You used it after the operation to remove your brain tumour. You had savage headaches for a while. We understand Fentanyl took the edge off that pain but after a day or two, according to your consultant's notes, you stopped using the drug. True?'

'No comment.'

'In the first place, you were given a month's supply. We estimate you used only a tiny fraction of that prescription, yet a search of your flat at . . .' He peers down at his notes. 'Four hundred and three Greyfriars Court failed to find any trace of these tablets.' He looks up. 'What happened to them, Ms Andressen?'

Once again, I'm trapped. The truth is that the presence of the

Fentanyl coincided with the lowest point of my son's life. Malo was in his late teens. He was truanting full time, hanging out in very bad company, and getting stoned on whatever came his way. Fentanyl, from what I knew of the drug, would have been the end of him. And so I got rid of them.

I'm looking at Tony. He's not interested in any explanation, just shakes his head.

'No comment,' I mutter.

'Fine. At this point, for all our sakes, I'm afraid I'm obliged to reveal the findings of the post-mortem carried out on Ms Beaucarne. This took place at Wonford Hospital on the fourteenth of December. According to the pathologist's report, Ms Beaucarne's stomach contents were still intact. They revealed significant traces of Fentanyl.' Bullivant looks up. 'In other words, Ms Andressen, Fentanyl killed your friend. It also, I'm afraid, put paid to the dog. Do you have any comment?'

'None.'

'That might be something you regret. You can, of course, obtain Fentanyl via the internet. As you might imagine, we've been through Mr McFaul's laptop and found no trace of even a Google search, let alone an order. He doesn't have a smartphone, so he couldn't have used that. Neither has his doctor or Ms Beaucarne's issued any prescription for the drug. So, short of obtaining it from a street dealer in Budleigh Salterton, there has to be another source. You're following this, Ms Andressen? You understand where this might lead us?'

'No comment.'

'I'm not sure I blame you. Let's just pause a moment. Let's try and assess exactly how bad this is looking for you. Annie?'

Leadbetter has been keeping score. She tallies the case against me, item by item. That I probably knew Christianne far better than I've let on. That I was naturally a good friend of Andy's. That I was aware of her favourite clifftop spot. That I had dealings with the bloody dog. That I had access to the chaise longue on the night Christianne probably died. And that, in all probability, the drugs that killed her came from my private stash.

Most of this is nonsense, and I think I can prove it. Bill Penny's chaise, for instance, was delivered to McFaul's bungalow a couple of days *after* Christianne's disappearance. And when I was wearing Christianne's plastic mac, I never went near the bloody dog. Yet without the chance to answer back, to make my case, to dispute all this crap, I'm totally helpless.

Alas, it isn't over. Once Bullivant is certain that I've registered the gravity of the situation in which I find myself, he raises one last issue, a hanging thread which might just need a tug or two before I break down and confess all.

'We need to talk a little more about your friend, Andy McFaul. As I'm sure you know, he broke his bail conditions and absconded. To be specific, he was due to report to Exmouth police station as part of his bail conditions on the twenty-fifth of September, but failed to do so. You're aware of this?'

'No comment.'

'We've been looking for him ever since, of course, but we now have grounds to believe that he may have left the country. Without a passport, that would present difficulties, as I expect you can imagine.'

'No comment.'

'We understand you went for a flight yesterday with Mr Nathan Kline. True?'

'No comment.'

'Fine. According to an account from a witness at the airfield yesterday, you were certainly present in the aircraft. That would suggest to us that you know Mr Kline well, and that you might have approached him on McFaul's behalf with a view to getting out of the country.'

'No comment.'

'We're not suggesting for a moment that Mr Kline flew McFaul himself, but we've made enquiries and we've established that McFaul was probably in a light aircraft that took off from a private strip in mid-Devon on the morning of the . . .' He checks his pad. 'Twenty-fourth of September. All cross-Channel flights are mandated to file a General Aviation Report and land at entry airfields in France. This one didn't. We have grounds to believe that it landed at a private strip inland from the Brittany coast. It would have refuelled there before the aircraft took off again and returned to the UK.' Bullivant looks up. 'Our belief is that McFaul was a passenger on the southbound leg of that journey, and that he was dropped off at the private strip. The nearest hamlet is called . . .' He glances down to find the name. 'Poullaouen Le Stancou. Do you know it?'

'No comment.'

'Let's assume you do. It's a tiny place, just a handful of inhabitants, but that's not the point because it's only thirty miles from Perros-Guirec. We understand you have family connections in Perros-Guirec. Is that true?'

'No comment.'

'Your mother still lives there?'

'No comment.'

'We suspect McFaul had been in touch with your mother, or perhaps you had. We think she arranged for someone to meet him at or near the airstrip to help him on his way. With a car, or even a motorbike, he could be anywhere in Europe. In the Schengen Area, borders are porous. Few checks. Little paperwork. In other words, Ms Andressen, thanks to help from you and your family, Mr McFaul thinks he's home safe. That may turn out to be wildly optimistic, of course, but for now we think it serves as an explanation.'

I hold his gaze. The only thing that can make this nightmare worse is the involvement of my lovely mum, and now it's happened. I want to find out whether they've been to knock on her door, or whether they've alerted the French police, or taken any number of other measures that would make her life a misery. Under certain circumstances, French bureaucracy can be unforgiving and this might well be a case in point.

'You couldn't be more wrong,' I say softly.

'About McFaul?'

'About everything.'

The interview, mercifully, comes to an end. Both Bullivant and Leadbetter leave the interview suite without a backward glance, and Tony returns from a brief chat with the custody sergeant to confirm that the time allowed for detention has been extended to thirty-six hours. By seven o'clock tomorrow evening, unless they apply to the magistrates for yet another extension, Operation *Bulldog* must release me.

'Given today's developments, they may decide to bail you,' he adds.

'Like McFaul?'

'Exactly. Take a hint, my darling. Find yourself a private pilot and go home.'

'You mean France?'

He shakes his head. He's joking, he says, but I don't find it the least bit funny. The day the consultant told me I had a tumour in my brain rapidly became surreal. Not me. No way. Not at my age. This, years later, isn't life-threatening but I feel exactly the same sense of dislocation, of fragments of the world I thought I knew whirling away in some cosmic wind. Helplessness is too small a word. A bunch of strangers have taken a very close look at Christianne's departure and decided that I'm to blame. Telling them they're wrong, trying to point out that the whole thing is absurd, simply confirms their suspicions. And now, the one man who might – just conceivably – make a difference is about to climb in his car and hit the road.

'Are the rest still banged up as well? Are you allowed to tell me?'

'All but one. Beth. They released her an hour ago.'

'On police bail?'

'It seems not.'

I nod. She must have painted the inside of that coffin. How on earth did she explain that?

Tony is itching to get away. He's made some calls and a solicitor called Andrea Gifford will be down to the custody centre first thing tomorrow morning. She'll press for fresh disclosure from DI Bullivant, and Tony has already briefed her on the thrust of today's interviews.

'I'm guessing that was a long conversation.' I'm trying to muster a smile.

'You guess right. Did today go well? Not really. Do we now know where they're headed with this thing? Absolutely. And can we head them off at the pass? No question about it. Andrea's good. Take her advice, my darling. Who knows, it might come better from a woman.'

He gives me a brief hug, wishes me all the luck in the world, and consigns me to the care of a hovering turnkey. My last image of him is that trademark way he flips up the collar of his cashmere coat as he steps into the gathering dusk.

The turnkey returns me to my cell. Its very bareness is deeply depressing, giving me no choice but to lie on my side on the thin mattress, and close my eyes against the brightness of the overhead light. As far as I can tell, it's early evening. They may or may not bring me something to eat, but even the prospect of food makes me nauseous. Earlier, around lunchtime, I'd smelled chips in the closeness of the corridors outside. Burgers, I suspect. Probably imported from the McDonald's up the road.

For what feels like hours, I try and kid myself to sleep, but it doesn't work. Time and again, my dizzy brain returns to the memory of those brief moments I shared with Christianne on the clifftop. Maybe, that Saturday afternoon, I should have anticipated everything that was going to follow, but how could I? Where, in Pavel's phrase, were the narrative clues? No question, I should have thought harder about Christianne's clumsiness, about the way she'd fight to keep her balance, and about the little vignettes I witnessed between her and Andy in the privacy of their back garden. The way he was trying to school her putting on his immaculate lawn. The way he protected her around the kitchen. The care he took of her. But the harder I try and get all this into focus, the more I realize that it's all way too late.

Someone else is in charge of this story now. Someone else is wielding the editor's pencil, and I have the darkest misgivings about what tomorrow might bring. How much evidence do they need before they formally charge me? And if that happens, do I swap this perch in Heavitree police station for a prison cell while the lawyers attend to their business and the wheels of justice grind little me to dust?

The key word here, oddly enough, is prison. My lovely mum, who now dominates my thoughts, never spoiled me for a moment. On the contrary, she had a very Catholic view of the wages of sin and always warned me that Hell awaits both the guilty and the weak. The latter, I always suspected, fully deserved damnation in her eyes when it came to the judgement call, and as soon as I was big enough to listen properly, she preached the virtues of strength, and something she called fortitude. The latter concept I never fully understood until I met Pavel, but after I witnessed what he could make of his life, regardless of the odds stacked against him, the more I realized that my mum was right. In the tightest corners, like now, you never bow your head, never succumb, never admit defeat. *Au contraire*, you fight your basest instincts and turn them on their head.

Supper arrives at what I assume to be mid-evening. A key turns in the lock and I'm looking at a microwaved Ginsters pasty with a small sachet of brown sauce.

'Lovely.' I sit up on the mattress. 'You must have read my mind.'

THIRTY-FIVE

Andrea Gifford, when I meet her next day, turns out to be a delight. She must be a year or two older than me. The darkness beneath her eyes suggests late nights and a crippling work schedule, yet she has a patience and a quiet sense of humour that I take as a kind of blessing. That we might be like-minded under these circumstances is a lifeline. For one thing, she's wearing a pair of my favourite Boden ankle boots. And for another, she's had the foresight to arrive with a decent cup of coffee, a takeout from some Costa down the road.

'Treating you OK?' She nods towards the door. We're back in the room with no windows.

'No complaints,' I say brightly. 'Microwaved pasty like last night's, I could live here forever.'

She has the grace to share my little joke. One day, God willing, we might end up splitting a bottle or two of decent Merlot in her favourite wine bar, but for the time being we have to attend to business. She's reviewed her notes from last night's conversation with Tony Morse, and has a suggestion to make, but first she needs to ask me a straight question.

'How much did you know about Christianne's death?'

'Nothing. Swear to God.'

'The dog thing?'

'Pardon my French but it's bollocks. I met the dog once. Yes, I picked it up, gave it a cuddle, but no, I wasn't wearing the bloody mac. They make this stuff up.'

'The chaise?'

'They've got the timeline wrong. It was still at Bill's until way after she disappeared.'

'The Fentanyl?'

'They're right that I had a month's supply, but I flushed them down the loo. This was years ago.'

'Why?'

'My son was zombied out at the time, totally off his head. Spice is evil, but I'm guessing you know that.'

She nods, says nothing, then lightly touches the flesh above her right eyebrow.

'And the tumour?'

'Better, I think.'

'Gone?'

'Not quite. But it knows the end is near.'

'Unlike you?'

'Unlike me.'

When she asks her last question, about masterminding McFaul's flight to France, I once again tell her that it's nonsense. It's true that I accepted a flight from Nathan Kline, but the man would never take no for an answer. The phrase sparks a nod and a smile.

'I know Nathan,' she says. 'You have my sympathies.'

The coffee, after this morning's cornflakes, is delicious. Andrea talks me through the likely course of the day's events, and when I press her for a game plan, something simple even I can understand, she understands at once.

'They need to back off,' she says. 'And you need to make that happen.'

Back off? I have a very clear memory of each of yesterday's sessions and the sheer weight of the evidence they seem to have amassed against me still makes my pulse quicken, yet I believe this woman when she advises me to simply be myself.

'Tony says you're an actress by trade.'

'That's true.'

'And is yourself a role you might play to some effect? Because he thinks it is.'

'I'm flattered.'

'Don't be. The police don't take prisoners, not in the way that you and I understand, and neither do lawyers. Bullivant can be a real monster, especially around women. He might not look the part, but lie down and he'll kick you to death. This happens to be his last big case. Which gives him every incentive to misbehave.'

'I know that.'

'Brett told you? Tony said you two were buddies.'

'That's true. On both counts.'

'Good.' She gathers her papers together and swallows the remains of her coffee. 'That's something else I've had a word about. Putting you in with young Brett breaks every rule in the book.'

We have to wait a while before Bullivant and Leadbetter appear. The atmosphere in the interview suite is immediately different. Bullivant is more cautious. Yesterday, he was far from cavalier, because he doesn't do reckless, but I get the feeling my insistence on hiding behind 'no comment' gave him ample scope to put his jewels on the table, fix me with that dead stare, and browbeat me into submission. This doesn't work with Andrea. She clearly comes with a reputation, or perhaps a health warning. Tread carefully. Treat with care.

She begins by suggesting to Bullivant that I might like to make a statement. This I'm more than happy to do. I tell him that I knew Christianne for just three days, and that there's absolutely no evidence they'll ever find to suggest otherwise. Christianne was French, like me. We got on incredibly well. We laughed a good deal. And we compared notes on what our lives had taught us with that candour that only a brand-new friendship can spark. Should I have been more curious about little physical problems she seemed to have? The answer is yes. Did she ever admit to having MND? Absolutely not. The issue of what she might have in mind to do about it therefore never arose. We were briefly mates. In French, *le mot juste* would be *copine*.

'That's c-o-p-i-n-e.' I spell it for Bullivant's benefit. 'I imagine you might like to write it down.'

I'm aware of a tiny shake of the head from Andrea, a shot across my bows. Softly, softly, she's telling me. Don't antagonize these people. Don't piss them off. But I don't care because I'm feeling far, far stronger and now is pay-back time. Yesterday this man humiliated me. Now I might regain just a little self-respect.

For the next hour or so, referring constantly to his notes, Bullivant explores and re-explores the key elements of his case against me, constantly changing his angle of attack, always trying to throw me off balance, but this time it doesn't begin to work, chiefly because I have so little to remember. Stick to the known facts, I keep telling myself. And don't stray off-piste.

Mid-morning, we take a break. Andrea pays another visit to the Costa down the road and I wait for her return, wondering how we're doing. The answer, to my intense relief, is well. She's pleased. Bullivant, she says, is beginning to repeat himself, and – something that's obvious to both of us – he knows it. More, please. But steady as she goes.

The second session occupies the rest of the morning. So far, Bullivant hasn't mentioned the night I went to dinner at Bill's place, but now he must have caught wind of that little gathering.

'This was the day we arrested McFaul. Am I right?'

'You are.'

'Did you regard that as a coincidence?'

'Yes. Anything else never occurred to me. Bill phoned at the last moment. I thought I was there to make up the numbers.'

'What did you talk about?'

'Christianne, obviously. They knew her far better than I did, but we all missed her.'

'You assumed she was dead?'

'Yes.'

'Dead how?'

'Drowned.'

'Did anyone else at the table have views about that?'

For the first time, I hesitate. I have no idea what anyone else has said about what really happened round that table, but I've no intention of sharing Beth's little fantasy about the ebb tide thundering past Exmouth Dock.

'No comment,' I say.

'So, you did talk about how she might have died? Is that what I'm hearing?'

'No comment.'

Bullivant is frowning now and, looking at his hands, I realize that he picks his fingers. The skin around the nails is reddened and angry.

'So, what impression did you get of these people?' he asks.

'I thought they were fine. Very different but very interesting.'

'Different how?'

'Background? Age? I don't know really. One was an ex-ambassador. Another was a carpenter. Beth runs a shop. Nathan used to be a QC.'

'Precisely. And didn't you wonder what brought them together that night? Round that table? Within hours of McFaul's arrest?'

'No, I didn't. Should I have done?'

'Yes, I suspect you should. And more to the point, I think you did. In fact, it's our belief that you were there for the same reason everyone else was there.'

'Which was?'

'To anticipate how much McFaul would tell us, and to come up with some kind of plan.'

'I don't understand what you mean.'

'Of course you do, Ms Andressen. The people round that table, you included, were complicit in Ms Beaucarne's disappearance. You all knew what had really happened. You all knew where she was buried, doubtless because you'd all helped carry the coffin. That explains this odd gathering around the table. What all of you had in common is the question we need to ask. And the answer, we think, is the night you buried Ms Beaucarne. Isn't that the truth?'

I've thought a great deal about that meal at Bill's over the last twenty-four hours, and I suspect Bullivant's got most of it right. Except, of course, for my own role.

'No comment.'

'So be it. Let's move on.' He turns to Leadbetter. 'Annie?'

Leadbetter checks a date on her notes, and then looks up. Overnight, she seems to have developed a cold sore on her lower lip.

'I want to take you on to Sunday the twenty-second of September. That was the end of the week of Ms Beaucarne's disappearance. There was a gathering on the beach. You were there. Am I right?'

'Yes. We came to say goodbye.'

'There was a ceremony of some sort, music, and then some of you went afloat with a wreath. Yes?'

'Yes. I was asked to say a few words about Christianne.'

'Really?' This appears to surprise her.

'Yes.'

'After you'd known her for just a couple of days? Doesn't that strike you as odd?'

'Not at all. I'm an actress. I also speak French. This was private but it was an event nonetheless. Bill was the one who asked me to do a reading. It was a performance really. He knows my work. He thought I could do the moment full justice.'

'And afterwards? After the reading?'

'We dropped a wreath. There were swimmers in the water, ladies who knew Christianne well. It was very moving.'

'But what was the point of the wreath?'

'To mark her passing.'

'Because she'd drowned?'

'Of course.'

'But she hadn't. And you knew that. Because you'd buried her.'

'Wrong. I didn't bury her, didn't carry the coffin, didn't supply the drugs, didn't even know any of that stuff had happened.'

'And the others? Those people round the dinner table?'

'I've no idea.'

'No *idea*? Not even the faintest suspicion? The faintest doubt?'

'None. None at all.'

'Really? And you really expect us to believe that?'

'I do, yes. Because it's true.'

Leadbetter holds my gaze for a long moment, then shrugs and makes herself a note.

'There was a reporter on that beach.' This from Bullivant. 'I was there. I saw him myself. He was taking photos.'

'That's right.'

'So, who invited him along? And why?'

'I've no idea. Christianne going missing was a big story. The search was huge. That kind of stuff sells newspapers.'

'Indeed. And a photo appeared in the *Journal* the following Wednesday, did it not?'

Unprompted, Leadbetter produces a copy of the paper's front page. The photo shows the boat offshore, listing slightly as we gather to watch the wreath drifting away on the tide. Bill Penny has lowered his head. I'm still holding my copy of the young *resistant's* last letter. *Town mourns missing swimmer*, runs the headline.

'This was a ploy, was it not, Ms Andressen? A red herring? Confirmation that this friend of yours had been lost at sea? Wasn't that the purpose of the gathering? And doesn't that explain the presence of the reporter? By Friday, thousands of people knew Ms Beaucarne had drowned. Why? Because the *Journal* said so. Very clever, very artful. But a lie. Isn't that the case, Ms Andressen? Weren't you all there in the knowledge that this whole episode – the woman dancing round the towel, the face paint, the dropping of the wreath at sea – was a pantomime? To lead us all astray? To disguise the truth of what really happened?'

'No comment.'

I resist the temptation to glance at Andrea. This is beginning to get tricky again and I'm very aware that not answering questions puts me in a very bad light indeed. Bullivant seems to sense this.

'Well, Ms Andressen?'

'I was there in good faith. I missed my friend. By then, McFaul had told me about the MND and I thought she'd drowned herself on purpose.'

'And it never occurred to you that there might be another explanation?'

'God, no. Why should it?'

'Not even with your background? Movies? Plot twists? All that?'

'This was different. This was real life.'

'And you think that makes a difference?'

'Of course it does. What I do for a living is entertainment. Drowning at sea is something very different.'

'But she didn't drown, Ms Andressen. She died of a drug overdose. Thanks to Fentanyl that we suspect you supplied. You were there. You watched. You may have held her hand, tried to comfort her. You *knew*. On that beach, in that boat, you *knew*. Please don't go through this charade again. You might not like us, Ms Andressen, but we're not as stupid as you might think. Just admit it. You were there when she died. You *knew.*'

'Wrong. I didn't.'

Bullivant studies me for a while. Then he extends a hand towards Leadbetter. I sense that they've probably rehearsed this moment. The file at her elbow is already open. She extracts a single sheet of paper and gives it to Bullivant. He's about to slide it across the table but then he changes his mind. McFaul, it appears, has left me a second note, recovered from his bungalow after he'd disappeared.

Bullivant adjusts his glasses. He wants to read it to me.

Thank you for helping Chrissie on her way, McFaul has written. *You'll never know what that meant to both of us. You're a true friend.* Bullivant looks up. Then he passes me the note. 'Well, Ms Andressen?'

I'm staring at the message. McFaul has written it in capital letters, very carefully, the way a child might. 'Friend', I like a lot. The rest will probably put me in prison. My mouth is dry, and I have trouble trying to swallow.

'No comment,' I say.

THIRTY-SIX

Andrea thinks the note is inconclusive. You can, she says, parse it a number of ways. 'Parse' is a wonderful verb and I haven't heard it for years. It means analyse or interpret. When I summon a smile and thank her for trying to cheer me up, she shakes her head.

'I mean it,' she says. 'Christianne was on a journey. Wittingly or otherwise, you offered support. She liked you very much. We have that in writing. Twice. You should feel proud about that.'

'*Helped her on her way?* Isn't that a gift to someone like Bullivant?'

'It's not Bullivant we have to worry about. He gathers the evidence, as he's doubtless told you. Then it goes in front of the CPS. They won't take it to court unless they think there's a realistic chance of getting a result, and even then they have to convince a jury. These hurdles are much higher than people think. There's also an issue with funding. This government have put the legal sector on a starvation diet. Court time costs a fortune and we're running out of money.'

'You're telling me they can't afford to take me to court?'

'I'm telling you they've got a very thin case. Mercy killings are notoriously difficult and in your case, I doubt they can prove you were there at the time.'

'Good.' I manage a smile. 'Because I wasn't.'

Andrea pops out to fetch us a spot of lunch, and when she returns, she has the broadest of smiles on her face. She's been talking to the custody sergeant and it appears that I'm free to leave.

'You mean it's over?' I can't believe it. In her absence I've been fretting again about McFaul's note. Now this.

'Not quite,' she says. 'They're not insisting on police bail, but Bullivant is making it very clear that he hasn't finished with you. He's the senior investigating officer. What he says matters. Given what I know about him, I suspect he won't give up.'

'And this goes on for how long?'

'Until they make a charging decision.' She smiles again. 'Or not. They call the latter NFA.'

No further action? Just now, nothing could seem less likely, but I tuck this little phrase away like an amulet, something to protect me in the days and weeks to come. Andrea has been honest enough to make it clear that my trials are far from over, but she's happy with my performance in the interview suite and is certain that I've given DI Bullivant something to think about.

'First thing this morning,' she says, 'he assumed it was all over. I can read the bloody man like a book. He thought he'd have a cough by lunchtime, latest.'

'Cough?'

'Full confession. Happily, it turned out he was wrong. Never make any assumptions in this game. They always come back to haunt you.'

'And the others?'

'They've all gone "no comment", not a peep from any of them.

They'll be released, too. You'll all get together, I'm sure you
will, but just a word of advice. Do I hear a yes?'

'Of course.'

'Be very careful what you say. To anyone. Just stick to your
story. You tell it very well, as you should, but if this little saga
is to have a happy ending, you've got to button your lip. By all
means get blind drunk tonight, but take care about the company
you keep. Bullivant hates losing. He won't give up, I promise
you.'

Take care about the company you keep. Andrea offers me a
lift back to Budleigh, but I can imagine how busy she is, and I
tell her I'm happy to take the bus. I've never been on the 58
service before but my perch on the back seat, with my cheek
pressed to the coldness of the window, feels inexpressibly
wonderful. This is freedom, I tell myself, all the sweeter for
being so unexpected. The rest of the day I shall spend with
Evelyn. I trust her completely, and in the light of Andrea's
warning that might be important.

Fat chance. When I finally get to the bungalow, it's Mitch who
opens the front door.

'Christ,' he says. 'You've escaped.'

He has his mobile pressed to his ear. Evelyn must have been
feeding him again because he has crumbs of toast all over his
Liverpool shirt. I step inside, glad of the sudden warmth. Evelyn
appears from the kitchen, stares at me as if I wasn't quite real,
and then gives me a long hug, just to check.

'You're all right?' She's holding me at arm's length.

'I'm fine. A bit tired, but OK.'

'They didn't hurt you?'

'Of course they didn't hurt me. No bruises. No missing teeth.'

'But in here, my lovely.' She has a hand clasped to her chest.
'That kind of hurt.'

'Ah . . .' I manage to summon a smile, and then nod towards
the kitchen. 'Tea, maybe?'

Mitch joins us shortly afterwards. He's finished his phone call
but leaves the mobile on the kitchen table where he can see it.
It seems to be ringing non-stop. He checks caller ID each time
but resists the temptation to pick it up.

'So, tell me what happened,' he grunts.

'Us,' Evelyn says. 'Tell *us* what happened.'

I do my best. Both of these people, I tell myself, have my best interests at heart, though possibly for different reasons, but the more detail I get into, the more uneasy I feel. In the end, I try to boil it down to a single proposition.

'They want me to admit that I was there when she died,' I say.

'But you weren't.' This from Evelyn.

'I know. That's what I kept telling them. The police live in a world of their own. And they're not great listeners.'

'You mean they didn't believe you?' Mitch seems amused.

'Not at all. They've built themselves a little fantasy about the way Christianne died. I suppose that's their job, but I'm the one they want to put beside her when she left us. Me and Andy. The long goodbye.'

'Nice title.'

'Horrible title. Excuse my French but they fuck with your head, turn you round and round until you've no idea where you are, who you are, or even what matters any more. Maybe I should treat it as some kind of masterclass. What it really feels like to be on the receiving end. Next time I play the innocent victim, I promise you I'll win an award.'

Mitch's phone is buzzing yet again. This time, he picks it up, listens to the voice at the other end, then hands it across.

'For you,' he says. 'Beth.'

Beth announces she'll be arriving at the bungalow within minutes. By now, we've decamped to Evelyn's lounge, and I'm inspecting a poster that Mitch has commissioned from a local graphics studio. I'm about to tell Beth she's welcome, but it's too late because she's hung up.

'It's just a rough proof.' Mitch nods at the poster. 'We'll obviously have to change the shoutline.'

The poster features mug shots of myself, Bill Penny, Sylvester, Nathan, Beth and Presley. God knows where Mitch laid hands on them, but what really grabs my attention is the bannered line across the top, and the three lines of text beneath.

'*Free the Budleigh Six?*' I shake my head. 'Is this some kind of joke?'

'Not at all. We'll need to change it now. You're on bail?'

'No.'

'Shame. Have they abandoned the enquiry?'

'Far from it.'

'Then we'll go for *Clear the Budleigh Six.*' He nods at the copy beneath. 'Read on.'

I do his bidding. A meeting has been convened in the public hall tomorrow night. It will start at half past seven and people with an interest in a decent society are urged to attend. Speakers will include a stand-up comic, huge on Channel Four, plus a handful of local luminaries.

A ring on the front doorbell brings Beth into the room. I can always tell when she's excited because she has a tendency to catch her breath. Just now, she's hyperventilating.

'Thank God.' She throws her arms round me. 'We were all fearing the worst.'

'We?'

'The rest of us.' She nods at the poster of the Budleigh Six. 'What do you think?'

'I don't know.' I shake my head. 'I'm not being a wuss, but I truly don't. A couple of hours ago I was anticipating the rest of my life in jail. Now this.'

'They've charged you?'

'Not yet.'

'Excellent. Join the gang.'

The gang? I'm looking at Mitch. I'm very keen for someone to tease just a splinter of sense from all this clamour, and he's the only one I really trust. Beth, typically, is about to take over because that's the role God's assigned her, but just now I need a little peace.

'Come with me.' I take Mitch by the arm. 'Please.'

We return to the kitchen. I shut the door and wedge a chair beneath the handle. Then I join him at the table.

'Just tell me what's going on. That's all I want to know.'

Mitch nods. He seems to understand. The mass arrests, he says, have gone viral. Social media is firing on all cylinders – Facebook, Twitter, God knows where else – and the developing story has built up a massive head of steam. First the landslip. Then the coffin and the body on the beach. And now an ex-ambassador and a QC, to name but two upstanding citizens of this little town, dragged from their beds and placed under arrest. Not for something of passing interest. But for conspiracy to murder.

'Have we got this wrong?' Mitch enquires. 'Is this something we've invented?'

'Of course not.'

'We agree on the facts? You were all arrested? Photographed? Fingerprinted? Held overnight? Interviewed God knows how many times? Was that what happened?'

'Yes.' I can't disagree.

'And you don't think people, a wider audience, the whole fucking world, doesn't need to be aware of what's going on?'

I stare at him. I'm lost for words. I haven't a clue what to say. All I can hear is a voice in my head and it belongs to Bullivant. We gather the evidence, he's insisting. And the rest will be down to a jury.

'They want to put us on trial,' I manage at last. 'For breaking the law.'

'I'm sure they do. All we're doing now is speeding things up a little. We need people to have their say. First here. Then a much wider audience. The point is this. The poor bloody woman was heading for a death most of us can't imagine. Tomorrow night we're going to explore what that death would have been like.'

'How?'

'We've got permission to use the Palo Alto footage. The *Guardian* has commissioned its video unit to knock some other stuff together. MND families. First-person witness. Other victims nearing the end. We'll screen it all, then have a debate. It'll be a clusterfuck, I guarantee it, but that's in all our interests, most of all – dare I say it – yours.'

'Clusterfuck?' I'm losing it again. This is becoming a habit.

'Huge media interest. The tabloids *en masse*. Three of the grown-up papers. Half a dozen news crews. Think satellite trucks. Think Channel Four News. Think Emily Maitlis. This will be the party no one dare miss. You thought the cliff fall turned into a media circus?' Mitch rarely grins. 'Just wait until tomorrow night.'

I nod, trying to keep my head above water beneath this torrential flood of images.

'Sounds like a crusade,' I mutter.

'Exactly.' The irony, for once, is lost on Mitch. 'And you know the best of it? We're catching a brand-new government as it's beginning to hatch. That makes it a political story. Johnson thinks in headlines. Tabloid approval is meat and drink to him. Lose the *Telegraph* or the *Daily Mail*, and he can't sleep at night. They're both sending feature people down today to write colour pieces. These are their top writers, the scribblers who really know how to stir the pot, and they know exactly how to touch the nerve that matters. Christianne should have been allowed to die in peace. That cliff fall was nobody's fault, but what's happened since *is*. Leave her memory alone. Stop wasting public money. Call the dogs off. Put Bullivant out to grass.' Another grin. 'Clear the Budleigh Six.'

The Budleigh Six? Would I really choose to share a poster with company like this? The whole thing, I tell myself, is bizarre, but just now I don't appear to have a choice. I don't doubt Mitch's sincerity for a moment. He's forever trying to give the Tories a kicking and just now must feel like the perfect opportunity. A chance to get the people on their feet, he'll tell me. An opportunity to listen to the true voice of the masses. Parliament's moment has come and gone. MPs of every stripe have blown it. Ignore democracy's middlemen. Go straight to where it matters, to our sainted grass roots.

I accompany Mitch back to the lounge. Beth, predictably, is on her phone. She brings the conversation to an abrupt end and tells me that she's already made contact with the feature writer from the *Daily Telegraph* and expects to be interviewed any time now. In the meantime, the *Sun* is offering her a sizeable sum of money for what she calls 'the inside story', and only her lawyer stands between her and national celebrity. The investigation is ongoing. Any revelations might be prejudicial. Only if the police drop the case, and abandon the investigation, will any of us be free to talk.

'So what's the point of tomorrow night?' I'm looking at the bloody poster. 'Or you talking to the *Telegraph*?'

'Because it's about Chris, about euthanasia, about the principle of the thing, not about us. I was talking to the guys in Palo Alto about an hour ago. They agree it's a real opportunity to bust the whole issue wide open. We have to do it, Enora. And with your profile, you have to join us.'

Bust wide open? I can't help thinking of the coffin on the beach, of the splintered marine ply, of the remains of Beth's farewell artwork, and of the shrouded figure that was once Christianne.

'They told you about the dog?' I'm looking at Beth. 'About finding Hundchen?'

'They did. And I've forgiven him.'

'Forgiven who?'

'Bill, of course. He told me she'd gone missing, just wandered off, and I believed him. In fact, he told everyone.'

'So, you didn't know?'

'Know what?'

'That she was in that coffin? With Christianne?'

'God, no.' She's looking at her mobile again. 'How could I?'

I watch her for a moment, her long fingers busy on the keypad tapping out a reply to some text, and I know that Andrea was right. Step back into the maze that is Operation *Bulldog*, try to sieve fact from fantasy, and my grip on what matters immediately begins to weaken. Was Beth there when they buried Christianne? Did she help carry the coffin? Does she have a tame dealer with access to limitless quantities of Fentanyl? And would she ever tell me if any of those things happened to be true? Not only do I doubt it, but I'm fast coming to the conclusion that I don't really care. All that matters is keeping Bullivant at arm's length.

'I haven't been sleeping too well.' I'm looking at Mitch. 'I might go upstairs for a nap.'

THIRTY-SEVEN

I must have been asleep for a while because it's dark outside when I hear a tap on the bedroom door. It's Beth. The woman from the *Telegraph* is downstairs and wants a word with me. She's really nice, too, and sees the issue exactly our way.

'Tell her I'm asleep,' I mutter. 'Maybe tomorrow.'

'She's filing tonight. She needs quotes. Her circulation's

massive. She's truly out there. Just half an hour? Is that asking too much?'

Beth never takes no for an answer. I struggle out of bed. A single glance in the mirror confirms I'm not fit for a meeting like this.

'Don't worry.' Beth is watching me like a hawk. 'Mitch says she'll use a stock photo. In fact, she's already been in touch with your agent.'

'She's talked to Rosa?'

'I imagine so.'

'Oh, Christ.'

I suspect that Rosa, who thrives on a good crisis, will be having the time of her life. With luck, she'll use this media shit storm to break the news about the French series. *Dimanche*, I think grimly. Starring a suspected murderer.

Downstairs, Evelyn has assigned the woman from the *Telegraph* a seat at the kitchen table. She's petite, pretty under a layer of make-up, and far younger than I'd imagined.

'Carole-Anne.' She gets up and extends a limp hand. 'I loved *Arpeggio*.'

'That's kind. This is all a bit sudden. I'm not quite sure how I can help you.'

'No problem. It won't take long. You mind if I record this?' She swipes her mobile without waiting for an answer, and finds the right icon, and watching her flip back through her notepad, I feel like I'm in the hands of a hard-pressed dentist. Ten minutes max. And it won't hurt.

'You don't really know this place. Am I right?'

'You are, yes.'

'Outsider? Would that be fair?'

'Yes.'

'So, what do you make of it?'

This is a clever question and there's absolutely no legal reason why I shouldn't answer it.

'It's a little bit of England writ small,' I say carefully. 'A lot of people here have money. Many of them have come down from London. They've been successful. They're used to what success and money and making your own decisions does to your life. They take all of that for granted.'

'Post-aspirational? Does that nail it?'

It's a beguiling phrase, and I wonder whether it's original.

'Yes,' I say. 'It does. This place is beautiful. It's quiet. It minds its own business.'

'Wants to be left alone?'

'Absolutely.'

'On its own terms?'

'Yes.'

I can see where this little exchange is headed, and I start to wonder whether Carole-Anne has been talking to Mitch. He, too, paints a picture of an entire town, a whole community, turning its back on the rest of the kingdom. Much like the Brits and Europe.

Carole-Anne is writing herself a note. She wants to know about Christianne. Was she, too, an outsider?

'She was French,' I say at once. 'That may be the same thing. She'd lived all over the world, often in some bloody awful places. That gives you a certain mindset. You know how to look after yourself. You make your own way.'

'A bit like the town itself?'

I gaze at her a moment. In truth, I've never made this particular link, but now she's pointed it out, I can only agree.

'That's right,' I say.

'And is that why she made so many friends? Fitted in so perfectly?' She gestures at her notepad. 'I must have done a dozen little interviews already and I've yet to meet anyone who won't be at that meeting tomorrow night. People want to protect her memory, and they think the police are way out of line. That speaks for itself, doesn't it?'

'About Christianne?'

'Of course.' She's smiling now. 'But about this little place, too.'

Brilliant, I think. Embattled Budleigh taking up the cudgels on behalf of its own. What a great headline. No wonder half the London media are already on the road, heading south-west.

At this point, I hear a voice in the hall, a male voice, a voice I know very well indeed, and moments later I'm looking round to see that familiar face at the door.

'Mum.' It's Malo. 'I've been really worried about you.'

*   *   *

As Evelyn's little bungalow begins to fill with more faces – some familiar, others not – I take my wayward son downtown for a drink. Carole-Anne, who seems more than happy with our brief little exchange, has joined the others in the lounge, but just now I can't face any more harangues from Beth, and a corner table in The Feathers turns out to be a much better idea.

On the walk down to the High Street, I've established that talk of Malo getting married is a little premature. Sylvester's a lovely guy, he says, but he has a habit of jumping the gun. He and Clem are back in harness, and whenever he's in London they're out on training runs together. If I really want to know, he'd love to move the relationship on, but he thinks she's not quite ready.

'For marriage?'

'For me. She wants to give it more time. Like she can't believe I'm not drinking any more. And that's just one thing I've knocked on the head.'

It's true. I'm looking at his glass. My son? Necking pints of fizzy water? We're sitting side by side. I give him a kiss, which he normally hates, but this time he doesn't even flinch.

'So, what happened?' He wants the details. 'They really banged you up?'

'They did.'

'And?'

'It was horrible. You go in good faith. You expect them to believe you, but it turns out they don't. They think I was there when Christianne died. That makes me an accessory to murder.'

'And were you?'

'What?'

'There? When she died?'

'Of course I wasn't.' I'm getting angry again. Even my son doesn't believe me. 'Don't you remember me coming home that Sunday? Driving back? You were in the flat.'

'I was. You're right. And they checked up on me, too. A policewoman. Tracked me down to Clemmie's place. Quite fit, actually.'

'Fit?'

'The policewoman. How come Asians are always so pretty?'

I ignore the question. I need to know when this happened.

'This morning. That's why I came down. They arrested

Sylvester, too. I saw that poster. The Budleigh Six? You're going to be famous, Mum.' He's grinning fit to bust. 'Brilliant.'

I shake my head. There's been nothing brilliant about the Heavitree custody centre, about DI Bullivant, about accusations of murder, about the prospect of a lengthy jail sentence, and the news that Bullivant's still checking my alibi has spilled the wind from my sails. The sheer momentum of the campaign that Mitch and Beth have launched has – just for an hour or two – convinced me that the nightmare is over. Wrong.

I want to change the subject. I want us back on safer ground. Doomsday and the Twilight Fund seem a much brighter prospect than whatever the next few days might hold.

'It's going well?' I ask. 'You and Sylvester?'

'It's going fine. Sylvester says it's a slow burn, bound to be, but the Doomsday Clock thing is only a month away and he says that's sure to make a difference.'

Doomsday Clock? In all the excitement of resisting a murder charge, I'd forgotten about the end of the world.

'This is when they adjust their predictions? Am I right?'

'January twenty-third. Sylv expects a spike in solid leads within a week. All we have to do is close them.'

Sylv, I think. Definitely mates. Is this a triumph of optimism on Malo's part? Or even Sylvester's? Or might my son's wildest dreams – of profile, of celebrity, of limitless wealth – really come to pass? Here and now, in a companionable corner of The Feathers, I could press the issue, play parental, but I know I've run out of energy.

My glass is empty. I'm looking at Malo.

'Another?' I reach for his hand and give it a squeeze. 'Please?'

By the time we get back to the bungalow, the poster has changed yet again. Instead of *Clear the Budleigh Six*, Mitch has decided on *Support the Budleigh Six*.

'This has become an issue thing. We need to reflect that.'

'Euthanasia? Mercy killings?'

'Yeah, for sure. But police harassment, too. I was talking to the guy from the *Sun* just now. Say what you like about the tabloids, but they always cut straight to the chase. They've done the sums on Operation *Bulldog*. They reckon half a million quid already, and still climbing. Is that true? I doubt it, but who's going to argue? Most people have given up on the police. Report a theft, or even some lowlife who breaks into your house, and fuck all happens. Yet here they are, burning through the budget, scooping up ex-ambassadors, ex-QCs, pillars of the community, just for doing a mate a favour? That has to be the allegation. That's where it's all heading. Worst case, you lot were guilty of helping a woman to the death she wanted. So, pardon me for asking, but where's the big deal?'

This has the makings of a speech, and I wonder if Mitch is rehearsing for tomorrow night.

'You're going to chair this thing? Pull it all together? Keep it on the road?'

'No.' He shakes his head.

'Beth, then?' My heart sinks.

'No way. She's still pushing, but it won't happen. I expect she'll have her say, but she'll be in the audience.'

'With the groundlings?' I laugh at the thought. 'She'll hate it.'

'Too bad. This is a once-off. That's not my phrase, by the way, it's the woman from Palo Alto. We've really got her attention. They're sending some video from the dead guy's wife as we speak. That'll go straight to the *Guardian* for tomorrow night's presentation. How often do we get a chance to change the fucking law?'

I nod. I agree. But he still hasn't answered my question. 'Just who will be in charge tomorrow night?'

'Evelyn.' Mitch is looking down at me. 'You ought to have a chat with her.'

THIRTY-EIGHT

That proves impossible. For one thing, Beth has whisked her off to Bill's house for a council of war with the other escapees from the Heavitree custody centre, and for another, I'm exhausted. I share a mug of cocoa with Malo and by ten o'clock, I'm asleep in bed.

This morning finds me alone in the kitchen, watching Evelyn preparing Mitch's usual full fried breakfast.

'You volunteered for tonight?' I ask her.

'I did.'

'Why?'

'Partly because Mitch asked me. That man can be very persuasive. Women my age are far too susceptible to compliments, and he knows that.'

'So, what did he say?'

'He told me about all the folk who'd been at that little thing I did in St Peter's, that weekend you first came down. Apparently, he's talked to some of them. They thought I was OK, perhaps better than OK. He also said tonight was about stories, about Christianne, about that poor man Adam we saw on YouTube, and if anyone knew about storytelling, then it had to be me. So . . .' She reaches for the frying pan and gives a sausage a poke. 'I said yes. Is it vanity? Probably. Am I terrified by the prospect? Of course I am.'

'But you don't agree with euthanasia. We had a bit of a debate. Remember?'

'That's true, and oddly enough, that's the other reason I said yes. Mitch thinks we need a moderating voice, and I agree. This little town is spitting bullets. Some of the people at Bill's last night? They're outraged. A lot of them think that we should have the right to die the death of our choice, and I suspect they really believe that, but this whole thing goes way, way further. They think people like you, and Bill, and Nathan have no place in a police cell, and I must say I agree with them. It's excessive, and it's spiteful, and they should be ashamed of themselves.'

'You're slapping their hands?'

'Of course I am, and they deserve it, especially that man Bulliwhatsit, but there's something else, my lovely, since you've asked.' She pauses to break a second egg into the hot oil. 'I had a long talk to Bill Penny last night, as you might imagine. They've all compared notes, everyone who got arrested, and they agree that you're Bulliwhatsit's prime suspect. Bill thinks it has to do with your profile, that stellar career of yours. You in the dock, he says, will put Bulliwhatsit on the front page of every newspaper in the country.'

'And that's where all this leads?'

'It does, my lovely, unless we can head that frightful man off.'

'And that's why you volunteered? For my sake? For little me?'

'Of course.' She turns from the stove and presents her cheek for a kiss. 'It's the least you deserve.'

The rest of the day becomes increasingly surreal. Evelyn and I mount a brief expedition to the Co-op to lay in supplies for what we hope will be a post-event party, but I'm totally unprepared for the number of people, most of them strangers, who stop me in the street, pump my hand, or even give me a hug.

Mitch, and Malo, and a small army of volunteers have been busy all morning. Mitch has had two hundred posters printed overnight, and now they're everywhere, in shop windows, taped to trees outside the public hall, mounted on oblongs of hardboard and propped against the traffic lights, a rogue's gallery of local faces snatched from their beds and driven away. *Support the Budleigh Six.* East Devon's call to arms.

One woman, who has to be eighty at least, peers up at me from her wheelchair. She says she remembers the war as a child. She gives me a gummy smile and waves one bent finger at some nameless enemy. 'We beat them then,' she says. 'And we'll beat them again. We're a free people. They should damn well remember that.'

They? In exchange after exchange, the pronoun comes up again and again. *They* meddle where they shouldn't. *They* should leave people to die in peace. *They* should be chasing foul-mouthed kids and internet scammers. *They* don't have a clue what people like us are really like. By the time we emerge from the Co-op, having bought a dozen bottles of wine for home delivery, I'm beginning to suspect that the entire town has slipped its moorings and drifted away into deepest space. Just like Christianne.

Evelyn agrees. This, she says, is the first time she's been able to put her finger on the pulse of the town and its heartbeat turns out to be agreeably strong. That, I tell her, is a nice place to be, and as we walk back up the hill towards Evelyn's cul-de-sac, we pass yet more posters. One of them has been taped to a pillar box and I pause beside it for a moment's reflection. I've been a working thesp for most of my life, but I've never had a starring role like this before, and the current production is all the scarier because, for once, the denouement is still wildly uncertain. A prison sentence, I wonder, or the A303 and the blessed anonymity of Holland Park? The jury, I know, is still out. And that's another thought that scares me witless.

In the afternoon, I take another nap. Evelyn brings me tea around half past five and we spend a girly half hour debating what to wear for the coming event. My choices are very limited. I've only brought a single suitcase but that doesn't matter because I feel very happy in black jeans and a loose crimson top. Evelyn, on the other hand, has an entire wardrobe at her disposal.

After trying on various outfits, we agree that none of them quite hits the mark, and in the end she settles for the beautifully subdued two-piece – a sublime confection in soft blues and greys – that she wore for her event in St Peter's Church. This, I tell her, has the merit of reminding certain members of the audience about her London pedigree. All those books, all those bestselling authors. Mitch, newly returned from setting up the public hall, agrees.

'It'll work for the media people, too,' he says. 'They love all that literary shit.'

We set off for the public hall with half an hour in hand. Mitch offers to drive us but both Evelyn and I prefer to go on foot. It's a lovely evening, still and cold. A full moon is rising above the line of rooftops as we leave the cul-de-sac and link arms and walk down the hill. Already, couples are emerging from their front doors, checking their watches, and setting off in the same direction. Might these people be heading for the public hall as well? The answer, we quickly discover, is yes.

By the time we arrive, the hall is already packed, standing room only at the back and along the side aisles. Mitch has had the foresight to run cables out for a pair of loudspeakers on the apron of hardstanding in front of the hall, and his trusty volunteers have been despatched for supplies of garden chairs to let these good folk take the weight off their feet. Cars and trailers are arriving from every direction, and men twice my age stand ready to offload yet another stack of plastic chairs. Among them,

I recognize Bill Penny. He's supervising the layout of this supplementary arena, a shallow crescent of white and dark green plastic seating, fast filling up.

'Thank God for the croquet club.' He's beaming. 'I knew those bloody awful chairs would come in handy.'

Inside the hall, arriving townspeople, eager for a peek at this extraordinary turn-out, must run the gauntlet of camera crews. Each proffered microphone is badged – ITV, Channel Four, Sky, BBC Spotlight – and the reporters are hunting for screen-ready soundbites they can build into an opening sequence. I pause while Mitch takes charge of Evelyn, trying to catch just a flavour of some of these brief interviews, gladdened by this very special mix of courtesy and outrage. This is a reprise of my earlier conversations up and down the High Street. People are deeply unhappy. They're protecting their turf. And tonight, God willing, they'll make their feelings more than plain.

The event kicks off a little late, thanks to a problem in Mitch's makeshift sound system. A retired BT senior manager locates the fault and restores the sound feed to the hundreds of latecomers outside. Bill, bless him, has laid hands on a supply of blankets from somewhere or other and I'm only too happy to help him pass them round.

Back inside the hall, the event has begun. Evelyn has prepared a set of opening remarks. She thanks everyone for turning out on such a cold night, especially so close to Christmas, and asks that we all try and limit our contributions to no more than a minute, once the debate begins. She then apologizes for the non-appearance of Mitch's stand-up comic but reads out a message of support. It's on the brief side, and just a tad cheesy. *We all feel your pain down there*, he's texted. *Viva Budleigh!* This is met with silence until a lone voice, oldish, growls something about standing on our own two feet. Do we need support from London? he asks. The answer, dozens of voices this time, is an emphatic No.

Evelyn is getting in her stride now, walking the mic up and down the stage like a pro. She talks about living next door to Christianne, about getting to know her, about realizing what a special person she was, and then – after she'd disappeared –

learning from her partner that she'd been diagnosed with motor neurone disease.

'That changed everything,' she says quietly. 'Both for Christianne, and now – dare I say it – for us. There are some of you in this gathering tonight who may be deeply uncomfortable with the very thought of euthanasia, and I happen to be one of them, but that's not the issue. The issue touches above all on respect. Not just for Christianne, God rest her soul, but of that handful of precious friends who may have helped her on her way. Neither the law, nor those who enforce it, should ever penalize courage, and good works, and neighbourliness, and all the other blessings of a community like this that works so tirelessly for each other. In my view, that's what has brought us together tonight, and – from the bottom of my heart – I thank you once again.'

Her pause is perfectly judged. She's centre stage, a slim, slightly stooped figure, peering out at the sea of faces below her, and in that brief, brief moment of time I know exactly what she's going to look like when she gets properly old. But that's not the point, because what she's just voiced is bringing the bulk of this audience to their feet. Couples help each other up. Eighty-year-olds clutch the back of the chair in front for support. Everyone's clapping, while Beth – subdued until now – mounts the stage to give Evelyn a showy hug.

The assembled media love it. Cameramen are picking their way along the side aisles, trying to avoid the tangle of bodies, hunting for those telling close-ups in the audience that will – fingers crossed – make the ten o'clock news. Old faces. Concerned faces. Affronted. Offended. Deeply upset. Leave us alone, please. Mind your own business.

Evelyn, I can see, is delighted as well as relieved. She may, or may not, have spent time this afternoon rehearsing that little speech, but either way it doesn't matter because it had a spontaneity, and a heart, that even seasoned thesps can't feign. As the applause begins to die, she invites contributions from the audience, and tells those outside in the cold to write down whatever questions they might have and give them to the nearest volunteer. These will come to her direct, and she'll deal with them as best she can.

The debate begins after a showing of Mitch's video, and it's quickly evident that these people, hundreds and hundreds of them, are four-square behind everything that Evelyn has touched on in her opening remarks. Many of them knew, and miss, Christianne. People who never had the pleasure of her company applaud her courage in taking her life, quite literally, into her own hands. One fit-looking eighty-five-year-old hopes that he, too, will summon that kind of pluck when the time comes.

'Here's to the Budleigh Six.' He raises a glass of red wine he's managed to smuggle in. '*Santé*.'

As the evening progresses, there's only one dissenting voice, an ex-property developer who bewails the money and resources wasted on the initial search for Christianne's body. It must have cost thousands, he says. It turned out to be a red herring and someone should be made to pay for that. It's an entirely reasonable point, but this man has badly misjudged the evening's mood. Instead of the support he's obviously expecting, he's met with a chorus of boos. The police, at that point, were doing their job. It's what's happened since that matters.

The debate – well-mannered, quietly passionate – goes on for the best part of an hour and a half. Sparked by the Palo Alto footage, contributions have flooded in from every corner of the hall, and from the half-darkness outside. Evelyn presides over this exquisitely local occasion with good humour and impeccable judgement. Inviting her to MC the event was, on Mitch's part, a stroke of genius. Towards the very end of the debate, when people are beginning to check their watches, Evelyn redirects all our thoughts to Christianne.

'She came to the right place,' she says quietly. 'And we were very lucky to have her.'

Watching from the back of the hall, I can only shake my head in wonderment and admiration. Beautifully put, I think. Just perfect.

The debate over, people stream out towards the car park, pausing to drop money in buckets for the Palo Alto appeal. Meanwhile, I succumb to a series of TV interviews, two of them live, refusing to rise to questions about my arrest and my treatment at the hands of the police. I'm very happy to talk about Christianne, and about the wider issue of so-called mercy killings, but when a woman from Sky News asks me whether I'm comfortable sharing a poster that might have come out of the Wild West, I offer a rueful smile.

'I never auditioned for Annie Oakley,' I say. 'Maybe now's the time.'

Evelyn and I accept a lift home. The bungalow quickly fills with faces from the public hall. We break out the wine, distribute glasses, fill bowls with crisps and olives, and ask people to help themselves. Mitch has turned on the TV and fired up a collection of laptops and iPads. That way, he says, we can keep tabs on the coverage, assuming any channel has decided to give it screen time.

The answer dumbfounds us all. Lead story on the BBC news, and on ITN as well. Extended coverage on Sky and the promise of a special on tomorrow evening's BBC Spotlight half hour. Thanks to Christianne, little Budleigh Salterton is well and truly on the national radar. By now, with most of the wine gone, we're all euphoric, Beth especially. Mitch, trapped in the bay window, is mobbed. Women embrace him. Men pump his hand. Everyone agrees he's played a blinder. I seize a passing bottle and pour the remains into his empty glass. Then I turn to the crush between us and the door.

'To Mitch.' I raise the empty bottle. 'And to our lovely Evelyn.'

THIRTY-NINE

We get up late next day. Thanks to resupplies from Bill and Nathan, we drank until three in the morning, reliving every moment from that extraordinary gathering in the public hall. Word about the Budleigh Six has spilled on to social media, a flood of postings, the huge bulk of them beyond supportive. People, in Mitch's phrase, love to stick it to authority, and here is the perfect opportunity. The target of choice, perhaps inevitably, is the police and literally millions of voices are raised on the internet. Much of this stuff is unprintable, but a small circle of us spend the early hours reading out post after post. One of them, a personal favourite, reads, *How come you spend all that money when you couldn't be arsed to even look for my stolen gnomes?*

I totter downstairs at eleven. Mitch is already at the kitchen table. He's been out for the newspapers and has a selection spread before him. Last night's event was too late to make this morning's edition but many of the tabloids, and even some of the broadsheets, have run feature pieces to steal a march on broadcast coverage. Once again, Budleigh Salterton is hogging the limelight. Reminder photos of the coffin at the foot of the cliff. Nicely framed shots of the curl of pebble beach and the sun on the water beyond. God's waiting room has become a national treasure.

Mitch directs my attention to my mobile. I must have left it in the kitchen last night.

'It's been ringing all morning,' he says. 'You'd better take a look.'

I scroll through a long list of messages. They're mostly from friends and colleagues. Rosa says she's proud of me. A fellow thesp thinks I've been following the wrong career all these years. *Stick to campaigning*, she's written. *You've done so, so well.* Then, towards the end of the messages, another name catches my eye. Brett Atkinson.

Shit. I glance up, feeling a sudden chill in the kitchen.

'You OK?' This from Mitch.

'I'm fine.' I'm looking at my mobile again. 'Something might have come up.'

'Like what?'

'I don't know.'

Brett has sent me an email. It comes from a police computer. He wants a private meeting. And he says it's urgent.

I'm looking at Mitch again. Is it too late to take a plane to South America? Or the Far East? Or New Zealand? Somewhere Bullivant will never find me? While I've still got my passport, should I simply beg a lift to Heathrow, blow a heap of money on a ticket, and flee?

I shake my head. I can hear my mum again. Face whatever's coming your way, she'd say. And never turn your back.

I decide to ring Brett. He answers the call at once.

'Enora?' He's sounding almost cheerful.

'Me.'

'We need to talk.'

'Why?'

'Just say yes. You know the big car park at the foot of the hill? The one on the seafront? I'll be there in forty minutes. Look for the same shit Ford Focus. Nothing changes in this life.'

Abruptly, before I have a chance to ask anything else, he's gone. Should I bring a solicitor? Should I ring Tony or Andrea and ask for advice? Should I lean on Mitch to accompany me down? In the end, I do none of those things. My mum, again. Man up, girl. Take it on the chin.

When Mitch asks where I'm going, I tell him I need the fresh air. This has the merit of being true. The inside of what passes for my head is befogged. Too much red wine. Too much excitement. I take the long way down to the seafront, and then march along the pebbles to clear my tubes. By the time I finally make it to the car park, Brett has already arrived and I'm feeling a whole lot better.

He watches me coming towards him and leans across to open the passenger door.

'Top night,' he says at once.

'You were there?'

'Of course I was there. Incredible turnout. Total triumph.'

This is truly the last thing I'm expecting. Part of me, to be frank, doesn't believe him.

'So why? Why were you there?'

'They sent me.'

'They? You mean Bullivant?'

'No. I'm afraid Bullivant's history, poor bugger. He fought and lost. Our lot can be unforgiving, believe me.'

I shake my head. I don't understand a word he's saying. Fought? Lost? What the fuck's going on?

'Operation *Bulldog* was nothing when it started.' Brett has lowered his voice, as if someone else is listening. 'Just a routine misper enquiry. We searched for a body and didn't find it. That can happen. Then Bullivant was tasked to take a look, just a precaution, and decided it was dodgy. You remember the ten grand McFaul had transferred to his account? That did it for Bullivant. He made a case for a closer look and they appointed him SIO. Happy days, for Frank. He's retiring in March but now he's in sole charge. One last bid for glory.'

Arresting McFaul, he said, was a bold step and took *Bulldog* nowhere. McFaul went 'no comment', but Bullivant wouldn't leave the misper enquiry alone.

'He came down here on a *Sunday*, can you believe that? Put on his leathers, fired up the bike and hit the road. You'd have seen him. You were all on the beach over there, some send-off or other. All those photos he took. He showed me every single one. "They're taking the piss," he told me. "And they'll live to regret it."'

'He thought we were lying? Some of us?'

'He was certain. And what's more, he was right. That morning the cliff collapsed, he was like a dog with two dicks. *Bulldog* went to Major Crimes, but he stayed SIO. And then it started to fall apart.'

'Fall apart how?'

'McFaul had done a runner. Very wise. That left us trying to stand up some kind of conspiracy. To his credit, Bullivant was right. Getting a coffin to a location like that would have taken some doing, which probably meant at least four other people, but facts are still facts. The woman had a horrible disease. She didn't want to hang around. Helping her leave was a favour, not a crime.'

'And Bullivant?'

'He thought otherwise. The man's a pedant. Everything's black and white with Frank, not a single shade of grey. Helping someone die is a crime. End of. We put the timeline together. We establish the likely order of events. We identify the key suspects. And then we arrest them. Bold, bold move. Alas, he chose the wrong town.'

I'm smiling now. This is very definitely the fifth act. I'm beginning to suspect I'm not going to be re-arrested, after all.

'And?'

'We've got a newish system in the force. It's called downstream monitoring. I won't bother you with the details, but it enables anyone with the right seniority to log into any live interview at any custody centre from here to Penzance. If anything troubling's about to kick off, the management can tune in and watch. This goes right to the top. Assistant chief constable, deputy, the chief himself, the lot.'

'And *Bulldog*?' I think I'm beginning to get the picture.

'Total nightmare. Bullivant's still SIO. The man can't help himself. He has no off switch. With Frank it's all or nothing. After he scooped you all up, and then released you, the management were getting very worried. And that's before last night.'

'Worried how? Why?'

'Harassment? Waste of resources? Aggressive interview tactics? No feel for the public mood? You want the whole list?'

'So, what happened?'

'We had a Gold Group meet yesterday afternoon. Twenty bodies round the table on the senior management corridor. Everyone from the ACC who chaired it to little me. Legal services. Head of Media. CID and uniform at Superintendent rank. Coroner. Everyone with an ear to the ground. Everyone who knew anything about where *Bulldog* was headed. You talk for a couple of hours, then there's another meeting, just the key players, just the four of them, and that's where the real decision is made.'

'And Bullivant? He was there?'

'No. Bullivant was transferred off *Bulldog* yesterday morning. He's been given a project. Aligning our IT systems with the Dorset force. Kiss of death, believe me. The guy's gutted. He may even try and fight it, but if that happens, they'll take a look at his disclosure record and hang him out to dry. He knows that so my guess is he'll take it on the chin. In any case, he retires in a couple of months. Keeping the pension intact trumps everything else.'

I nod. Am I pleased? Very.

'And *Bulldog*?' I query.

Brett looks at me for a moment or two, then smiles.

'They sent me over to that meeting of yours last night. I was told to take a look, gauge the mood, and report back in person. By the time I got to headquarters, they'd all been watching the news.'

'They?'

'ACC. Deputy. Chief.'

'And?'

'Their biggest worry is risk to the organization. Putting it bluntly, you've put the shits up them.'

'They took a decision?'

'They did. Which is why I'm here.'

'And?'

'NFA.' He leans across and gives me a hug. 'No further action.'

FORTY

C hristmas has come and gone. We're a week into the New Year when, back in London, I get the message in person from Nathan Kline. No email. No text. No WhatsApp. Not even a phone call. He appears on my video entry phone in Holland Park early on a Wednesday afternoon. He'd appreciate a cup of tea, but he won't be staying long.

I buzz him in and put the kettle on. He says he's come up for some lawyerly get together, which may or may not be true. He has ten minutes to kill and a message to deliver.

'From?'

'Andy McFaul.'

'You're kidding.'

'I'm not. He's in Lisbon for the next couple of days. He'd appreciate a chat.'

'Face-to-face? He wants me to go down there?'

'Yes. To make it easier, I thought I'd give you this.'

He slips an envelope on to the table between us. Inside is an open return Air Portugal ticket to Lisbon, and another folded sheet of paper.

'All you have to do is quote the booking number and choose the flights.' He smiles, getting to his feet. 'There are directions to the rendezvous in the envelope. I get the impression he's looking forward to seeing you. Any questions?'

I'm staring up at him, the ticket still in my hand.

'No tea?'

'I'm afraid not.' He checks his watch. 'Time, I'm afraid, waits for no man. Least of all me.'

*   *   *

I fly to Lisbon two days later, having made contact with McFaul
on the phone. My flight gets in at 14.35. He confirms that he'll
be waiting at the Hotel Astoriam, from mid-afternoon onwards,
and will be very happy to buy me as many Portuguese stickies
as I can manage.

'Stickies?'

'Cakes. Treats. All of them delicious. The locals should be
fat, but they aren't. Christ knows how they manage it.'

The flight is late taking off, and it's gone four o'clock before
I step out of the taxi and make my way into the hotel. I've never
been to Lisbon before and I love it at once. Trams clanking up
the steepness of the hills. Glimpses of the river beyond terrace
after terrace of houses. Even a hint of warmth in the late-afternoon
sun.

The hotel is tiny, and McFaul is waiting for me in the first-
floor room that serves as a restaurant. There are only four tables,
none of the others occupied. McFaul is with a much younger
man, very black, beautiful suit, gleaming elasticated boots, perfect
teeth in a wide, wide smile.

'Raimundo,' he says. 'Domingos' boy.'

The name Domingos stirs a distant memory and I'm still trying
to hunt it down when McFaul supplies the answer.

'You remember me telling you about Angola? The minefields?
The local man I employed?'

'Domingos.' I've got it at last. 'And Celestina.'

Mention of his mother's name sparks another smile from
Raimundo, and we all sit down. There's a tiny bell on the bareness of the tablecloth, and moments after McFaul gives it a shake,
a woman appears with a towering display of tiny cakes.

'You want coffee? Tea?' She has a hand draped over McFaul's
shoulder. She seems to know him very well.

I settle for coffee. The woman nods, distributes three plates,
and disappears. To break the silence that follows, I tell McFaul
he's looking well.

'You too.'

'You're living here?'

'In the hotel? Christ, no.'

'In Lisbon?'

'No.'

'Somewhere else then?'

'Obviously.' He offers a rare smile, and then nods at the cake stand. 'Try the *pastéis de nata*, egg and cinnamon. They're wonderful.'

He's right. I demolish the first in a couple of bites and help myself to another.

'You know what happened?' I reach for a serviette to wipe my mouth. 'To Christianne?'

'Yeah.'

'The problem with the cliff? All that?'

'Yeah.'

'The police have given up now. It's all over, finished, done.'

'Sure.'

'So, what really happened? Is that why you asked me down? Is that why I'm here?'

'Not really, but since you ask . . .' He shrugs. 'Why not?'

Christianne, he confirms, had made a decision to call it quits. What had finally made a difference was the Sunday morning she'd woken up and had difficulty swallowing.

'She was terrified of not being able to eat properly, not being able to take liquid, not being able to talk. She knew her body was telling her something and she no longer wanted to be around when it decided to pack up completely. Odd, really. Because in most other respects she was really patient.'

'You're blaming her?'

'Not at all. It was a gutsy decision. I was with her all the way.'

All the way. I nod. I bet he was.

'She had access to Fentanyl?'

'She did. She'd been saving it up, squirreling it away.'

'How? Where from?'

'It doesn't matter. She had enough tablets. More than enough. That's all you need to know.'

'So how did she take it?'

'Crushed. With a glass of red wine. Alta 904 Gran Reserva if you want the full story. Cost us a fortune.'

I nod, trying to imagine what a lethal dose of Fentanyl married to a vintage Rioja must taste like.

'So, where did this take place?'

'At Bill's. We'd worked it out weeks before. We knew it was

going to happen sooner or later. Presley had made the coffin. Beth had painted it, her own design of course, not to my taste at all, but then I wasn't doing the dying. It was the Sunday night. Chris hadn't been at all well. I drove her round to Bill's and Presley and Beth joined us later. By that time, Chris had gone.'

'Just the three of you, then? You, Chris, and Bill?'

'Just the two of us. Chris wanted to die on that chaise longue of Bill's. She loved it, and she loved the view from that window as well. Bill stayed downstairs until it was over.'

Over. Dear God.

'She was happy? At the end?'

'No. But that's another story.'

'You want to share it? Tell me?'

'No.' He shakes his head. 'Bill's son was in the house as well. He was staying the weekend. Between us, we got Chris into the coffin and put her in the back of Presley's van. Nathan had arrived by now. We drove across to the golf club and he showed Presley the way to the bit of the fence we needed.'

'You'd already dug the grave?'

'We both had, Bill and me. We were doing National Trust work at the time. We waited for rain to soften the earth, and then used their spades. The hole was deep enough to keep the foxes out. Took maybe ten hours, off and on, between us.'

'And the dog? Hundchen?'

'That was Chris's last wish. She loved the dog, and the dog loved her. You might have seen it. Old. Half blind. Bill thought it was a blessing.'

'Fentanyl again?'

'Injected. In a solution of warm water.'

'I see.'

Throughout this story, Raimundo has been keeping a discreet distance, his back half-turned, smoking a small cheroot, but I get the impression he's heard it before.

'So, you buried her?' I'm back with McFaul.

'Yes. Full moon. Stars. Birds calling from down below.' He frowns, then studies his hands. 'You want me to go on?'

'No, of course not. I'm really, really sorry. Truly I am. But maybe it was for the best, eh?'

I put my hand over his. When he looks up, I think I detect just a glint of a tear.

'She loved you,' he says. 'She really did.'

At my insistence, we abandon the rest of the cakes, and find a nearby bar. I very badly need a drink, and so does McFaul, and we both agree to change the subject. The bar is perfect: small, intimate, shadowed spaces with just a thin scatter of other drinkers, most of them solitary men. McFaul confesses that he comes here a lot when he's in town, and looking round I believe him.

Raimundo, it turns out, has a new job, working in a bigger bank. It's given him a substantial salary raise plus two days off every month that he never expected.

'Raimundo wants to be a writer,' McFaul announces. 'But he's far too shy to admit it.'

'That's true?' I've been watching him taking the occasional sip of Diet Coke.

'It is, yes.' His English is near perfect, all the sweeter for just a hint of a lisp. 'I used to write stories when I was a kid, back in Africa. I read all the time, books and books and books. Just recently, with this new job . . .' He smiles.

'You've started writing again?'

'Yes.'

'Short stories? Poetry?'

'Neither.' McFaul nods at the briefcase beside Raimundo's chair. 'You want to show her?'

Raimundo looks a little awkward. I can tell he's hating this.

'I'd love to see it,' I tell him. 'May I?'

With some reluctance, he bends to the briefcase and extracts a yellow file.

'For you.' He gives me the file. 'I have another copy.'

'For me?' I'm looking at McFaul again. Raimundo's file is heavier than I'd expected.

'It's a novella.' McFaul empties his glass and checks his watch. 'We thought we'd put it in for that competition Evelyn announced. Back last year. In the church.'

FORTY-ONE

J ust over a week later, Evelyn and I take an early Eurostar to Brussels, en route for Prague. Pavel comes with us, his ashes still contained in the plastic urn I failed to get through the security checks at Gatwick last year. In this respect, and many others, the train does the business. There's an X-ray machine at St Pancras International, but no one is the least bit troubled by the ghostly image of Pavel passing through.

By the time we change trains at Brussels, Evelyn has brought me up to speed with the latest Budleigh gossip. After the excitement of last month, life has settled down. Passing conversation on the street or in the butcher's, says Evelyn, still returns by some strange magnetic force to that evening when we took on the forces of law and order and won. People still treasure those wonderful moments in the public hall, and the organizers of this year's literary festival have asked Evelyn to deliver another talk, which she describes as a riff on the perils and rewards of civil disobedience. This sounds a bit worthy but Evelyn assures me that it'll be anything but.

Mention of the literary festival is the perfect cue for the next stage of our journey. Once we've settled down on the train that will take us to Frankfurt, and then Prague, I fetch out a biggish envelope and lay it carefully on the table between us.

'What on earth's that?'

'It's an entry,' I tell her. 'For your Golden Nymph competition.'

'Really?' She's intrigued already. 'May I?'

She slips out the manuscript and studies the title page. Raimundo has titled his story *Sheppey*, and as Evelyn begins to flick through the opening pages, I tell her about my recent trip to Lisbon.

'You *met* him? Andy?' She is astonished. 'How is he?'

'Much the same. Solitary. Not a lot of small talk.'

'But he told you what really happened?'

'Yes.'

I repeat McFaul's account of that Sunday night, Christianne not well, the Fentanyl readied, her favourite chaise longue waiting at Bill's house, the grave already dug, Presley's van bumping over the golf course, willing hands only too ready to help with her final journey through the undergrowth and on to the clifftop.

'And that's really how it happened?'

'Yes, according to Andy.'

'And you believe him?'

'I do, yes.' I nod at the pile of manuscript and explain briefly about Raimundo. 'It's very good. Very impressive. See what you think.'

Evelyn, as you might expect, is a quick reader and by the time we get to the Czech border, she's finished. She sits back, staring out at the last of the daylight, her fingers drumming lightly on the final page of Raimundo's manuscript.

Sheppey is a dystopian vision of what life might be like in post-Brexit England. The Scots have declared independence, Ireland is reunited, and Wales is on the verge of rebellion. On the Isle of Sheppey, meanwhile, the second Johnson administration has built a multi-acre detention centre that houses the many prisoners, political and otherwise, that the State has seen fit to bang up. It's a tale of despair and defiance, and touches on some of the stories that came out of The Jungle camp for marooned asylum seekers at Calais. It's relentlessly claustrophobic, and in places extremely violent. The writing is both vivid and tender, a kick in the ribs, and the softest of embraces. By the end, even the second time I read it, I was nearly in tears.

'It's brilliant,' Evelyn murmurs at last. 'I doubt we'll get anything else in this league. I'd publish it tomorrow.'

'That good?'

'That good. Maybe even better.'

We spend the weekend in Prague. Evelyn has never been here before, and she loves it. I've taken the precaution of consulting the local weather forecast and I've decided that late afternoon on the Sunday offers the best setting for the moment I unscrew Pavel's lid, upend the container over the balustrade of the bridge, give it a good shake, and watch his ash-grey remains settle on the river and drift slowly away downstream.

The forecast delivers all that it's promised. By Sunday afternoon, we've attended a couple of concerts, eaten in a wonderful restaurant on the other side of the river, and walked our legs off exploring corners of the city where, according to the receptionist at our hotel, tourists never go. On Sunday morning, as a gesture, I even accompanied Evelyn to church.

Now, the light is dying over the domes and spires of this wonderful city, and as we choose a spot for me to say goodbye to Pavel, I realize just why he loved the place so much. Unscrewing the lid of the container proves far harder than I'd ever imagined, and in the end we have to enlist the help of a young passer-by, who speaks no English. He has a go himself, but it's only with a penknife that he manages to get the lid off. By now, mercifully, it's nearly dark, but he shows no curiosity about what's inside the container, and leaves us with a nod and a cheery smile.

'Well, my lovely?' Evelyn is looking at the container. 'You want me to leave you alone?'

'Yes, please.' I nod. 'Just give me a minute.'

'Take as long as you like.' She gestures towards the end of the bridge. 'I'll be waiting when you're ready.'

I watch her walking slowly away. I know she's loved our weekend together, but we must have trudged miles and miles between churches, and bars, and galleries, and all the other must-visit delights, and it shows. When she gets to the end of the bridge, she stops, sits down on a bench, and gives me a tiny wave. I'm here, she's saying. Join me when you can.

I turn towards the river. The water is nearly black in what's left of the daylight, the ripples of current barely visible. I peer briefly into the container. Pavel dying has made remarkably little difference to our relationship. I still talk to him most days, and most days he answers back.

Now, I have some news for him.

'That missing file of yours,' I murmur. 'A man called Andy found it in the end. It's a wonderful story, truly wonderful, and we think *Sheppey* is going to win someone very deserving the star prize. Ten thousand pounds goes a long way in rural Angola, as I'm sure you know. Something else, though, dearest Pavel. That little fable of yours also got me into serious shit with MI5, thanks to the bits in The Jungle camp, but that's another story. So well done for writing it, and here's hoping they never knock on my door again.'

I wait, in vain, for an answer, or even a brief comment, and then decide he must be impatient to leave. And so I lean out over the balustrade of the bridge, murmur the key lines from an Auden poem I know he loves, and turn the container upside down. A thin cloud of ash is caught in the wind, unfurling like a flag, and then the grittier bits disappear soundlessly into the darkness below.

I gaze down for what seems like a very long moment, blow the remains of Pavel a kiss, then screw the lid back on to the container. When I check the end of the bridge, Evelyn – bless her – is still waiting.

AFTERWARDS

From the *Bulletin of the Atomic Scientists*, released on Thursday 23 January 2020 and widely reproduced.

As seasoned watchers know, the Doomsday Clock did not move in 2019. But the clock's minute hand was set forward in January 2018 by 30 seconds, to two minutes before midnight, the closest it had been to midnight since 1953 in the early years of the Cold War. This year, the Science and Security Board moved the time from two minutes to 100 seconds to midnight, a decision taken in full recognition of its historic nature.